TOOLS OF ENGAGEMENT

By Tessa Bailey

TOOLS OF ENGAGEMENT

A NOVEL

TESSA BAILEY

AVON

An Imprint of HarperCollinsPublishers

TOOLS OF ENGAGEMENT. Copyright © 2020 by Tessa Bailey. All rights reserved. Printed in the United States of America. No part of this book may be used or reproduced in any manner whatsoever without written permission except in the case of brief quotations embodied in critical articles and reviews. For information, address HarperCollins Publishers, 195 Broadway, New York, NY 10007.

HarperCollins books may be purchased for educational, business, or sales promotional use. For information, please email the Special Markets Department at SPsales@harpercollins.com.

FIRST EDITION

Designed by Diahann Sturge
Emoji on page 211 © Art studio G / Shutterstock, Inc.

Library of Congress Cataloging-in-Publication Data has been applied for.

ISBN 978-0-06-287293-7 (paperback)
ISBN 978-0-06-303484-6 (hardcover library edition)

20 21 22 23 24   LSC   10 9 8 7 6 5 4 3 2 1

To those who overanalyze

ACKNOWLEDGMENTS

It's here! Wes and Bethany's story! I tend to save my favorite couple for last. This time was no exception, but I didn't expect to relate so hard to Bethany. Over the course of writing this book and talking to readers during the process, I realized just how many of us share Bethany's need to keep up appearances. Even though she most definitely does *not* have it all together, she wants people to think she does. It's not enough that she's a good friend, daughter, club president, and house stager. Nothing is ever enough—and I think we all feel like that some days. We could have done more. We could *be* more. We could look, act, and vacation like the people we see on the internet. The truth is, we're doing just fine, each and every one of us. We're enough just as we are. We're the glue that holds our families together, we're the encouraging commenter on a Facebook post that might save someone's day, we're the ones whose imaginations bring words on a page to life—and that's enough. So let's all take it freaking easy on ourselves, all right?

Thank you, as always, to my family; my editor, Nicole Fischer; marketing and publicity gurus Kayleigh Webb and

Imani Gary; the incredible cover designers who worked on this series; and the readers who continue to pick up my stories.

A special thanks to the nurses and aides at my daughter's school—Nora, Sarah, and Joanna—who take care of my third grader, who is a type 1 diabetic (and an absolute warrior), so I can concentrate on working.

Enjoy the book!

CHAPTER ONE

Wes Daniels cracked an eyelid.

The streetlamp outside the house let in just enough light for him to make out the silhouette of his five-year-old niece sitting on the end of his bed, wearing his cowboy hat. If these freaky wake-up calls weren't a regular occurrence, it would have scared the living shit out of him. The first time, he'd almost started shouting for the ghost child to go toward the light. His niece was an early riser, however, and this routine had been well established over the last month.

Didn't mean he had to accept it.

"Nope. Still dark." Wes pulled the comforter up over his head. "You have to stay in bed until the clock says six, two dots, double zero, kid. We talked about this."

"But I don't want to go to school today."

"School isn't for . . ." He lifted his head and checked the clock. "Lord. School isn't until nine A.M. That's four hours from now. You could fit one and a half major league baseball games into that."

She was silent a moment. "I don't have any friends at school."

"Sure you do." When she didn't respond, Wes sighed, reaching over and turning on the lamp, finding a super-serious child peeking at him from beneath the brim of his tan felt hat. *How on God's green earth am I responsible for a five-year-old?* He asked himself that question several times a day, but the absurdity of the arrangement struck harder in the morning time. Wes cleared the sleep from his voice. "What about the girl with the Minnie backpack? You two seemed pretty chummy when I dropped you off yesterday."

"She's best friends with Hallie."

"That means she can't be your friend, too?"

Laura shrugged and pursed her lips, a clear indication she was about to change tactics. "My stomach is going to hurt in four hours."

Time to face facts. He wasn't getting that extra hour of sleep. Hell, he couldn't remember the last time he'd woken up in the actual daylight. *If only my friends could see me now.* In the not-so-distant past, Wes would have slept straight through a hangover and woken up just in time to hit the San Antonio bars all over again with whatever cash he'd managed to scrape together rodeo riding. Even now—he was just shy of his twenty-fourth birthday—this was prime oats-sewing time.

But everything had changed with one phone call. He'd been yanked from a party lifestyle free of responsibilities in Texas and dropped onto a foreign planet, also known as Port Jefferson, Long Island. To raise a child.

Good thing it was temporary.

And hell, what wasn't?

Wes swallowed the hard object in his throat and rolled into a sitting position at the edge of the bed, reaching for his discarded shirt on the floor and tugging it on over his head. "Come on, kid. Let's go see what infomercials are on. Maybe we'll get lucky with some cooking demonstrations."

Laura brightened. "Maybe Instant Pot."

He ruffled her hair and helped her off the bed. "Here's hoping."

No sooner had Wes gotten Laura settled on the couch with a blanket did she request apple juice. While retrieving it from the kitchen, he leaned down and scanned the various schedules taped to his refrigerator. There were goddamn four of them. Four schedules. To say it was a rough transition, going from no schedules to four, would be putting it lightly.

Schedule one: kindergarten. Every day was a something day. Bring a silly poem to share with the class. Wear yellow. Dress like a superhero. For the love of God, wasn't homework enough? Wes wasn't even sure what PTA stood for, but when he found out, he was going to show up at a meeting and solve the mystery of who was behind these crazy-ass *something* days. He or she probably had fangs and a maniacal laugh.

He sighed and rested his head on the fridge a moment before focusing on schedule two, aka the Almighty Food Rotation. There was a local group of women called the Just Us League and they'd taken it upon themselves to bring him and Laura labeled containers of food when they found out about his situation. At first, he'd been pleased as hell to inform them he didn't need charity, but he had just enough humility to admit they'd be eating pizza every night without the meals.

Not to mention, the Just Us League organizer was Bethany Castle, and Wes didn't turn down chances to be in her vicinity. No, sir. Only an idiot would. He might have taken a few hits to the noggin after being tossed off the backs of some angry bulls, but Wes wasn't a fool. He knew a ten when he saw one.

Bethany was a fifteen.

Which brought him to the third schedule: childcare. It was written in Bethany's handwriting, and he ran his finger over the neat, feminine letters now, smiling over her color-coded system of deciding which Just Us League member would babysit Laura until he got home from work each day. She was never on the schedule herself, of course. Kids weren't exactly her area of expertise.

Join the club, gorgeous.

What were her areas of expertise?

Turning him on and driving him nuts. And she excelled at them.

Good thing he was an expert at driving her nuts right back. Which brought Wes to his fourth and final schedule. Work.

Starting Monday morning, he'd have the opportunity to get under Bethany's skin on an *extended* basis. When Wes landed in Port Jefferson last month, he'd had just enough construction experience on his résumé to land a gig with the local house-flipping gods, Brick & Morty. Their next project happened to be located right across the street from Bethany's house. Yes, sir. Come Monday morning, he would be driving Bethany nuttier than ever.

Bring it on.

"Uncle Wes!" Laura shouted over an infomercial about revolutionary mops. "Apple juice!"

"Damn, kid. What did your last maid die from?" he drawled, prying open the fridge and taking out the yellow-and-gold container. "Do you want Cheerios?" he called over his shoulder. "Don't wait for me to sit down to ask. Tell me now."

"'Kay. Cheerios."

A smile played around his mouth as he took down a bowl, dumping in a handful of dry cereal. He might be a far cry from the ideal father figure, but he had this kid's quirks down to a science. They would need to begin figuring out her outfit by seven o'clock or she would panic and melt down. He frowned, trying to remember if he threw her favorite pink jean shorts into the washer.

"Apple juice!" his niece shrieked from the living room.

"Coming," he droned, walking to the couch and handing her the cup before wedging the small bowl of Cheerios between her knees. "Don't spill. This isn't my couch."

Laura sent him an uneasy glance and Wes cursed inwardly. Why had he gone and said that? She didn't need the reminder her parents had split and left her in the care of a clueless bachelor. Wasn't Wes being here in their place reminder enough? After the failure of his sister's relationship, she'd called him claiming to need a breather from her responsibilities, including motherhood. With no childcare experience to speak of, he'd gotten on a plane in San Antonio and flew to New York, only to realize this shit was *complicated*. Raising a child was a damn sight more than providing food and shelter; it also involved a fair amount of mind reading, multitasking, and patience—all on a very small quantity of sleep.

Good thing Wes was only there to fill in the gap until his sister decided to be a mother again and came home. *Just until I get my act together*, she'd said, but a month had come and gone without so much as a text. Still, Laura didn't need him reminding her their arrangement was temporary.

Wes sat down beside Laura and tucked her into his side. He waited a few minutes but she didn't eat a single Cheerio, making his stomach sink. His dumb comment was just another prime example of his inability to do this. To be here, attempting to be a child's caregiver. Knowing what would distract her and get her spirits back up, he snuck a Cheerio and popped it into his mouth.

"Hey," she complained.

"Couch snacks are fair game. You want food all to yourself, you sit at the table. Everyone knows that."

"No."

He shrugged. "Better eat them fast, before I snag some more."

Laura turned her body to shield the bowl of dry cereal and shoveled a fistful into her mouth. Better. She was still mid-chew when her spine snapped straight and she pointed at the television. "Oooh. Instant Pot."

Wes cozied deeper into the couch cushions. "Now we're

talking, kid." He waited until she was distracted by the info-mercial to work his mind voodoo. "You know, I'm no expert on making friends. But if I was hanging out in the classroom, pasting macaroni onto construction paper and stuff, just minding my own business . . . and one of the other kids did a *perfect* Scooby-Doo impression, I would want her at my craft table. Hundred percent."

She sucked in a breath. "*I* do a good Scooby-Doo impression."

"Oh, that's *right*." He snapped his fingers. "You do. How's that go again?"

"Scooby-Dooby-Dooooo," she howled, eyes crossing a little. "That one?"

Was he biased or should there be a talent scout knocking on their door? "That's quality work, Laura. It's like I'm in the room with Scooby."

She beamed. "Now you do it."

He did it terribly on purpose. "I can't compete. You're the master."

"Thanks." His niece crawled up under his arm and laid her head on his chest. "We don't glue macaroni to paper at school anymore. We have iPads now."

Instead of addressing her implication that he was out of touch, Wes looked down at the top of Laura's head, frozen. This was new. She'd never cuddled up to him before.

Unsure exactly how to proceed, he relaxed his arm around her shoulders, settled them in as a unit, and went back to watching the television. If there was a weird flip in the middle of his chest, he ignored it. Probably just fatigue or something.

Bethany walked through her living room, toothbrush stuck in her mouth. Using one hand to scrub her pearly whites, she ran the admiring, opposite hand over the jeweled throw pillows that decorated her couch. She wiggled her toes in her thick white carpet and sighed happily, moving the brush to her back teeth and cleaning them with a vigorous circling of bristles.

Tonight's Just Us League meeting was set to begin in an hour. Their official positivity whiteboard was arranged at the perfect angle in the living room, and the blinds were drawn to an optimal position, allowing in the right amount of Saturday evening light, made hazy by late-fall weather. Champagne flutes were arranged on the kitchen island, waiting to be filled with bubbly. She'd lit a candy-apple candle upon returning from her hair appointment, and the interior of her home called to mind a small-town harvest festival.

"God, I'm good," she said, the words garbled by her toothbrush. A dribble of white foam cascaded down her chin and she swiped it away. "Ew, Beth."

She jogged up the stairs to her en suite bathroom, the glowing flicker of her favorite vanilla candles swaying against the white tile, before she spit into the sink and wiped her mouth. She turned her good side to the mirror and smiled, giving her blond hair a gentle tousle.

"Welcome, everyone. What smell? Oh, the candle? I picked it up at an outdoor bazaar in the Hamptons while shopping for artwork to stage our latest flip." She leaned close to the mirror and ran her tongue along her top row of teeth. "Glamorous? Me? No. You're so sweet."

She pushed away from her marble vanity, turning on her big toe and entering the bedroom. Two outfits were laid out on the bed. A cream-colored cashmere sweater that left one shoulder bare, paired with black leather leggings. And a red turtleneck dress. Since she usually wore the former with boots and wouldn't be leaving the house, she went with option one and slipped on a pair of gold ballet flats to complement the ensemble.

"You'll do," she whispered, looking over her reflection with a critical eye. "You've worn this before, though."

Bethany scratched at the side of her neck on her way into the walk-in closet. Her pulse started to hammer beneath her fingertips and she forced herself to stop scratching before she left red marks. She didn't have time for an outfit change now. Georgie and Rosie would be arriving any minute to help set up for the meeting—

The front door opened and closed downstairs, the voices of her younger sister and their best friend drifting up the stairs.

She took a centering deep breath. "Be there in just a minute!" she called cheerfully, yanking hangers off the racks and running a mental checklist of the outfits she'd worn since the inception of their women-powered support group. If the members knew she was agonizing over her outfit, they would laugh at her. Tell her she was being silly. Heck, some of them wore variations of the same ensemble to every meeting, didn't they?

They weren't Bethany Castle, though.

No. They were a hell of a lot more authentic.

Realizing she was scratching at her neck again, Bethany forced herself to stop, finding a silk emerald-green tunic at the back of her closet with the tags still hanging from the wrist. She snapped them off and pulled the garment over her head, speed-walking toward the stairs. Before descending, she tucked her hair artfully behind one ear and fanned the irritated skin at her neck. Then, fingertips casually trailing down the banister, she greeted Georgie and Rosie with a smile. "You ladies look like I need a cocktail."

Georgie laughed from her perch on the kitchen stool. "On it," she said, popping the cork from a chilling bottle of champagne Bethany had arranged in a silver bucket beside the flutes.

"I'm on food," Rosie called, sticking a tray of something delicious looking into the oven. "Beth, we need to have a serious talk about Georgie."

"I'm right here," Georgie protested. "You can't miss me."

"Let me guess." Bethany accepted a glass of champagne and took a small sip. "This is bachelorette party related."

Rosie nodded. "She won't commit to a plan. She's noncommittal."

Georgie threw up her hands, splashing champagne onto the island. "I don't want one. The wedding is the party. I don't need a pre-party party."

Bethany stuck out her bottom lip. "Pre-parties serve a purpose. It will save you from drinking too much and stumbling through the cha-cha slide on your wedding day. You'll have gotten it out of your system." She grabbed a folded kitchen towel and wiped up the fizzy splotch of alcohol.

"Besides, I've already planned it. There's a binder with colored tabs and everything."

Rosie snorted into the back of her wrist. "Knew it."

"What?" Georgie sputtered, before falling silent for a moment. "Details, please." She shifted on her stool. "You know . . . so I can say no. Firmly."

Bethany smiled into a sip of champagne. "You won't say no."

Her certainty wasn't unfounded. As a professional house stager for her family's company, Brick & Morty, planning, executing, and beautifying was Bethany's purpose on this earth. When presented with a blank canvas, she took light, shadow, spacing, practicality, and wow factor into account—and she turned an empty shell into a home. No stitch out of place or book spine askew. Perfection. Something inside her never stopped yearning for that tip-top mountain peak. That awed reaction she received at the end of her stages. That rush of accomplishment.

At some point that quest for perfection had bled into every other aspect of her life and continued to bleed, and bleed, but that was a positive thing. Right?

When she realized her hand was curled too tightly around the champagne flute, she set it down with a flourish and smiled. "We're starting with brunch at the Four Seasons, moving on to an afternoon of pampering—you'll be getting married hairless and shiny, you're welcome—and we'll round the night out with a harmless orgy. What's not to love?"

"Stop. Oh God." Georgie coughed, eyes tearing. "Champagne. Burning the insides of my nose. So painful."

"Tell her the real plan, you evil woman," Rosie scolded, biting back a smile.

Bethany rolled her eyes. "Fine. We're ending the night with a combined bachelor-bachelorette dinner at Buena Onda. Mom and Dad will be there, too. I knew that's what you'd want. Travis and Georgie forever. Yada yada. You make me sick."

Georgie jumped off her stool and threw her arms around Bethany's middle. "I love it. I can commit to this." She squealed and attempted to crush Bethany's ribs. "Thank you. It's perfect."

Bethany kissed her cheek and waved her off. "You're welcome."

The doorbell rang. Bethany picked up her champagne flute again, holding it with a loose wrist, and put on a bright hostess smile on her way to the door. Details mattered. Every detail mattered. When she opened the door with a flick of her wrist, leaned a hand high on the doorframe, and tossed her hair, taking a dramatic sip of champagne, the women on her porch saw exactly what she wanted them to see. A woman who had it all together.

A woman who made everything look effortless.

Ten minutes later, two dozen women were settled in, some on the couch, others sitting cross-legged on the floor or even standing. Bethany took her place in front of the whiteboard and picked up her marker, twirling it between her fingers and giving the room a sly look.

"Shall we open with our song?"

A cheer lifted the already-joyful atmosphere. Their theme

song was totally ridiculous, had been cobbled together after way too many drinks, and was sung to the tune of "Jingle Bells," but it was theirs. This *club* was theirs. It was hard to believe they'd grown from three members who'd had the misfortune of being early to Zumba class . . . into this.

That night, she'd been good and fed up with the male population, having been cheated on by a community theater director. She'd noticed her friends were in similar situations and decided to bolster her journey to a man-free lifestyle with a club where women supported women. Now they were a veritable faction of ass kickers who met weekly to discuss their goals and support one another in that journey. She'd watched the meek grow mighty in this very room, witnessed her own sister and best friend reach for their professional dreams.

Each week, Bethany stood at the whiteboard and listed accomplishments so they could be seen in black and white. Or gold metallic, as it were.

If she continued to razzle-dazzle them with proof of their own amazingness, maybe they wouldn't realize she was long overdue to add her own triumph to the board. Oh, she'd made a lot of noise about branching out from the family business on her own.

I want to swing a sledgehammer.

At the time, she'd meant it. Even now, she meant it. The actual swinging was yet to happen.

Bethany clicked her heels together, holding the marker like a mic. "I'll start." She made a show of clearing her throat, garnering a few chuckles from the room. "Lady balls, lady balls, we're not on short supply . . ."

Everyone picked up where she left off. "If a challenge seems too tough, just poke it in the eye!"

"Olé!" Georgie finished.

With the notes still hanging in the air, Bethany tapped her fingernails on the whiteboard. "Who would like to go first?" She squinted at Cheryl, who'd been struggling with her new job hunt. "How did the interview go this week?"

"Well." Cheryl pressed her lips together. "Very well, actually. The firm made me an offer and I used it to leverage a raise from my current employer. So . . . I booked a trip to Barbados." She slapped her hands to her cheeks. "Is that crazy? I haven't had a vacation in four years."

"Not crazy!" Georgie called on her trip back from the fridge, a fresh bottle of chilled champagne in her hand. "You've definitely earned the right to lounge on the beach and drink rum out of a coconut. Or a scuba instructor's navel. Dealer's choice! Three cheers for Cheryl."

Clapping and whistling filled the room.

Bethany wrote "leverage/Barbados/navel drinking" on the board and turned back to the room. "Who is nex—"

"What about you, Bethany?" Cheryl asked, still flushed from the applause. "You were so excited to try and flip a house by yourself, without your family breathing down your neck. You applied for those construction permits months ago, right? Have they come through?"

Bethany retained her wide smile, but a screw seemed to loosen in her belly button, dropping her stomach to the carpet. In her mind's eye, she could see the thick envelope where she'd stashed it inside her suitcase and shoved it to the back of her closet. It had been there for weeks, taunting her.

What were you thinking, striking off on your own?

Since graduating college, Bethany had been staging houses for Brick & Morty, but there was a part of her that had grown restless with paint swatches and shiplap and tasteful greenery, while having no say on layout.

She'd been *so sure* she wanted that to change.

"No, I haven't received the permits yet," she breathed, her thumb biting into the dry-erase marker when her voice didn't sound quite natural enough. "But you better believe I'll hear back soon. I didn't want to resort to calling in favors, but desperate times . . ."

A bead of perspiration slid down her spine.

"Would someone else like to—"

"It's a little odd, isn't it? Stephen seems to get his permits so fast," Cheryl continued, referring to Bethany's older brother. Also known as the CEO of Brick & Morty, who wanted to keep everything—including Bethany—in her place. Cheryl gestured toward the front window. "The house across the street only went on sale last month. I heard they're already starting demo on Monday! He must be bribing someone at the permit office."

A buzzing started in Bethany's skull. "I'm sorry. Did you say Brick and Morty is starting a flip on Monday across the street from my house?"

"Mom might have mentioned during my final dress fitting," Georgie said from her lean against the wall, wincing. "Sorry, Beth. I thought Stephen told you."

"He did not, but it's fine. I mean"—Bethany let out a casual laugh, tucking a loose strand of hair behind her ear— "with a construction crew across the street, I guess I'll have to start wearing pants to the mailbox. A little annoying, but I'll cope."

Laughter spilled out around the room and Bethany used the moment to divert focus from herself. Carrying on the rest of the meeting was not easy, however, because her mind kept returning to two very alarming facts.

One: she couldn't stall any longer. Either she started her own flip or she backed out—and the latter wasn't an option if she wanted to retain her pride.

Two: Wes Daniels, the man who drove her insane with his Texas twang and eyes that scrutinized her far too closely, would be working across the street for the foreseeable future. She saw him on job sites during the final stages, when measuring for furniture or instructing painters. But across the street from her home, Wes would be impossible to avoid.

A twist in Bethany's belly told her World War III was on the horizon.

Bring it on.

CHAPTER TWO

Bethany stared down at the paperwork spread across her bed.

Every time she started to gather up the construction permits, she dropped them again and paced instead.

It was now or never. Put up or shut up. Shit or get off the pot.

If she waited any longer to commence her solo flip, people were going to grow suspicious. They might not peg Bethany as a coward, but they were going to keep asking questions. A couple of months ago, she'd announced to the family that she would be striking out on her own, since Stephen refused to let her run a solo flip.

They'd been aghast. And she would be lying if she said that hadn't shaken her already shaky confidence.

Bethany understood their desire to maintain the status quo. After all, she kept everything, from her thoughts to her sports bras, in neat little categorized compartments. It was a family trait and she'd been given the biggest dose of control freakitude.

So why was flipping a house alone so important to her?

Why had she made such a massive issue of the whole thing?

Why not stick to staging, a practice in which she was actually skilled?

Bethany sat down on the floor and arranged herself in a meditative position. She rested the backs of her hands on her knees and breathed in deeply, desperately trying to exhale the stress of what she needed to do this morning.

Visualize.

See yourself walking across the street where Brick & Morty have already banged the company's signature sign into the front lawn and started demo.

See it happening and then do it.

Wes Daniels's smirk appeared in her head and she fell backward onto a cloud of fluffy white carpet with a groan. The younger man always seemed to make it his mission to needle her until her cool, calm, and collected demeanor faltered. His presence was going to make this already-terrifying morning worse.

"Why?" She scratched at the spot on her neck. "Why am I doing this to myself?"

She knew the answer, but her moment of courage had been buried by the passage of time. Making her forget the tingling sensation in her belly, the scary excitement of deciding to test herself. Yes, she was a great stager. Yes, it was still something she enjoyed, but . . . did she have to remain in one lane forever?

Staying low to the ground, Bethany got on her hands and knees and crawled to her bedroom window, peeking over the sill at the house across the street. In the short amount of time since the crew arrived, there were already tools strewn across the lawn, a sawhorse in the driveway, noise. So much noise.

Construction was not neat.

She'd been an idiot to visualize herself with a perfect ponytail and high-waisted jeans, sashaying her way into a fixer-upper and demolishing walls in style. Real life was not HGTV. There was no thirty-second take of the host burying an ax in a wall before the director yelled "Cut!" and the real crew took over again. When she headed her own flip, she would be making all the decisions, doing all the work.

And it might turn out less than perfect.

It might turn out terrible.

Bethany turned away from the window and leaned back against the wall, pressing her fingers tightly to the center of her forehead and breathing, in and out. In and out. Maybe it was time to talk to a therapist. Knowing one's worst faults didn't mean one could fix them alone.

Bethany was a prime example of that.

When she was thirteen, she'd bought a pair of uncomfortable Mary Janes with a wedge heel. Her mother had warned her not to wear them to school without breaking them in first. Had she listened? No. But she'd come home with a smile on her face, danced up the stairs, and closed herself inside her bedroom—before falling to the floor with a gasp of pain and prying off the shoes to reveal twin, bleeding blisters. Then she'd bandaged them up and worn the shoes again the following day.

She was one stubborn bitch. And the thing she was most stubborn about was always, without fail, getting everything just right.

If this flip ended up less than amazing, she wouldn't be able to slap a Band-Aid on it. She'd have to face everyone's inevitable disappointment. She'd have to watch the dawning realization on their faces that she wasn't perfect.

It took Bethany a few more bracing breaths to climb to her feet. She stood in the center of her room for a moment, the crisp, white décor and tasteful Tiffany picture frames making her feel slightly more in control.

Well.

If she was going to make a statement this morning, she'd better look good doing it. With a resolve she didn't necessarily feel, Bethany threw back her shoulders and marched into her walk-in closet, silk robe fluttering in her wake.

Wes paused with the water bottle halfway to his lips, eyebrows lifting at the sight of Bethany crossing the street. With a runway walk like that, the woman was on some kind of mission. He couldn't help but take a moment to appreciate being in the presence of a living, breathing goddess, because soon enough, she was sure to rain down holy hell on somebody's head. *Probably mine.*

To Wes, the nonstop contention between him and Bethany was foreplay. Plain and simple. But the more time that passed, the more he was starting to think that Bethany was on a different wavelength. One that didn't include them sweating it out between the sheets. Which, Lord, he'd been fantasizing about daily and nightly since jump street.

Based on the information he'd been able to glean via Travis, who took pride in having the gossip through his fiancée, Bethany wasn't the kind of woman who took part in a fling. Until recently, she'd been interested in the whole relationship thing, but with the inception of the Just Us League, she'd gone on a man hiatus. So even if Wes *was* in Port Jefferson for the long haul, his chances were slim.

His slim chances might *also* be due to the addictive vitriol they'd developed, but stopping was easier said than done. At this point, he couldn't very well show up on her doorstep with a dozen long-stemmed roses and tell her she was the most breathtaking woman he'd ever met.

She'd roundhouse him in the nuts.

They were halfway through October, but nobody would guess it based on the way Bethany was dressed. She was wearing a white strapless tube top tucked into a long, flowing skirt with some kind of girly flower pattern on it. Her hair was down, curled a little, and blowing in the wind, showing off her pretty neck.

"Hell," he muttered, shaking his head. The woman's brother was no more than ten feet away, but even that wasn't enough to stop Wes from appreciating the shake of her tits, the way her skirt's thin material outlined her swaying hips.

There was nothing, *nothing*, more beautiful than what he was looking at right now. His palms started to perspire inside his work gloves, a fireball of lust lighting up and starting to spin in his belly. He'd been the one to wake up early this morning, instead of Laura, anticipating the extra chances to see Bethany. Be in her environment. Maybe even speak with her, get a rise out of her with a joke about their age difference, make her blush or her blue eyes flash. It got his blood moving like nothing else. Not even the danger of a sold-out Saturday-night rodeo.

Bethany Castle. The ultimate thrill ride.

It shouldn't excite him to see her so determined to shake up their orderly construction zone, but hell, did it ever. *Come on then, darlin'. Don't hold back.*

When she reached the door's threshold, Wes leaned a hip against the wall and did his best to look bored, when in reality, his senses were sharpened like the tip of a number-two pencil before a test.

Bethany breezed through the opening left by the missing front door, and the cacophony of male voices and Sheetrock mutilation ceased. Her scent, an expensive mixture of tea and flowers, reached him through the cloud of sawdust, sending a rippling tightness through his abdomen. She was holding a manila envelope in her right hand and he caught the slightest tremor pass through her fingers before she crossed her arms over her chest.

"Hey, Beth," Stephen called from the back of the house, his voice growing closer as he progressed to where they were standing, swiping a wrist across his sweaty forehead. "You need something? It's a little early for measurements, isn't it? We've barely finished gutting the place." Bethany's brother gestured to the carnage surrounding his work boots. "Won't need couches for a while."

Wes heard her long intake of breath. Did it . . . hitch there in the middle?

He narrowed his eyes.

There had been some tension between Bethany and Stephen since Wes had arrived in Port Jefferson. Without appearing too interested, he'd managed to gather a little intel from Travis and knew Bethany was looking to forsake the family business and strike out on her own, leading to the siblings being at odds. But it didn't get in the way of their jobs and they still shared a wisecrack on occasion, so he'd let the whole notion of a rift fall by the wayside.

That said, he definitely caught the flash in Bethany's eyes when Stephen reduced her job to couches.

Not that he would ever let on that he paid such close attention, but he'd seen one of the finished houses put up for sale by Brick & Morty. The men might be responsible for the heavy lifting, but Bethany's staging sold the damn place. She worked a certain magic that turned a place from four empty walls to a . . . lifestyle. God, that sounded uppity as shit, but it was true. She created a better version of whatever life buyers were leading and made them envision themselves within it, almost like a challenge. Even Wes had been compelled to up his decorating game, so he'd brought Laura to Target and came home with an area rug, two new lamps, and a pumpkin pie–scented candle.

He'd lie about that under oath.

Bottom line, he didn't appreciate the way Bethany's big brother had whittled it all down to couches. More like couches, paint color, shelving, storage, character. He bit down hard on his bottom lip to stop himself from speaking up. The inner workings of the Castle family was none of his business. He was an extra in a movie that would continue long after he'd gone back to Texas.

Trying to ignore the sweep of disquiet in his chest, Wes focused on Bethany. There was something off about her today and it was making him extra reckless. Her usual composure was there, but it was on the blink. Coming and going, as if she could only hang on to it for a moment, before it slipped away.

There. She found her confidence, firming her shoulders and pinning Stephen with a look. "I'm not going to need measurements for this flip." She pried the paperwork from where she'd stuffed it beneath her arm, then promptly shoved it back into place. "My permits arrived for the project across town, so . . . that's it. I'm going to begin work on it next week."

Stephen cocked an eyebrow. "You can't do both?"

"No."

"Why the hell not?"

"Because I want to give this job my whole focus." She shrugged a shoulder. "And if you think it's just a matter of picking out couches, get Kristin to do it."

The oldest Castle paled a little. Not surprising. Stephen's wife was slightly unbalanced and even she knew it. If Kristin was put in charge of staging, she would probably do a horrific job on purpose, just so Stephen would have to hurt her feelings, giving her an opportunity to milk his guilt afterward.

Men and women and their mind games. Hell, he despised that shit, and yet, look at him and Bethany. They danced around each other with insults, making a big show of being incompatible when Christ knew that was the furthest thing from the truth.

Wes knew what incompatible looked like. Hell, he grew up in foster care. He could probably write a book about the way people could make each other unhappy. In the epilogue, he'd let everyone know he'd never be one of them.

Yes, sir. He would be shackle-free forever.

But Stephen almost seemed to enjoy those shackles and the mind games his wife inflicted. A damned confusing anomaly, to be sure.

"Bethany." Stephen sighed. "Be reasonable about this."

She rolled her eyes. "You've known about this since the beginning of fall. I'm sorry if you didn't take me seriously enough to plan accordingly."

Stephen's nostrils flared, his silence in the wake of Bethany's barb making the crew shift nervously. "I would have taken you seriously if the permits hadn't been issued weeks ago."

Bethany jolted and dropped the envelope, sending paperwork spewing out onto the ground. She bent down to pick it up quickly, those tremors back in her fingers. "Go to hell, Stephen," she muttered under her breath. "You shouldn't have been checking up on me with your friends at the permit office."

Wes noticed that Stephen looked regretful over what he'd said, but Wes was more concerned about Bethany. What the hell did Stephen mean, she'd gotten the permits weeks ago? Why would she wait this long to start the job? Or even say anything?

She straightened with red cheeks and Wes ground his back teeth together.

Whatever was going on here, he didn't like it. Sure, he got a rise out of her once in a while, but she always hit back. Bethany didn't get shaken up like this.

"Come on, Beth." Stephen sighed again. "Where are you going to get a crew by next week? Let me finish here and I'll reschedule my next job so I can help you out."

Her laugh was short. "By help out, you mean take over."

Stephen didn't bother denying it. "We're heading into winter in a few months. You're not going to find anyone good who's looking for a gig that short. Trust me. Everyone worth a damn is already in this room." He gestured to his sister. "Including you."

"Oh, come on, jackass," she returned. "Don't backpedal now. You were doing so well at being condescending."

Wes breathed a little easier with her tone back to normal, but his optimism dipped again when he saw how tightly she was holding the envelope. Her gaze flitted over to him and the color of her cheeks deepened another shade.

Shit.

Was it possible she'd put off starting the flip because she was nervous? That didn't track, considering what he knew about Bethany and her ball-buster nature. But his eyes were telling him a different story altogether. She was vulnerable in front of the entire crew right now, and her throat seemed to be stuck in a permanent state of swallowing. A lot like his own.

Shit.

"I'm going with her," Wes said, stripping off his gloves.

Someone dropped a sledgehammer in the back of the house.

"W-wait. What?" Stephen sputtered. "Now?"

"Yup." He finally made eye contact with a stupefied Bethany. "We better get a game plan together and start rounding up materials."

She couldn't seem to land on a response. "I . . . I . . ."

"You what?"

"I mean, this is all very Renée Zellweger in *Jerry Maguire* of you, but . . ."

He knew exactly which scene from *Jerry Maguire* she was referring to—when Tom Cruise quits his fancy sports agent job and Renée is the only one who joins him, even though he's been reduced to stealing the office goldfish— but Bethany needed to know accepting his help wouldn't change anything between them. Otherwise she might turn him down, and he got a weird pinch in his throat when he thought of her all alone, trying to install drywall without breaking a nail. "*Jerry Maguire*? Never heard of it. That one of your generation's black-and-white films or something?"

That spark zipped back into her eyes and relief caused a hitch in his chest. "Apologies. I should have referenced *Fast & Furious Nine*."

He bit back a smile. "You ready to go yet?"

She seemed to remember everyone was watching them and started chewing on that sexy bottom lip. "I'm thinking."

"Bethany," Stephen cut in. "You're really going to come up in here and steal one of my best guys—"

"Thanks, pal," Wes said, tipping an invisible hat.

"What do you think Dad is going to say about this?" Stephen finished.

"Really?" Bethany intoned. "'I'm telling Dad'? Are we back in the station wagon driving to Hershey Park when we were eight?"

Face slightly red, Stephen looked over his shoulder at the men behind him. "I only meant it's going to stress him out, us moving in separate directions. We're supposed to be one team."

"Well, you know what they say, Stephen," Bethany said breezily. "There's no asshole in team."

Wes coughed a laugh into his fist.

Bethany caught him, her lips jumping at one corner before she sobered. "Before I agree to anything"—she shot a look at their audience and moved closer to Wes, lowering her voice—"I think we should try and get through a planning-stage meeting first. You know, just to confirm we can actually do it."

He matched her quiet tone. "I was thinking the same thing. We should do it first. Cut the tension."

"I can hear you," Stephen wailed.

"You know what I mean," Bethany snapped under her breath, all worked up and beautiful. So close he could taste the expensive coffee she'd drank that morning in the air between them. "If we can get through a meeting without biting each other's heads off, then we'll consider working together."

"We're just going to pretend you have other options, huh?"

She blinked and drew in a deep breath. "Are we having a meeting or not?"

Sharpness jabbed him in the middle. "Yeah."

His answer surprised her, but she only let him see it for a second, before she turned on a sandaled heel with a hair flip. "Stephen, if you bring this up at the rehearsal dinner and ruin the evening, I'll castrate you. As you were, boys." She stopped at the door to glance back at Wes and he held his breath. "Meet you at the house."

CHAPTER THREE

*W*hat happened to my neat, orderly life?

Bethany sat in the driver's side of her Mercedes, staring at the busted childhood home of Travis Ford, her sister's fiancé. She still couldn't believe he'd given her the house free and clear. Sure, it had been part of his plan to win back Georgie after their epic breakup, but still, the move had been generous, to say the least.

Even though said house was literally falling down.

If they didn't demolish it themselves, the next stiff breeze would probably do the job on their behalf. Overgrown weeds and gnarled trees all but obscured the view of the house from the driveway and main road. Bethany hadn't even been inside yet, but the interior had to be even worse.

Starting from scratch was not in her wheelhouse. She usually walked into a fully finished home and applied the final brushstrokes.

What if she buried a sledgehammer into a wall and a colony of spiders burst out like a geyser? Hopefully she could duck in time so they all landed on Wes.

Wes.

What just happened?

Out of everyone in Port Jefferson, Wes was the last person she would expect to volunteer to help her. Sleep with her, yes. Confine himself to close quarters with her and take direction? No. No, she definitely hadn't expected that.

It was almost as if he'd seen through the bravado that fooled everyone else, straight to the mess beneath. Had that left him no choice but to help, whether he wanted to or not? If that was the case, she needed to do a way better job of masking her insecurities and flaws. Especially from Wes, with whom she waged a constant war of words. And now they were working together.

In the space of a single morning, nothing was neat and orderly anymore.

The road ahead was a dramatic curve, and she couldn't see far enough into the distance. As a thorough planner, the uncertainty made her feel like a balloon floating aimlessly into the clouds, no idea when she would burst.

Would there be nothing but air inside of her, too?

Bethany jumped when her cell phone buzzed on the console.

When Georgie's name blinked on the screen, she picked it up and hit talk. "Really? News has spread already? I just left Stephen's job site ten minutes ago."

"You know how it works. Stephen told Dad, Dad told Mom, Mom called me like a cat with a cross-eyed canary in her mouth."

Her nose wrinkled. "That imagery is unsettling."

"I want your side of the story while you bandy about a

glass of wine. I won't rest until it happens. Is it true that Wes pulled a Zellweger?"

Bethany laughed despite her nerves. "I'll oblige you tomorrow night at Zumba class."

"Oh my God. I forgot."

"Nope. Kristin is torturing us for guessing she was pregnant before she could do a big, dramatic reveal."

"*You* guessed, not me, and when is she going to tell Stephen?"

"Probably a split second before you say 'I do.' It would satisfy our sister-in-law's sense of drama. Picture it. Gender reveal by way of wedding objection." With Georgie laughing in her ear, Bethany checked the rearview mirror in time to see Wes's truck turn into the driveway. "Tomorrow night, Georgie. There might even be more to tell by then."

"Are you sure? I was kind of hoping for right the hell now."

"One does not simply bandy wine before noon."

"It's my pre-wedding week," Georgie disagreed. "Day drinking is not only allowed, but encouraged. I've already got Rosie on the other line awaiting a time and locale."

"Are you avoiding working on your vows?"

"Yes, of course I am!"

Bethany snorted. "See you tomorrow, nutcase."

She cut off her sister mid-wail and schooled her features, climbing out of her car at the same time Wes unfolded his lean, muscled body out of his truck. Momentarily forgetting about the professionalism she wanted to present, her traitorous gaze wandered up the worn material of his dusty jeans, taking its time moving over his thick thighs and the old gray T-shirt where it brushed his hard-working zipper.

Come on, she couldn't help but notice the way those metal teeth strained to keep his package from unwrapping itself.

Men from Long Island wore looser jeans.

He was living here now—shouldn't he abide by the customary wardrobe?

Annoyed at the steam swirling in her belly, Bethany zoomed her attention to his face with resolve, only to catch his knowing wink. "Here I am, boss," he said gruffly. "Put me to work."

She was silent for a full minute.

What body language did a woman display when she got wet? Did she press her thighs together or lick her lips? *Do not do any of those things. Stand still. Just let the moisture spread and those intimate muscles coil without any outward reaction.*

Bethany cleared her throat and focused on preparing her words. This morning might have moved faster than the speed of light, but she'd had some time to think on the drive to her solo flip. She'd always kind of disregarded Wes's advances as something of a joke being played at her expense. How many times had he made cracks about her age? Sometimes she believed that he was physically interested in her, and other times she told herself not to be sucked into whatever game he was playing. Still, just in case he was really interested in taking her to bed, she needed to manage his expectations.

"Wes?"

"Yes, Bethany."

"If you volunteered to help me thinking it might be a nifty

little inroad to sleeping together, you can forget it. Even if I wasn't on a voluntary man hiatus, it wouldn't be happening."

Her stomach knitted waiting for his response. Why was she so worried he might disappoint her and renege on his offer to help? They didn't have the kind of relationship where one could let the other down. They didn't have a relationship, period.

Wes's expression hadn't changed a single iota. And it remained impassive as he used a booted foot to push off his truck. "If we're going to work together," he responded slowly, "you're going to start giving me a little more credit."

"Um, okay? Let me sift through the sexual innuendoes you've been making for a month and find this credit you speak of."

He sliced a hand through the air between them. "Sex is off the table."

Bethany reared back, truly awkward sounds sputtering in her throat. "It was never on the table, cowboy."

His skeptical expression said he thought otherwise, but he wisely refrained from voicing his incorrect opinion out loud. "Look. I'm attracted to you, Bethany. Like hell. Would I like to spend a couple sweaty afternoons with you in the sack finding out if you fuck as well as you fight, yeah. I really would. But I wouldn't use this job as leverage to make it happen. So like I said, sex is off the table now."

"This isn't going to work," she wheezed.

"Because you want sex on the table?"

"Stop phrasing it like that! It's sex. Not a placemat." This was already spiraling out of control. "And this isn't going to work because of the way you—"

"Get under your skin like an itch you can't find with two hands? Feeling's mutual and I can't do anything about that." He held out his palm faceup. "Keys?"

"Drop dead."

Wes was already striding past her. "I only spent a year working construction when I was nineteen, but it was enough to know this. First thing you're going to want to do is give this flip a name. Personalize it. Make it matter." He reached the front door, stopped, backed up, then kicked it open while Bethany gaped. "How does War of the Roses sound? Seems appropriate."

Bethany hustled past Wes into the house, careful not to brush against him. "Now who's making old-timey film references?"

"I'm not too proud to suck up to the boss . . ."

Wes's voice trailed off when he stepped into the house beside Bethany.

Their sight adjusted to the lack of light at the same time.

"Shit," they whispered in unison.

They might as well have been standing outside. Bethany didn't know where to look first. The dirt caking the walls and floor? The boulder-sized hole in the ceiling, complete with tree branches snaking inside and growing along the exposed beams? Two windows were broken. The *drip-drip-drip* of water came from down the hallway, which was especially ominous because it hadn't rained in a week.

"We're calling it the Doomsday Flip." She sensed Wes watching her.

"We?"

Bethany hedged. "I don't think I can . . . well, that is to say, surely one person couldn't tackle this alone, so . . ."

"Hate to break it to you, darlin', but I don't think two people can tackle this one. Not if you want to stick to a reasonable time frame." He squinted his right eye. "We have a hiring budget?"

There was no mistaking the easing of pressure in her chest when he used the word "we." "Considering Travis gifted me the house, it's a pretty healthy budget. We can afford additional labor." She shifted. "But I want to make the decisions."

He nodded once. "I'm hearing you, Bethany."

How was this the same man who talked so bluntly about fucking back in the driveway? Who *was* Wes Daniels? A crass, innuendo-cracking good ol' boy? An honorable guy who showed up to raise his niece at a moment's notice and Zellweger'd in front of his bros? He vacillated too quickly between the opposite sides of himself. God help her if there were more layers to this man. Two was already confusing enough.

Wes produced a pencil from behind his ear and a notebook from his back pocket, flipping it open to the middle. "Let's talk floor plan. What do you have in mind?"

You would think she'd never set foot inside a house before. Or logged a million hours listening to Stephen and her father talk measurements and layout. The very fundamentals of construction had been her bedtime stories. Now, given a blank canvas for the first time, as soon as she had a burgeoning idea, she discarded it, mentally citing a reason someone wouldn't like it. Or it wouldn't be exactly right. How long had she been standing there in silence, staring at the walls and begging them to inspire her?

"Talk it out," Wes said, sounding almost bored, but when she glanced up, he was watching her intently.

Bethany swallowed hard and turned in a circle, her sandals making a sifting sound on the dirty floor. "We need it fully gutted, obviously. The kitchen needs to be twice as large, which will mean sacrificing the tiny dining room for a cozy breakfast nook." She wet her lips. "This is a starter house for sure. Which means kids. Parents needing to watch them from the kitchen at all times. They'll need extra dining space, so we can put in a chest-high dividing wall to double as a breakfast bar. Can we make the whole front of the house visible from the kitchen?"

"Is that what you want?"

What she wanted was a *Yes, that's a great idea.* Apparently she wasn't getting it, though. "Yes," she forced herself to say. An answer that required relying totally on her own instincts. "That's what I want."

He made some notes on his pad, looking much older with his furrowed brow. "You brave enough to tour the rest of the house?"

She gave him an eye roll. "I think I can handle it," she muttered, already stepping over some broken glass and picking her way down the hallway.

A rat came careening out of the first doorway and trucked a path right across Bethany's foot. "Oh! Rat rat rat. No. Noooo!" With her screech echoing off the hallway walls, and potentially putting them in danger of the house collapsing, Bethany turned and scaled Wes's body like a hysterical rock climber.

He dropped his pad and pencil just in time to accommodate her, his only reaction to raise an eyebrow. Getting her feet off the floor required locking her ankles at the small of his back and if she hadn't been so squicked-out over her brush with rodentia, she would have noticed he didn't so much as flinch or strain under her weight. She would think of it later, though. A lot. "First, we exterminate," she heaved breathily beside his ear, patting him twice on the shoulder. "Can you take me outside, please?"

"Uh-huh." In the slowest turn ever executed by man or animal, Wes started a sloth-like trek back the way they'd come.

"Can't you go any faster?"

She ignored the shiver that traveled down her spine when his laugh tickled her neck. "Wouldn't want to drop you, darlin'."

"Your arms aren't even around me. It's all cling."

"I just don't want to lead you on. Sex is off the table, remember?"

"Move! My legs are starting to shake."

He groaned and wrapped her in his arms, one beneath her butt, the other locking around the center of her back. "Bethany, I'm starting to think you say this shit on purpose to torture me."

She struggled to formulate a response but couldn't locate one. Not when synapses were firing in her brain, like coffee had been poured on a circuit board. She'd be lying if she claimed she'd never once wondered how Wes's body would meld with hers. She'd also be lying if she claimed the reality wasn't unnervingly better. His shoulders were the kind a woman could press her face into and laugh. They were . . . inviting. Warm. Strong. And they connected to a tan throat with lots of interesting stubble. Too interesting.

"You want me to disrobe for this exam?"

"What?" She jolted and slipped slightly lower in his hold and felt it. Felt his erection through the film of her skirt. Wes hissed, his gait slowing to a stop, and they just kind of hovered there in the entryway, gravity pressing her softness down on his thick sex, his breath rasping in her ear, Bethany's trapped in her lungs. "Labor," she forced out. "We need to hire labor. Let's talk about that."

The forearm resting on the small of her back flexed—and was it her imagination or did his lips brush her hair? "Labor. Right."

A tremor meandered through her limbs. "We'll have to look outside Port Jeff."

She felt Wes's internal vibration. One of his hands fisted in her skirt. "Bethany, if you expect me to focus on a goddamn word you're saying, we can't be one lowered zipper away from f—"

"Whoa. Don't finish that sentence." Wes acknowledging their compromising position out loud had the effect of a paintball to the face. What was she doing? She didn't even *like* this man. She couldn't nail him down as a type—and she never had that problem with men. They were self-involved pretending *not* to be self-involved, lazy, overly ambitious, or downright liars. Wes? He was just messy. That was the only category he fit into. No, wait, he was also too young. How could she forget that little piece of the pie? With a stern directive to stop being an idiot, Bethany unhooked her ankles, let her legs drop, and pushed away from his tense body. "There was a rat," she said to defend herself. "He had bloodstains on his teeth and a definite air of menace."

With a humorless laugh, Wes turned and stamped out of the house, leaving his back muscles rippling in his wake.

He started talking as soon as Bethany exited the still-open door behind him. "If it's all right with you, I'll round up some men to put on the payroll." As he said it, he settled his thumbs in the loops of his jeans, like he was going out to wrangle some cattle in a few minutes. "I can't be here every minute of the day. I'll have to leave to collect Laura from school and I won't feel comfortable leaving you with just anyone."

Her right eye twitched at his high-handed tone. "You'll be leaving me with myself, cowboy. A responsible human woman."

"Bethany, you can make the rules about everything else. But you're going to learn real quick that I won't compromise your safety."

"My God." She slapped her hands over her face. "This is a scene straight out of a Western. Next you're going to call me little lady and hock a loogie into a spittoon."

Wes tossed back his head and laughed.

"I'll be in charge of hiring," she said with a tight smile, gliding to her car.

The infuriating man stepped into her path, the humor bleeding quickly from his face. "I'm taking care of it. No compromises."

She poked him in the right pec. "This feels suspiciously like a macho male ritual where you insinuate yourself as leader of the pack, then make the rules of engagement regarding the available female."

"Allow me to clear up your suspicions. That's exactly what this is."

Bethany blinked at least seventeen times. "We agreed sex was off the table! Even though it was never even remotely on the table!"

Wes crossed his arms. "Doesn't mean I want it on the table for anyone else."

A look of wonder wafted across her face. Why was she even surprised by this behavior? One evening several weeks back, while Rosie and Dominic had been smack in the middle of splitsville, the girls had embarked upon a night out in the city that was promptly crashed by the men. Wes included.

A very nice downtown-finance-style gentleman had just purchased her a cocktail and was complimenting her dress when Wes plucked the drink out of her hand and slid the guy a twenty to cover it, his gaze telling him pointedly to *Beat it, bitch.*

"This chauvinism is unacceptable in the golden age of female superheroes and pegging, Wes."

She sensed he was trying not to laugh. "You know, I kind of sensed you'd be into tying up a man and prodding him to death."

Bethany waved her hands. "I didn't say I was into it."

"Sure about that?" He tucked his tongue into his cheek. "It was right there on the tip of your tongue."

"I'd like to shove my foot up your ass right now. Does that count?"

His eyes crinkled at the corners. "I'll do the hiring. You call an exterminator and a landscaper. Carve out some time this week to go pick out materials. Tile, flooring, cabinets."

Bethany hedged.

"The wedding is coming up this Sunday. No sense in taking on the job of finding a crew when you're already swamped."

She could concede this one thing or stand there arguing for another month, and frankly, she was beginning to almost enjoy sparring with Wes a little too much. Best to get out of there now. "Fine. You're in charge of hiring."

"Great. Let's aim to demo next week."

Bethany nodded and gave him a wide berth as she headed to her car. She settled her hand on the driver's-side door and stopped, tapping her nails on the white curve. Wes's eyes were on her. She could feel them. Climbing into her car and driving away without another word would be exactly what he expected, but she couldn't bring herself to do it just yet. Because as obnoxious as this man could be, she didn't feel nearly as alone or daunted as she had this morning.

Galling, really.

"Wes?"

"Yeah."

"Thank you." She sniffed. "Okay?"

"Okay." He winked at her. "We can still pretend to hate each other, if it makes you feel better about accepting my help."

She brushed her hair back. "Who's pretending?"

His lopsided smile was a fixture in her rearview mirror as she drove away.

What in God's name had she gotten herself into?

CHAPTER FOUR

This was Long Island, not Texas, but Wes was banking on some things never changing. And in Texas, when a man needed help, he went to the local hardware store. There was a good reason for that. In a hardware store, a man only had to drop the barest hint about his project and dudes started pouring out of the aisles touting the best advice. This was a ritual that saved men from having to actually ask for help while also making other men feel useful. Kind of like the "leave a penny, take a penny" of masculinity.

Being that Brick & Morty had all the best construction hands from Port Jefferson on the payroll, Wes picked up Laura from school and drove to the neighboring town of Brookhaven. She rode on his shoulders through the sticker-covered front door, making the overhead bell tinkle a second time with her fingers.

He breathed in the competing smells of paint, polyurethane, and sawdust, taking his time toward the back of the store. No need to appear too eager for advice. This kind of thing required timing and a visible lack of enthusiasm.

"Uncle Wes, can we get that?"

Wes's steps slowed even more. It never failed to jar him a little when Laura referred to him as Uncle Wes. Hell, after a month of five A.M. wake-up calls, he'd earned the title, hadn't he? And they *were* related by blood, even if Becky, Laura's mother, was only his half sister.

The fact that he'd had *any* family had come as a shock to him. Becky had shown up where he'd been living just before his sixteenth birthday, at a temporary foster home in San Antonio. A year younger than Wes, she'd been skinny and wary of her new, temporary parents. Wes had been wary, too. Especially when he found out, via their foster father, that he and Becky shared a mother and thus, the state had been attempting to place them together for a long time.

He'd been transferred among enough families at that point to know getting attached to anyone was stupid. So he'd ignored Becky for a while, until she started following him around, living in his shadow. She didn't need to say a word for him to surmise she'd had it worse than him. Her deer-in-the-headlights expression told him the ugly gist of the story. Because of that, because he knew the system could be harder on girls, he'd broken his rule and started covering for her when she didn't wake up in time to complete her chores. When they were moved to separate houses, she continued to call on him when she needed to be bailed out or when she was scared and needed a place to sleep, which usually ended up being his closet.

Not for the first time in the last couple of days, Wes wondered where Becky's "breather" from motherhood had taken her. Back to Texas? Further up the East Coast? It was anyone's guess. The one predictable thing about his sister was her unpredictability. She'd proven that many times, not the least of which was getting pregnant with Laura at seventeen.

"Uncle *Wes.*"

Shaking himself, he followed the direction indicated by Laura's grubby finger—really, he needed to start carrying baby wipes or something—landing on a garden gnome. He'd learned quickly that no matter where he brought his niece, be it the post office or a walk down the dang street, she would find something for sale she desperately needed. An outright "no" never worked, because a denial was always followed by no less than seventy-five groans of "PLEASE, UNCLE WES." So he'd started getting creative and distracting her with bullshit.

"A garden gnome?" He snorted. "Why do we need a fake one when we've got the real thing?"

Her knee jerked and caught him in the chin. "What?"

Wes tested his jaw. "You heard me. We've got a whole colony of them protecting the house. They don't get to running around until you start snoring, but I've caught them in action a time or two."

"You're lying." She paused and he could picture her pursing her lips, brow furrowed in thought. "What were they doing?"

"Playing ring-around-the-rosy. Chasing cats. Trying to steal my truck."

Her giggle made him smile. "Can we get McDonald's for dinner?"

"Depends. What's on our food calendar for tonight?"

"Green bean casserole."

Wes winced. "I could go for a Big Mac."

"Yay!" She folded her hands on his head. "What are we doing here?"

"I'm being a chauvinist. You're just along for the ride."

"What's a chauvinist?"

"In my case, it's someone who's being a damn fool over a woman."

Laura sighed. "Oh." Her fingers fidgeted in his hair and he could almost sense her working up to something. "I think my mom called my dad that name once."

"A chauvinist?"

Her voice was glum. "Yeah."

Something pointy turned over in his middle. "Did they call each other names a lot?"

She didn't answer right away. "Yes. It's a lot quieter without them home." A moment passed. "Do you know when my mom is coming back?"

"Soon, kid," he lied, feeling like a bastard. "Probably real soon." Not for the first time, he attempted to mentally reach out to his sister and nudge her into coming back, doing the right thing, even though he wasn't capable of telepathy. "Hey, I was thinking, there's no reason you can't get double toys at McDonald's tonight."

Her heels rebounded off his chest. "*Yes!*"

Crisis averted. For now. How many more weeks or, hell, months would pass without word from Becky?

Trying to focus on the task at hand, Wes made a casual pass in front of the register, only stopping when the most Italian man he'd ever seen propped his meaty forearms on the counter. "Help you find something?"

"Maybe," he answered, still scanning the shop, as if a construction crew might be sitting on one of the shelves. "I'm working on a flip over in Port Jeff."

Dark bushy eyebrows went up. "A flip, heh?"

"That's right." Wes shrugged. "I guess if you knew some locals looking for something to keep them busy, we've got room for a few more."

Laura pulled on his ears. "Uncle Wes is a show-va-vist."

"Is he?" the man said, handing Laura a lollipop from under the counter without missing a beat, thankfully distracting her from embarrassing him any more while he was pretending not to desperately need help. The Italian shrugged back. "Might know a guy or two. The job going to pay well?"

Wes inclined his head. "It'll pay well for the right crew."

"My boys might be able to help out. They're in college at night—"

"They ugly?"

The man reared back. "Hell no, they ain't ugly. What kind of question is that?"

"Who else you got?"

"Uncle Wes, can we get that?"

This time his niece was pointing to a box full of laser

pointers. "No way. I'm not waking up tomorrow with that thing shining directly into my eyes."

She laughed. "How did you know? Can I get a shake at McDonald's?"

The hardware store ritual was not going according to plan. Time to abort. "Listen, do you have anyone else in mind, or not?"

A man in overalls materialized to Wes's right, wiping his hands on a greasy rag. With his salt-and-pepper mustache, Wes judged him to be in his late fifties. "Couldn't help but overhear."

Maybe the ritual was intact after all.

Keeping hold of Laura's knee with one hand, Wes reached for a stack of paint sample pamphlets that sat near the register with the other, casually thumbing through the glossy pages. "Overhear . . . ?"

"You mentioned a flip, son?"

"Might have."

Overalls lifted up his cap. "Well. There are a dozen more ugly, retired sons of guns just like me in this town."

"It's true. They live in my shop. They never leave."

"We keep you in business."

"You never buy anything!"

Ignoring the owner's outburst, Overalls held out his hand for a shake. "Carl Knight. Good to meet you."

"Ollie," piped up another voice behind Wes. He turned to find an African American man with a WORLD'S BEST GRANDPA T-shirt, roughly the same age as Carl. "I'm not ugly, but I know my way around some plumbing."

Carl smacked the counter. "We've still got some juice left in us, don't we, Ollie?"

"Juice for days. At the very least, a couple hours."

Wes's lips tugged at the corner. "You two mind taking directions from a woman?"

"We're married," both men responded in unison.

Wes picked a pen up off the counter and wrote down the address to the flip. "See you boys on Wednesday."

Bethany stood side by side with Georgie and Rosie, all three of them hunched over with hands on their knees. At the front of the workout room, Kristin bounced away to a remixed version of "Sweet Dreams," her blond ponytail swinging right to left, her eyes closed, totally oblivious that everyone had stopped following her lead.

"Start from the beginning," Rosie instructed, swiping at the perspiration on her brow. "You stormed the construction site . . ."

"I don't storm. I glide."

"What were you wearing?"

This from her sister, who'd been content with hand-me-downs until the age of twenty-three but could now tell the difference between business casual and smart casual. "An ankle-length floral skirt with my white strapless top."

Rosie poked her in the side. "Oooh. Hair?"

"Down, wavy. I looked great."

"You always do," Georgie assured her. "What happened next?"

"I showed him the paperwork and announced my defection." She bobbed a shoulder and followed a couple of Kristin's dance moves, which—if she recalled 2008 correctly—were straight out of Britney's "Womanizer" video. "That's all. It really wasn't that dramatic."

Georgie rolled her eyes. "You know, sis, it's actually more telling that you're leaving out the Zellweger moment."

"I'm not leaving it out," Bethany rushed to say. "It's just . . . inconsequential."

"I don't know," Rosie said, delivering a healthy dose of side-eye. "My husband was present during said Zellwegering—"

"Okay, ladies, it's not a verb. Can it stop being a verb?"

"And Dominic said it was quite a scene."

"I suppose it was scene-ish," Bethany hedged, ignoring the goosebumps that climbed her skin when she thought of Wes announcing he'd be going with her and stripping off his gloves. Why was it so annoyingly hot that he took off his gloves? "As soon as we met at the house, I made it perfectly clear that our temporary partnership would not include any physical benefits."

"Besides you watching him work shirtless, you mean?" Georgie wiggled her hips. "I'd say that classifies as a major benefit."

"Georgie, you're getting married on Sunday. Wait at least a month after the honeymoon to commence your role as a horny old married lady."

"Aw. Why else would I get married?"

Bethany's laugh was pained. "Rosie, help me."

"Sorry, Beth. Shirtless Wes is a definite benefit." She bit her bottom lip. "You think he'll wear his cowboy boots?"

Georgie reached across Bethany for a high five. "I was wondering the same thing."

"Your husbands should be worried," Bethany muttered, though she didn't really mean it. Rosie and Georgie were facedown in a mud puddle of everlasting love with their dudes and they would be forevermore. Bethany couldn't be happier for them. If there were two women who deserved men with unquestionable loyalty who worshiped the ground they walked on, it was her sister and Rosie.

Bethany would be lying, however, if her little sister getting married first didn't bring about a certain . . . self-reflection. Seeing Georgie and Rosie so happy made her doubt, on occasion, that she'd been built for happiness herself. The kind of relationships they had with Dominic and Travis, the kind where all the walls were down? Didn't that ever terrify them? Bethany didn't even like her *parents* knowing she didn't have her shit together, let alone someone she expected to be devoted, faithful, and sexually attracted to her. How could one just be themselves, be completely honest, and trust that it wouldn't eventually send the person on his merry way?

Yes, while Bethany was totally thrilled for her sister and best friend, she could admit to being a little baffled by how the blind trust/unconditional love thing worked. She might have purported on occasion to being somewhat well versed in the world of men, but truthfully? She didn't know a damn thing about the opposite sex—and it had taken her until exactly this second to admit it. To herself, anyway.

In high school and college, she'd dated liberally and without major commitments, more focused on getting her degree in design and carving out a long-term way to practice what she loved. When she'd settled back in Port Jefferson after four years at Columbia, she'd started seeing men in a more permanent light. Her first serious boyfriend was a bond trader named Rivers. They'd dated exclusively for six months before she found out he'd been back together with his old girlfriend for five. And thus had begun a steady stream of handsome, exciting, successful men who would later prove to be less substantial than dust.

She'd been on a mighty tear the night they formed the Just Us League, in this very room, as the theater director boyfriend she'd been seeing had made for greener pastures, claiming her work schedule didn't leave enough time for him. A lot of her boyfriends had made this same complaint. A lot of them had pursued *other* female company because of it, when in truth, her working hours weren't *that* demanding.

But the more time she spent around someone, the higher the chance that they would see her faults. They might force her to accept that she wasn't the warm, fuzzy relationship type, and in reality, she was kind of . . . *cold* when it came to men. When it came to a lot of things, really. She didn't seem capable of relaxation or contentment. Her agenda always seemed to include moving and planning. If she stopped and let herself try to enjoy life, enjoy men . . . maybe she wouldn't.

Couldn't, even. Maybe some of her past boyfriends' claims that Bethany was cold were correct.

So, simple solution, right? Avoid men.

She avoided her own boyfriends.

"Bethany?" Georgie hip-checked her. "You're thinking about Wes's nipples covered in sweat, aren't you?"

"What?" *Well, now I am.* "No."

"Is anyone following the moves?" Kristin demanded from the front of the class, scanning the room as if there were a hundred people present instead of three. "I'm not just up here for my health, you know."

"You don't exercise for your health?" Georgie asked.

"Oh, hush, smartass. You know what I mean," their sister-in-law scolded, cradling her nonexistent baby bump with a scowl. She turned back around with an elaborate shoulder roll and fell into rhythm with Katy Perry.

"Pregnancy is making her mean," Rosie remarked with a shiver.

"Yeah, maybe we better dance," Georgie muttered, beginning the most basic of foot shuffles. "Keep talking, though."

"Yeah," Rosie whispered, cautious eyes on Kristin, like she might turn and spew venom at any moment. "What did Wes say when you told him there wouldn't be any benefits?"

"Nothing. He said nothing," Bethany answered, too quickly.

"Come on," Georgie said. "That man never says nothing."

Bethany sighed. "He might have said"—she fluttered a hand around her high bun—"sex is no longer an option, anyway."

Georgie stopped dancing. So did Rosie. They stared at her. And promptly burst into laughter.

Bethany spoke over them. "I, of course, told him it was never going to happen in the first place, so his point is moot." She searched for a way to distract them. "And then a rat scurried over my foot."

"Oh, ew," Rosie said, consoling her with a pat on the shoulder.

"Yeah." Sober now, Georgie reached for her throat. "I'm so sorry."

"I bet you feel bad about laughing now."

"Not really," Georgie said with a straight face.

Rosie shook her head. "Sorry, no."

"You two are the worst," Bethany grumbled. "There is nothing going on with Wes. Nothing will ever go on with Wes. If we make it through this without clubbing each other to death, I'll be grateful."

But a few minutes later, when Kristin browbeat them into silence, Bethany thought of how her legs felt wrapped around his hips and wondered if clubbing each other to death was what she should be worried about.

CHAPTER FIVE

Wes checked his reflection in Buena Onda's glass door, giving himself a moment to collect his thoughts before heading inside. He was still getting used to having . . . people. Making friends during his temporary stay in Port Jefferson was something he *definitely* hadn't expected. Casual acquaintances were more his stride. But a few beers with the guys after work had led to a standing happy hour hangout . . . and eventually transitioned into this. An invitation to Georgie and Travis's rehearsal dinner.

There might have also been the bonding experience of traveling into Manhattan like a pack of scorned idiots to drag home the womenfolk when they'd had the *utter nerve* to take a ladies' night out, but he digressed.

Apparently he had friends now, but he was still getting used to that fact . . .

And knowing Bethany would be there tonight had gone a damn long way toward his decision to put on nice clothes and call the babysitter.

His gaze found her the second he walked into Buena Onda.

Since she was busy fussing with a flower arrangement and paying him no attention, he stopped just inside the door and allowed himself a few moments to appreciate her. Good Lord. The woman had no right to be so fine. No right.

It was Friday night and the restaurant was packed. Waiters and waitresses in black, white, and red moved with seamless choreography through the maze of tables, dropping off drinks and clearing dishes. Sconces flickered, highlighting the gold walls and framed photos. Colorful scenes straight out of Argentina. Snippets of conversations reached his ears from nearby tables, emerging and weaving back into the overall drone of the crowd.

Wes only registered his surroundings in passing, because Bethany had his attention and that's where it would stay, mainly to get her all worked up and flushed. It really wasn't fair of him to take these precious moments to prepare himself for their upcoming battle. It gave him an advantage.

Then again, maybe he needed an edge. Continuing their war of words wouldn't be easy when she looked like a fucking queen tonight. Bethany Castle never had a hair out of place, but there was something extra happening with her this evening and it damn near made his blood run backward.

Her hair was in a perfect ponytail—and he knew a perfect ponytail when he saw one. Laura pointed them out on the Disney Channel stars constantly. *See, Uncle Wes. That's what a ponytail looks like. Not what you do.*

All right, so his technique was a work in progress.

Bethany's smooth waterfall of blond hair brushed the

center of her bare back, drawing Wes's attention to her delicate shoulders, only a slim strap of ice blue decorating them. Silk. She was wearing silk and Wes could hear the sound of it brushing her glowing skin. The hem of the dress met her knees, but the modest length did nothing to curtail his hungry thoughts. How many nights had he lain awake in bed, imagining himself standing behind Bethany, gathering her dress in his hands while exploring the curve of her neck with his tongue?

As if his thoughts had been broadcast aloud, Bethany straightened from her lean across the long banquet table and pinned him with a look that could only be described as *haughty*—and Wes barely knew what the hell that word meant.

We can still pretend to hate each other, if it makes you feel better about accepting my help. Hadn't Wes given her that assurance?

Looked like she'd taken it to heart.

Bethany turned fully and cocked a hip, sweeping him with a concerned glance. "Wow, get a load of you. Did you get lost on the way to a cattle auction or something?"

Wes's lips tried their damndest to curl into a smile, but sheer will and a lot of practice kept his expression bland. "Nope, I'm in the right place," Wes said, sauntering toward Bethany. "The directions said if I passed Resting Bitch Face, I've gone too far."

Her smile was sweet. "Feel free to keep going until you fall off a cliff."

He tucked his tongue into his cheek and leaned in to speak near her ear—and if she thought he didn't notice the goosebumps that appeared on her neck, she was sorely mistaken. "You smell different. Where've you been all day?"

Her quick intake of breath turned into a scoff. "None of your business, knockoff Lone Ranger." With a single finger planted in the center of his chest, she pushed him back several inches. "But if you must know, we've been at the spa. Massages, facials, and waxing." She used that same finger to tap his upper lip. "Someday when you're old enough to grow facial hair, I'll make you an appointment."

Wes could only laugh at the ridiculousness of that insult. "And I'll book a specialist to saw down your cloven hooves."

"I like them sharp."

"Yeah?" He stepped back into her personal space, just enough to feel the tips of her breasts against his chest. "Well, come on, then, darlin'. Dig them in."

Pink coasted over her complexion and satisfaction fisted in his gut. Sparring with Bethany was better than sex. What was it about this woman that made him feel like his skin was elastic? He could still remember the first time she'd stepped out of her Mercedes on the construction site, all sleek composure, gorgeous legs, and attitude. Before she'd taken two steps, he'd made up his mind to sleep with her. She'd had other ideas.

"I thought we only hired college kids in the summertime," she'd said to her brother, eyeing Wes with distaste.

Wes had crossed his arms. "That must be hard, considering you probably create winter wherever you go."

She'd gasped. "Are you calling me an ice princess?"

"If the tiara fits."

"I'll take a tiara over your Clint Eastwood hand-me-downs."

"Remind me who that is? He might be better known among your generation."

Funny, the memory didn't give him the same kick of satisfaction it used to. Maybe it had something to do with that peek beneath her perfect top coat when he'd quit Brick & Morty to help her on the Doomsday Flip? Was a glimpse underneath her exterior his objective all along, with all the teasing and name-calling? Now that he'd gotten that preview of the real Bethany Castle, he surely wouldn't mind seeing more.

Although, had he already screwed himself by becoming the man who bit back?

Wes stepped back. "Where is everyone?"

"I dropped the ladies off at my place to change. My parents are picking them up on the way." She straightened a napkin, but he noticed her flush was still intact. "I came early to make sure everything was just right."

Although his knowledge was slim to none when it came to tabletop design—or design of any kind, really—Wes had to admit she'd killed it. There were little fresh white flowers cut short and arranged in mason jars filled with fairy lights. Tasteful stands spaced evenly apart on the table held candid pictures of Georgie and Travis. Notecards with everyone's names written on them in script sat in the center of each plate. He didn't have to do any sleuthing to know she'd placed him as far away from her as possible.

He pointed toward the far end of the table. "That wine glass has a smudge."

"What?"

As soon as Bethany turned to handle the phantom smudge, Wes pilfered Stephen's name card and switched it with his, putting him on Bethany's right.

"I don't see anything," Bethany said, lifting the glass to inspect it. Their eyes met through the goblet, magnifying her sexy pout. "Very funny."

"No one would have noticed a smudge."

"I would have."

"You notice everything."

"Mmm-hmm."

Wes smiled.

She narrowed her eyes at him suspiciously, but he was saved from her finding out about the name-card switch when the rest of their party appeared at the restaurant's entrance.

Wes saluted the new arrivals. Dominic kept his head down and stuck to the sidelines, scouting for Rosie. Stephen rolled in like a ball of nervous energy and Travis strutted through the awestruck patrons like the goddamn mayor. If Wes didn't like the son of a bitch so much, he'd hate him.

The Castle parents walked in behind Travis, their entrance causing a ripple of comforting energy in the small room. Everyone in town revered Morty and adored Vivian. In the short time he'd lived in Port Jefferson, he'd learned they were an institution. Half the town had either sold their homes to the Castles or purchased one from them—and the rest would get there all in good time.

Wes hung back and watched Bethany, as was becoming

his unbreakable habit. How she kissed her parents, guiding her father to his seat with one hand, taking her mother's coat with the other. She nailed Travis with a well-placed quip, softening it with a grudging smile. Then she mouthed Dominic his wife's ETA.

Bethany was a graceful, flawless one-woman welcoming committee, and she was ridiculously out of Wes's league. That unfortunate fact didn't keep him from thinking about her nonstop, now, did it?

She turned and caught his eye over her shoulder, the candlelight giving her complexion a rosy glow, and something heavy clenched in his gut. Not sure if he wanted to explore the growing frequency of that reaction, Wes pulled out his chair and sat down. Bethany's mouth formed an *O*, her attention dropping to the swapped name card. "Wes," she said through her teeth.

He winked. "Howdy, neighbor."

Lucky for Wes, the female contingency joined the party at that moment, or Bethany might have stabbed him with a butter knife. Instead, she was rendered speechless by her little sister. Georgie was dressed in an off-white, form-fitting dress with long sleeves and an abbreviated hem and her legs looked about fifteen miles long in the silver pumps she'd borrowed from Bethany's closet. How could this be the same person who'd once gotten her braces stuck to a radiator valve?

Bethany had almost missed the chance to know Georgie better. What if they hadn't ended up in that stupid Zumba class all those months ago? They'd opened up to each other by accident that night, sprawled on the floor in their workout gear. Sure, Bethany would still have planned this party. They would still be sisters, break bread on the occasional Sunday, buy each other Christmas presents. But they were *friends* now, too.

God, she was so grateful for that. And now, in just two short days, the scruffy tomboy was getting married. Bethany's sight started to blur and, with visions of running mascara in mind, she tipped her face up toward the ceiling, begging the tears to ebb. She couldn't very well host this dinner with raccoon eyes. *Pull it together.*

Something soft pressed into Bethany's hand and she looked down to find Wes passing her a cloth napkin. "Oh, but it'll ruin the table's flow," she mumbled, fanning her eyes. "You're behind me. How did you know I was crying?"

"Maybe you're not the only one who notices things, darlin'."

Even as his low tone blew an unwanted shiver down her spine, Bethany turned slightly to slide him some side-eye. It was her default where Wes was concerned. Sighing in the face of her skepticism, Wes took off his cowboy hat and dropped it on the table. "Fine. Your ass was clenched."

A surprise laugh rocketed its way out of Bethany. She threw the napkin at Wes and he caught it in midair. "Idiot."

As Bethany went to greet her sister, she couldn't help but notice the tears no longer threatened to erupt from her eyeballs. Wes had said the exact right thing. By accident, of course. And wow. Her standards must be dropping at an exponential rate if that jackass admitting he'd been staring at her ass was now the right thing to say.

Her man hiatus was responsible for this attraction to Wes. It had to be. Maybe it was time to consider getting back on the market. Because if she continued at this rate, she might actually start considering one of Wes's not-so-subtle invitations to jump each other's bones—and that surmounted to the worst idea in life. In history.

Not happening. Never happening.

Even if she didn't hate him, even if he wasn't seven years her junior, Wes was messy. Not literally. Gun to her head, she could admit he actually cleaned up pretty well. Very well, in fact. The removal of his cowboy hat had revealed his shock of dirty-blond hair that never seemed to fall in the same direction, amber eyes that held a perpetual humorous twinkle, and richly sun-loved skin that called to mind farmer tans and Texas back roads and—what was she doing? Writing lyrics for a country-western song now?

The man's attractiveness was neither here nor there.

The real problem was, Wes knew she wasn't perfect and put together and effortless. She hadn't fooled him, not for a second—and that was unacceptable. His awareness of her faults was one of the main reasons Bethany had such a hard time believing he was actually interested and not just amusing himself with an older woman who could play a decent game of hard to get. But did he actually *want* to catch her? His irreverence made it so hard to tell.

Okay, so he *had* gotten hard for her when she'd jumped him to avoid the rat.

Wouldn't a stiff breeze make a twenty-three-year-old hard?

Stop thinking about erections at your sister's rehearsal dinner.

"Georgie," Bethany breathed, finally having reached her sister. At the sight of Georgie dressed to the nines, hot moisture crowded the backs of her eyelids again and she almost wished for another inappropriate comment from Wes before she caught herself. "You look magical."

"Did you have something to do with this?" Travis asked at her elbow, sounding as if he'd slipped into a daze. "How am I supposed to sit through a three-hour dinner with her looking like that?"

Georgie poked her fiancé. "You're talking about me like I'm not here."

"You're not here. You're a hologram. That belief is the only thing that's going to keep my hands off you." Travis dragged a hand down his face. "Can we move this dinner along, please?"

Unable to keep the smugness off her face, Bethany wedged herself in between the bride- and groom-to-be and guided them toward the table, standing behind their place settings. "Everyone, please take your seats." She snapped a look at the college-student waiter and he lurched forward, pouring champagne into everyone's glasses, one by one. When the final flute was bubbling with Dom Pérignon, she picked up her own and held it high. "Stephen gets to say his piece as the best man at the reception, so it's only fair that I get to put in my two cents now."

She sniffed, shooting playful dagger eyes at her older

brother, who mostly looked confused as to why he'd been seated three spots away from his wife.

"It's no secret that it took me a while to warm up to Travis. Decades. I'm still reserving the tiniest bit of judgment. We're, like, ninety percent there." She patted her future brother-in-law on the shoulder. "However. I am one hundred percent positive that no one else could make my sister this happy. Or get her, quite like Travis. They're a match made in heaven and I'm definitely not bitter about being the last single Castle. Pay no attention to my mile-long therapy bill." Bethany squeezed them close, emotion catching her in the throat. "On a serious note, I'm so happy for you both. I mean that. This is what the real thing looks like." She raised her glass a touch higher. "To Travis and Georgie."

"To Travis and Georgie," repeated everyone.

Bethany eased out from between the future newlyweds and took her seat, enjoying the way conversation unfolded around her naturally, drinks being refilled before they were fully empty. The evening had been set into motion without a hitch. Second by second, the tension in her chest eased until she was once again all too aware of the man sitting beside her.

"Nice speech," Wes drawled. "If I didn't know better, I'd almost be fooled into thinking you have a heart."

"Oh, but I do. In the same place as yours." She sipped her champagne. "It's located about nine inches below where your brain should be." He opened his mouth to respond, but Bethany cut him off. "If you make a 'nine inches' joke, I'll dump candle wax on your head."

"Damn, girl, that's kinky as hell." He winked. "I like it."

She ground her back teeth. "Is this why you wanted to sit next to me? So you could poke me all night?"

He bit his lip.

Bethany pinched her eyes shut. "Say it and die."

Wes leaned back in his chair, wisely refraining from another innuendo. Yet she still couldn't keep her knee from bouncing beneath the table. Why did this man thwart her composure like this? No one else could get under her skin with such efficiency. Or scramble her brain with a well-placed grin.

A grin that said, *I see your flaws. I see them all.*

God, she couldn't stand him.

As if it wasn't bad enough that Wes seemed to see straight through her, it was impossible to reconcile all of his moving parts (thank goodness she hadn't said that out loud). According to Stephen . . . and perhaps some Web sleuthing, Wes was a good ol' boy with a wild streak. She'd confirmed that one evening after too much wine via his long-neglected Instagram account, which was essentially just photo upon photo of him riding bulls, being treated for injuries in the ER—usually with a thumbs-up and a smile—or pounding a pint while his buddies egged him on in the background.

Such evidence should validate her utter dislike of Wes. She'd dated irreverent party guys who could become the center of her universe simply by being the most interesting dude at the bar. She was past men like that. They never failed to turn into bitter douchebags when they weren't the center of attention.

And yet.

He'd come to Port Jefferson to raise his niece.

He didn't seem to want a cookie for it, either.

Curious.

Bethany realized she and Wes were sitting a little too near, scrutinizing each other way too closely. She abruptly leaned away.

"Did you manage to find some capable souls to help us on the flip?"

Wes remained focused on her mouth for a few beats. "Oh yeah," he said, nodding. "They are . . . something else."

She let her suspicion over *that* vague response show, but chose not to comment. "I'm going shopping tomorrow for bathroom materials—"

"Great. When and where? I'll meet you."

She was already shaking her head. Spending time with Wes when it wasn't absolutely necessary? Not a good idea. They were going to be in close enough proximity on the job site. They didn't need to become shopping buddies. Besides . . . she didn't exactly know what to buy for the bathroom and she didn't need a witness there to watch her muddling through every purchase. "That's not necessary."

"As foreman, I'd really like to be aware of all details, big and small."

Bethany reared back. "Foreman? Who gave you *that* title?"

He eyed her curiously. "Which title would you suggest for me?"

"I don't know. Head clown?"

Humor rippled across his features. "If it makes you feel better, I was mentally referring to you as manager."

"Oh." Feeling silly for being so defensive, she shifted in her seat. "Then . . . I suppose those titles work."

He winked. "Just trying to please the boss."

The guilt over her defensiveness spun like a stupid lead ball in her belly. "I'll text you the address of the bathroom supply place. We'll meet there in the morning. Just . . ."

"What?"

The irritated skin on her neck glowed hot, so she squeezed her hands together in her lap. "I don't know exactly *what* we need."

Some of Wes's amusement faded. "I got you."

Exposed, Bethany pushed back from the table and stood so fast, she almost knocked over her chair, but Wes caught it in time. With a mumbled thank-you, she went to make sure everyone had fresh glasses for the switch from champagne to red wine, very aware of Wes cataloguing her every move.

Tomorrow morning suddenly loomed much closer than before.

CHAPTER SIX

He'd been a complete idiot for telling Bethany sex was off the table.

That was Wes's first thought when she strolled into the bathroom supply showroom in high-waisted jeans that looked like someone painted them on with a brush and a loose T-shirt tucked into the front—just the front. Why was that hot? And heels. He'd never paid much attention to clothing women wore, definitely not the finer details, but there was so much thought put into every garment that Bethany chose to put on her body, it felt like a sin not to catalogue them.

There was a pencil holding her bun together on the top of her head, almost like she wanted people to believe she hadn't spent actual time making herself look delicious. What would she look like first thing in the morning? Without a scrap of clothing on, fucked-up hair and no makeup? That's what he wanted to know. She looked beautiful put together like this, but he had a feeling she'd be something else altogether if he took her apart. Laid her out bare.

Bethany stopped in front of him with a smile. "Nope."

"Sorry, was I talking out loud?"

"Your horndog expression was speaking on your behalf."

"It's your fault. Thanks to that rat, now I've had those legs wrapped around me."

She took off her sunglasses and snapped them closed, sliding them into a hidden compartment in her purse. "Well, I hope you enjoyed the first and last time."

"Come on, now. You've still got a few good years left in you."

Wes frowned when she faltered a little, a rejoinder seeming to die on her lips. Instead of cutting him off at the knees like she normally would, she moved past him and beckoned to one of the sales clerks. "Hello!" Of course her smile was one hundred watts for the thirty-something dude in ill-fitting khakis and company polo shirt. "Kirk," she said warmly, reading his name off the tag fastened to his shirt. "We need to place an order for bathroom supplies. Would you mind setting us up with some catalogues and a place to sit?"

Kirk almost sprained an ankle scrambling off to do her bidding. "Sure thing."

Wes followed her to the back of the showroom, but he still had an itch under the collar over her reaction to his stupid joke about her age. She knew he needled her about being older in the name of sarcasm, right? The seven years between them was nothing but a puddle jump. Thirty was young. Hell, she could be forty-five and he'd still be panting after it. So why had she clammed up on him?

He took a seat beside a straight-backed Bethany at a

cluttered table and studied her profile. Something told him he needed to smooth out this one misconception—that he actually thought she was ready for pasture—or he'd regret it. Before he could say anything, though, Kirk came back with a stack of books up to his chin, dropping them on the table with a slap. "Here you go, Miss Castle."

"Oh." She beamed up at him. "You know my name."

"Sure. You're Stephen Castle's sister."

Some of the spark faded from her eyes and Wes wanted to throttle the dumbass. "Right," Bethany said, opening one of the books. "We'll let you know when we're ready to put in the order."

Captain Foot in Mouth took his exit and Wes leaned back in his chair, wondering why the hell he felt so jumpy all of a sudden. Lust was an inevitability when he was in the same room with Bethany, but right now, he was more interested in holding her hand. Or cupping the nape of her neck and running a thumb up into her hairline to comfort her. And that rattled him a little.

Maybe there was a way to comfort her without being too obvious. She'd admitted at last night's rehearsal dinner that she was nervous about picking out bathroom supplies when she didn't know where to start, hadn't she?

Wes cleared his throat hard and slipped his cell out of his pocket, pulling up the picture app and thumbing through a couple pictures of Laura dancing on the front porch be-fore finding what he wanted. "Went back into the house last night and grabbed some pictures of the bathroom. Took measurements."

Bethany blinked at him and Wes could see her playing back their conversation from last night, too. *I told you I got you.* That's what he wanted to say, but . . . it wasn't gratitude he was after. What was it? Her trust?

"Oh. Oh . . . good," she breathed finally, squaring her shoulders. "Thank you. My plan was to order extra tile and return what we didn't use, but this is better." She snuck another glance at him before resolutely focusing on his phone. "Did you run into the rat again?"

"No, but I had the pleasure of making the acquaintance of his children." Wes shivered. "Several of them."

Bethany made a sound. "I wish you hadn't told me that. Now I feel guilty about calling the exterminator."

"They were squealers."

"May they burn in hell," she deadpanned, going back to trading glances between his cell phone and the book. "Should I be worried about inappropriate text messages popping up on your screen and scarring me for life?"

Wes reached over and stopped her from turning a page, tapping a square of tile that was moderately priced and on trend. "Inappropriate texts from who?"

Bethany slapped his hand away from the book and flipped to the next page. "I don't know," she muttered, distractedly. "Women."

A smile prodded him. "I'll admit I receive a pretty high volume of texts from women."

Her shrug was jerky. "Well, you can put it away now. I know what the bathroom looks like—"

Casually, Wes picked up the phone and navigated over

to his text messages, reading aloud. "Three forty-seven P.M., yesterday. 'Laura won't eat her granola bar.' My reply: 'Tell her she can dip it in pudding.'" Wes caught a hint of a smile curving Bethany's mouth before she reinvested herself in the sample book. "A day earlier: 'Laura claims you let her watch *Judge Judy.*' My reply: 'You're damn right I do.' Real scandalous stuff here, Bethany."

"Those are Laura's babysitters."

"Call them what they are. Heroes."

She flicked him a surprised glance. "It's nice of you to acknowledge them like that."

"Before you go giving me credit, please know I have them listed in my phone as"—he scrolled through his most recent texts—"Green Bean Casserole, *Outlander* Ringtone—"

"How did you recognize the *Outlander* ringtone?"

"She told me when I asked. And now I know way too much about a redhead named Jamie." He shook his head. "Faded Calf Tattoo—she's my favorite—and Let's Color. She's always got a fresh pack of Crayons holstered like some kind of blue-haired gunslinger."

Bethany was having a harder time not smiling now and Wes was enjoying the hell out of watching her fight the amusement. "I fear you've made the classic male error of assuming women aren't in a constant state of evolution. What happens if *Outlander* Ringtone switches to *The Crown* theme song, or Faded Calf Tattoo starts wearing her winter jeans?"

Now he hadn't really considered that, but Bethany had a point. He'd never been around a woman long enough to watch one evolve, but he reckoned they must. Hell, he'd been a bull rider until early this fall and now he was a substitute dad. If that wasn't an evolution, he didn't know the meaning of the word.

Had Bethany evolved?

Would she evolve after he left?

Wes shooed away the weird tightening in his throat. "And here I thought my nickname system was foolproof."

"Good thing you don't have my number." She flipped the page a little quickly. "I'd hate to find out what I'd be listed under."

"Who says I don't have your number?"

Her blue gaze slowly met his and he was momentarily hypnotized by the lighter flecks just around her pupil. "Excuse me? You *do* have my number?"

"Faded Calf Tattoo coughed it up." He winked. "Told you she was my favorite."

"Marjorie?" She gasped. "She's a retired human resources manager."

Wes stretched his legs out. "Ethics are no match for charm, darlin'."

"Oh, shut up." She eyed his phone, looked away, came back. "How am I listed?"

"Don't worry about it."

"Show me."

"Uh-uh."

She drummed her nails on the tile samples for several seconds. "Fine." Her spine ironed out. "Doesn't matter to me anyway."

"I can see that," he drawled.

Captain Foot in Mouth materialized in front of them. "Are you finding everything okay? Can I help or make suggestions?"

"We're good," Wes and Bethany said at the same time.

Off he went again.

Wes watched Bethany pet a square of gray-and-white speckled tile while he played back their conversation. By asking who had been texting him, she'd definitely been fishing to find out if he was dating, although she'd probably go with an orange-and-lime-green theme in the bathroom before admitting even a remote interest. Still, it was progress. Maybe he could make some more.

"Marjorie is coming to the wedding on Sunday," Bethany murmured, almost to herself. "I'll look forward to teasing her about being susceptible to cowboys."

"*All* my babysitters are going to the wedding. Had to take Laura out shopping for a fancy dress so I could bring her along."

Bethany turned those sparkling eyes on him again and his stomach rippled. "What kind of dress did she pick?"

He fought off a wave of uncertainty over his styling abilities—of which he had few. "I don't know." His shrug was jerky. "We bought some pink deal."

"Pink. That's all you've got?"

"It has sleeves."

"Oh. Well." She shook her head at Wes and he cursed himself for not spending more time on Google before taking Laura shopping. Sue him for being overwhelmed by the astronomical number of websites dedicated to children's fashion. Bethany didn't seem inclined to take him to task over his ineptitude, but he was surprised when she asked, "Do you have any idea when Laura's mother is coming back to Port Jefferson?"

"No. Soon, probably," he said too quickly.

She studied him a moment. "You don't sound confident in that."

He swallowed. "That might be because . . . I'm not." Wes wasn't used to the soft way Bethany was looking at him and he caught himself leaning closer before she could notice. "I just wish she'd give me a call. For Laura's sake."

There was a slight scratch to Bethany's voice when she responded. "Of course you do," she said, shifting in her seat. "In the meantime, my mom will make a huge deal out of Laura at the wedding. She misses us being miniature."

When he would have made a crack about her being old, this time he zipped it.

"So I've got my date for Sunday," Wes said slowly, a truly hideous thought occurring to him. "What about you, Bethany? You bringing some chump in a designer suit?"

"Maybe." She hoisted a blond eyebrow. "How will you pay him back for my drinks this time? It's an open bar."

Wes ground his back teeth.

"Relax, cowboy. I'm still on my man hiatus." She turned another page. "Not that it's any of your business."

He begged to differ. "What exactly prompted this hiatus?"

"The realization that men are so simplistic they keep women listed in their phones under names like Let's Color."

"Jesus, Bethany. I know her name is Donna. Sue me for

cheating a little with reminders after you introduced me to forty women of roughly the same age and physical description in one night."

He was referring to the evening the Just Us League got wind of him, a single twenty-three-year-old man taking care of a child on his own, and they'd arrived on his doorstep like Port Jefferson's version of FEMA. He'd woken up the next day wondering if he'd dreamed middle-aged women organizing his underwear drawer, but no. His jocks were now rolled up in balls according to color.

She pursed her lips and cut him a look. "I'm . . . sorry. For that one little assumption, nothing else."

"Well, shit." He kicked up his boot, crossing it over the opposite knee. "Are pigs flying outside?"

Bethany didn't respond right away. "I'm on hiatus because my last boyfriend cheated on me. When I caught him texting one of his theater students, he told me I was distant and cold. Basically it was my fault. It wasn't the first time that had happened with a boyfriend, either. In fact, it was becoming something of a pattern. And I guess I need a little time to recover before trying again. *If* I try again. Are we even now?"

Fire ants crawled up his throat. How badly had she been hurt to swear off men? Had she been in love with these pieces of shit? "I didn't need you to cut yourself down to size for me. I'd never ask that or enjoy it."

"You'd rather do it for me?"

"I'm just giving as good as I get, darlin'. Sounds like you picked men who couldn't keep up like I do." A pink blush stained her cheeks and there it was, that same way she'd looked at him Monday morning, when she'd felt his cock between her legs. Her lips parted and she appeared to be controlling her breathing with a hard-fought effort. Those blue eyes swam with awareness and caution—a combination that made his jeans all the more confining. "I'll show you how I've got you listed in my phone if you dance with me at the wedding on Sunday."

She snapped out of her trance with a scoff. "Forget it."

He waved his phone. "Sure about that?"

A few beats passed. "One dance?"

"If you can pry yourself off me afterward."

"I think I'll manage." She plucked the phone out of his hand between her finger and thumb, looking all prim and sexy as she scrolled. "Bethany Motherfucking Castle," she read, wrinkling her nose. "Is that meant to be a negative connotation or a positive one?"

"I said I'd let you look. Didn't say I'd explain."

Cogs turned behind her eyes. "Well, I suppose since you have my number and we're flipping a house together, I should probably have your number, too."

She sifted through her purse and extricated her phone, trailing her finger in zigzags over the screen before arriving at her contacts. She punched in a few letters before sliding it in front of him.

"Cute," said Wes, typing in his number under the heading Send to Voicemail.

Leaning in close, he stopped just short of brushing her hair with his lips, noticing the way her fingers curled on the tile samples. "I pick the dance. Think you can keep from climbing me?"

"There was a rat."

"Keep telling yourself that's all it was."

He heard Bethany swallow. "Can we pick some tile now?"

"You're in charge. I'm just here for moral support."

"Your morals are in need of more support than mine."

He couldn't help but breathe a laugh at her clever word-play, his smile widening when she laughed reluctantly, too. Her gaze strayed to his mouth for a split second before it shot back to the sample book.

Progress?

Hard to tell. But he was damn well counting the minutes to Sunday.

CHAPTER SEVEN

Bethany popped the cork on a bottle of Moët, pouring the fizzing champagne into a neat line of crystal flutes. She'd woken up early that morning and turned her mother's bedroom into a glamorous changing room, stringing up white lights along the edges of the ceiling, lighting candles, arranging seating. Georgie had balked at a bigger wedding venue, opting to marry Travis in their parents' backyard, but that didn't mean luxury had to be forgone entirely.

Champagne in hand, Bethany turned to offer her sister a glass only to find her sprawled out faceup on their parents' bed. "I just spent two hours on your hair, woman." Bethany nudged her foot. "Sit up."

"Sorry, this is the only way I can breathe in this bustier."

"You'll thank me when Travis gets a load of your tits."

"He's gotten many a load on them. That's why he's wifing me."

"Georgie Castle," their mother admonished, sashaying into the room in her new blue mother-of-the-bride dress. "You can't stand before God with that mouth."

"He's aware of her mouth by now, Mother." Bethany

handed Vivian a glass of champagne. "He also knows where she got it."

"I beg your pardon." Vivian took a long sip of bubbly. "Damn. That's good."

"Only the best," Bethany said briskly, though excitement was making her fingertips sizzle. "Up with you, Georgie. It's time to put on your dress."

Georgie rolled onto her stomach, pushed up, and slid backward off the bed, gaining her feet. "Is Travis here? Are guests arriving?"

Bethany drew back the bedroom curtain and craned her neck to get eyes on the street. "Yes, he's changing in the pool house. And it would appear we have some arrivals. Who is that slick-looking fellow with the equally slick-looking lady on his arm?"

Georgie sidled up to the window. "That's Travis's agent, Donny—and his date, I guess?" She smiled. "Donny really is every inch the wheeler-dealer sports agent, but I secretly love him. If he hadn't told Travis to spruce up his image to score the commentator gig, we never would have pretended to date, and, well . . ." Still blushing from earlier, she gestured to her fancy wedding hair. "You know how that turned out."

"You would have ended up together no matter what," Vivian said, draining her champagne and setting it down on the dresser. "I saw it coming a mile away."

The sisters traded a smirk. "Let's get this dress on."

"Ooh," Georgie said. "Let's wait for Rosie—"

"I'm here!" The third member of their trio slipped in

through the door and closed it behind her without a sound. "Sorry I'm late. Dominic always conveniently forgets how to tie a tie when we have one damn minute to leave the house."

Bethany hummed. "And then said tie ended up on the floor . . ."

"Girls," Vivian huffed, smoothing her updo. "Knowing those two, the tie probably ended up around her wrists."

"Mom!" Bethany and Georgie squawked.

"What? I'm a card-carrying member of the Just Us League. It's not my fault you overshare at meetings after too much tequila."

Bethany took a moment to recover, then crossed to Rosie, whose bronze skin was glowing in a deep-green silk dress identical to Bethany's. "You look amazing."

"Likewise. I'm so glad we went with the shorter length. I plan on dancing." Rosie twisted her hips, causing the dress's hem to brush mid-thigh. "But I'm more interested in seeing Georgie in white." She stepped toward Georgie and pulled her into a squeezing embrace. "Let's make you a bride."

There wasn't an unused tissue to be found during the ceremony. Travis and Georgie exchanged vows beneath the trees in the Castle backyard—the same trees where Georgie used to hide to spy on Travis while pretending to read *Tiger Beat*. Smoke practically came out of the man's ears when his bride proceeded down the aisle in her clingy silk gown with embellished bodice, escorted by Morty. Travis didn't take his eyes off her for a single second, as if she might turn tail, speed off in a taxi, and join the circus.

Rosie and Bethany stood to Georgie's left. Stephen and

Dominic were positioned at Travis's right. All the tension between Bethany and her brother were forgotten in those moments beneath the twinkling, ethereal lights and twilight sky. There were no houses being flipped, only their sister marrying a man who believed she'd hung the moon.

Feeling eyes on her in the crowd, however, and knowing Wes watched her, Bethany couldn't help but remember she'd agreed to a dance.

It was just one little dance.

Only, was it? From her maid of honor position at the front of the crowd, Bethany couldn't stop herself from searching the sea of faces for Wes. Under the guise of welcoming guests with her smile, of course. At first she didn't see him. Even while listening to the minister expound on the virtues of love, she despaired over her disappointment that he'd missed the wedding—

His head popped up in one of the center rows, cowboy hat and all.

The corner of her mouth tugged up when she realized he'd been hunting in a bag for Goldfish crackers to hand his fidgeting niece. Honestly. Where did he get off serving "James Bond meets Daddy of the Year" vibes tonight?

Slowly, his gaze lifted to meet Bethany's and he winked, giving her a blatant once-over that made her grateful she was shielding her excited nipples with a bouquet of roses.

It cost her an effort to focus back in on the ceremony, but she managed it, well aware of Wes's rapt attention on her from start to finish. Once the bride had been kissed, there was a rush to change Georgie into her reception dress and make sure the music for her and Travis's entrance was cued up.

In the romantic, starlight-dappled setting, with "The Way You Look Tonight" playing softly from a string quartet, the dance she'd promised Wes felt the furthest thing from inconsequential.

Bethany watched him out of the corner of her eye as she spoke with one of the caterer waiters. Now that she could see Wes better, she noted he'd traded in his cowboy boots for shiny black loafers. Still, every time Stephen introduced him to someone new, he swept off his cowboy hat and pressed it to his chest, like Buffalo goddamn Bill, the college years. That flash of white teeth and accentuated jawline every time he smiled was so distracting that Bethany almost walked straight into the ice sculpture.

"Pull yourself together," she muttered, batting a nonexistent wrinkle out of her bridesmaid's dress. "You are mature enough to know better—"

"Are you talking to yourself or the ice sculpture, darlin'?" His shoulders shook with silent laughter. "What the hell is that supposed to be anyway?"

Bethany's chin went up a notch. "It's two swans with their heads bent together, thus creating a heart. Obviously."

Wes winked. "Did they model it after your frigid heart?"

"Yes. Didn't they do an amazing job?" Bethany erected her middle finger on the far side of the sculpture, making it visible through the ice. "If you look closely you can see which part of my heart you occupy."

"Let me guess. That would be the fuck-off zone?"

"Bravo, Wes. You can't discern the basic shapes of animals, but you know your geography."

Bethany had the strong, stupid urge to laugh. Not a mean laugh, either. A good, long, belly laugh. Sparring with Wes had always been kind of a fun pastime, but it was alarming how much she'd been enjoying it lately. For the most part. Every once in a while, he made her stomach jolt with a barb about their age difference. Like yesterday afternoon when they'd met to pick out tiles and he'd joked that she had a few good years left in her. Those comments didn't roll off her back quite as easily as the others. As much as she wanted to disregard them . . . they smarted.

But why? Shouldn't she be grateful for the reminder that they'd been born seven years apart and were totally unsuitable for each other?

Yes. Yes, she should be. Totally grateful.

"So. I was thinking of squaring off those archways in the house—"

"Uncle Wes!"

A blond streak of lightning split the atoms between Wes and Bethany. A second later, the laughing child was tossed up on his wide shoulders, knocking Wes's cowboy hat to the ground and leaving his hair in some kind of . . . mesmerizing mess. Needing a distraction from his warm chuckle and haphazard hair, Bethany stooped down and picked up the hat, holding it awkwardly.

"Hi, Laura," she greeted the child. "Are you enjoying the party—"

"Elsa!" Laura's eyes lit up. "How come you don't babysit me?"

It took Bethany a moment to recover from the odd rush of pleasure she experienced over the child recalling her. Even if she remembered her by the wrong name and as a Disney character whom she apparently resembled. "I . . . well, I leave that in more capable hands."

Laura's forehead wrinkled. "What?"

Wes patted the child's knee. "What Elsa is trying to say, kid, is that she ain't the babysitting type."

"What type is she?"

"Less make-believe, more make-miserable."

Bethany and Wes traded toothy smiles.

"Did you make that ice, Elsa?" Laura pointed past her shoulder at the frozen swans. "With your powers?"

Not wanting to disappoint, Bethany leaned in and whispered in her ear, "Yes, but you can't tell anyone. Our secret, okay?"

"Okay," she responded in a hushed tone, though her feet were kicking in tandem against Wes's shoulders. "Uncle Wes, make her babysit. Please?"

Wes was looking at her in a quiet way that made her dumb stomach flutter. "I can't make her do anything, kid."

Bethany opened her mouth, then closed it just as fast. Was she really about to offer to babysit? She didn't know the first thing about entertaining a child. No, it was definitely better to have Laura believe her to be a fictional princess than to bring that illusion crashing down. And it would. "Um." She clasped her hands together at her waist. "The cake is coming soon. You don't like cake, do you?"

"I love it!"

Having distracted Laura, Bethany let out a relieved breath, but it caught when she saw Wes was still watching her in that knowing manner. Like he was trying to navigate the landscape of her mind and was making headway.

Or thought he was.

Good luck, buddy. I can't even find my own footing in there.

"Bethany!"

She turned to find Stephen approaching with a bottle of Sam Adams in his hand—and she braced herself. Her brother drinking alcohol was never a good thing. He seldom imbibed, usually sticking to energy drinks and smoothies. He couldn't hold his liquor to save his life, either becoming competitive or so sentimental about the past it made everyone uncomfortable. He was well within his rights to drink on Georgie and Travis's wedding day, but she couldn't help but think, *Here comes something stupid.*

"Hey there, Stephen," Bethany said, looking pointedly at the little girl sitting on Wes's shoulders so her brother would remember not to curse.

"Hey there," he repeated, snickering. "I want to introduce you to Travis's agent, Donny, and his girlfriend." He turned in a circle. "Hey, where'd they go?" He waved at someone in the distance, who indeed turned out to be the slick couple Bethany had seen arriving earlier. They were flashy Manhattan types, comfortable in their formalwear, and they extended their hands to Bethany with practiced ease.

"Donny Lynch," started the agent, bringing the woman forward with a hand on the small of her back. "This is Justine, my girlfriend."

"Thank you for coming," Bethany said, shaking both of their hands. "So nice to meet you."

Stephen tipped his beer bottle toward the dark-haired woman. "Justine is a television producer."

Justine lifted a shoulder. "Guilty."

"I've been telling her Brick and Morty is prime reality-show material."

Bethany sighed. Didn't she have enough on her mind tonight? The caterers were making passes with hors d'oeuvre trays, but she'd only spotted a single cocktail waiter and the sit-down dinner courses would start soon. One of a thousand things could go wrong at any second. "Um. Why is it reality-show material? Because of the family drama?"

Justine perked up. "Family drama?"

"No," Stephen said firmly, lowering his beer bottle. "Because of our unrivaled craftsmanship. We blow those HGTV hacks out of the water."

"Now that's a stretch," Wes said out of the side of his mouth.

"I see," Bethany said, sipping her champagne.

"I'm still interested in the family drama," Justine pressed with a wide smile. "I'm sure it's unavoidable, right?"

"We managed to avoid it for a long time," Stephen answered before Bethany could confirm that yes, family drama ran in their veins. Apparently the drama only affected those who didn't get to make the rules. "We'd still be avoiding it if Bethany didn't ditch the dream team for a vanity project."

Bethany's mouth fell open at his casual description of something that could make or break her. Prove she was as perfect as everyone assumed . . . or fallible. "Vanity project? Really?"

Wes whistled under his breath. "That's not how I'd have put it."

"You've broken rank, have you, Bethany?" Justine prompted casually.

Her laugh sounded unnatural. "I am leading my own flip, yes, but—"

"You're flipping houses at the same time. In the same town."

"Yes," Bethany and Stephen responded at the same time.

Justine whipped out her cell phone and pressed the button on what looked like a voice memo app. "Brother and sister, dueling flips, only one will emerge victorious. We'll call it *Flip Off.*"

"I'm sorry, what?" Bethany broke in, her nerves beginning to crackle. "There's no competition."

"Isn't there?" Justine raised a brow. "Even unspoken?"

"I mean"—Stephen shrugged—"I was certainly planning on kicking your butt."

Bethany shot a pleading look in Wes's direction, but he seemed a little preoccupied glaring at Stephen. How weird. She returned her attention to her brother. "We are not doing this at our sister's wedding."

"What am I doing?" Stephen asked, slapping a hand to

his chest—great, he'd decided to go with competitive and defensive. When it came to being annoying, drunk men were right up there with telemarketers and thirty-second advertisements in the middle of an internet video.

"I'll tell you what you're doing—" Wes started in on Stephen, but Bethany laid a hand on his arm to waylay whatever he was going to say.

"Look." Bethany gave Justine her best smile, noting absently that Donny was scrolling through his emails. "There's really nothing interesting going on. Just a difference of opinion between siblings. Happens every day."

"Right." Justine nodded. "Stephen thinks he's the only game in town and your flip couldn't possibly compete . . ."

"And I know that's bull—" She winced in Laura's direction. "Baloney."

"You think your flip will earn a higher appraisal."

Bethany knew she was being manipulated, but that knowledge didn't stop her hackles from rising. Maybe it was being in their parents' backyard, the scene of countless races and rivalries with her brother. Maybe it was the desperate need to believe in herself out loud, since she couldn't do it on the inside. But with all eyes on her and the producer's question hanging in the air, Bethany heard herself say, "I know it will."

Stephen sputtered. "You're on."

Wes dragged a hand down his face.

Laura mimicked him.

"Let's see. Today is Sunday. If I manage to move a few mountains, I can have cameras at both properties on Wednesday morning. I'll just need your contact information so my assistant can send you the details." Justine tapped notes into her cell phone. "There will be some waivers and insurance, blah blah, but I know my boss is going to go nuts for this."

"*Flip Off* is a great title," Donny murmured without looking up from his phone. "Edgy. Cool. Good work, babe."

"This is all happening so fast," Bethany breathed.

"Yeah," Wes spoke up. "Maybe we should talk about this?"

"Who is he?" Justine's gaze ricocheted between Wes and Bethany. "Is this the boyfriend? Husband? What's the connection?"

"That's what I'd like to know," Stephen thundered. "Actually, never mind. Please don't tell me. My little sister literally just married my best friend."

"He's my foreman," Bethany stated, handing Wes his hat back finally. How long had she been holding it? "That's all."

"He's being a damn fool over her," Laura said brightly, intercepting the hat and plopping it on her head.

Justine fanned herself. "Oh, this is gold."

Bethany snorted, mentally sidetracked by what Laura had said. Was that something Wes had said out loud? Did he talk to his niece about her? Why did that make her insides feel like they'd been coated in warm wax? "I-it's just run-of-the-mill family politics—"

"I assure you it's not. You're interesting, not to mention very attractive. Viewers like watching good-looking people sweat." Justine paused the million-miles-an-hour typing on her phone. "There will be a prize, too, of course."

Stephen crossed his arms. "What about a title?"

"Why, whoever wins will be the Flipping King or Queen of Port Jefferson. Crowned on television and everything."

Oh, dammit. Justine had them.

They were way too immature to turn down a shot at those bragging rights.

Bethany should not do this. The house they were flipping was a certified wreck with a fucking rat colony, in far worse condition that Stephen's, and her lack of experience already had them at a disadvantage. She was on shaky ground when it came to her abilities to turn the house into a livable home, let alone an award-winning one. A home that people would see dissected on television.

She would be dissected on television, along with her talent for construction.

Or lack thereof.

Stephen and Bethany traded measuring looks.

Scared? mouthed her brother.

The dare twisted in the side of her neck like a corkscrew. "Nope," she drawled, sounding a little like Wes. "We're going to put you to shame."

Stephen reared back with a harsh laugh. "It's on."

"Bring it, bozo."

Bethany turned on a heel and left her audience gaping after her.

She made it around the corner of the house before she succumbed to the inundation of sheer, utter panic.

CHAPTER EIGHT

Wes had no trouble finding someone to keep an eye on Laura for a few minutes, since all four of her rotating baby-sitters were present at the wedding reception. As soon as his niece disappeared into a flurry of floral perfume and chiffon, he stalked off into the darkness where he'd seen Bethany disappear.

He was going to give her hell.

What in God's name was she thinking signing them up to be guinea pigs for a new reality show? They had two senior-citizen crew members, no blueprints, and a decaying shell of a house to make presentable. They were looking at months of work and a shit ton of setbacks. He'd been prepared to tackle all of it head-on, but not with a camera in his face.

Or her face.

That's what annoyed him the most—the thought of a film crew following Bethany around and catching all her little idiosyncrasies like fireflies in a jar. Sending out her image to thousands upon thousands of televisions. His back teeth ground together at the idea of her being consumed by any-one but him.

Wes stopped short and ran a hand through his hair, realizing he'd left his hat on Laura's head. Before he confronted Bethany and asked her if she'd lost her ever-loving mind, he needed to get his shit together and stop thinking like a jealous boyfriend.

Sure, he was protective of her. Possessive, too. He put it down to a combination of respecting Bethany and being attracted to her, more than he'd ever been attracted to anyone. But his heart was not involved. It *couldn't* be. If she chose to broadcast herself to households all across the country, there was nothing he could do about it—and furthermore, he didn't have a say in that decision.

So rein it the fuck in, man.

Wes started toward the back of the house again, toward where he'd watched Bethany vanish. All right, he wouldn't bitch at her about the cameras and make her believe him an even bigger chauvinist than she already did, but she was sure as hell going to hear about entering the contest, period. They weren't prepared and—

Was that wheezing?

Wes spurred into a jog and turned the corner into mostly darkness, but there was just enough light from the festivities to see Bethany's doubled-over form leaning against the house. His next step crunched some leaves and she straightened with a gasp, her hands immediately fluttering up to smooth her hair.

"Sorry." Her voice was hoarse. "Sorry, is someone looking for me?"

She tried to breeze past Wes, but he caught her around the

waist, bringing her close so he could study her face. No sign of tears, but her skin was flushed, eyes bright. Too bright. "Hey. What's wrong?"

"Nothing. I'm fine." She blew out a breath. "I'm going to head back."

She rested a hesitant hand on his shoulder, contradicting her words.

Wes's throat tightened. Just what exactly had he stumbled upon here? Bethany Castle was supposed to be cool as a cucumber, in charge, infallible. Not hyperventilating in private. "See, I was thinking of collecting that dance."

"Right now?"

"Right now."

Disbelief tackled him when Bethany seemed almost relieved, her other hand sliding up onto his other shoulder, meeting its mate behind Wes's neck. If he breathed the wrong way, the moment was going to blow away like pieces of a dandelion, so Wes oh-so-carefully placed his hands on Bethany's hips and eased her closer. She let him, her still-shallow breaths bathing his throat. "I know it looked like I was upset, but I wasn't. I was just . . ."

He grazed the top of her head with his cheek. "You don't have to say anything. Not unless you want to."

"You're learning, cowboy."

"I'm learning how to say the right thing. Not necessarily think it."

"Baby steps."

Oh Jesus, did he love holding her like this. All of her weight leaned on him, her mouth near his neck, belly cushioning his lap. He was getting a hard-on and knew she could feel it, but she seemed inclined to excuse what his body couldn't help. Not with her so close, so pliant. Watching her walk down the aisle earlier in her short green silk dress, Wes hadn't taken so much as a breath. Never mind what the whole getup did for her body, cupping and draping in places he shouldn't be thinking about during a religious ceremony. With light shining down on her smiling face, she'd been . . . angelic.

For a split second, just a split second, he'd pictured her walking that same aisle in a wedding gown, and, hours later, he was still confused by the pressure around his windpipe. He couldn't account for it. Marriage wasn't for him. His life was a series of temporary situations and had been since he could remember. This—his life in Port Jefferson—was definitely temporary. Bethany's life here was permanent, however, which meant she might very well walk down the aisle in white one day. And that thought kept replaying in his head like an aggravating pop song on repeat.

Wes brushed his thumb across her bare shoulder and she sighed, drawing his brows together. More than anything, he wanted to continue dancing with her like this, in the quiet privacy, savoring their truce, but something was bothering her. Enough to send her running from the wedding into hiding. He couldn't force her to tell him what exactly was wrong, but maybe he could make her feel better.

Yeah, he wanted that more than anything.

"You know, we can still turn down this whole reality-show nonsense."

Bethany laughed into his shoulder and he closed his eyes, tugging her just a little closer and praying he got away with it. "Thank you for toning down what you actually want to say." She looked up at him. "You were coming back here to yell at me for being an impulsive idiot, weren't you?"

"Yes."

Her low laugh wreaked havoc in his chest. "Go ahead. No one's stopping you."

"I'd rather know why you accepted the offer if it stresses you out."

"I . . ." She seemed to be searching for an answer while staring at his throat. "I'm not sure there is one thing that doesn't stress me out."

He continued to turn them in a slow circle. "Grocery shopping?"

"Sure. A good hostess always has the right items on hand at all times. The Just Us League meetings are held at my house, and dairy allergies, gluten-free diets, vegan regimes . . . all of them have to be accounted for."

"All right. How about baths? Those can't stress you out."

"Not if I add the right amount of essential oil."

"Christ. Sex?"

"Sex? Are you kidding me?" She wet her lips. "How is my lighting, is the man present, can he tell I'm *not* present, am I really as cold as men say because I can't lose myself in these moments, is this creating an expectation, how does my butt look, where is his dog? I could go on." A beat passed. "I shouldn't be telling you any of this. You're just going to use it against me."

Damn. How did she make everyone think she had the world on a string when, in actuality, the world was holding her by one? Wes put his surprise aside and tipped her chin up. "I hereby solemnly swear to use nothing you said tonight against you." His fingers spread out to span her jaw, his thumb sliding across her bottom lip. "I'll just say this. If you've had time to think of all that bullshit during sex in the past, I completely understand the man hiatus you're on."

One of her hands smoothed down Wes's chest and he held in a groan. "Are you implying you'd wipe my mind clean"—she lifted on her toes and brought her lips within a breath of his—"of all those distracting thoughts?"

"I'm flat-out telling you, Bethany . . ." He ghosted his mouth over hers, tasting her uneven exhale on his tongue. "I'd keep you too busy to think."

She pressed her belly more securely to his lap. "Too bad sex is off the table."

"Weddings don't count." He tilted his hips to let her feel his arousal, grazing her bottom lip with his teeth at the same time. "Everyone knows that."

Her head fell back and he dragged his lips slowly up the smooth column of her neck, letting go of her chin in favor of drawing her tight against his body. Fuck, he was hard. Distantly, he heard some microphone feedback, the band hitting a bad note, and just assumed he was so horny, the whole damn party was being affected. No one was coming back here. God willing no one would come looking for them. Who knew if he'd ever get another chance like this with Bethany?

"Wes . . ."

He was already walking them further into the shadows. "I know, darlin'."

"Wes, I need you."

"Goddamn. Been dying to hear you say that." Still in motion, his hands found the hem of her dress and lifted it to her waist, leaving it bunched there so he could greedily palm her backside. "Hard and quick, baby? That what you need?"

"Hard and—what?" She shoved him away. "Jesus, Wes. I didn't mean I needed you for sex. Pull your life together."

A full five counts passed before he realized Bethany wasn't finally giving him the green light. Frustration and a whole lot of throbbing below the belt made his tone snappier than was warranted. "What the hell else do you need me for?"

His words were still hanging in the air when Bethany grabbed his elbow and started dragging him back toward the party. "Kristin. I knew she'd try and pull something like this. You have to help me stop her."

"Stop . . . Stephen's wife? Do what? Bethany, you bring me down there right now, I'm going to take someone's eye out with this erection."

She wasn't hearing him. "My sister-in-law is nuts. And pregnant. She's been pregnant for months and hasn't told Stephen." She pointed toward where the band was gathered and, sure enough, there was Kristin trying to pry the microphone out of the band leader's hand. "She's going to announce the pregnancy right here and now, the wacko."

"At someone else's wedding?" The urgency of the situation finally punctured his need for the woman beside him. Kind of. Okay, barely. "That's pretty messed up."

"Yes, it is. Thank you." She looked down at the swell behind his fly and chewed her lip. "Can you get that thing under control?"

"It's not a puppy, Bethany," he said through his teeth.

"Sorry." The only saving grace of this situation was the fact that she seemed impressed, her gaze continually returning to the scene of the crime. "Can I help?"

"I thought that's what you were doing." He dragged a hand down his face. "You putting our reputations in the hands of reality-show editors who can manipulate whatever they film to make us look like jackasses. I'll think of that. It should take care of the problem in no time."

"As if you need any help looking like a jackass," she shot back. "And I *knew* you were coming to yell at me!"

The pretty blush he'd put on her cheeks was replaced by an irritated red and he wished he'd just kept his mouth shut. Blame the boner. More microphone feedback made its way to where they stood and Wes sighed. "You want my help or not?"

"I'm not exactly flush with choices." She tapped her chin. "I'll take Kristin. You cause a diversion." She pointed to his—finally—subsiding hard-on. "A diversion without the use of that, please. I'd rather Kristin announce she's having quadruplets."

Wes winked at her while adjusting himself. "Now who's possessive of who?"

Pink climbed her neck, her eyes following his movements. "Oh, shut up."

He laughed and they started walking side by side toward the dance floor. "Is she really having quadruplets?"

"Probably. Just to show off." She squared her shoulders. "Don't let me down, Wes. I'm counting on you."

Just before they parted ways at the edge of the dance floor, Wes snagged her hand and leaned down to speak beside her ear. "You look fucking beautiful tonight, in case no one told you."

He left her standing with her jaw on the floor and slid seamlessly into a huddled group of women, who just happened to be Let's Color, Faded Calf Tattoo, Green Bean Casserole, and *Outlander* Ringtone.

"What did you ladies do with my niece?" They stepped aside to give him a view of Laura dancing with Georgie. His laugh turned her head and she waved at him enthusiastically, creating a suspicious tug in his throat. "Well, ladies. Are we going to give them a run for their money or not?"

Wes spun Faded Calf Tattoo around, much to her delight, and then took the opportunity to check on Bethany's progress across the dance floor. Lord. She looked ready to strangle her sister-in-law with the microphone cord, but Rosie had gotten involved, too, and appeared to be talking some sense into the pissed-off pregnant woman. Trying to hold up his end of the bargain, Wes twirled Faded Calf Tattoo one more time, then multitasked while she turned, dropping *Outlander* Ringtone back into a dip. Their antics, as expected, were drawing a lot of attention, even

Bethany's—and she sent him a small, secret, grateful smile that, dammit . . . had him thinking about her walking down the aisle in a wedding dress again.

Wes was just about to bring a third lady into the dance and really ratchet up the diversion when Travis, obviously oblivious to the drama, saved the day by casually plucking the microphone out of the band leader's hand. "Excuse me, everyone. I have an announcement." He smiled at the guests, seeming to notice for the first time that Kristin was two feet away, scowling at him. "Er . . . did I . . ."

"Nope!" Bethany said brightly. "Go ahead. Make your announcement."

Bethany wrapped an arm around Kristin, who tried to dig in her heels, and escorted her out of sight.

"Okay." Confidence restored, Travis lifted a pint of beer. "I just want to make a toast to my wife." He stopped, his composure slipping again, his eyes developing a sheen. "Wow. First time I've gotten to say that. My wife, Georgette Castle." There wasn't a sound to be heard, save the wind rustling the trees in the backyard. "You made me the happiest man alive today. And I know you don't need a single thing. I don't, either, now that I've got you. But I can't help wanting to give you everything in the world, so bear with me. Okay? Buckle up, baby girl, because we're going to Italy. Tonight. Your bags are already packed."

A gasp went up, followed by a loud cheer.

Somewhere outside the limelight, Kristin wailed miserably.

Wes laughed. A few minutes later, Bethany locked eyes

with him across the dance floor. Slowly, some might say grudgingly on her end, they made their way back to each other, meeting in the center of the celebrants. They were the only ones who weren't dancing, but there were almost enough sparks leaping in her eyes to qualify. After dancing with her behind the house, feeling her let go and breathe up against his chest, it was nearly impossible not to reach for her now. How could touching her be wrong when his hands felt empty without her?

"Thank you for the diversion," she started.

He winked and it seemed to momentarily distract her. "Any time."

"It occurred to me"—she crossed her arms at a very precise angle—"that I never asked if you were comfortable being involved in the reality show. If you want out, I'll totally understand—"

"I don't scare that easy."

She inclined her head, her body sagging ever so slightly. With relief? "Then I guess I'll see you on Wednesday."

"I guess so." She started to turn away, but he stopped her. "Hey, Bethany?"

"Yes?"

The words seemed to come from the dead center of his stomach. "Maybe I could be the one thing you don't overthink, all right?"

The music faded a little around them. Wes could see the pulse at the base of her neck going a thousand miles an hour, despite her collected expression. For a few moments, they were back behind the house and she was baring her vulnerabilities to him, but just as quickly, she snatched them back up with a sly smile. "Who says I think about you at all?"

Wes's low laugh followed her back to the other side of the dance floor. Goddamn, she was something else. He couldn't wait for Wednesday when he'd get the honor of matching wits with her again. Hell, just being around her. Seeing her, this time with the added knowledge of how she ticked. They were going to be on the same team. It would be an understood fact, if only for the time it took to renovate the house.

Although, for the first time, the finish line at the end of his stay in Port Jefferson was obscured by a fine layer of mist. A *someday* as opposed to a soon. With an alarmed shake of his head, he cleared the mist and went to find his niece, calling himself ten times a fool.

CHAPTER NINE

Bethany got to the site early on Wednesday morning and parked on the street, as they'd been advised to do via the furious rounds of emails that had arrived since the wedding. As of Sunday, she'd had zero clue how television productions came together.

Today she considered herself a reluctant expert.

Though she'd agreed to appear on the show, she'd nearly escaped her panic by reasoning there was *no way* the filming of a television show could be pulled together so quickly. Surely she'd be let off the hook.

Apparently she'd underestimated a motivated producer with a flexible budget. Since Sunday night, a full camera crew, complete with director, had been pulled off an in-progress reality show called *AirBn'Ballers*, which had been set to film in the Hamptons. *That* gem having been put on hold, the crew made their way to Port Jefferson instead.

Now the driveway was reserved for the cameras, producers, director, sound and lighting crew, not to mention about a dozen production assistants—the imminent presence of whom made her want to puke her breakfast into the ratty-ass lawn.

She was equal parts thrilled for her sister's Italian honeymoon and sad that she didn't have Georgie's irreverent banter in her ear. It definitely would have helped her get through demo day.

It wasn't as though she'd never been present during the demolition of a home's interior. As kids, their father had brought them along to witness the gutting of houses many times. Even as an adult, she'd watched walls being ripped down, floorboards being pried up. Seen debris tossed out windows or carried to dumpsters. There was something indescribably satisfying about breaking down the old to make way for the new. That sense of exhilaration displayed by others had sparked her interest in heading her own flip in the first place. She wanted to experience that rush of pleasure.

So few things gave her that reduction of tension. Would burying a sledgehammer in some drywall leave her boneless and too depleted to think of what came next for five minutes? God, she hoped so. She was starting to worry about her inability to sit still. Was it normal? This total failure to be happy with any of her efforts or be satisfied with her accomplishments?

She hadn't been lying when she told Wes *way too much* at the wedding. It had been a weak moment, nothing more . . . though she trusted that he wouldn't use her revelations against her. She wasn't sure why she held that trust in him, only that it was rock solid.

Bethany caught sight of her thoughtful frown in the rearview mirror and shook herself.

Since the final guest had left on Sunday night, she'd been cleaning her parents' backyard, returning the catering company equipment, packing up the gifts and leaving them arranged just so in Georgie and Travis's living room, so they could open them upon returning from Florence.

Everyone had left the wedding happy and loaded, as was always the hope. So why had she lain awake for the last two nights trying to pick every moment apart for something that hadn't been perfect? There was food left over. Did that mean people didn't like it? Should she have provided a coat check? Why the hell hadn't she considered a damn coat check? Now those jackets draped on the backs of chairs would be in photographs photobombing for all eternity. That's how people would remember the wedding, wouldn't they?

Conversely, when Bethany thought of the wedding, she would remember how much of her ass cheek could fit in Wes's hand. As in, the whole thing. She'd never had her butt gripped with such authority before—and why couldn't she dredge up some more indignation about it? He'd lifted her dress and grabbed two handfuls and she could only work up the barest irritation. There was something definitely wrong with her. It was the lack of sleep. Definitely.

She certainly hadn't liked it.

Or humped her vibrator thinking about it until she strained a hamstring.

Bethany slapped open the driver's-side vanity mirror and smoothed a ridge of unblended concealer beneath her eye with the pad of her pinky. Her movements paused when she heard the crunch of gravel behind her, excitement leaping in her belly before she could stop it. That would be Wes arriving, but she wouldn't get out to greet him. No, she'd stay locked in her car where she was safe from bad ideas.

Bethany only made it to a count of ten before tightening her ponytail and climbing out of the car. She drew up short when, instead of Wes and his dinged-up truck, she saw a very attractive man leaning against a black town car, complete with driver. The James Marsden lookalike was laughing at something on the screen of his cell phone, ankles crossed in a careless way.

"Can I help you?"

The man seemed disinclined to look up from his phone, but he finally did, performing a double take. "Oh." He pushed off the town car. "Hello there. Did they bring in another host to replace me?"

Bethany frowned. "Sorry?"

"Well, you can't be the homeowner." He put his hand out for a shake, sliding it smoothly into hers, holding. "With that face, they'd be bad at their jobs if they put you in the background, instead of front and center."

Wow. Bethany was ashamed to admit that line might have worked on her before. This guy was so her usual type, it hurt. She tended to gravitate toward men with impeccable style. Complimentary men. Men who saw the best in her and pointed it out, rather than bring up her worst qualities constantly, like a certain someone she knew.

You look fucking beautiful tonight, in case no one told you.

Warmth flooded her stomach at the memory of Wes say-ing those words to her at the wedding, hasty and oddly timed as they'd been. Why did Wes's compliments get a physical reaction out of her while this man's praise left her totally cold?

She didn't know. But the hiatus train rolled on.

"I am the homeowner, actually." Bethany shook his hand firmly and let go. "And you are?"

"Slade Hogan." His teeth almost blinded her when he smiled. "Can't lie, I'm glad I picked today to show up early. That almost never happens."

"Crazy."

He laughed even though she hadn't made a joke. "You probably recognize me from *Insane Porches*? It ran for two seasons."

"Oh, right." She didn't. "I thought you looked familiar."

"I get that a lot." He squinted past her toward the house. "Ouch, they really think the crew can get this done in two and a half weeks?"

"Excuse me?" Bethany blinked. *"Two and a half weeks?"*

Slade shrugged a shoulder. "That's the term of my con-tract. Being that I'm a vital part of the show—"

"The show they created on the fly three days ago?"

"Yes." He stopped and considered her, as though decid-ing whether or not he'd been insulted. "Anyway, my agent tells me this particular film crew has to resume production of *AirBn'Ballers* in three weeks, so there is a tight deadline to film this pilot. Not to worry, though, I'm sure you've got a capable team."

"Sure do."

The sound of an approaching engine turned both of their heads and Bethany almost laughed. Of course Wes took that moment to pull up. Her unlikely foreman climbed out of his truck with all the aplomb of a gunslinger dismounting his horse. He eyeballed Bethany and Slade from beneath the brim of his cowboy hat, tucked his fingers into the loops of his jeans, and traversed the driveway with his long-legged stride. "Morning."

"Morning," Bethany replied, mentally berating her hormones for responding to the sight of his freshly shaven jaw, the wet ends of his hair. The morning breeze plastered his long-sleeved, paint-splashed shirt to his body and it really should have annoyed her that he'd shown up to be filmed for television in an old stained shirt. But it didn't. It made her . . . glad to see him. For some reason. A lot gladder than she'd been to see the hot show host. "This is Slade Hogan," she said, introducing the man when Wes drew even. "He's going to host the show."

Wes raised an eyebrow at Bethany.

She raised one back. *Don't you dare laugh at his name.*

Wes sighed.

There was no mistaking Slade's wince when the men shook. "You planning on pitching in?" Wes asked Slade.

"Me?" Slade laughed. "No. I only hold a hammer for promotional purposes."

He seemed to be waiting for Bethany to laugh, so she obliged him in the hopes of balancing the awkwardness Wes was working to create. Her hostess mentality didn't come and go at will, and there was no point in making Slade uncomfortable. Especially when it looked like they'd be stuck with one another's company for over two weeks.

"I'm sure you'll find something to keep you busy," Wes drawled, taking a step toward Bethany. "Something else, that is."

Silence landed, the men staring hard at each other.

"I'm sure there will be plenty of photo ops," Bethany said without missing a beat, taking hold of Wes's arm and tugging him into the scrappy side yard. "Can I talk to you?"

He was still looking at Slade. "Sure, darlin'."

"No problem. Go ahead." Slade's voice was tighter than before. "I have a million calls to make."

"Better get to it," Wes said, tugging down the brim of his hat. "Slade."

With her back turned away from the host, Bethany rolled her eyes like an exasperated twelve-year-old. She cast a glance over her shoulder to make sure they weren't being watched—and then she jabbed her finger into Wes's chest. "I am only going to say this one more time. I am not your chew toy. We are not involved and therefore you are not allowed to tell other men to back off. I make that decision! Me!"

Wes snorted. "I did you a favor. Any man with hands that soft will only steal your moisturizer."

The urge to laugh was seriously inconvenient. "I didn't ask you to do me a favor, cowboy."

"Aha! So you're admitting it was a favor?"

"No, I am not," she enunciated. "I am admitting nothing."

Wes contemplated her quietly for a full five seconds. "You really interested in Hammer Promo Guy, Bethany?"

She wasn't. In fact, she was painfully disinterested. Which was alarming, to say the least. Normally, she would still be working over a man like Slade with charm. Instead, she was arguing with Wes. Again. How did she keep ending up here? And why wasn't she doing more to avoid it?

"I don't have to answer that," she whisper-screeched. "But if I decided I was interested, that would be okay. I'm allowed."

His jaw flexed. "Let's say the host was the female version of Slade. You'd just be fine watching me flip my hair around and flirting?"

Bethany battled a smile. "Actually, I'd pay good money to watch you flip your hair around. Can I film?"

"You know what I meant," he growled. "Answer the question."

She envisioned herself pulling her car into the driveway and finding Wes putting the moves on some faceless woman, all twinkling eyes and Wrangler-booty swagger. The lining of her stomach turned to acid. "I wasn't flipping my hair," she croaked, caught off guard by her own reaction.

Wes stepped closer and their fingers brushed. "Admit you wouldn't like it."

Bethany's headshake was a little too vigorous.

Enough to carry some warmth into his expression. "What you told me at the wedding about your sex life . . . I know I promised I wouldn't use it against you, so this is totally unrelated."

She snorted. "I knew you wouldn't be able to resist."

"Ah, come on. It's just the two of us standing here," he murmured, twining their index fingers together. "If you date guys like that, it doesn't surprise me you can't relax and stop overthinking everything. They're not doing any of the thinking for you."

God help her, she actually wanted to hear his logic, because she needed all the advice she could get. She'd once had a perfect plan to find someone as driven and successful as herself. That plan hadn't panned out. Now, she'd kind of just . . . given up. So what would it hurt to consider someone else's opinion? Even Wes's? Not that she would let him know she was listening to his spiel willingly. "I had no idea you were an expert on sex and relationships."

"I'm not. But I'm guessing Slade would be overthinking in the sack, too." He traded the Texas accent for a distinctly Hollywood millennial one. "'Why did my latest Instagram post only hit four thousand likes? Did I remember to make my toe waxing appointment? Should I try a side part?'"

Bethany laughed and lightness filtered into her chest. It was . . . nice laughing at things that would normally stress her out, even if she couldn't make it a habit. Wait. How long had they been holding hands? Out in the open? "Men don't have to ride bulls to be masculine like you—"

He reared back a little, amusement written on his features. "How did you know I rode bulls?"

"I . . ." Panicking, she tugged her hand away, shoving it into her pocket. "That was a wild stab. A mere example."

"No, it wasn't." A slow smile spread across his face.

"Speaking of Instagram, you've been doing a little cyber-stalking, haven't you, baby?"

Bethany took a step back, but he followed. "Hardly. I just wanted to make sure my foreman had a savory online presence."

"And?" He winked. "Did you savor it?"

"Shut up."

He caught her wrist and pulled her close, making her stomach flip like she was on a roller coaster. "I looked at yours, too." She didn't have a chance to process that before he continued. "I like being referred to as your foreman," he mused. "It's got a nice ring."

"Especially compared to what I usually call you."

"Truth. It's a definite improvement from dickhead." His thumb brushed over the pulse in her wrist. "Tell me you're not interested in him, Bethany."

Her hold on good sense slipped. "I'm not interested in him," she murmured, shaking her head at the triumphant blaze in his eyes. "But . . . Wes, I don't get . . . this. You're not in town permanently. I'm not interested in a fling—and even if I was, you've wisely removed sex from the equation—"

"Deepest regret of my life."

"Yeah, pretty shortsighted of you."

"I'll bring sex back into the equation when you know I didn't just take this job to improve my chances of sleeping with you."

"I—" She'd almost said *I do know that now*. Like a total moron. "That still wouldn't inspire me to end my man hiatus."

Gaze lingering on the neckline of her T-shirt, Wes licked

the corner of his mouth. "Keep telling yourself that." He considered her for a beat—above the neck this time. "I don't have answers to all of your questions. I can't define what's going on between us, either. But maybe that's exactly what you need."

"Oh Jesus. Every time I start to think you're redeemable, you say something so fucking stupid, I wish for a time machine so I can go back and never hear it." She went up on her toes to get in his face. "Don't tell me what I need."

"You'd like me to demonstrate instead?"

I would. But don't let him know it. "I mean." She tilted her head to expose her neck. As in, *Look, here's my neck, by accident.* "How can I answer that when I have no idea what a demonstration might entail?"

His lips paused just above her pulse. "Come closer and I'll show you."

"Fine. Just so I can paint an accurate picture," she managed, heat starting to pump in places only Wes seemed capable of accessing. Cautiously, her toes pushed her up another inch toward his face.

Chuckling, Wes dropped his mouth the remaining distance to her neck, trailing up the curve—lightly, so lightly—and pausing at her ear. Oh, that was good. *Too* good. "Took those bulls a good long while to buck me off, baby. Think you could do it?"

"We're not going to find out," she breathed, her nipples tightening like bolts and making her sound like a liar. "By the way, that kind of talk doesn't do much to dampen my belief that you're here to get laid."

"You love it just the same," he rasped against her mouth. "Same way I love it when your eyes get all unfocused, like you're trying to remember why I'm a bad idea."

"Hey, folks!" A camera crew was walking up the driveway, Justine leading the way with a headset and a clipboard. They appeared to be . . . rolling. As in, filming her and Wes in a near lip-lock. "I had a feeling this shoot would be a jackpot," Justine called, waving her clipboard. "Please continue to prove me right."

Bethany took a backward lunge away from Wes. "Just discussing plans!"

Wes smiled without so much as acknowledging the camera. "I'll say."

CHAPTER TEN

Bethany stood shoulder to shoulder with Wes.

They'd both been positioned behind an animated Slade, who was taping his introduction in front of two cameras, a boom mic operator, and a lighting crew. It was crazy to witness how quickly he'd shifted from miffed prima donna to jocular construction guru as soon as the cameras started rolling. It probably helped that he was reading off a prompter.

"Greetings, DIY junkies, you've tuned in to *Flip Off*—a new drama-fueled competition show where family members flip two different houses and vie for the ultimate bragging rights. Who flipped it best? We're coming to you from Port Jefferson, Long Island, and boy oh boy, do we have a treat for you! Although the word 'treat' might be pushing it, because our first featured property is quite frankly the worst home I've had the pleasure of seeing restored to its former glory. And that's exactly what you plan to do here, isn't it, Bethany?"

The camera swung in her direction and Bethany's heart climbed until it was clogging her throat. She looked to Justine, but the producer only provided an encouraging finger roll.

"Um . . ." *Come on. Pull it together.* She'd gotten herself into this mess; the least she could do was fake it until she made it. And God knew, she faked having her shit together often enough that she should know the drill.

The stakes were a lot higher this time, though. She wasn't planning a party or styling the perfect outfit. Or even going on a date and trying to represent a much more together version of herself than really existed. If a crack formed in her walls—literally and figuratively—she wouldn't be able to hide it.

She smiled brightly. "Yes, that's the plan!"

"Fantastic!" Slade sidled to the right. "And who are you here with today?"

"This is my foreman, Wes. He's—"

"Folks at home, this is where things get even more juicy. See, Bethany is competing against her own brother, Stephen, who is flipping a house across town. Wes here is his former crew member. Ooooh, baby, things are going to get interesting. You don't want to miss it. Stay tuned for this family drama on *Flip Off.* Next up: demo."

"Cut!" called the director. "Did we get our before shots? Inside and out?"

"Still need to get the master!" a disembodied voice called from behind the blinding lights. "Backyard, too. Give us ten."

"Great." Justine made some notes on her clipboard. "We have to get across town for Stephen's introduction, so let's get some good demo footage. After that, we need some individual on-camera interviews with Wes and Bethany, together and separate. We'll be doing this frequently to get your reactions."

"To what?" Wes wanted to know.

"To everything. Construction progress, tension among the crew . . ." Justine looked around. "Speaking of your crew, do you have one?"

"That would be us, ma'am."

Bethany shielded her eyes from the light, ducking down until she brought two senior-citizen men into view. One had a pair of cheater glasses tucked into the collar of his shirt; the other one appeared to be rubbing a bum leg.

Cheater Glasses waved at her, accidentally bumping his friend with a stray elbow. Which led to them griping at each other. "Didn't know we were going to be on TV," said Cheater Glasses. "I'm not going to be required to carry anything, am I? My back isn't what it used to be."

Back teeth grinding together, Bethany looked at Wes. "Where did you find them?"

He avoided making eye contact. "The hardware store."

She stared.

"There's a system," he said curtly. "You're not meant to understand it."

"And thank God for that."

Justine approached her, head buried in her clipboard. "Right. We'll bring in some interns to help . . . flesh out your *amazing* crew. Note my sarcasm."

Heat swamped Bethany's face. The operation was already

showing cracks, meaning *she* was showing them. *It's already happening.* "We'd appreciate that, thanks."

Justine sailed away, muttering something about rounding out the *Grumpy Old Men* franchise into a trilogy. Before Wes could introduce her to Cheater Glasses and Bum Leg, one of the college-age production assistants approached her with a sledgehammer. "Miss Castle, if you could come with me, please? We want to check the lighting on the wall you plan on demolishing first."

She accepted the heavy tool. "Right. Which wall is that?"

The young man blinked. "You don't have a starting point?"

"Oh, me? I have a starting point. Sure." Bethany turned in a circle, the sledgehammer rebounding off her calf muscle. "That one?" She pointed at the water-damaged living room wall, consulting with Wes out of the corner of her eye. When he gave her an imperceptible nod, she let out the breath she'd been holding. "Yes, that one."

"Great."

Off went the PA, already throwing hand signals to the mobile lighting crew.

"So I'm just supposed to bury this hammer into the wall?" she whispered to Wes. "Just . . . make a mess? No exact science to it?"

"Not for this particular wall, no. There's no plumbing, gas lines—I came through last week and marked them." He indicated the orange spray-painted Xs in the kitchen and dining room that she'd neglected to notice until now. "We've got three load-bearing walls: one in the living room, one in the back bedroom, and the other in the hallway, but we'll cross that bridge when we come to it."

Load-bearing walls? Gas lines? If Wes weren't here, she could have started a fire or collapsed the roof on day one. What had she been thinking agreeing to have this process broadcasted? What had she been thinking taking on this flip at all? Bethany wrangled her runaway panic and tried to focus on the here and now. "Okay. What if I hit the wall and it doesn't even crack?"

"Bethany, you could probably flick a rubber band at that wall and it would cave faster than my niece when I accuse her of stealing cookies."

Still . . . "Maybe you should demo the wall."

Wes turned, giving his back to the room full of people and blocking her from sight. "You wanted to get dirty, Bethany. Lead your own project. That's why we're here. Now that it's time to get started you've got stage fright? Shake it off."

Easier for the rough-and-tumble cowboy to say. No one expected him to get through life without a single misstep. People had expectations for her and she couldn't simply disregard her need to fulfill them. "When I made the decision to do this . . . I-I didn't expect so many people to see me dirty."

"Look here, darlin'. You're the one who decided to compete with Stephen. This reality-show bullshit is on you."

Heat wove its way up the back of her neck. "Does it really seem like a good time to remind me of that?"

"The perfect time, actually," he said without hesitation. "It won't hurt to be a little pissed when you swing that hammer."

Bethany tilted her head. "That's why you riled me up, isn't it?" She waited but he said nothing. "You did the same thing when I was getting emotional at Georgie and Travis's rehearsal dinner. Irritated me until I stopped tearing up—"

"I irritate you because it's fun," he said, chuckling. "No other reason."

She narrowed her eyes at Wes's odd tone. He seemed almost nervous over her believing there could be more to the timing of his ribbing. There was no time to analyze Wes's reaction too deeply, however, because the director was watching them impatiently near the wall they'd designated as the first to go. "Okay, Bethany. Our production schedule is tight. Let's make this a good take."

Sledgehammer in hand and goggles in place, she swallowed and stepped into the brightly illuminated space. Through the refracted lens, she could see two dozen pairs of eyes on her, the stillness of the bodies making her stomach flip-flop. They were waiting. Watching her do something she hadn't perfected. Oh God. They would be witnessing her employ untested skills for two weeks. They were going to know she was out of her element, a fraud, starting now. She didn't have entertaining skills or the perfect outfit to fall back on. It was just her and a hammer—and two cameras capturing her every move.

When the director coughed, she turned to face the wall and ordered her arms to lift the sledgehammer. But nothing happened. Her hands started to shake on the wooden handle, her mouth losing all moisture. *I'm going to be sick.*

"Turn off the cameras," Wes said.

"Excuse me? I'm not—"

"I said turn them off." A presence warmed her back. *Wes.* His palm skimmed down her forearm and settled on her hand where it gripped the handle. "Hey."

"Hey," she whispered back.

"What's wrong?" he asked into her hair.

Bethany couldn't come up with a lie. It wasn't merely the wall that had left her stalled out—it was the whole job. The whole house that surrounded them and what it meant. A test of her mettle. A barrier she would normally avoid, for fear she would run into it headfirst. It was just like her relationships with men. As soon as her past boyfriends started to become suspicious that she wasn't Mary Make It Look Effortless, the persona she'd sold them, she started pulling back. Dodging calls, canceling dates, until they burned her by cheating or breaking up via an impersonal text.

It was almost a relief when that happened.

There was no more fear of being discovered.

She could start over again with a fresh slate and pretend like the last relationship never happened. But a house was different. It was forever. It was visible proof of her efforts and what they could yield. It couldn't be erased by changing her status on Facebook and purging a handful of pictures.

"I'm really afraid to be bad at this," she said now, the confession leaving her mouth unchecked. "At anything. It scares me. Like, a lot."

"Great. Do it anyway."

She huffed a laugh.

"If people were good at everything on the first try, they

wouldn't appreciate the journey to getting better," he murmured against her ear, his fingers trailing back and forth across her knuckles. "Why are you really here?"

She wet her lips. "Because I want to prove I can . . . I want to know if I can do more than make things pretty. I'm getting too comfortable staying in my lane and . . . I never get a sense of accomplishment anymore. Everything always could have been better. Always. Maybe if I push and do something harder . . . I'll feel it again."

Somehow, she could sense his thoughtfulness. It was nice having someone shoulder her inadequacy issues for a few seconds. Even though she would surely regret telling him these personal things any time now.

"Bethany."

"Yes?"

"Your brother fucks up constantly."

She perked up. "What?"

"You heard me. On our last job, he didn't measure the bathroom door's swing correctly, so it smacked off the toilet every time we opened it. Same job, he damn near electrocuted himself putting in the basement track lighting. The man yelped like a poodle who'd gotten his tail stepped on. And how many flips do you reckon he's done?"

"At least thirty."

"Right. Stephen has the most experience out of anyone, but he still messes up. *We* will mess something up, baby, but any mistake you make on this house is one that can be corrected, okay?"

The pressure in her chest lessened, slowly but surely. Was

it insane that she . . . believed him? He was so unflinching. So sure. He didn't seem thrown off by her admissions at all. "Okay."

"Aim and swing. Hard. Let these folks get their shots, we'll do our stupid interviews, and then it'll just be you, me, and two geriatrics."

Her laugh caught her off guard, as did the loosening in her middle. He'd done it again. Thinned out her worries like cookie dough under a rolling pin. The more often it happened, the less she believed his casual heroics were a mistake. Maybe he was just . . . heroic. On occasion. "That sounds good."

"Doesn't it?" He kissed her temple so quickly, she almost thought it was a figment of her imagination. "Give that wall hell, darlin'."

"Can we record now?" the director asked drily, not waiting for a response. "And we're rolling in three . . . two . . . one."

Bethany heaved the sledgehammer up onto her shoulder, rested it a second, then used every ounce of force in her body to smash the metal into the Sheetrock. It split wide open and debris flew everywhere, leaving a giant hole behind. A few of the crew members whistled and Wes boomed a laugh. But she barely heard any of it over the wild applause in her own head. It matched the fast-paced tempo of her heart. It sped and sped like a propeller until she worried it might carry her away. In search of an anchor, she turned and found Wes amongst the lighting.

He was smiling broadly at her when she turned, but

whatever he saw on her face caused it to slip, his Adam's apple rising and falling in his throat. His recovery was far from instantaneous, but he eventually gave her a jerky nod.

There was a strong—horribly conceived—urge inside her to go to Wes, to see if he'd put his arms around her, but thankfully she was stayed by the sudden putrescent smell that filled the room.

"Aw, shit," called one of the PAs. "We've got a dead rat in the wall."

"We'll do the interviews outside. Someone get an intern to bag the rat."

Everyone groaned and filed out of the room.

Bethany followed the flow of people, still dragging the sledgehammer behind her until Wes took it out of her hands and propped it against his shoulder. Not looking like a sexy Paul Bunyan or anything. Definitely not.

Just before she exited through the front door, Bethany turned and glanced back at the house. She'd made one hole in the wall. Only one. But she wasn't as apprehensive as before to commence the flip—and she couldn't deny that the man walking beside her scowling at the cameramen had a lot to do with it.

Not good. Not good at all.

CHAPTER ELEVEN

Wes watched Bethany work across the debris-strewn floor, wood and ancient drywall littering the space between them. Thanks to Rat-Gate, followed by the start and stop of on-camera interviews that had taken over an hour yesterday, they were still only halfway finished with demo on Project Doomsday.

Bethany was avoiding him, as much as she could in a confined space where they could hear each other breathing. He supposed he was avoiding her a little, too, not that he could stop drooling over her in those dusty pink yoga pants. Where was her panty line? Would he be able to slide his hands down into those tight little things and get a hold of her butt cheeks? Would she like it?

Try not to get an erection while operating heavy destructive equipment, would you, asshole?

Besides, he was still unnerved by the way his heart had shaken like a martini when she'd laid into that wall yesterday, then turned around with that unchecked smile on her beautiful face. She'd looked right to him, dropping that happiness directly into his lap—and the subsequent squeeze between his pecs had landed like an attack. It hadn't gone away, either. Was it . . . permanent?

Couldn't be.

Bethany grabbed his attention when she moved to the kitchen, attempting to pry tile off the wall. When she couldn't get one unstuck and whacked it with her crowbar in frustration, he set down his sledgehammer, fished a metal wedge out of his toolbox, and joined her. "Here." He slid the tip of the tool in behind the tile and gestured for Bethany to hand him the crowbar, which she did. "Now you tap it. Like so." The tile hit the floor. "The sucker'll pop right off."

"Oh, uh. Thanks." She accepted the crowbar back and followed his instructions on the next one, smiling when she executed the move perfectly. "I like that. It's clean."

He leaned a shoulder on the wall, biting back on the urge to brush a layer of dust from her nose. "Do you like anything messy?"

Bethany narrowed her eyes at him and he held up his hands in innocence, letting her know he wasn't trying to make the conversation dirty. Though he easily could have. Find him a twenty-three-year-old man who *didn't* relate everything back to sex.

Her suspicions seemed to fade and she pursed her lips. "I allow my bun to be a tad haphazard on a Sunday morning. That's about it." She popped off another tile and gave a satisfied swing of her ponytail. "Don't you like anything neat and orderly?"

Damn, she never failed to make him think. He liked it. In the past, women were just another part of his life he didn't have to consider too hard. They were either coming home with him, or they weren't. What was there to stress about?

With Bethany, he could almost see her filing away every piece of information he dropped, so he wanted to say the right thing. The honest thing. Not simply whatever she wanted to hear. She was too smart for that, anyway.

"I dust my cowboy hat off every night and I, uh . . ." Unbelievable. He could feel the tips of his goddamn ears turning red. "I store it in my closet in a hatbox."

"You do?" Her eyes turned distant, like she was trying to picture him completing the nightly ritual. "What does the box look like? Is there tissue paper?"

"Hell, no, there isn't any tissue paper." He laughed, scratching the side of his chin. "There might be some shredded newspaper."

Her gasp turned into a giggle. "That's not even remotely different."

Oh, hey. She'd never made that sound before. It was adorable and feminine and he'd let her watch him dust the hat off if she made that noise again. "Yes, it is. It's entirely different," he managed finally. "And Jesus, look at you. Turned on by the idea of proper hat storage."

He watched her struggle through subduing her amusement and realized there was a smile stretching its way across his face. Hot damn. They were flirting without it devolving into a name-calling competition, and the relief of that, knowing they *could* manage that feat, was enormous.

"Listen," she said. "I do the same thing with my Louboutins."

His smile dropped. "Jesus Christ. Now you've gone and compared my manly hat to a lady shoe."

She buried her face in the crook of her elbow, her shoulders shaking with mirth. In that moment, he could picture himself tickling her, maybe taking a playful bite out of her neck. Boyfriend-girlfriend behavior.

It brought Wes up short. He definitely didn't want permanent. Settling down and walking one straight path for the rest of his life didn't appeal to him. He always needed to be ready to move on, so he wouldn't be caught floundering when the moment arrived. Quick, painless, easy. That's how he lived.

A man who grew too comfortable and left himself no escape hatches eventually ended up stranded. A couple of times growing up, he'd let himself get comfortable with a foster family, only to find out they'd never gotten comfortable with *him*. They'd been angling to steer clear of him the whole time.

No one had ever needed him.

No one, except for his half sister. She'd relied on him to get her out of trouble so many times it had become draining, disappointing, but he couldn't help answering the call. A small part of him *wanted* to be depended on. Even by someone who didn't appreciate it or, hell, even thank him most of the time.

Bethany certainly didn't need him. Sure she'd had a couple of weak moments, but if he wasn't around, she'd simply get encouragement from her local support group. He'd merely been handy. Within reaching distance.

No, he definitely didn't have any notions of staying in Port Jefferson. Still, every time Bethany glanced over and their eyes locked, his stomach wrapped itself around his fucking spleen. Yeah, it was safe to say his preoccupation with her went far beyond the average, casual hookup. The word "hookup" wasn't even worthy of being mentioned in the same breath as Bethany—and that became more and more true every time she made Wes privy to her thoughts.

I never get a sense of accomplishment anymore. Maybe if I push and do something harder . . . I'll feel it again.

Wes always knew there were several leagues below Bethany's surface, but she kept surprising him with another one. His sense of self-preservation told him to stop trying to locate her ocean floor, but this morning upon arriving at the house, he'd found himself vowing to aid her in finding that feeling. Accomplishment. He wanted to help give that satisfaction to her so goddamn bad.

Probably sensing his stare, Bethany looked up from her task of prying off a skirting board with the crowbar. "Um, hey," she said. "How's it going over there?"

"It's going. How about you?"

"The mess is killing me."

"Figured it might be." He pressed his tongue to the inside of his cheek to subdue a smile. "It may not look like progress, but it is."

"Progress needs a scented candle and a dustpan." Bethany paused, looking like she had something else to say, but a grunt turned both of their heads to find Carl wiping sweat off his forehead with a rag and passing it to Ollie.

"My sciatica is on the fritz," Ollie complained, leaning his side against the wall. "Hurts like hell."

"My leg is still swelled up from yesterday," Carl said.

"All you did yesterday was wipe out the craft service table," Wes pointed out.

Carl snorted. "I wasn't passing up those little rolled-up cold cuts. My wife made us go vegan. Cut out my sugar and coffee, too. If you thought she was miserable before, you should see her now."

"Why can't they just let us be retired?" Ollie intoned, staring off into space. "It's like they were waiting for us to finally relax to start unleashing hell."

"Mine did run me a bath yesterday," Carl said. "Helped my leg some."

Ollie elbowed him, looking like a cat with a canary. "I got a massage."

Their sighs faded into groans, both men rubbing at their respective injuries. "Damn, that hurts," Carl moaned.

"I think I pinched a nerve," Ollie said.

"Are you sure you guys are up for this job?" Bethany asked.

"What?" Carl called. "We're having a great time."

Ollie snorted. "Best two days I've had in years."

She shook her head at Wes, but there was a smile playing around her mouth. One that made the pad of his thumb itch to smooth over her lower lip. Maybe he should ask her out. Nothing that would spook her. Just a last-minute-drink-between-coworkers kind of thing. Lord knew he went drinking with Stephen, Travis, and Dominic down at Grumpy Tom's often enough. This wouldn't be any different.

At least that's how he'd present it.

Wes cleared his throat hard. "Listen, Bethany—"

His phone rang noisily in his pocket. With a mental curse, he slipped off his working glove and took it out. Faded Calf Tattoo was calling him. She was his babysitter for that afternoon, which meant she would pick up Laura from school, bring her home, and watch her for the two hours that remained of Wes's workday.

"Hello?"

"Oh, hello, Wes." Her voice wobbled with worry. "I'm so sorry to do this to you, but I can't watch Laura today. My sister is having an emergency operation and I'm already on my way to New Jersey to be with her."

"I'm sorry to hear that. I hope it's not serious."

"Oh, she's lived through three dirtbag husbands, so I doubt a gall bladder is going to take her down now. But she'll need some coddling."

Wes chuckled. Dang it, he was really starting to grow fond of these babysitters. "Let me know if I can do anything for you."

"Will do. Sorry again."

"Don't be. See you soon."

He hung up and checked the clock on his phone. Too late to call for a replacement, and even if it wasn't, he didn't like being a bother, especially when these women were already doing enough. Too much to be sent running to the school at the last minute on their day off. It would have to be him.

"That didn't sound good," Bethany said, having come closer during his conversation. "What's wrong?"

It took him a second to collect his thoughts, thanks to the cute smudge of dirt on her nose. "I'm sorry, but I have to knock off early to pick up Laura from school. Marjorie had a family emergency."

"Oh. Sure." She tried to hide her panic, but didn't quite succeed. "Sure, of course. You have to go."

"I'll make up for lost time tomorrow."

Her shoulders relaxed by approximately one degree. "We will."

"Right."

"Were you going to ask me something?"

Yeah. Out for a friendly drink, when he really wanted to kiss her senseless. Right here and now, their audience of two be damned. She was looking at him differently today, her eyes more curious than disdainful. After that day she'd stormed the jobsite and he'd unexpectedly seen below her surface, he'd started wishing she'd change her attitude toward him. Now that she had, right on the heels of him acknowledging the temptation to try and be more to her, something inside him screamed to lighten the moment. Whether it was out of fear of the unfamiliar or simply not knowing how to be around someone he needed—how could he when he'd never experienced it before?—Wes gave her a slow once-over and spoke for her ears alone.

"Why don't you give me some motivation and tell me you're going to wear those extra-thin pink pants again tomorrow, darlin'?"

She cracked a disbelieving laugh. "Wear the same pants two days in a row?"

Wes fought a laugh. *"That's* the part you took offense to?"

"I-I . . . no." Her face colored. "I'll wear the pink pants if you wear your flea collar."

"First you talk about pegging and now I'm wearing a collar." He rocked back on his heels. "The plot thickens."

"It'll never be as thick as your skull." She dismissed him with a sniff, crunching through construction rubble on her way to her post. "Go home."

"See you tomorrow, Bethany."

"If only I had a choice, Wes," she sang sweetly.

His encounters with Bethany used to leave him feeling charged up. If not satisfied, he'd damn well gotten pleasure out of it. While there was a definite spark in his belly after their exchange, it now felt unfinished. Their barbs were supposed to lead somewhere, weren't they? Yeah. And he wanted to go there. Crazy enough, he wasn't sure *there* was just sex. Instead of walking away and leaving her frowning, he wanted to keep going until it became a grudging smile.

That would satisfy him almost as much as sex.

Jesus. What the hell was wrong with him?

Wes felt Bethany's questioning gaze on his back as he left the house. He got into his truck and drove to the school, arriving in the pick-up line just in time for Laura to begin her journey down the walkway. He hadn't picked her up many times this year, but based on her complaints that she didn't have any friends, Wes didn't expect her to be flanked by two girls her age. They were lost in an animated conversation complete with hand signals and giggles, while his niece appeared to be floating on cloud nine between them.

He lowered the passenger-side window at the exact moment Laura did her Scooby-Doo impression, making the other girls laugh, and an odd sound puffed out of him.

Laura spotted him idling at the curb and waved enthusiastically.

Warmth spread downward from his collarbone. "Hey, kid," he called. "Hop in."

"Wait. Uncle Wes, Uncle Wes, can Megan and Danielle come over?" His niece literally shrieked the question at him from fifteen yards away. "Please? If their mom says it's all right? Please?"

No. No way. He'd just figured out how to be passably decent at taking care of Laura. Throwing two more children into the mix could be disastrous. He searched for a distraction. Distractions always worked. "Maybe not today. I was planning on renting *Tangled* for us—"

"I love *Tangled*," Danielle or Megan squealed. "I want to watch it, too."

Rookie move, idiot. "I'm sure their mother has plans—"

A woman's face filled his passenger window. "Hi, I'm Judy. Danielle and Megan's mom. You're Wes, right? Laura's uncle?"

She stuck out her hand for a shake. He held up his grimy one apologetically. "Sorry, I just came from a construction site. Might want to steer clear."

Judy's expression was amused, but mostly distracted. "So, you're taking the girls today?"

"Oh." He scratched at his five o'clock shadow. "I . . . Am I?"

"I don't think these sassy ladies are going to take no for an answer!" What started off as a jovial laugh turned dark, Judy's expression becoming infinitely more intense. She leaned into his truck, knuckles turning white on the frame. "Please, take them. Even if it's just an hour."

Wes forced himself not to jerk back. "Think they can all fit in my truck?"

"We'll make them fit." Her smile returned, brighter than ever. "Girls," she called over her shoulder. "Good news. Laura's uncle is taking you for a few hours."

"Wait. A few?"

Ignoring him, Judy pried open the passenger door and ushered the celebrating girls into the cab, throwing one seatbelt around all three of them. "Pick you up after dinner."

Dinner?

She looked across at Wes. "My cell number is on the class contact list, if you need anything—along with yours. You got that email, right?" said Judy, closing the door without waiting for a response. Through the glass, she called, "Bye now!"

Wes pulled away from the curb in a state of shock and stayed parked at a red light until it turned green and the person behind him laid on the horn. A peek in the rearview told him it was Judy. To his right, the three girls were singing a song about raining tacos at the top of their lungs. What the hell was he supposed to do with them?

Nothing. He had to bring them home. He did not sign up for this.

He wasn't a dad. He was a drifter, a former orphan, a man without ties, and that's how he liked it. That's how it had always been.

Wes was on the verge of asking Danielle or Megan for their address so he could drop them off, but his niece caught his eye. It was obvious she was reading his mind and knew he was already throwing in the towel. Her eyes pleaded with him silently to reconsider and something unfurled in the center of his chest. Something that had been wrapped up tight for as long as he could remember. He'd kept this box sealed shut for safety's sake, but his niece climbed inside and made herself at home.

Before he registered the turns and avenues, Wes found himself on his porch, unlocking the door and making way for three tiny people to bound inside. While the newbies sprinted toward Laura's bedroom, his niece stopped and put her arms around his waist, squeezing with all her might.

"I don't know what happened, but I think I have friends now and they wanted to come over and what are we going to do, Uncle Wes?"

"You're asking me?"

"Please! I have friends!"

She ran after her pals before he could ask what on God's green earth she wanted from him. "Please, what?" he muttered under his breath, going to the fridge and starting to take out a beer before stopping himself. Without overthinking too much, he pulled out his cell and called Bethany. Because it felt right.

She answered on the second ring, her tone indicating she

was still sore over his request that she wear the pink pants tomorrow. "Yes?"

"Is the adult supervision allowed to have a beer while hosting a playdate?"

"How should I know?" There was some background shuffling. "Are you in charge of *multiple* children right now?"

"It all happened so fast."

A couple seconds ticked by. What the hell had he been thinking calling her? He hadn't relied on anyone else to solve even his most insignificant problems since he was a child. If this wasn't dangerous proof that he'd started to ask himself *what if,* he didn't know what was. "Why are you calling me?" she asked.

"To find out if I can have a beer," he answered, striving like hell to make the call casual, instead of letting himself need her. "Listen, never mind—"

"My father drank during our playdates," she blurted. "Pour it into a mug and pop in a breath mint before their parents show up." A moment passed. "You're going to do fine. Easily better than I could."

There she went again. Hinting at her own insecurities and making it impossible not to be one hundred percent honest. Wes stared hard at the reflective surface of the refrigerator. "Laura has been kind of down lately, saying she doesn't have any friends. Which . . . I guess I brushed it off because of course she must have them. She's cool and funny, right? But I think this is kind of important and I don't know how to come through for her." He turned and leaned back against the appliance. "We don't have a lot of toys. I don't even know if they're still young enough to play with toys."

"I played with my Barbies until I was nine."

"Come over." The request was out before he could lasso it, but he'd pictured Bethany throwing fancy dinner parties with dolls and he'd just . . . wanted to see her. Wanted her *there.* "I mean, come over?"

Silence. Then, "I mean . . . I guess two partially inept grown-ups equal one decent adult."

Wes pushed off the fridge. "You'll come?"

"It wouldn't be a big deal," Bethany said quickly.

"No, definitely not. Not a big deal."

It was a *huge* deal. He'd asked for help and he was getting it.

Relying on someone else who seemed to have the power to make him happy, horny, frustrated, introspective, or pissed as hell. He'd kicked the rodeo gate open.

"I'd be doing it to help out Laura, of course. So she can make a good impression on her new friends."

"Of course."

"Do you have snacks?"

Wes turned on a dime and started to rummage through his cabinets. "Some stale pretzel goldfish . . ."

"Keep looking."

His lips quirked up. "A bag of microwave popcorn."

"Bingo. Fire that up and give them juice boxes."

He listened to her footsteps on the other end of the phone and pictured her gorgeous ass twitching through the construction zone. Did he really ask her to wear those pink things again tomorrow? When the cameras would be back with all that lighting and zoom ability? "I changed my mind about the pants. Burn them."

"I'm still expecting the flea collar." He heard a door close. "I'll just swing by my house to get out of these clothes—"

"By all means, get out of them here."

"I'm not coming over if you're going to act like a pervert."

"It's out of my system now. Promise."

"Good. I'm hanging up now."

"Bethany?"

"What?"

"Thanks."

A beat passed. "It's for Laura."

"Of course."

"Bye."

"Bye."

CHAPTER TWELVE

Bethany kicked off her nasty work boots on the porch and stumbled into her house, already stripping off her smelly T-shirt and yoga pants. She started to leave them in a heap in the entryway, only making it two steps before going back, gathering them up, and putting them neatly in the laundry basket.

"What are you thinking?" she whispered to herself on the way up the stairs. By the time she finished scrubbing her grimy skin and rinsing off, a full five minutes had passed and she still hadn't answered her own question. Already she was spending entirely too much time with Wes; now she was going over to help him babysit? Multiple kids? What she knew about children could fit inside of a shot glass. She knew even less about them than she knew about renovating a house. What had possessed her to take both of these new challenges on in the same week?

Careful not to slip on the tile floor, Bethany wrapped a towel around her body and stood in front of the bathroom mirror. No time to fix her hair and that was a shame. Clean, straightened hair always boosted her confidence. Her shot glass of children knowledge consisted of one fact—they preyed on the weak. She could remember her own glee as a third grader when a substitute teacher waltzed in, thinking they were going to follow the lesson plan. Sorry, sucker. Not today.

Now she was going to be the sucker.

She'd *volunteered* to be one.

"Okay, okay," she breathed, moisturizing quickly and applying the barest layer of foundation, followed by a swipe of mascara. "You entertain dozens of women every week. You can handle some kindergartners."

It was true, she did entertain the Just Us League members every Saturday night, but she only made it *look* easy when in truth she was overthinking every word out of her mouth, analyzing her friends' comments to death, looking for some proof they were aware of her flaws. She loved the club. Loved the spirit and honesty and the women. But some part of her had always seen it as temporary. How long could she make them believe she was graceful and funny and dazzlingly carefree? What happened when they started to see through her?

Not wanting to examine those fears too deeply, Bethany hung up the towel, hunkering down to make sure the corners lined up, then marched through her bedroom to the closet. On the drive home, she'd mentally set aside an outfit and she reached for the ruffled denim romper now, putting it on and then sliding her feet into a pair of pointed white flats. She ran a brush through her hair and put it back in a high ponytail and, after stopping at the fridge to grab a slab of leftover wedding cake, then sailed out of the house with far more confidence than she felt.

In a matter of minutes, she was pulling into Wes's driveway, parking behind his truck. "You can do this," she said brightly to her reflection. "You can help babysit three little girls and leave them none the wiser that you're a shocking mess."

Cake in hand, she climbed the steps to Wes's front door.

She'd barely raised her hand to knock when it flew open.

"What took you so long? They're down to kernels, woman."

She came very close to smashing the cake in his face. And seriously, why did her brain force her to register how sexy he looked even when his mouth was letting out rude shit? He hadn't even bothered to change, still decked out in his worksite finest, hair mussed with dust, T-shirt wrinkled with dry sweat and plaster flakes. When he leaned a forearm on the doorjamb and made a sound of approval while looking her over, top to bottom, she refused to acknowledge the sliver of tight stomach revealed by his elevated T-shirt.

Or the fact that she'd gone home to change just so he'd look at her like this.

Dammit, though. She had, hadn't she?

Someone really needed to overthrow her as leader of the Just Us League. She was a total fraud. It was just that no one had ever seen her in the states of dishevelment to which Wes had borne witness. He'd had the audacity to see her angry, crying, racked with stress, dirty. The utter nerve of him.

Was it so much to ask that she be allowed to cast her usual spell for one afternoon?

"Step aside, cowboy. I brought cake."

"And here I thought you were dessert."

She held up a single finger. "You get one pass. That was it."

His smile flashed white in his stubbled face and for a few, valuable seconds, she almost forgot he was twenty-damn-three. "I've been suitably warned." He pushed the door open wider and eased out of her way. "Is that wedding cake?"

"Yes." She stopped short in the entryway, her fingers dancing over the plastic wrap. "Did you . . . like the cake at the wedding?"

He crossed his arms over his big chest. "Never met one I didn't like."

She hummed. "And what about the food?"

"Before I moved to Port Jeff, I was existing on Subway and whiskey."

"Well, that was predictably unhelpful," she muttered, starting to walk away.

"Hold up." Wes ceased her movements by wrapping a warm hand around her elbow. "Someone say they didn't like the food?"

Her stomach pitched. "Did someone say that to you?"

"No. The food was great. My five-year-old had to remind me it's rude to take home shrimp in my pockets." He stumbled over the last word, frowning to himself. "I mean, not *my* five-year-old—"

"I know what you mean," she breathed softly, alarmed

by the scratch in her throat. "So, um . . . you liked it, then? There was so much left over . . ."

He raised a brow. "And you've been worried all this time the guests hated the food. Food you didn't even cook?"

"I arranged it."

"Did I mention the open bar?"

"Okay, you've made your point." She turned and strutted into the living space, all too aware that she definitely felt better about the leftover wedding food. Like, completely better. Absolved. So much so that she was breathing easier than she had since Sunday night. "Where are the girls?"

"ELSA!"

Three little girls barreled into the living room from the hallway and proceeded to jump up and down in front of her. Expectantly. "Oh, um. I have cake," she rasped, apprehension starting to sneak into her belly.

"Cake and popcorn! Don't tell our mom."

"Your secret is safe," Bethany said quickly, searching her memory bank for some hint as to what five-year-olds were into. Wait. Rewind. There it was. Inspiration had struck and not a moment too soon. Laura was looking up at her with big round eyes as if Bethany held the secrets to pre-pre-preteen happiness. "And . . . you know, the best way to eat cake is with tea."

All three children grew very still and unnervingly quiet. Had she flubbed it?

She adjusted the plastic wrap, even though it was perfect. Not a single bubble or overlap. "T-tea party?"

An eruption of happy, ear-splitting shrieks sent Bethany back a step, her relief followed by a laugh. She bit her bottom lip to keep her smile from dominating her whole face and met Wes's gaze where he stood in the kitchen, a coffee mug poised halfway to his mouth. And oh. Just ohhh. He didn't hide the way he was looking at her fast enough and Bethany knew she'd wake up tonight thinking about the mixture of admiration, gratitude, and pure, bottomless longing in his eyes.

Her body reacted like she was sitting on a dryer during the spin cycle, heating and tightening in kind of an embarrassing way that definitely wasn't appropriate for a children's tea party. "Well," she managed. "You need guests, don't you? Go round up some dolls or stuffed animals and I'll set up the table."

They moved down the hall in a commotion of flailing limbs, speaking over one another. Bethany crossed to the kitchen table and set down the cake, tucking a loose hair back into her ponytail.

"She does have some stuffed animals, right?" Bethany whispered to Wes, who nodded slowly while sipping from his mug, eyes steady on her over the rim. "Good."

"What I don't have is tea. I'm guessing that's mandatory for a tea party."

Bethany winced. "Who lives next door?"

"The Santangelos."

"Ah! They went to school with my parents. I'll be right back."

Five minutes later, after persuading Mrs. Santangelo into

giving them an assortment of decaf tea, Bethany reentered the house to find the girls arranging teddy bears and a family of stuffed penguins around the table, talking animatedly. While Wes continued to hide in the deep recesses of the kitchen.

"You look terrified. Go sit down."

Wes hesitated. "I've seen this movie. As soon as I pull my chair out, one of them is going to ask where babies come from."

A snort-laugh flew out of Bethany without warning and she smacked a hand over her mouth, too late to stop the cringeworthy sound. "Pretend you didn't hear that," she said briskly, dropping her hand away.

"Why? I liked it."

"You love when I give you new reasons to make fun of me."

Wes dipped his chin and gave her a look that said *Oh, come on.* "All right, let's clear this up now, since you're here saving my biscuit." He crossed the kitchen in her direction. "Am I actually making fun of you, Bethany? Or am I just riling you up because it's the only way you'll give me the time of day?"

His question thwarted her concentration, and she paused in the middle of searching for a teakettle in the pantry, finally spying one near the back. "What? That's not true."

"It is. You decided you wanted nothing to do with me the first time we met."

She frowned while putting the kettle under the sink tap and turning on the water. "You tried to run game on me in front of my brother."

"I did, didn't I?" He gave her a slow wink. "Reckon I couldn't help it."

Bethany ignored the weight that continued to sink lower and lower in her belly. "Yes, you're falling all over yourself to sleep with a woman you find so ancient you can't even comprehend her movie references." She moved to the stove and situated the kettle over a burner. "That's probably why when you hit on me, it feels like a trap."

Wes was silent so long, she had to look over to make sure he hadn't left the room. But no, there he was, frowning at her from the shadows. "A trap?" he said, finally, his voice hard. "Explain that."

There was a nervous flutter in her throat she couldn't explain. "I don't know. Why are we talking about this?"

"Because we are."

She rolled her eyes. "I guess it feels like . . . when you proposition me, it's just another way of poking fun. At me. Okay? Fine, you're attracted to me, but maybe it's just the chase making you that way. You've only pointed out how much freaking older I am nine hundred times, so you don't really . . . want me like that." With a hard swallow, she removed the lukewarm water from over the flame. "You're waiting for me to accept so you can have the ultimate laugh at this old witch's expense. I actually admire this long game you're playing."

He was staring at her like she'd just risen from the floor in a plume of smoke. "Jesus Christ, you really believe that bullshit, don't you?"

Yes. Until that very second, Bethany didn't realize how

deep she'd shoved the insecurities regarding their age difference. Could anyone blame her for thinking his intentions toward her were less than sincere? Every man she'd ever dated had been a flatterer. Compliments were an indication that a man wanted to sleep with a woman, wasn't it? Not outright vitriol, like the kind she shared with Wes. If there were some lines she was supposed to read between, she didn't have the right decoder ring—and that was a *Christmas Story* reference he would probably laugh at her over.

Bethany started opening cabinets. "Could you help me set the table? I need plates, cups, napkins—"

"I made a mistake."

"What?"

He took her wrists and turned her to face him. "Hey, I made a mistake." His chest rose and fell. "I should have left our age difference alone."

Bethany looked everywhere but at him, because his intensity was doing weird things to her midsection. "Wes. You're making a big deal out of nothing."

"Out of nothing? You've been doubting how I feel about you this whole time—"

"How you feel about me?" In a rush of panic, she tried to pry her wrists free, but he held on. "Back the truck up."

He closed his eyes, appearing to count to ten. "Fine. I'll back up. You've been doubting how bad I want you because I made some stupid jokes."

"I . . ." She attempted a casual laugh. "I guess? Sure."

"How?" He was visibly bewildered. "Bethany, you know you're a fucking masterpiece, right?"

Her legs turned to gelatin, a foreign emotion swelling inside her. A big, heavy feeling with untapped power. "I . . . um. Um."

Wes let go of her wrists and fell back a step. "My God, you don't," he said dazedly. "You don't know."

Bethany's hands remained suspended in midair, a lot like the breath in her lungs that refused to come in or out. Part of her wanted to run from the kitchen, but the other part kept her planted. In front of Wes. *You know you're a fucking masterpiece, right?* He couldn't really mean that, could he? She was at her worst in front of him. This had to be a simple case of lusting for something he couldn't have.

Yes. Obviously. He was a gorgeous man who'd been continually turned down by a woman. Getting her to cave might be nothing more than a point of pride.

Wes turned her until he could press her against the counter . . . and her noodle legs went from al dente to limp. "Don't kiss me," she whispered.

His sigh warmed her mouth. "I have to, baby. You're ridiculous."

"And that makes you want to kiss me?"

Blue eyes searched hers. "I don't understand it, either. Just know once you've got my tongue in your mouth, you're going to feel my lack of fucks that you're thirty and I'm twenty-three. Those seven years don't mean a damn thing to me . . ." He trailed his open lips along her jaw. "If anything, they'll make us moan a little louder, won't they, darlin'?"

Their mouths were so close, his breath was leaving the most delicious condensation on her lips. Oh God. This was it, he was going to kiss her. Right here, right now. She wasn't going to be able to hide behind sharp words or snappy comebacks with her mouth occupied and *shitshitshit* this was going to be bad. He'd know by the time this kiss was over that he affected her. Physically . . . and more. Dammit, there was more, wasn't there?

How was she supposed to be around him and like him at the same time?

Ughhhhhhhh.

"Elsa!"

"Uncle Wes! Elsa! Can we have our tea party now?"

Record scratch.

He pushed his face into the curve of her neck, latching onto a patch of sensitive flesh with his teeth, groaning in a way that sent a thrill screaming down to her toes. "God help me, I won't survive these blue balls."

Laughter shivered through her, but she was too stupefied by the state of her body and the things he'd said to respond.

"You think it's funny? I come home on my lunch breaks while she's in school and sometimes I just sit in the quiet, staring at the wall." He made a pained sound, dipping his mouth to the hollow of her neck and licking, all the way around to her earlobe. "That's a lie. I think about you."

"Wes."

"You think about me, too."

Her nod was subtle and grudging and she couldn't take it

back. Another impatient plea from the dining room had her sliding out from underneath Wes's rigid body. "Remind me what I was doing."

He ground the heel of his hand into one eye. "Plates, cups . . ."

"Forks. Tea. Okay."

They both took fortifying breaths, then broke for the tea party.

Oh mama.

As soon as this tea party ended, she needed to get the heck out of Dodge.

What was that saying about the best-laid plans?

CHAPTER THIRTEEN

From his reclined position in a beanbag chair in the corner of Laura's bedroom, Wes watched Bethany pause in the doorway. His intention had been to observe the tea party from the safety of the kitchen, but damn, was he ever glad he'd let Laura drag him to her bedroom to await Bethany's official escort to the dining room table—and thus, the start of the game.

She swept in with an air of drama, pausing for several beats without saying a word, heightening the anticipation. "Attention! Attention, please," she called to the three little girls who were already squealing and essentially losing their minds, simply because Bethany was taking their make-believe seriously, British accent and all. "May I speak to the lady of the house? I have a formal invitation from Her Majesty, the Queen."

"Me!" Laura almost landed facefirst on the carpet diving for the letter Bethany held in her hands. "I'm the lady of the house!"

"Brilliant." Bethany handed Laura a folded-up page

they'd torn out of his latest *Sports Illustrated.* "The Queen requires your presence at afternoon tea."

Laura pretended to read the royal invitation. "It says we're all invited."

Megan and Danielle cheered and hopped to their feet, joining Laura in a stampede that almost knocked Bethany on her gorgeous ass. She traded a dazed look with Wes. "They almost knocked me down to get to the drinks. This isn't that different from a Just Us League meeting."

Wes heaved himself out of the beanbag chair with a chuckle. "Hopefully the similarities end there. The last thing we need is these kids going home chanting about lady balls."

Bethany's mouth formed an *O.* "I'm going to start having the members sign an NDA. All of this leaking of important procedures is getting out of hand."

"After Marjorie sang the song for me, it got stuck in my head, if that helps."

"It does, actually," she said, letting him see just a hint of her smile, before she turned to walk down the hallway and join the tea party. "Now, ladies," Bethany said, clasping her hands together. "If I could have your attention, please, I would like to introduce your butler for this afternoon, Wes Dorkingham. He's taking a break from his duties as court jester to serve the tea."

The polite applause from the three girls lasted all of three seconds, before they started waving their teacups in the air and erupted with choruses of "Tea! Where's my tea, Dorkingham?"

With narrowed eyes in Bethany's direction, Wes picked

up the plastic pitcher they were using as a teapot and poured lukewarm liquid into each of the cups. When he reached Laura and filled her cup, he didn't even think, he just leaned down and kissed her on the crown of the head. He hovered there for a few seconds, wondering what the hell had possessed him to do something so . . . fatherly. She'd only cuddled up to him once on the couch—now he was kissing her on the head?

Laura tilted her head back slowly and smiled at him. It wasn't the going-through-the-motions smile she'd painted on a lot when he first got to Port Jefferson. Now that he thought about it, he hadn't seen that one in about a week. This one was bursting with something he couldn't really name. It was definitely on the happy end of the spectrum, though, wasn't it?

Yeah. His niece was happy.

Was it crazy to think he'd helped her get there?

Pressure started in his throat and cascaded downward. He almost had to set down the pitcher so he could feel around in his chest for the twisting sensation.

"What about dinner?" Danielle singsonged, breaking the spell. "We can't have cake without dinner first."

Wes cleared his throat. Noticing Bethany was watching him thoughtfully, he made his voice light. "Dang, girl. You haven't even tried the tea yet. Are you one of those difficult customers?" On his second pass around the table, he spoke from the side of his mouth to Bethany. "Seriously, though. It's almost dinnertime and I seriously doubt they want green bean casserole."

"Oh God." Bethany hid behind the fall of her hair, but not before he saw her watching him and Laura with a curious sheen in her eyes. "Um. Which Just Us League member made you that?"

"Come on, now." Desperate to lighten the mood, he gave Bethany a light hip-check. "You know I call her Green Bean Casserole."

Thankfully back to normal, she snorted. "You're impossible." She chewed her lip for a moment. "Go order some pizzas and I'll stall."

"On it."

Wes set down the tea pitcher with a clunk and whipped out his cell, which, of course, had the closest pizza place on speed dial. They put him on hold and, with the music playing in his ear, he watched Bethany further work her magic—and that's exactly what it was.

"All right, ladies, if we've all had our fill of tea, the time has come for the princess ceremony."

"The what?" Laura asked, in a trance.

"The princess ceremony, of course." Bethany clapped her hands together. "The Queen has brought you all here today to make you all official princesses."

Wes was surprised when the roar of excitement didn't shatter a window.

Bethany was killing it. And the craziest part of the whole situation was . . . she only seemed capable of enjoying their reactions for approximately two seconds before she visibly started worrying about what came next. Didn't she know how far out of the park she was hitting this? She claimed to know nothing about kids, but she'd won them over faster than a seasoned babysitter could ever hope to do. He'd put money on it.

What the hell had made her so unsure of herself? His earlier epiphany that he'd contributed to her insecurities sat in his gut like a lump of lead.

He wasn't done making it up to her. Not by a long shot.

Was it wishful thinking, or did Laura seem . . . happy? Very happy. She'd seemed that way all through the tea party and dinner. Afterward, Megan and Danielle had been picked up by their mother, but Laura didn't seem to want Bethany to leave yet, asking her to read a story. And seemingly enjoying it. Bethany was struck by how satisfying that was. It was nice to know that someone was content, thanks to her efforts. Instead of wondering if they were disappointed in her or the job she'd done or a million other possibilities.

She'd felt the same way when she swung the sledgehammer into the wall and turned to look at Wes—

She really, really needed to go home.

"And that is the story of how Fancy Nancy triumphed in her quest to find the unicorn," Bethany finished, closing the book. "Good night, Laura."

Laura put her arms up. "Hug."

"From me?"

The little girl nodded.

"Oh." Bethany leaned down and let Laura wrap her in a hug that pulled her hair and put a twinge in her neck, but was somehow the loveliest hug she'd ever received. "Would you like me to send in your Uncle Wes?"

"Way ahead of you," said the man as he entered the room. "Did Nancy get that unicorn?"

Laura grinned. "Yes."

"Oh good. I'm always worried." Wes went down on his knees on the opposite side of the bed from Bethany and dropped a kiss on Laura's cheek, chuckling when she strangled him with a fierce hug.

"I can't wait for school tomorrow," she said.

A smile was blooming on Wes's face when he pulled back. "That's great, kid."

Laura snuggled into the sheets, turning onto her side. Almost as an afterthought, she said, "I love you."

Bethany held her breath as she watched Wes's easygoing expression be replaced with dumbstruck awe. "I love you, too," he said, gruffly. "See you in the morning."

Both adults left the room. Before they'd even reached the door, soft snores were coming from the bed. Quietly, they stepped into the hallway and Wes closed the door behind them. Then he just kind of stood there, staring into space.

"Is that the first time she's said that to you?" Bethany asked.

"Yeah." He scrubbed at the back of his neck. "Shit."

"Shit, what?"

"Shit . . . no one's ever said that to me before," he said, dazedly. "Have a beer with me?"

"I really should go," Bethany said, too quickly. No one had ever said *I love you* to this man? She was already having a very hard time remaining detached after watching such a personal exchange between Wes and his niece. Now her fingertips were numb from his admission. He looked like he'd been smacked in the face with a two-by-four and her own dumb heart was pumping like a revved motor in response.

This whole evening had already been an out-of-body experience, but she'd managed to retain a scrap of objectivity. After all, she couldn't very well make it a regular occurrence. Reading bedtime stories to the adorable niece and spinning tea party narratives. *Honestly, Bethany.* Shouldn't she be home updating her professional social media or tackling a design plan for the flip? Something productive?

As if he hadn't heard her response, Wes herded her down the hallway—and she went, feeling a little like a pirate prisoner walking the plank. They stepped over stuffed animals and crayons until they reached the kitchen. Bethany hugged her elbows until Wes handed her an open bottle of beer, clinking his glass neck with hers.

"Come on." He padded on bare feet to the back door, flipped the lock, and opened it, summoning her into the backyard with an inviting chin jerk. If she'd sensed she was walking to her doom before, she'd been wrong. The real trouble lay in the romantic outdoor setting.

Neither one of them was wearing shoes and the damp fall grass threaded through her toes. The beer was cold in her hand, the moon was bright, and the wind held just the right amount of chill. Plus he still had that kind of delighted shock on his face that was so sweet, she almost wished she'd never seen it. How was she supposed to go back to disliking him?

Wes tilted his face up at the moon and took several sips of his beer. She was helpless to do anything but watch the silhouette of his strong throat gulping down the liquid.

He squinted over at her. "Do you think she meant it?"

"Yes," she answered honestly, pressing her beer bottle to the unusual tug in her chest. "Did you mean it?"

A beat passed. "Yeah."

She swallowed. "Will you leave right away when her mother comes back?"

"That's the plan. Move on and hope I made a small difference." He blew out a breath. "There were people along the way that did that for me, when I was moving in and out of new homes. Teachers or a good foster parent who turned me toward a certain path and kicked me in the ass to get me moving. It doesn't seem like much at the time and maybe it was nothing to them, but it was something to me. Maybe . . . for her, it'll be me who does that."

Her stomach jolted. "I didn't know you were in foster care."

He nodded once, but didn't respond. In the glory of the moonlight, he looked older, more worldly and weathered. Or maybe it was the words coming out of his mouth. She didn't know what it was, but all of it, everything, drew her closer.

"So Laura's mother isn't your real sister?"

"She is. Half. We have the same mother." He seemed to gather his thoughts. "Becky had it a lot harder than me growing up. I could get hired to do manual labor and that made it easier to stay out of our foster home. Out of the way.

There are good families out there helping kids, but the one where we were placed together . . . we weren't as fortunate. Our foster parents had an issue with liquor and fighting. Money troubles, on top of it." He squinted into the darkness. "Becky used drugs to cope. She stayed off them when she got pregnant with Laura and I thought she'd carved this new life out for herself in New York. But I don't know. It worries me that she's run off like this."

Bethany couldn't help but glance back toward the house, where Laura lay sleeping. What would this little girl have done without her uncle? As far as she could tell, no one in Port Jefferson had been aware of any discord between Laura's parents. Definitely no one had spotted any drug use or she'd have heard. "Thank God you're here, Wes," she whispered. "You really stepped up."

Her praise earned her a sharp look. A surprised one? "Yeah, well. I'm far from a saint. There've been a lot of times I've wanted to ignore Becky's calls. I've just learned it's easier . . . letting people pass in and out without trying to hold on or they just slip through anyway. But I'm glad I didn't this time." He made a jerky movement and took another pull of his beer. "This was one of those good stops along the way."

"Along the way to what?"

He winked at her in the moonlight. "Gray hair and sciatica, I guess."

She puffed a laugh, though she had a weight on her chest. "This isn't just another stop along the way for you."

He sobered. "It doesn't feel like I'm supposed to . . . leave here. But I've thought that before."

"Because of a woman?"

Now why did she ask that? Bethany mentally kicked herself. But before she could take back the question, Wes looked away from the moon and over at her, a combination of humor and heat snapping in his eyes. "No, not because of a woman." He set his beer down on the back windowsill and came toward her slowly. "I spent eighteen years in and out of foster care. Lived in single-parent homes, stayed with married couples, retirees. When I was seven, the Kolkers took me in. They were warm and welcoming in the beginning. Happy. I let myself feel secure. But they eventually split over money troubles and I was spit right back into the system." His throat worked. "I've found situations that felt right. Friends, a job, a foster family. I thought that was it. I'd stick. But it turned out I was just a stop along the way for someone else."

Bethany could only partially relate to that. Her relationships had never been anything but pit stops, but at least she had a family and friends. They were constants for her. Constants Wes never had. "I'm sorry."

Without sacrificing their cemented eye contact, he took out her ponytail and worked his fingers through her hair. "I don't want sorrys from you."

"No," she whispered, wetting her lips. "You just want me to make this stop along the way more interesting."

Conflict tightened his features. "Never lied about that."

"No, you haven't."

His mouth was closer now, hovering just above hers. "Goddamn." His gaze trailed over every inch of her face. "If there was ever a woman I'd stick for, darlin'—"

Bethany surged up on her toes and locked their mouths together. What was her other option? Hearing the rest of that sentence? No. No, sir . . .

Oh good God, his mouth felt great.

He didn't lead her into some perfected dance or impose his will on her. He just let the kiss happen, let it unfold like an unwritten story. His uneven exhale filled her mouth and his body pressed close, slowly, swaying with the breeze as their lips parted and the tips of their tongues met once, twice. It was the exact opposite of what she would have expected from kissing a twenty-three-year-old man. It was unique to them and the moment and she could barely feel her fingertips.

Keep your head. Keep your balance.

Wes sipped at her upper lip and she quite helplessly melted against him, still on her toes, letting him guide his tongue into her mouth, sweeping it across hers. His fingers were gentle and reverent in her hair, his opposite arm finding a place wrapped around her hips, urging her close until their lower bodies pressed and they moaned into each other's mouths.

That's when Bethany expected him to turn it on, to impress his masculinity upon her, but he continued to slant his mouth over hers in savoring slides, rubbing the base of her spine with his thumb and brushing her hair sweetly. His worship of her was too much, too unexpectedly perfect that she started to panic, but he pulled away before she could stop the kiss. "I know you didn't want to hear the end of what I was telling you," he rasped, brushing their mouths together. "But I just told you anyway."

I'm in trouble.

He didn't allow her to acknowledge more than that single coherent thought before he swept her back into the tornado. Their lust had gone from a slow leak to a broken dam and Bethany had no choice but to ride the tide. His tongue played with hers almost tauntingly and when she tried to get a satisfying taste, he tugged away and snapped at her lower lip instead. "Got something else to tell you now."

"No," she breathed. "Shut up."

Wes laughed low and husky while walking her backward into the shadows and steadying himself with a hand on the side of the house. "What did I say would happen when I got my tongue in your mouth?"

His hips pinned hers and she gasped. "That I would feel your, uhhm . . ."

"My lack of fucks about our age difference." He captured her chin and tilted it up, his hips cinching forward so she could feel the thick jut of his erection. "Someone is finally paying attention."

Her panties grew damp. Or damper, rather. "Don't talk to me like that—"

Wes's mouth stamped down over hers and made love to it. She couldn't describe it any other way. He owned her tongue with possessive strokes, his hold firm on her chin to keep her mouth pried open. It was nothing like their first kiss and all the better for the contrast. Knowing he could do both, be gentle and demanding, was such a turn-on, her head was going to pop like a balloon.

After me! called her ovaries.

Wes broke off with a growl and pressed his open mouth to her forehead. "You feel my lack of fucks yet?"

Wait, what? How was she supposed to concentrate on anything when he kissed her like that?

"Guess I better speak a little louder," he said gruffly, one of his hands leaving the wall, fingers sliding under the strap of her romper. "That what you want, Bethany?"

"What are you asking me?"

He bent his knees and rose, grinding their sexes together. The friction was so raw and welcome and unexpected, she whimpered at the resulting flex of her feminine muscles. "I'm asking to suck your tits," he said, his hot eyes dropping to her neckline. "Climb on up here so I can play with them. Bet they're so fucking pretty."

"They are," she asserted, trying to regain some of the control that was quickly slipping through her fingers. "Wes, I . . . This is . . ."

His fingers slipped back and forth beneath her strap, his hips rocking between her legs. "This is what?"

The first time I've ever been desperate.

The first time I've been so needy I'm not sure I could stop.

Wes looked down at their lower bodies and Bethany realized she'd wrapped her right leg around him and was meeting his slow bumps and grinds. "Looks like you're the one telling me something now, baby."

"Shut up," she breathed.

The corner of his lips lifted. "Words. I need to hear them. You want me licking all over those nipples like I licked inside that smart mouth?"

Her nod was vigorous and totally involuntary.

Right.

"Thank God," he growled, boosting her up and smacking her back against the house. His big shaft hit her in a new spot between her thighs, but Wes gave her no time to recover from the *amazing* friction. No, he was already yanking down one strap of her romper, using his teeth to draw down the other. "Show 'em off now. Show me how much you don't care that I'm younger." Bethany arched off the house with a moan, her angle causing the top of her denim romper to fall to her waist, revealing two things to him. Her lack of a bra and how hard he'd made her nipples. "Fucking hell, Bethany."

"T-told you they were pretty," she murmured, even as she checked his eyes for signs that he was disappointed.

His scoff filled the dark backyard. "Pretty doesn't do them justice. Not sure there's a word that would." He leaned down and brushed his lip against her nipples, one by one, groaning when the tight buds puckered all the more. "I've finally got you where I want you, baby. Can't believe it." He dragged the length of his tongue side to side on top of her right nipple. "Fuck that, it's where I need you, isn't it?"

"Yes," she said, her eyes closing, legs tightening around his hips. "Please."

She'd always rushed men through using their mouths on her breasts—and that was when they deigned to try. Most of them . . . okay, *all* of them lacked Wes's finesse. Although could she call it finesse when his enjoyment was so authentic? As he took her left bud into his mouth and drew on it hungrily, she could feel him pulse against the seam of her romper, could feel the vibration of his groans straight through to her core. His hands were everywhere. In her hair, squeezing her waist, molding her opposite breast in his palm while he took liberties with the first.

I want him inside me.

Badly. Not once in her entire life had she been this wet, this eager, this hungry to feel that first pump of a man's thickness between her legs, the roughness that came after. She wanted it all.

What if he lost interest after that?

When did she start caring if Wes was interested?

Did she care now?

What was he thinking right now?

Was she exceeding expectations or merely meeting them—

"Bethany." She opened her eyes to find Wes looking at her from beneath heavy eyelids, his breath coming in short spurts. "What happened? I lost you."

"I don't know." Honesty came to her lips without even a smidgen of coaxing or consideration. "I started thinking *I want sex* and then I spiraled."

"Into what?"

"Wondering if you'd . . ."

He narrowed one eye. "If I'd . . ."

"Hit it and quit it."

Wes was silent a moment, pensive even, which was kind of funny considering he was still skillfully kneading her right breast. Which, in turn, was still making her flesh contract and slicken. "Those kind of doubts about me are why sex ain't happening yet." Bethany opened her mouth to speak, but he beat her to it. "Your trust matters. It matters whether I'm leaving or staying. It just matters. You matter." His forehead pressed against hers. "Now let me get you off like I've been dreaming about for weeks."

She was a can of Pepsi and someone had shaken her and flipped open the tab. Her fears and follow-up questions went in ninety messy directions and canceled each other out. All she could do was hold on and feel. His mouth captured her right nipple and he circled his tongue around it, grazing it with his teeth and making her thighs jerk. A cry shot from her mouth. His hands pushed down the sagging back of her romper and landed on bare bottom cheeks, separated by whatever thong she'd put on after her shower. She couldn't even remember the color.

"One thing at a time," he rasped, seemingly to himself, rubbing his scruff over one of her puckered nipples. "Right now, I want to hear our ages don't mean shit. Say out loud that they don't mean a damn thing to either of us."

"They don't," she managed, the pulse between her legs thickening and growing more urgent. "They don't mean anything."

He sucked a nipple into his mouth and let it go with a pop. "My mouth will always be the perfect age to make you come." His hips thrust up into the notch of her thighs and bounced her three times. "That's what counts, baby."

Heat didn't just permeate her loins, it bit in and twisted—and she was coming. Right there against the house, with her top down and this man she thought she hated providing her with friction for days. She sobbed through it with trembling legs and Wes staring her right in the eye. That was the part that robbed her of breath, of boundaries. She stared back and let him see how thoroughly he milked her orgasm. Continued to prolong it with sharp rolls of his lower body as if he'd read a freaking dossier on her preferences. She bit her lip and whined for him, telling him without coherent sentences that her pussy was spasming in his name. The connection she shared with him in those extended seconds was almost as satisfying as her climax. It went beyond intimacy—and it was making her painfully aware that she'd never really shared intimacy with anyone.

Never before had she given herself over to a man completely. She'd been faking, only letting them see what she *chose* to show them. With Wes, she had no choice but to let him in deeper. To stop thinking and feel. Without her overly analytical mind holding her back, her body let him take without reservation.

"There you are, darlin'," he ground out against her mouth, his hands still exploring her bottom, using his grip to ride her up and down. "There the hell you are, leaving the proof of what I did to you all over me. Right where I want it. Good girl."

The strain of relief left Bethany and she slumped, depleted, over his shoulder. Wes turned and walked them into the house, her legs dangling around his hips. All the way through the kitchen, the living room, and the hallway, she told herself to put her damn feet on the ground and go home, but she kept silencing herself in favor of one more minute in his arms. She had a million questions, like . . . mainly, didn't *he* want an orgasm? That erection pointed toward an enthusiastic yes. But also, what happened now? Were they completely done being enemies? Did he expect to hook up with her again? Like on a regular basis? Was she okay with that?

Wes slapped her on the ass. "Stop thinking so hard."

Bethany's mouth fell open and she started to sputter a protest. What came out instead was, "What about you?" All breathy-like and simpering. "Don't you want me to take care of, um . . . that?"

A male grunt. "I'm good." He let her down in front of the door and laid a final firm kiss on her mouth. "It's going to drive you nuts leaving something undone and that guarantees me a next time with you." He winked. "Good night, Bethany."

She walked to her car on Rubbermaid legs, wondering if the whole afternoon had been a dream. And refusing to acknowledge how much she wanted to stay asleep.

CHAPTER FOURTEEN

It was still dark the following morning when Wes walked into Grinders, the coffee shop on Main Street. He was gritty-eyed and more than a little cranky, to tell the truth. Sending Bethany on her merry way when she'd been inclined to return sexual favors had seemed like the only option at the time, but around two in the morning, he'd started wondering if he'd fallen out of the Stupid Tree and smacked his head on a couple of branches.

There in the darkness, he'd envisioned himself putting down roots in Port Jefferson, maybe even trying for something real and lasting with Bethany. Something more than sex. Or the wanting of it, rather.

He'd been up and pacing before the ink dried on that thought.

It was getting harder and harder to deny that Bethany made him wonder if more than a vagabond existence was possible. If maybe his presence in Laura's life was positive and could continue to be that way.

Indefinitely.

But what about the hard lessons he'd learned in foster care? Was he going to completely disregard them now? Life could seem stable one minute and get shaken up like a martini in the next. Without warning or a satisfying reason. Was he setting himself up for disappointment? Loss?

Needing to clear his head with some manual labor, Wes had dropped off Laura at *Outlander* Ringtone's house early this morning so he could make up for the time he'd lost on the flip yesterday. Demo was complete, thanks to Ollie and Carl proving their salt (and pepper), and this morning he was getting to work on framing out the walls they'd knocked down due to water damage. Bethany's budget had allowed him to hire some garbage removers to haul off the debris, including the mangled floorboards, ancient appliances, and old insulation.

Wes could only hope a full day of woodwork would keep his mind off his own wood. But he wasn't holding his breath. Not when he was already counting the minutes until Bethany showed up on the site. God help him, he couldn't wait to see how she'd act around him now that he'd rung her bell a little bit.

Had she been everything he'd fantasized about?

Not even close.

She'd eclipsed anything his brain could have conjured up by a good thousand miles or so. All those times he'd gone home to his empty house during lunch breaks and beat off in Bethany's honor, he'd imagined angry sex. Hate-fucking, to be exact. That wasn't what he'd gotten. *You didn't have sex*, Wes's dick reminded him.

"No shit," he muttered, sidling up to the counter of the sleepy coffee shop and waiting for the owner to mosey out of the back room. Oldies played from a radio on a corner shelf, just below a sign that read PILATES? I THOUGHT YOU SAID PIE AND LATTES.

Damn, that usually got a laugh out of him.

Wes leaned onto his elbows and buried his face in his hands, memories from the night before infiltrating like ninjas. No, there hadn't been anything angry about last night. The whole evening, even before he'd brought Bethany out into the backyard, had been so . . . nice. The tea party, stealing touches with Bethany in the kitchen, putting Laura to bed and getting the *L* word dropped on him like a sack of stones. For the first time in a long time, he'd just lived in the moment without reminding himself it would end.

He'd let himself *belong*.

Bethany had a hell of a lot to do with that. Yesterday, they'd both been feeling their way in the dark. Together. Learning as they went.

Their relationship was supposed to be simple. They were going to swipe at each other until one of them gave in and pounced. But when it came time to pounce last night, he'd been more concerned with trust. Building a foundation. His mind kept telling him things weren't possible, but his . . . heart had cotton stuffed into its ears.

Two college-aged kids, a guy and a girl, stumbled out of the back room, tangling ankles, both of their faces inching toward fuchsia. "Sorry for the wait," said the girl. "What can I get you?"

Wes tried not to let his theory that they'd been making out show on his face. "Large coffee, please. Black."

Before he'd finished placing his order, the bell rang over the door and in walked Stephen. Bethany's brother had a frown on his unshaven face, distracted by a note in his hand, so it took him a moment to register Wes standing at the counter. Wes tipped his hat. "Morning."

Stephen rolled back his shoulders. "Well, well. If it isn't the competition." He sauntered his way through a few tables, the note at his side. "I see I'm not the only one getting an early start. Where's your partner in crime? Powdering her nose?"

A bug of irritation crawled up his neck. "Women don't powder their noses anymore, man. This isn't the fifties."

The eldest Castle slowed his gait. "What do they do?"

"I don't know, but it's liquid and it lasts all day. That's what the commercials tell me." Wes took out his wallet and dropped the appropriate amount of singles on the counter. "And anyway, Bethany has been getting her hands dirty, just like she said she would. Don't underestimate her."

"Ah, Jesus. I know that tone you're throwing at me. I know it because I heard it from Travis when he innocently started hanging out with Georgie." He put air quotes around the word "innocently," causing him to drop the note in his hand. With a curse, he stooped down to pick it back up. "All of a sudden, he was an expert on my kid sister and now you're doing it, too. Well, I hate to be the bearer of bad news, but this time it's not going to end in an Italian honeymoon."

"What the hell is that supposed to mean—" Wes reeled

his curiosity back in like a ten-pound trout. "You know what? Keep it to yourself."

Stephen crossed his arms, leaned back against a table, and waited.

Wes took his time with his first sip of coffee. "I mean it. I don't want to know."

"Uh-huh."

"Can I get you something?" called the guy behind the counter.

Stephen pushed off the table. "I'll have a fresh squeezed orange juice, please." He sniffed at Wes's coffee. "Some of us want to live long, healthy lives."

"Then I'd stop trying to piss everyone off."

His old boss barked a laugh. "You're in a mood." He drummed casual fingers on the counter. "Maybe you want to talk through your renovation plans?"

Wes tilted his head. "Now, Stephen. You wouldn't be asking me for inside information on the competition, would you?"

"Please. Like I need help winning." Stephen unwrapped a straw and attempted to pop it into his orange juice cup, missing the hole several times. He stopped trying with a withering sigh. "I do need help with something, though."

"What's that?"

"What else? Kristin. She's been leaving me these notes around the house." He waved the piece of paper still wedged between his knuckles. "There's some kind of significance to them, but I can't figure it out."

Wes held out his hand. "Want me to give it a read?"

Stephen hesitated. "As long as you don't tell anyone the contents. Especially my sister," he stressed. "Not that I can even decipher the contents, but still."

"Not surprised. You still think women powder their noses." Wes took the note and read the handwritten lines.

Things are going to change. Yes, sir. You can count on that.
Signed, your steadfast wife

Wes kept his features schooled. He was seriously regretting his promise not to tell Bethany the contents of the note, because he knew she'd get a kick out of them. Her sister-in-law was definitely as crazy as Bethany claimed. She was obviously hinting at the fact that she was pregnant, but instead of outright telling Stephen, she'd decided to terrorize him first. After that snide comment about Bethany, Wes couldn't resist getting in on the fun.

He handed the note back to Stephen on a blown-out breath. "I don't know, man. Sounds like she's mighty unhappy. You been giving her problems?"

Stephen paled. "No. I-I . . . I mean, I don't think so. You never know with Kristin. One minute she's smiling at me like I hung the moon. The next, she's watching me and chopping onions in this kind of focused, bone-chilling way . . ."

"Sure. Sure."

"You don't think she means things are going to change for the better?"

He was now Jim from *The Office* messing with Dwight. If only there was a camera lens he could shrug at sheepishly.

"I don't know, man. If I know one thing about women, it's that you can always tell when they're happy," he said, pulling from his total lack of experience. "But when they're suffering in silence? That shit creeps up and bites you."

Stephen's head bobbed. "You're right about that, my friend." He carefully folded the note and tucked it into his pocket. "I have some work to do."

"Sounds like it."

Wes contained his chuckle until Stephen left the coffee shop. He started to follow, but went back and bought a brownie with pink sprinkles for Bethany, rolling his eyes at the sappy gesture. Which was exactly the reaction she would probably give him, too. If he was trying to scare her off, tokens of his admiration ought to do it.

Fifteen minutes later, he arrived at the jobsite. He left Bethany's brownie wrapped in a paper bag on the sawhorse and brought his coffee outside to get started on the framework. For the next two hours, he went back and forth, inside and out, using the table saw inside since construction couldn't legally begin until eight o'clock in the morning and he didn't want the neighbors complaining. He was so focused on his task that he barely noticed when people started to arrive, glancing around from behind his work goggles to find the film crew setting up.

Ollie and Carl were there, too, carting in the insulation and Sheetrock he'd asked them to pick up. They still had a couple of days before they could utilize those materials, since the plumber and electrician were set to arrive today. If they got the all-clear—and that was a pretty huge *if*—they'd keep on schedule, but Wes was pretty sure the electrical would need to be upgraded, to say nothing of the leaky pipes.

The sound of Bethany's voice in the distance broke into his thoughts. Eager to lay eyes on her, Wes pushed his goggles back on his head and crunched through leaves and broken-up concrete on his way around the side of the house. Familiar voices reached him before he got to the driveway, one belonging to Bethany. The owner of the other one was Slade.

Something sharp drilled into his gut. Instead of making himself known and telling the cheesy host to get lost, he forced himself to wait and listen.

"You look beautiful today, Bethany," Slade said.

Wes ground his teeth.

"Thanks. You look nice, too."

He ground them harder.

"So listen, I was thinking . . ." Here it came. Slade was making a move. "I'm staying in town while we film and I don't know any of the local spots. Would you be interested in showing me the best place to get dinner? My treat."

Wes turned and braced his hands on the house, his gut a lake of fire, and it was in that moment he realized there was no turning back. He was invested in this thing between him and Bethany. Like, send-a-motherfucker-to-the-hospital-for-looking-at-her-twice invested. Their mouths and bodies had been in perfect sync last night, but there was more here. He didn't just like her. Or lust after her.

He was falling for her.

This feeling wasn't a fleeting one; it was sticking around.

Did that mean . . . he *was* considering sticking around?

His throat grew tighter while he waited for Bethany's answer.

It finally came. "That's a great offer, but . . ."

"But?"

Don't push her, Slade.

"Are you involved with your foreman? That might have been insinuated, but I just couldn't see the fit. If I'm being brutally honest."

Wes ground his fist into the wall of the house.

"Um . . ." Bethany again. "'Involved' is a strong word. But it's definitely complicated, I guess you could say. With Wes."

He threw up a victorious fist. *It's complicated.* She'd said it was complicated.

He'd fucking take it.

"I see," Slade said. "Well, if something changes, I hope I'll be the first to know."

"Sure," she said with a smile in her voice.

Footsteps moved in Wes's direction and he arranged himself in a casual lean against the side of the house, ankles and arms crossed. Bethany entered his line of vision with two to-go coffee cups in her hands and stopped dead, flushing to the roots of her hair. "How much did you hear?"

Wes rubbed his jaw with the backs of his knuckles, unable to subdue his grin. "Exactly how complicated is it, darlin'?"

She put her cute nose in the air and breezed past him. "I hate you."

"You do not," he said, hot on her heels. "Who is that second coffee for, because it sure as hell ain't for Slade. He's

off somewhere right now trying to piece his balls back together, baby. That was poetic."

"Your epitaph is going to be poetic once I strangle you."

"Having your hands on me is the ideal way to go."

She stopped on a dime, gave him a prim look that made
his fly feel tight . . . and then she started to dump one of the
coffees on the ground.

"You're going to feel real guilty when you find out I
brought you a brownie with pink sprinkles."

Her wrist twisted, saving a couple inches of coffee from
spilling out. "You did?"

Wes hummed an affirmation. "To match those pants that
make your buns look all tight and sexy."

With a slow shake of her head, she finished dumping the
contents of the cup on the ground. "I can't believe I let you
kiss me."

"We did more than kiss and you want to do it again."

Continuing her journey toward the back of the house,
she threw him a snort over her shoulder. "It's sad how delu-
sional you are."

"I could say the same to you."

"Not unless you want *this* coffee on your head." She
slowed to a halt in front of the frames he'd spent the morning building. "When did this happen?"

Wes came up beside her and let their shoulders brush.
Let himself take a whiff of her magnolia scent. "Told you I'd
make up for the time I lost yesterday. I keep my word."

"So you do." Her light brows pulled together. "Who took
Laura to school?"

Her concern for his niece and her routine bled warmth into his chest. "*Outlander* Ringtone is an early riser. She was excited for the company."

"Oh. Good." Bethany firmed her shoulders, her gaze dancing up to meet his and flitting away just as fast. But not before he saw that she remembered last night, every beat of it. The way he'd nibbled on her delicious tits until she came, the way their mouths felt like they'd been reunited after a long absence. She remembered and was in the middle of being thrown for a loop, same as him. "Well, um . . . the window guy is here to take measurements. I guess I better get to work."

Wes nodded, reluctant to part ways with her. "Okay."

She turned toward the house, but made no move to go inside. "Wes?"

He followed her line of vision to where a cameraman was taking a panning shot of the backyard, including them in it. "Yes?"

"Is this going all right?" She gestured to the house. "Everything?"

By sheer force of will, he stopped himself from reaching for her. Burying her face in his neck and talking away her worry. Jesus, he loved this woman asking him for reassurance. "It's going just fine, Bethany."

She turned to him with her lip caught between her teeth. "Fine?"

"Renovations are messy right up until the last stroke of paint, baby. That's just how it goes," he said. "That's . . . hard for you?"

Her nod was slight. "It has to be perfect."

Tell me everything. Lay it on me. "Why?"

"Why what?" she asked, confused. "Why does it have to be perfect? Because that's what people expect from me. It's what I expect from myself."

"Well, don't. Expecting perfect can only lead to disappointment. Besides, it's the flaws that give a person character. That's where the beauty hides."

She seemed to chew that over and disregard it. "We're talking about the house, not a person."

"Right." He caught her hand trembling and frowned. Upon studying her closer, he noticed the little red patch of skin on her neck. Without thinking, he reached up and brushed it with the pads of his fingers. "What's this?"

Quickly, she stepped out of his reach. "Nothing. Just some irritation."

"It wasn't there last night. I remember every inch you showed me."

"It's nothing."

"Then let me see it." She rolled her eyes at him and cocked a sassy hip, but went still as a statue when he came closer, easing down the collar of her white cotton T-shirt. Outwardly, he gave no reaction, but a tractor plowed through his middle, turning over soil. "You do this to yourself, darlin'?"

"It's not a big deal. It's just a stress thing."

"When things aren't going perfect."

"Yes. Sometimes." He heard her swallow. "All the time."

The plow dug deeper. It killed him to know he'd once

believed she had it all together, when in actuality, she'd needed someone to confide in. She wasn't cool and unflappable the way people assumed. Not by a damn stretch. "I've got a first-aid kit in my truck. Let me put something on it and then you'll leave it the hell alone for the day."

"Don't boss me around."

Honesty made his voice raw. "I don't like seeing this mark on you."

Her lips parted on a puff of breath. "You can't see it unless you get really close, but people will be able to see a bandage if you put one on. It'll peek out."

"Who cares?"

"I do," she muttered. "I do."

There was a lot going on here. Wes wanted to know every doubt and insecurity in her head, but he suspected if he pushed any more, she'd dig in her heels. In fact, he was going to be grateful for as much as she'd revealed this morning. He was willing to bet she didn't do that with many people, if anyone. But she'd done it for the man she'd once claimed to hate.

It's complicated, indeed.

"Just some salve, then, all right?"

She gave him a grudging nod and Wes led her to his truck, a hand on the small of her back. He kept an eye on her while retrieving the kit, in case she tried to make a break for it. She settled for drinking coffee and looking impatient instead, but he could see through her. Giving him access to the red blemish probably hadn't been easy for her and he was . . . humbled.

A lot like he'd been last night when Laura said *I love you.*

These females were carving him up like a Thanksgiving turkey.

He wanted to kiss this one in the worst way, though, and the resulting knots in his stomach made his fingers unsteady as he applied the salve to the smooth base of her neck. But he'd never been a coward. Not a single day in his life. Plus she'd given him a strip of pride by letting him fix up her neck. Now it was his turn. "At the risk of complicating this more, Bethany, I want to take you out."

"What?"

"Don't act like it's some crazy-ass notion. You'd have let me take you to bed last night if I hadn't sent you home."

She gaped at him, but Wes could see gratitude in her eyes. This woman preferred sparring over coddling and he'd given her a way to stomach the latter. "I went home voluntarily, thank you very much. But even if I'd stayed, it's a huge leap—huge—to land on dating."

"I didn't say dating. I said a date. But if you insist we're dating, I'm not going to contradict you."

"Were you working with polyurethane this morning? Did you sniff it?"

Wes laughed. "So you're telling me you need some convincing."

Bethany moved out of his reach. "I am not encouraging that."

"You said it's complicated, baby. Heard it plain as day."

"I meant you give me indigestion."

This woman. She was such a fucking work of art, it was

torturous standing this close without holding her, kissing her, tickling her. Something. "One drink. Think about it. We already had a beer in my backyard. It's not such a stretch."

"In this town, it would be. One drink and people would start asking me if we're planning on having one or two kids and if we've decided on a color scheme for the nursery."

"A neutral yellow sounds about right."

She dismissed him with a groan, leaving him standing at his truck. Right before she turned away, though, Wes caught sight of her blooming smile and he held on to that memory for the next half hour while Slade interviewed him on what would eventually be the porch. He was forced to pretend like the son of a bitch hadn't tried to ask out his woman while answering questions like "Are you worried about losing? How worried? Do you wish you'd stayed with your original team? Would you like to know which team is farther ahead?"

Wes answered no to everything and didn't elaborate, no matter how vigorously the director rolled his finger, begging Wes to keep going. Out of the corner of his eye, he watched Bethany and the window guy moving from room to room, the middle-aged man taking notes on a clipboard until they were finished. Finally, the producers let Wes get back to work and called Bethany over for the same interrogation.

It wasn't easy working with the cameras in his face all day, but they made a hell of a lot of progress while listening to Slade do the same pun-tastic takes twenty times. Bethany worked on sanding down the salvageable walls in the back bedrooms. Wes, Ollie, and Carl started framing the new floor plan, which would transform the dining and living room into the open concept space Bethany wanted.

The film crew started packing it in for the day around three o'clock, thank Christ. If someone approached Wes with a boom mic one more time and asked how he felt about their progress, he was going to snap that thing over his knee. Thankful for the chance to work a few hours in peace before heading home, Wes was getting ready to staple insulation into the frame he'd just installed when his phone rang.

His head fell back and he issued a prayer at the ceiling that it wasn't the babysitter canceling again. If he kept cutting out early, they weren't going to finish this job in time. But when he looked at the screen, ice prickled along his skin. It wasn't *Outlander* Ringtone calling, it was his sister.

"Hello?"

"Wes. Hey."

Hearing the anxious note in her voice, he slowly set down his staple gun. "Becky. What's up? Where are you?"

"I'm back. I'm in town." Traffic buzzed past in the background. "I'm at the train station. Can you come pick me up?"

Bethany appeared in the room to his left, but stopped moving when she saw whatever expression was on his face. Shock? Dread? Both? "Where is your car?"

"Had to sell it. Can you come or not?"

Her agitation was like worms burrowing in his bones. Was she using again? He'd have to see her to be sure, but the defensiveness she was already employing had him leaning toward yes. And that meant he didn't want her around Laura. Protectiveness lapped at his neck like a rising current, surprising him with its intensity. When he'd arrived in Port Jefferson, he'd been determined to do his best, but he'd never considered himself a better option than anyone, even his sister. He'd just been the only option. Now, though? He couldn't help feeling like the gatekeeper between his niece and anything remotely negative. Not happening.

Becky wasn't a bad person. She'd just grown up with very little guidance and it hadn't been enough to overcome the challenges that came with being orphaned and moved around so often she couldn't find stability. It was no wonder she didn't know how to provide it now. But his sympathy for her didn't override his need to do what was best for his niece.

"Yeah, stay where you are. I'll come get you and we'll talk, all right?"

Silence passed. "Fine."

"See you soon," Wes said, hanging up the phone. He smacked the device against his palm a few times, but didn't feel the impact. "That was my sister. I'm sorry, I have to go pick her up. She's at the train station." His hands were unsteady when he tried to dial the babysitter. "I should let the babysitter know I'm going to be late. I don't know what Becky'll be like . . ."

Bethany appeared frozen, but recovered to say, "Cancel the babysitter. I can go get Laura. I don't mind staying as late as you need."

"Really?"

"Yeah. Yes. I know how to order a pizza." She fussed with her ponytail. "Go."

Wes didn't think. He just did what felt right, leaning in and kissing Bethany hard on the mouth. "Thank you." He slipped his key ring out of his pocket and detached the house key, tucking it into the front pocket of her jeans. "I'll call the school on the way and let them know you're coming."

He only allowed himself a few seconds to watch the flush spread across her cheeks before he turned and left. On the way to the train station, one phrase repeated itself over and over in his head.

I'm not ready to go.

CHAPTER FIFTEEN

Bethany's life was a landscape that never stopped changing.

Last week, she'd thought the flip would shake things up. That it would riddle her with anxiety and force her to confront the woman she'd become at age thirty. Apparently she'd only been half right.

She was now a member of an It's Complicated arrangement.

Those words had come out of her very own mouth, despite her better judgment, and they'd never been truer than right now, with a five-year-old eating an ice cream cone in the backseat of her immaculate Mercedes, singing along to Katy Perry in between licks. What in the sweet hell was going on?

And why didn't she mind it?

Driving Laura home was exactly where she needed to be, but more than that, she'd probably be enjoying herself, if it weren't for the harbinger of Wes's imminent departure hanging over the sunroof like a thunderhead. Weren't they supposed to lock horns for at least another year? Was he going to leave now that his sister had come back on the scene? Why did that possibility make her short of breath?

What she should be was relieved that the man who seemed aware of her every flaw—and didn't hesitate to point them out—was leaving. No more cracks about her cloven hooves. No more inappropriate comments about how her ass looked in yoga pants.

No more breathless kisses, either. Or those unexpected moments when she couldn't help but unburden herself to Wes and, oddly, he didn't make her feel judged. No more of his amused smile. No more of him riling her up at the exact times she needed to be riled.

Bethany realized they'd been sitting in the driveway of his house for a good minute and cut off the engine. Her gaze strayed to Laura in the rearview mirror, then dipped to where the red spot had been on her neck. His salve had done the trick, hadn't it? But it hadn't just been the medicine. After they'd bickered in front of his truck, she'd simply lost the desire to attack the area with her nails. Her stress had dipped to nonexistent, because Wes had a way of talking her through her tension without her even realizing it.

Expecting perfect can only lead to disappointment. Besides, it's the flaws that give a person character. That's where the beauty hides.

Oh God.

I don't think I want him to go.

"Elsa, can we go inside?"

"Yes." Bethany shook herself and exited the car, rounding the bumper to let Laura out of her booster seat. When she'd arrived at the school and realized she needed a certain kind of child seat to legally transport Laura, she'd panicked, but Judy was kind enough to let her borrow an extra. Bethany wasn't even going to deduct points for the fossilized Cheerios inside the cup holder. "How's the strawberry? I would have pegged you for a chocolate girl."

"Uncle Wes likes strawberry," said the little girl, hopping out onto the ground, as if that explained everything. Uncle Wes liked something so she liked it, too. "Where is he?"

Would Wes want his niece to know her mother was in town? She wasn't sure. They hadn't spoken about it, so she settled on a lie, even though it made her feel yucky. "He's working a little late," she said breezily, using the loose key to let them into the house. "What do you usually do after school?"

"Ummm. If Let's Color is watching me, we color."

"I see Uncle Wes has you using their illustrious nicknames."

Laura giggled. "You talk weird. Can we watch infomercials?"

"Um, sure." Bethany's lips twitched. "Is that the norm in this household?"

"The what?" Laura asked, crunching into her waffle cone. "Uncle Wes watches them with me when I wake up too early."

"Oh." Somewhere in the region of her throat, her stupid heart was having an official summit with her ovaries. Translators and minute-takers were present and everything. A bagel tray had been ordered. It was all very alarming. "I'm sure we can find some infomercials. My favorites are the jewelry ones."

The little girl's eyes widened. "Like necklaces?"

"You like necklaces?"

"Yes! I don't have any."

"Well, we certainly can't have that. Next time I come over, I'll bring my costume jewelry and you can pick one."

Laura's resulting smile was a display of pink teeth and cone crumbles. "Are you my Uncle Wes's girlfriend?"

"No! No, we're just friends." Bethany set her purse on the back of the couch and played with the straps. "Why? Did he call me his girlfriend?"

"No, Megan and Danielle's mom did."

"Oh, did she?" Bethany smiled, filing away that information. "Isn't that swell."

Laura flopped onto the couch lengthways in an apparent ice cream coma and Bethany scrolled the channels until she landed on QVC, where they were showing off an exquisite solitaire peridot pendant in a white-gold setting. "Do you have one of those?" Laura used her toe to point at the television screen. "I want that one."

"We have so much in common," Bethany said, sinking down into the couch and promptly finding herself with a pair of little girl feet in her lap. It was nice.

Very nice.

They'd been watching QVC for fifteen minutes, discarding their previous favorites for whatever bling was on the screen several times, when Bethany heard a car stop at the curb outside. It didn't sound like Wes's truck. Maybe it was one of the neighbors? With a prickle on the back of her neck, Bethany carefully set Laura's feet back onto the cushion and crossed to the front window.

There was a woman climbing out of the back of what appeared to be an Uber. Her hair was unbrushed and she wore a man's flannel. Though her eyes were shadowed, there was no mistaking the resemblance to Laura.

Becky tripped a little on the path on her way toward the front door, and Bethany knew something was off. Way off. Bethany didn't know a lot about this woman, except that she'd been a foster child like Wes and hadn't been able to cope with raising a child alone, at least for the time being. She also knew that Becky had used drugs before—and that meant she could be using them now. In other words, she needed to intercept Becky before she came into the house. No question. At least until Wes could get there.

As quickly as she could, Bethany shot off a text to Wes and opened the front door without making a sound, slipping out onto the stoop. She descended with the brightest smile she could muster, highly aware that this woman's reception of her could range from friendly to hostile. Especially if she suspected Bethany was barring her entrance to the house. *Come on, Wes. Get here.*

"Hi," she said, trying to keep her voice low, so Laura wouldn't hear them from inside the house. "I'm Bethany."

The other woman's gait slowed, suspicion blanketing her features. "This is my house. What are you doing here?"

"I'm a guest. Of Wes."

"Oh." Becky rubbed her tongue along her gums. "He's not here, is he?"

"No, he went to pick you up."

She avoided Bethany's gaze, her hands disappearing and twisting in the cuffs of her flannel. "I'm just here to get my kid."

The bigger picture cleared. "You didn't want Wes to be here when you came."

"I don't need to talk to you. I don't even know you."

"No, you don't," Bethany said calmly. "But Wes is on his way. Why don't we just wait until he gets here?"

She coughed into the crook of her elbow. "I got a place to take her."

Bethany couldn't help the flame of anger igniting in her chest. Becky was just going to take Laura and go without telling Wes. She was trying her best to have empathy for this woman who was obviously going through something, possibly addiction, but she couldn't help but want to rage on Wes's behalf. He would have been devastated.

"Wes is coming. Let's just wait."

"I don't have to wait to go into my own house. To see my own kid."

"If you didn't want Wes here, you know there's a reason you shouldn't."

That logic took a moment to infiltrate, but when it did, Becky's eyes filled with tears. She started to issue a rejoinder, but Wes's truck came flying around the end of the block, braking hard where the Uber had been moments before.

His attention was locked on the window of the house when he climbed from the truck, relief crossing his features when he didn't see Laura. He must have put on his hat after leaving Project Doomsday, but he took it off now and slapped it against his thigh restlessly, as if unaware of the nervous gesture. "Why did you have to do that?" Wes said finally, addressing his sister with a thick voice. "You're unfit to see her if you're playing these kinds of games, Becky. You left me in charge until you sorted yourself out. You made me promise I wouldn't leave until you had. You haven't. So what the hell am I supposed to do?"

"I do have my shit together, Wes." She sniffed hard. "I'm living with my boyfriend in Linden. I got a job."

"Boyfriend," he echoed in disbelief. "You're not even divorced yet."

"If I could track his ass down, I would be!"

"Keep your voice quiet," he growled. "She doesn't need to see you like this."

"I'm fine."

Laughing without humor, he paced in a circle and came back. "You got a room for her in Linden? Babysitters? Have you enrolled her in school?"

Becky's expression was the very picture of a woman treading water. "I'm . . . I'm going to take care of all that. Jesus. Give me five seconds."

"Take care of it first and then we'll talk."

"You can't stop me from seeing her."

Strain appeared at the corners of Wes's eyes. "No, I can't. But do you really want her to see you like this? Or do you think you can do better?" Wes sent Bethany a pleading look. "Could you go inside and distract her? Please?"

"Yes, of course." Bethany wheeled around and started to walk up the path, but then stopped and looked back. "Wes, could you give her my number?" she said for his ears alone. "No pressure. I just want to help."

After a moment, he nodded, temporary warmth moving in his face. "Yeah, darlin'. I will."

Wes stared into the sunken eyes of his half sister and he could see her as she'd been at seventeen. Lonely, unsure of herself, just waiting for the other shoe to drop.

Like he'd told Bethany, Becky had a harder time than him. He suspected he only knew the half of what she'd gone through while being wrung out by the system. By the time he'd met her, the damage had already been done. To both of them. He'd been too jaded by his experience to love her the way a brother should. The guilt he'd harbored over that might even be part of the reason he'd gotten on the plane to New York—and thank Christ he had.

Never in his life had Wes felt like he was standing in the right spot. Until now.

Not only with Laura. Or Bethany. Or the friends he'd made in Port Jefferson.

No, he was meant to be there standing in front of Becky at this crossroads in *her* life. This wasn't about him. Or his pain. Or lack of belonging. It was bigger than any of those things. And for once, he wasn't thinking about skating away and avoiding entanglements. This was it. He was going to let himself get tangled up.

The cool sweep of relief in his chest only reinforced his decision.

"Hey." When his voice emerged unsteady, he took a long breath and centered himself. "Look at me and listen good."

She crossed her arms and waited, her stance belligerent but her eyes full of tears. Damn, he hadn't done enough for her. Not by a damn sight. But he could change that now. He could stop using his past to excuse his commitment issues and dig the hell in.

"You're my sister and I care about you."

Her arms dropped slowly to her sides.

"You're a survivor and a fighter, all right? You're going to come out clean on the other side of this and see your daughter again. You don't have a choice. Laura needs her mother. She needs *you*, Becky."

"That's why I'm here," she croaked.

"You're here because you love her. Of course you do." He stepped closer and put a hand on her shoulder, visibly stunning her. Had he ever even hugged his sister? "Look, there is no time limit on me being here. I've got Laura while you figure everything out. She's happy here."

His niece was happy . . . with *him*. It was still almost impossible to believe that he'd come here totally inept in all things family. All things children, love, and . . . permanence. But he'd created stability where none had existed before. Not only for Laura, but for himself. Jesus, he really wasn't going anywhere. He was in this. And it felt right.

"Look." Wes squeezed Becky's shoulder. "If I can figure this shit out, Becky, anyone can."

That got a watery laugh out of her. "Who are you anymore?"

"Your brother." He swallowed hard. "I know I wasn't a good one in the past. But you can count on me now, all right?"

Emotion clouded over her features. "I knew I shouldn't take her. I just thought . . . it's been so long. What kind of a mother am I, leaving her kid for over a month?"

"You made sure she'd have someone to care for her. That's more consideration than we were given a lot of the time."

"God knows that's true." She swiped curious eyes. "Who was that woman?"

Wes considered the question. "Let's call her my reluctant girlfriend."

They shared another bittersweet laugh and for the first time, he acknowledged the bond that lay between them. An acknowledgment that was a long time coming. Maybe it would change things. He didn't know, but he had hope, and he was pretty sure the two people waiting for him inside the house had a lot to do with it.

Having that safety net gave him the courage to say what came next. "I don't know how these things work, but I can find out about becoming Laura's temporary guardian. If you're open to that. It won't be forever, but I want her to have some proof I'm staying as long as she needs me. I would have killed for that when I was a kid, you know?"

His sister cast a wistful glance toward the house, not speaking for several moments. "I think that could be a good idea. I'll think about it."

Wes let out the breath he wasn't aware he'd been holding. "Becky . . ." He hesitated for a moment, then pulled her into a hug. "It's going to be all right."

Wes walked through the front door of the house, sending Bethany's heart into a marathon. He was alone and Bethany didn't know whether to be relieved or sad about that. For Laura's part, she bounded off the couch like a shot, squealing and skidding to a halt in front of her uncle. Without missing a beat, he tossed her up in the air like pizza dough, catching her on the way down in a hug. "Hey, kid."

She patted his back with sticky ice cream hands. "Hey."

There was a smile on his face, but when he met Bethany's eyes over his niece's back, there was unrest spinning in their depths. "I wasn't sure what to do about dinner, so I ordered pizza. Again. It's on the way," she said, her stomach full of helium. "I should go," she breathed, stuffing her cell into her purse.

"Wait." Wes set Laura down and ruffled her hair. "Can you go wash your hands for dinner and pick out a bedtime book for later? I need to talk to Bethany."

Laura gaped at Bethany. "Is she in trouble?"

"Naw, she's not in trouble." He tapped her nose. "Go ahead."

"Okay."

The little girl sped from the room, sliding in her socks as

she rounded first into the hallway. Bethany remained rooted to the spot beside the couch watching Wes enter the kitchen and return with two bottled beers. He offered her one and she declined with a headshake, waiting as he drained half of his own. Twice he opened his mouth to say something, but closed it and shook his head instead.

Bethany's feet were moving before her head issued the command. She stopped in front of Wes, plucked the beer out of his hand, and set it down on the table. And she put her arms around him.

Wes wrapped her in such a tight embrace, the breath in her lungs was expelled in a giant whoosh.

"I can't leave Laura," he muttered into the crook of her neck. "I can't."

Her fingers threaded into his hair. "No, of course not."

"I mean ever." He lifted his head, emotion rippling along his jawline. "I put Becky in another Uber back to Jersey. She's not going to push seeing her daughter for now, but even if my sister gets her life on track, I think . . ." Self-doubt flickered in his eyes. "Laura needs me, right?"

"Yes."

He let out a hard breath. "I have to stick, Bethany."

There was something familiar in the way he said those words. They sounded like every single time she'd questioned her own capabilities. Or done something that scared her, like flip a house, plan a wedding, lead a Just Us League meeting, or babysit a child. She knew that rush of fear for the unknown very well, and she suddenly felt connected to him in a way she didn't think could be severed easily, to this man she'd once loathed. Or thought she loathed, anyway. Had any of her vitriol toward him ever been real to begin with?

Bethany didn't know. She only knew she wanted to smooth the jaggedness inside of him now, the way she'd wished was possible for herself so many times.

"Wes," she whispered, levering herself up on her toes until her lips landed against his surprised ones . . . and they tripped slowly into a kiss that was equal parts voracious and pure. Honest. He let himself be kissed, let Bethany hum comfort in her throat while mating their tongues, let her fingers twist in his hair and drag him down, before he grunted and tried to yank her up into his body at the same time. His arms were still around her as far as they could go and the embrace was so intimate, she could feel his entire body pulse, his inhales and exhales, the thick swells and sensual dips of his muscle. Could smell his sweat and deodorant.

The tempo turned desperate, but her need to give solace never abated, and she could feel him being undone by it. And it gratified her when Wes reached out for more, attacking her mouth and taking possession of the understanding she offered.

His right hand dove into her hair, gripping and angling her for deeper tastes, his body bowing over hers until she was almost bent backward. God, it was glorious, being needed this badly. Needing in return. Being in wordless agreement and not having to guess what a man was thinking. She knew every thought in his head because he was expressing it with his tongue, lips, and teeth.

It got to be too much, the pulse points throughout her body hammering, her mind reeling, her balance obliterated. So much feeling directed at one person and she was afraid of defining it, so she forced herself to put an end to the kiss and there they stood, still wrapped in each other's arms, frantic breaths filling the scant space between them.

"Is that a yes to drinks?" he said, finally.

Bethany puffed a laugh. "Oh, now it's drinks, plural?"

He brushed a hand over her hair. "One of anything could never be enough with you."

There was a vicious tug in her middle. "Is that a fact?"

"Damn straight." He nipped at her bottom lip. "I'll ask you again, is that a yes?"

She drew a circle on his chest, finishing with a playful finger shove. "It's an I'll think about it."

Wes growled. "God, you make me fucking crazy, Bethany." He picked up a piece of her hair and twisted it around his finger. "When I walked back in here, I didn't know up from down. Now I'm halfway to solid. How'd you do it?"

"You should know," she whispered, unable to look him in the eye. "You've done it for me, more than once now."

Admitting that was so exposing, her body broke his hold involuntarily. Though she immediately wished to be back in his arms, she all but dove for her purse, slinging it over her shoulder. When she chanced a look at Wes, he was tracking her movements with single-minded intensity. "Stay."

"I . . . have plans," she blurted.

His eyebrow ticked up. "Come again?"

"With Rosie." Not that her friend knew about said plans, but Bethany was in sudden need of tequila and girl talk.

He grunted, but didn't relax. In fact, there were thoughts churning behind his gaze. A multitude of them. "I asked Becky to think about giving me guardianship. Of Laura." She was given no time to process that revelation, because Wes advanced on her, not stopping until her head was tilted back and their fingertips were brushing, his breath feathering her lips. "I'm not going anywhere. I'm here to stay, so when you get in bed tonight and think of me, remember to change the way you do it. Instead of that one sweaty session where we break the headboard, I'd be in your bed night after night after fucking night, learning what makes your thighs shake. We'd have to lose the headboard altogether."

Her ears turned into wind tunnels. "You don't make the design choices in this relation—"

"Relationship?" he prompted when she cut herself off, his tone triumphant. "When you're ready to say it out loud, I'll be waiting right here."

Catch your breath. "With your blue balls?"

"They're more of a blackish purple at this point."

"Ouch." The doorbell rang and she took the opportunity to escape his magnetism. "Good night, Wes."

He groaned. "Good night, Bethany."

Bethany opened the door to the pizza delivery guy and asked him to wait, unable to resist a final glance back at Wes over her shoulder. She found his powerful arms crossed, hair still mussed from her fingers. So masculine in his dirty work clothes, it should be a crime. "Your pizza is here," she said, her tone more suited to a poetry reading.

He reached for the wallet in his pocket. "Thanks."

"Wes?"

"Yeah?"

She swallowed hard. "If Becky says yes, you're going to do an amazing job."

A muscle popped in his cheek. "Thank you."

Get out of here while you still have the willpower.

Her reserve of the stuff was running dangerously low.

CHAPTER SIXTEEN

*E*very time Bethany walked into Buena Onda, something new had been woven seamlessly into the atmosphere. Rosie wanted the restaurant to be an experience, and Bethany could safely say she'd accomplished that task.

Tonight, there was a string of lights, an angled rug hugging the floorboards, a new picture on the wall. Only a decorator's eye would pick out the changes, they were so subtle, and the ambiance never changed. It was always a warm hustle-bustle. A noisy welcome that she could sink into and decide what journey to let the menu take her on.

She'd been right to come here tonight. Bethany weaved through the tables toward the back of the restaurant where Rosie would be putting together takeout orders and supervising the kitchen, and the sparkling depth swallowed her up in a hug. She waved at Dominic where he sat at his reserved table, sipping a beer and reading the evening edition of the *Daily News*. Several patrons called out to her or lifted their glass, not-too-discreetly whispering in her wake.

Nothing malicious, just Port Jeff gossip. Well earned, too. She'd given them quite a few topics to choose from by defecting from Brick & Morty, signing on for a reality-show competition, and being caught after sunset at Wes's house. Not to mention picking his niece up from school, a distinctly domestic activity.

Remembering the way Laura's feet felt in her lap, she experienced some hollowness in her throat. What were Wes and Laura doing right now? Eating pizza and watching infomercials? It scared her a little how badly she suddenly wanted to turn around, leave Buena Onda, and go back.

In other words, she definitely needed the break. She'd been around Wes so much during the flip, she was due some distance and perspective. He was getting to her in ways she didn't anticipate. Fine, she'd always been annoyingly attracted to him physically, even after she'd decreed him a low-down asshole. What was she going to do now that the truth had surfaced? Wes had more layers than she'd given him credit for. He was slightly damaged from an unstable past, funny, observant, and Jesus, he could kiss. She'd never, ever experienced kisses like the ones he'd laid on her.

Most important of all, he was a stand-up man. My God. He'd asked for guardianship of his niece tonight, taking on a challenge that would scare even the most independent adult.

Yes, Wes was brave and full of heart and . . . she really needed a reality check before she did something stupid like fall for the man.

A few yards away, Rosie passed through the swinging door out of the kitchen and into the staff station, a nook built by her husband that contained shelves laden with cutlery, coffee paraphernalia, hot sauces, and other condiments. She did a double take when she saw Bethany. "Hey, stranger! I haven't seen you since the wedding," Rosie said, stacking and organizing what looked like credit card receipts. "How is the flip going?"

Bethany clasped her hands beneath her chin. "Amazing, of course. I'm in charge."

Even though Bethany made her friend laugh, she didn't get as much pleasure out of it as usual. Because she wasn't being honest. In truth, she likened the flip to flying down railroad tracks without brakes. That would shatter the illusion she'd worked so hard to create, though, wouldn't it? Even with her best friend?

In the space of seconds, she'd gone back to being the woman who never showed a single weakness. The woman who hid behind style and bravado, who would never admit she didn't know how the hell the flip was going. Wes told her it was going fine and they'd been seeing daily progress, but arriving at the hazardous mess every morning made her stress and self-doubt flare up. Each day, she put her head down and focused on whatever project she'd chosen. It helped to put on blinders and do one thing, but stepping back and realizing what a massive undertaking she'd shouldered? It was hard. She wasn't coping the way she presented to the cameras. She wanted everything perfect *now*. Until then, the unfinished mess was a reflection of her.

Her fingers crept toward her neck, itching to attack the spot Wes had put salve on earlier this morning, but she forced it down to her side. "I can see you're swamped," she said to Rosie, waggling her eyebrows. "Definitely a good problem to have, right? I'll just grab a table and if you have time for a drink, come join me. No pressure!"

Rosie smiled. "Okay." She craned her neck to look past Bethany. "Take the two-top by the window. I'll send over the waitress."

"Two-top. Look at you with the restaurant lingo."

With a little shimmy, Bethany headed back toward the front of Buena Onda, winking at the people whom she suspected were whispering about her. Her smile remained intact, but on the inside, a million thoughts pinged around her skull. Were they laying odds that her brother was going to win *Flip Off*? Were they calling her a cougar for making time with a twenty-three-year-old man? Could they see her lack of a manicure, thanks to her grueling new gig?

Bethany curled her nails into her palm and took a seat at the table in front, thanking the waitress who handed her a menu. Though she was positive her appearance was serene, she was kind of sweating sitting alone, especially with all the whispers, so she took out her phone—and found a text from Wes. A laugh tumbled out of her before she could stop it.

It was a picture of him blowing on his credit card while QVC advertised a diamond broach in the background. But the best part was Laura mid-cheer on the couch, her delight obvious.

Bethany pressed her smiling lips together and texted back.

BETHANY: Always hold out for diamonds. The kid knows her stuff.

WES: This is bad. She's no longer accepting Cheerios as bribes. If I end up promising her jewelry to get five more minutes of sleep tomorrow morning, you're in trouble.

BETHANY: Am I? That's not my credit card.

WES: You'll have a cranky foreman on your hands.

BETHANY: Awww. Don't be cranky.

WES: How are you going to cheer me up?

Bethany coughed quietly and scanned her surroundings, wondering if anyone noticed the way she was pressing her thighs together. These text messages weren't even naughty. Not really, even if they seemed to be veering in that direction. But she could hear Wes's gruff Texas drawl in her ear and imagine his hands molding her hips, cheating lower to her butt, squeezing.

Seriously? Her panties were wet after a brief text exchange? She'd just showered and put on fresh clothes.

I'm not going to answer.

Bethany smacked the phone onto the table, facedown, but snatched it back up before five seconds had passed.

BETHANY: I'd take care of those nasty blue balls, of course.

WES: 🐻

BETHANY: With all that paint lying around, I can totally paint them a new color.

WES: If you were here, I'd have to spank you for that.

Her fingers hesitated over the screen, trembling. She couldn't reply or she'd send back gibberish. That was all her brain was capable of producing with that image in her head. Wes laying her facedown over his lap and walloping her bottom with that warm, calloused palm.

WES: Why aren't you here, Bethany?

That message, so different in tone from the last, struck a totally different chord. Now a pang of yearning joined her desire for physical contact. With Wes.

She missed him. After a matter of hours.

Bad. This is so bad.

"Hey!"

Rosie bounced into the seat across from Bethany and she yipped, fumbling her phone and knocking over the red rose flower arrangement in the center of the table. "Oh my God," she breathed, righting the vase before water could leak out and scanning the restaurant for signs that anyone had witnessed her clumsiness. "Sorry. I just didn't expect . . . I didn't think you'd be able to join me when you're this packed!"

"Here I am," Rosie said, watching Bethany with a bemused expression. "You looked deep in thought over here."

"Huh." She snuck the phone into her pocket. "Did I?"

"Uh-huh." Rosie kept an eye trained on Bethany while ordering for them. "So let's talk about Slade Hogan. He came in for lunch yesterday and I thought the waitresses were going to hyperventilate."

"Oh yeah." Bethany nodded enthusiastically and tried, without success, to recall the host's face. "He's a dish."

"Worthy of ending your man hiatus?"

Bethany kept right on nodding. Until she started shaking her head. "No."

Rosie arched a dark brow and leaned back with her just-delivered glass of wine. "Oh?"

"He did ask me out. I passed."

Her friend gasped. A little too theatrically. "Why would you do that?"

"I can see where you're going with this."

"Can you?"

"Is this thing where you answer a question with a question a product of couple's therapy?"

Rosie laughed into her sip of wine. "Sorry. It's just that I hear so much gossip being in this place all day and you and a certain cowboy have come under heavy speculation. I wanted to hear it from your mouth." She shrugged an elegant shoulder. "That wasn't going to happen without a little goading."

Bethany subdued her smile. "You've been spending too much time with my family." She tapped her tragically unfiled fingernails on the table. "I'm neither going to confirm nor deny that there is something worth speculating over."

"Okay."

She lowered her voice. "But if there was, I would need assurances that the phrase *I told you so* would not be uttered."

"You'd only have your sister to worry about. But since she's going to return from Italy in a sexual stupor, you've got a decent shot at her letting you off with a lofty sniff or two."

Bethany hummed. "I guess I can deal with that."

"Great. I'll intercept Georgie when she gets home." Rosie rubbed her hands together and leaned forward. "Tell this horny married lady everything."

The suspense built while Bethany unnecessarily straightened her fork. "There has been some kissing. I'm thinking of sleeping with him."

Rosie picked up her cloth napkin and hid her face in it, but not before Bethany caught her grinning. When she dropped it, her composure was back in place. "Oh?"

"Yes. I'm just not sure yet."

"You were texting with him when I walked over here, weren't you?"

"About the flip."

"Construction talk really gets you going, huh?"

Bethany cleared her throat. "Was I that obvious?"

Rosie's gaze meandered through the restaurant and landed on her husband, who—predictably—was already hard at work watching his wife. "Only to someone who's spent a lot of time trying to repress their sexual needs."

"There's that therapy talk again," Bethany said absently, drawing a pattern on the table. "Let's say . . . and this is totally hypothetical . . . Wes stayed in Port Jefferson." She laughed a little too brightly. "And wanted a"—she made air quotes—"relationship. Wouldn't that be crazy? I mean, woooo. Come on."

Rosie set down her drink. "Why would it be crazy?"

Bethany tried to be as casual as possible ticking off her fingers. "He's seven years younger than me, he doesn't have any career focus—construction is just what he's doing now. I mean, he was a *bull rider*. And we fight all the time. It would be a complete disaster, start to finish."

Her friend said nothing, simply waiting for her to elaborate.

"And . . . you know, he's just not thinking this all the way through." Her shoulder jerked. "Why would he want a relationship—hypothetically—with someone who can't relax until everything is exactly perfect, but it never is. Ever. It would just get exhausting for him, being around that anxiousness. You know how I am." She waved a hand. "I like things a certain way."

"Yes," Rosie said slowly. "But I never knew you second-guessed yourself. You always seem so confident."

"I am!" She picked up her wineglass, ignoring the drops that sloshed over the side onto her hand. "No, I totally am. I don't know what I'm talking about. Just thinking out loud." Her throat ached with the forced lie. "So, tell me. Did you add a new string of lights to the ceiling? It's an amazing touch."

Rosie was obviously hesitant to let her change the subject, but relented. They were able to steal a few more minutes before Rosie went back to work, but long after her friend left, Bethany's words hovered over the table. Until tonight, she'd never realized how firmly she kept her mask in place, even around her best friend. Even around her sister. She hadn't realized it until she'd started allowing herself to be less than perfect around Wes.

Of course, he'd kind of ripped the mask off, but that was splitting hairs.

The point was, she'd been a dishonest version of herself tonight and it had never been more obvious. She'd never actually considered a relationship with Wes. Until they'd started working together, the very idea would have been laughable. But now? When Bethany tried to picture them together, as a couple, the vision made her . . . warm. Hopeful.

Happy.

But those positive emotions didn't keep her old fears from coming back to roost. Wasn't there a reason she'd gone on a man hiatus in the first place?

She'd pushed her past boyfriends away for wanting to get too close.

For daring to expect *more* from her.

Knowing Wes would want more, total access to her heart, mind, and body—access she'd always been afraid to give anyone—made her want to backpedal before things got too comfortable. Too optimistic.

Before expectations were formed for a normal, healthy relationship that she had no earthly idea how she could fulfill. She definitely never had before.

How could Wes be happy with her when she didn't know how to be happy with herself? Despite what Bethany's heart was telling her to do, she could feel herself shifting back to her old patterns with men. If she didn't let things get too serious, he couldn't get sick of her, right?

A little time, a little space, and Wes would probably thank her for keeping things casual. And the disappointment she felt in herself?

It would fade with time. Wouldn't it?

Bethany hoped that once she'd had a Wes-free weekend of repeating the mantra that the distance between them would get easier and she'd stop second-guessing herself that she'd actually be closer to believing it. She doubted she would, but no one had ever accused her of lacking a strong will . . .

CHAPTER SEVENTEEN

Okay, folks, it is day four of the family-flip competition *Flip Off*, and the battle is certainly heating up! We're on the job-site that has been lovingly dubbed Project Doomsday." Wes's thumb and forefinger did their best to crush the bridge of his nose. At least if he ended up in the emergency room, he wouldn't have to listen to Slade fucking Hogan's made-for-television voice for a while.

Outside the window, Slade walked backward, the camera-man and lighting and sound guys following him to where Bethany was . . . Wait, was she carrying a ladder?

Why?

Wes didn't have a clue.

As a matter of fact, he didn't know a damn thing going on in her head because today was Monday and she'd been distant with him since Friday. Everything had been coming up roses when she left his house. They'd even traded some flirty text messages and he'd thought they'd well and truly turned a corner into . . . coupletown. Or at least approaching it. But all weekend, she'd been busy with the Just Us League and antique shopping for when she eventually staged the flip.

He'd missed her, but he hadn't panicked until coming face-to-face with her on the site this morning. Every time he moseyed in her direction to make small talk or maybe get himself another one of those life-altering kisses, she suddenly had to go pick up materials or make a coffee run. He'd joked with her about being a cranky foreman, but it had become reality and he still—still—had fucking blue balls.

Wes threw down the pair of pliers in his hand and stomped outside to see where the hell Bethany thought she was going with a ladder. Unless she was planning on creating some kind of avant-garde lawn sculpture out of it, he wasn't sure why she needed one. She was scheduled to work on the crown molding today, wasn't she?

It was a terrible idea to approach Bethany in this black mood, especially while the cameras were rolling, but a man could only take so much. She'd kissed him like a man ought to be kissed the other night. The sweetness of it, the way it had felt like a promise . . . well, it had rocked him. Rocked him real hard. It didn't make any damn sense that she should be avoiding him now. Unless something had happened between the time she'd texted him Friday night and now. But what?

"Bethany, I heard you've decided to retile the roof?"

At the sound of that question coming from Slade's mouth, the coffee Wes drank that morning turned to bitter acid in his stomach. Bethany on the roof? She wasn't trained for that. Hadn't gone through a safety course or even a casual tutorial with him or someone with construction experience. More than once, he'd worked with men who'd been injured in falls from roofs and ladders on the construction site. The thought of Bethany shattering a femur or breaking her back broke him out in a cold sweat.

"Yeah," he said slowly and, fine, maybe a touch sarcastically. "Mind if we put a pin in that genius idea for now?"

Bethany very carefully set down the ladder and crossed her arms. "I'm sorry. Does my foreman have a complaint to voice?"

"Your foreman," he said witheringly. "Sure, we'll go with that."

Twin sparks shot off in her eyes. "Good."

Wes reined in his frustration. What the hell had happened between them that he wasn't aware of? She almost seemed *relieved* to kick off this argument. "Let's turn off the camera and take a couple of hours to make sure you know what the hell you're doing, all right? I don't want you falling off the fucking roof."

"We'll have to bleep that," called the producer.

"Bleep it, then," Wes spat.

"I've watched plenty of roofs being tiled," Bethany said.

Wes closed some of the distance between him and Bethany. They were surrounded by at least thirty others, but they might as well have been the only people there, for all the attention he paid them. "Watching and doing are two different things. Either we do some training or you keep your feet on the ground where they belong."

She squared her shoulders. "You don't make decisions for me."

"Now, there is some truth to that, buddy," Slade had the stones to pipe in. "Bethany is the official homeowner—"

"Jesus, Slade," Wes interrupted, massaging his right eye with enough force to blind himself. "You are truly getting on my last fucking nerve."

"Bleep!"

"Wes," Bethany gasped.

"It's bad enough I've got to work with camera cords and spotlights and Slade in my way"—his shout lost some steam—"but I can deal with all of that if you're okay." It came to him at once that he'd just revealed a lot in front of a large crowd of people, not to mention two cameras. "It's a long fall," he finished, trying to recapture some of his angry tone, but it didn't work. Bethany's jaw had dropped open and silence—for once—had fallen among the crew.

Bethany recovered, visibly shaking herself. "I'll be careful. Ollie is going to show me what to do."

"Lord. Don't drag me into this," Ollie said from his hiding place behind the lighting guy. "I didn't think it would be a big deal."

"It's not a big deal," Bethany enunciated. "Thank you for your concern, but I can manage not to plummet to my death."

She had to go putting death in his head, sending his blood pressure sky-high. "You go up on that roof and I'll carry you down over my shoulder, Bethany. You hear me? Tiling the roof is not a job for you."

Yet. He should have said *yet*.

Her reaction had Wes regretting his words immediately. The stubbornness fled from her beautiful eyes, replaced with betrayal. It was too late for apologies or take-backs, though, wasn't it? He'd royally screwed himself now. The hardheaded woman was backed into a corner in front of God and everyone. She had no choice but to call his bluff.

"Well . . . you know." Her voice cracked, but she patched it fast. "You won't have a say if I fire you."

A sharp object got stuck in his throat. "Is that what you're doing?"

Fear crept into her eyes, but she blinked it away. "Yes," she said, lifting her chin.

They spent a good ten seconds in a stare down that Wes eventually won.

But as he stormed to his car, the ache in the center of his chest insisted he'd definitely lost.

Wes did what any self-respecting cowboy did when he had woman troubles.

He drowned his sorrows in a bottle of brew.

Outlander Ringtone had offered to give him the night off since she'd had an afternoon reprieve from picking Laura up from school yesterday. He'd jumped on it immediately. His mood was black and he didn't want it affecting his niece.

"Want another?" asked the bartender on his way to ring up a round.

Wes eyeballed his empty bottle of Bud, weighing the pros of oblivion versus the cons of getting a six o'clock in the morning wake-up call while nursing a hangover. Was this parenthood? Constantly having to decide if a hangover was worth it? Not only that, there was this icky, sticky guilt over being out in the first place urging him to turn down another beer. Why did he feel guilty when this was his first night out in a month?

Hell, it wasn't even nine thirty.

"Yeah," he muttered, pushing his empty bottle toward the bartender. "Thanks."

Truthfully, he'd rather be at home reading Laura a bed-time story instead of taking up space in Grumpy Tom's, but sometimes a man needed room to think. That went triple tonight.

How had everything gone to shit so fast?

He still couldn't make sense of it.

Three days prior to being fired by Bethany, they'd been right there on the edge of something more. God, he'd been ea-ger to get there, too. She'd been so close to giving in and say-ing yes to their date. He was going to take her out, open doors for her, treat her like a queen, and fuck her to high heaven.

Now he'd lost his shot and his job.

His world had turned upside down faster than a bull bucking him onto his ass—and right at the time he needed to have his life together. He was serious about taking guard-ianship of Laura if he could get his sister to agree to the ar-rangement. Wes didn't have any notions of keeping Becky from her daughter forever, but while he was her caretaker, he wanted to give her stability. He didn't want her waking up every morning wondering if today would be the day he lit out of Port Jefferson.

Which brought him to his most immediate problem. Stability for Laura meant a steady income—and as of this afternoon, he no longer had that.

He couldn't blame Bethany, either. All day he'd been replaying the scene outside the house. God, he'd been an idiot. Bethany's whole reason for wanting to head this flip was to prove herself capable. He'd tried to rob her of an opportunity to further her confidence in herself. Shit, he was as bad as Stephen.

As if his thoughts had put up a Stephen Bat-Signal, the man in question walked into the bar a few minutes later, holding another note in his hand. Deep in concentration, Bethany's brother almost walked right past Wes, but tripped to a halt before he could get too far.

"Wes. What are you doing here?"

"What's it look like?"

Stephen settled into the stool beside Wes and ordered a Coke, smoothing his crinkled note out on the bar while he waited. "Is my sister giving you headaches?"

Wes held up a hand. "Let me stop you right there. I'm not here to gossip like a middle schooler."

"Ah, you're no fun."

"Says the man who ordered a soda in a bar," Wes drawled, bottle to his lips. "I see you've got another cryptic note from Kristin. What does this one say?"

"'After every storm, there is a rainbow.'"

Lord, the woman was certifiable. "Let me ask you a question, man. Have you just come right out and asked her what the notes mean?"

"I can't do that." Stephen gaped at him like he'd just suggested they steal a cop car and do donuts in the town square. "She'll be disappointed in me if I can't figure it out on my own."

"But you can't."

Stephen faced Wes on his stool. "One year, Kristin knitted me some socks for Christmas and I didn't react with enough appreciation. I mean, they were socks. But she gave me the silent treatment straight through New Year's." He popped a straw into his Coke. "I finally figured out what was wrong. Turns out, they were exact replicas of my christening socks, right down to the little red crosses on the ankles."

Wes knew he must look stupefied. He was. "How the hell did you figure that out?"

"My mother came over for dinner and saw them. Kristin had left them out on the mantel, but I was too naive to realize she was trying to give me a hint." He nodded as if that explanation was completely normal. "Anyway, my mother knew right away and commented on the resemblance of the socks. So Kristin threw them in the fire."

"What?"

Stephen leaned in. "She wanted *me* to figure it out."

Was this Long Island or Mars? "That sounded like a horror film, but thank you, I guess."

"Thank you?"

"Yeah," Wes said, sipping his drink. "My own lady troubles don't seem quite as daunting now."

"I knew it." Stephen wrapped smug lips around his straw. "Bethany ghosted you, didn't she? Wasn't sure how she'd manage it since you're working together, but my sister is re-sourceful."

Goddammit. Why had be mentioned trouble? The last thing he wanted to do was listen to Stephen talk a bunch of nonsense about Bethany. But he was also one beer deep, heartsick, and confused about what had actually happened between them. He'd been caught in a weak moment. "What do you mean, she ghosted me?"

"That's her thing. She casts her line out into the water." Stephen moved his Coke aside so he could mimic fishing. "The man bites. And then she throws the whole damn rod back into the ocean while the poor sucker is still attached."

The back of his neck prickled ominously, but he scoffed. "How long have you been working on that metaphor?"

"It's my mother's, actually, and there's more," Stephen responded, squinting back down at his note. "So there's the rod floating on the ocean, the man is hooked at the end, and Bethany stands on the boat blaming the fish."

Wes's entire life, he'd avoided any kind of long-term relationships. This right here was why. Stephen had clearly lost his fucking mind and what was to blame?

Love.

Marriage.

Sure, Stephen's wife was a complete loony toon, but Wes would have been standing on the outside laughing at this manner of conversation a few months ago. He'd have ridiculed Stephen for letting himself get played like a fiddle. Now it wasn't so funny. Because he was the hooked fish and if he closed his eyes, he could see Bethany standing at the bow of a ship, watching him sink.

Yeah, she'd caught him, that was for damn sure. He'd never imagined how much he would love having a hook through his lip, either. But this woman. This woman had made him earn her trust, her respect, her laughter. Each of those accomplishments made him feel more capable as a man. A potential partner for her. Someone who could not only be in a lasting relationship, but maybe even be good at it.

Was he just going to swim off now when they'd come so far?

No. He was going to jump back into the goddamn boat and throw the rod down at her feet. Let her know he wasn't going anywhere. She'd caught herself a Texas man and he refused to sink like the chumps she'd dated before. More important, he was going to figure out *why* she continued to throw the fish out with the rod.

A crack of thunder sounded outside, as if the heavens approved of his new course of action, and rain began to pelt the windows of Grumpy Tom's. The downpour sent the smokers scurrying inside using their jackets as shelter.

Damn.

The forecast didn't call for rain. He'd checked as recently as this morning, to make sure there would be no bad weather causing them delays. Back when he'd been the foreman and he was paid to have contingency plans in place, anyway. He'd need to drive over to the jobsite and put some tarps on the roof.

With a sigh, he took out his wallet and signaled the bartender so he could settle up. "I need to get to the site," he told Stephen. "Fired or not, I can't let all that hard work go to waste."

Stephen spit Coke onto the bar, earning a stony look from the sleepy barman. "She fired you?"

"Yup."

"First of all, welcome back to the winning team," Stephen said magnanimously. "Second, I don't know why I'm surprised. This is classic Bethany."

Wes flicked an irritated wrist, sending a twenty fluttering down onto the bar. "Have you ever asked Bethany why she pushes people away or do you just bitch and moan about it behind her back? Maybe there's a good reason she does it. You ever thought of that?"

"You're defending her?" Stephen sputtered. "She fired you!"

"I pushed her to it. It's on me. And I don't want back on your team."

Stephen stayed silent a moment. "There's obviously something going on between you two or she wouldn't have pulled her parachute."

Ire pinched his nerve endings. "Oh, fuck off with your metaphors. What is wrong with everyone in this town? No one can just say what's on their minds?" Wes plucked the note up off the bar and tossed it into the air. "Your wife is pregnant, you moron."

"She is?"

"Yes. And I'm sure he or she will grow up completely stable."

To Wes's shock and horror, Stephen launched off the stool and threw his arms around Wes's shoulders, cry-laughing noisily. "I'm going to be a dad."

Wes sighed and patted him on the back. "Congratulations."

Finally, Stephen pulled back with moisture-filled eyes. A loud beep had Bethany's brother disengaging to pull his cell from his front pocket, his rapturous expression turning to exasperation. "Just got a text from Bethany. She wants to know if a staple gun is waterproof." He flicked a glance at Wes. "Sounds like she's way ahead of you on the roof situation. You better go."

Wes's heart took an elevator up to his throat. "What? Text her back. Tell her to wait for me—"

The phone beeped again. "Never mind," Stephen read aloud. "I googled it."

Wes propelled himself out of the bar into the rain, visions of Bethany slipping and falling chilling his blood.

Apparently one more fight was in order before he won her back.

Although, had he ever had her in the first place?

CHAPTER EIGHTEEN

*B*ethany spit rainwater out of her mouth and did her best to unfold the tarp blind. No matter how she positioned herself on the roof, the rain seemed to slant directly into her face, so she planted her feet shoulder-width apart and sarcastically thanked Mother Nature for this glorious piece of timing.

She was not too proud to admit she should be anywhere but a rain-slicked roof during a storm. In fact, she would even have given the job to Wes, if she hadn't fired him in the bonehead move of the century. But she'd spent six hours on that roof this afternoon, her hands were torn to shit, her back was sore, and something felt broken inside of her. So she was going to salvage her hard work, dammit, and everything in the line of fire beneath the leaks while she was at it.

Her right boot slid a little bit, but she righted her stance in time to get the tarp open. Going down on her hands and knees, she spread the blue covering and stapled it into place as close to the roof's edge as possible. The wind and needle-like raindrops made it almost impossible to see what she was doing, but surely the worst of it would be over any second? The forecast said overcast through tomorrow. They'd all been lied to! Who would be held accountable?

She was being dramatic, but whatever. She was soaking wet on a roof beneath a full moon and there'd been a rocky turbulence inside her since that afternoon. Even before the rain started, she'd been pacing in her living room, unable to sit still. This wasn't right. She shouldn't have this awful foreboding in her stomach because of a man.

It was never like this.

At worst, when she decided her association with a man had run its course, she felt mildly peeved when they didn't try and get back in her good graces. Not that she ever *let* them. But the chance of Wes deciding she was too much trouble . . . it really truly scared her.

He'd hung in there through countless traded insults and arguments. He'd witnessed a near panic attack at Georgie's wedding. He hadn't even flinched at the ugly mark on her neck. Would the blow she'd dealt to his pride be the final straw?

She hadn't wanted to fire him.

He was the Zellweger to her Cruise.

There were feelings. She had feelings.

Bethany adjusted the hood of her jacket so the rain would stop dripping in her eyes and set about laying out the second tarp. She secured one corner, then crawled slowly toward the opposite end of the roof as the blue tarp flapped in the wind. The coarse material of the shingles bit into her knees through her jeans, but she welcomed the distracting pain.

What was it that really scared her about Wes leaving this afternoon and not even looking back once? The slam of his truck door reverberated with such finality. It was the sum of her fears, wasn't it? That a guy would finally know all the negative things about her and leave. Isn't this what she'd been avoiding for so long?

The proof that she was imperfect.

Bethany swallowed hard and picked up the pace of her crawl. Making it across the roof, she applied the final staple. There. Done.

Still . . . maybe she should check for unsecured openings. She'd lost Wes today. She wasn't going to sacrifice all the hard work they'd accomplished together on the house, too. The added blow would be unbearable. Just a few more minutes and it would be perfect—

"Goddammit, Bethany!"

Wes?

She twisted toward the sound of his voice, though she couldn't be sure where it was coming from because the wind was so strong. As soon as her head turned, the rain lashed her in the face and she flinched, dropping the nail gun. She tried to snatch for it blindly, but missed and lost her balance.

Bethany slid on the part of the roof that hadn't yet been tiled, a scream ripping from her throat. There was an unnerving moment of clarity where she realized death was imminent, right before her body went sailing over the edge. In a sudden burst of self-preservation, her fingers caught on the ancient rain gutter and clung, but just like everything else attached to the house, it was too old to be viable and a snapping sound was her only warning before it gave, leaving Bethany dangling from the edge of the broken gutter.

"Wes!"

"I'm here. I've got you, baby. Let go."

"I can't. Are you insane?"

"I won't let you hit the ground, you know that." His voice was stronger than the storm, tunneling inside her and putting down roots. "Come on. I've got you."

It was the biggest leap of faith she'd ever taken. Perhaps she never would have realized that she did, in fact, trust Wes—maybe more than anyone—if she wasn't dangling from the roof like a sodden monkey. But she wholeheartedly trusted that he would catch her and she let go with a squeak. His arms banded around her a split second later, her body colliding with his hard one, and Wes stumbled back a pace. He positioned her more securely against his chest and then he was moving.

Bethany's view of Wes's face was obscured by the hood of her rain jacket, but she saw his leg strike out and kick open the door to the house. He stomped them both inside and set her down carefully in the pitch black, leaving her to shiver and drip onto the floor. A moment later, one of the hanging lights came on across the room, illuminating Wes—and wow, he was pissed.

The masculine planes of his face were highlighted on one side, blanketed by the darkness on the other. His breaths were harsh and uneven, joining the pelting rain as the only two sounds in the room. Besides her heartbeat, that was. The sight of him was so welcome, her heart seemed to be beating even harder than it had been while suspended from the gutter. She opened her mouth to say something, but nothing would come out. What could she say? This buildup inside of her was so unusual and it ached. She had no idea what kind of words it would produce.

Wes had no such problem finding something to say.

He took off his drenched hat and threw it across the room, where it slapped off one of the only finished walls in the house. "Goddammit, Bethany. Of all the stupid—" He pressed a fist to the center of his forehead, slowing his breathing. "I'm rehired. Simple as that. If only to keep you from killing yourself by being stubborn as shit. And it's permanent. You can haul off and fire me as many times as you want, baby, but I'm going to show up every morning like it never happened. Deal with it."

A warm cloak of relief landed on her shoulders, wrapping tight. The assurance that he would keep coming back, even if they fought, even if she freaked out and did something she regretted . . . God, she was already breathing easier. Like she'd had a sandbag on her lungs until now. Her knees started to shake, not from weakness, but with the need to go to Wes. She didn't question the impulse; she didn't have the willpower to quell it this time. Not after he'd shown up here, not after he'd caught her midair, not after she'd missed him so much.

Bethany walked straight into Wes's bristling frame and wrapped her arms around his neck. She was grateful for the rain still decorating her face because it camouflaged the warm, salty tears that fell from her eyes.

His arms wrapped around her tightly and her knees stopped shaking.

"Why did you come?" she asked, laying her cheek on his right pec.

"To put tarp down, same as you," he answered gruffly.

"Even though I fired you?"

He grunted and held her tighter. "You didn't want to fire me."

Bethany shook her head, a few more tears escaping. "No."

"It's behind us now," he said, swaying her side to side. "And if you get pissed at me again in a couple of days and we argue or storm off to lick our wounds, we'll put it behind us then, too."

"How many times can you put something behind you . . . before all those incidents crowd you out the door?"

"We're in construction, darlin'. We'll just build an addition to make them fit."

At that, Bethany teetered and fell messily into love with Wes. Not only because she believed what he said and the sentiment made her feel secure, possibly for the first time ever. But also because he'd said *we*.

We're in construction.

Wes lifted her chin and was visibly gutted by the sight of her tears. "Aw, Bethany." He brushed them away. "None of that, please. I can't take it."

"It's just rain," she said, unevenly.

"Sure, I'll play along." His fingers traced their way down to Bethany's lips and hunger darkened his eyes. "We're going to make a go of this, you and me."

"Are you asking or telling me?"

Humor reshaped his mouth. "All right, I'm asking."

Bethany hesitated in the face of the unknown. She'd never been in a relationship with someone for whom she'd felt this much. As much as she'd started trusting him, the problem was she didn't know if she trusted herself. Her patterns with men had never been so obvious as when she employed them with Wes. Someone she . . . oh God, loved? If she messed this up—and the odds were, she would—it would feel like today had, but in perpetuity.

Worst of all, she risked hurting Wes. Right now, that seemed so much worse than acting as her own worst enemy.

Wes saw her hesitation and visibly regrouped. "We can take it slow, all right?" He nodded on her behalf and dropped his mouth, leaving it an inch above hers. "But you're not going to avoid me. I'm not going to stay where you put me and wait for attention."

"No?" she managed, wetting her lips for the kiss that would surely come any second now. She needed it so badly.

"Uh-uh. When I want attention, I'm going to let you know."

"How?"

One of his hands had been slowly undoing the buttons of her rain jacket. He pushed the sides open now and yanked her dry body up against his soaked one, tilting his hips and breathing into her mouth at the same time. "How's this?"

A barrage of arousal-tipped arrows hit their target beneath her belly button, piercing her with bliss and sexual frustration. God, she'd tried to ignore how much this man turned her on for so long. Now that she'd given herself permission to embrace what he did to her body, her need was even more potent than she realized. Bethany wiggled her hips against Wes's distended fly, biting her lip over the way he groaned. "This is your way of showing me you're willing to go slow?"

"I meant it," he rasped, cradling her hips in desperate hands. "Bethany Castle, my dick has been hard for you since that first morning you climbed out of your Mercedes at that jobsite. All business, no time for anyone to step out of line, especially me." He licked into her mouth, but didn't kiss her, the smooth friction of his tongue causing a melting-butter sensation between her thighs. "Been wanting to prove you wrong ever since. You'll love making time for the way I step out of line. But I'm smart enough to know waiting will be worth the payoff of finally having you naked with your thighs open underneath me."

Oh, brother. On a surge of lust like she'd never known, she pressed up on her toes and kissed him. Her core clenched dramatically over the way he jerked her higher with one arm, shoving the jacket off her shoulders with his free hand before bringing it to her ass and kneading, kneading, his touch slow and possessive.

"How far can we take this and still go slow?" she gasped, letting her head fall back so he could suck and nibble on her neck.

"Long as you let me give this body what it needs, I can remember the boundaries tomorrow," he muttered into her hair.

What if my body needs everything? Right now?

And it did. Her feminine flesh was throbbing and it was

taking all her self-control not to wrap her legs around his hips and grind on him until she hit her peak. Unbelievably, though . . . she wanted to give him fulfillment even more. The way he'd done for her in his backyard, without taking anything in return. Knowing how long he'd spent wanting her from a distance made her desperate to give him relief. There might even have been a part of Bethany that wanted to apologize for scaring him while up on the roof. Whether that mentality was right or wrong, it stoked the flame already flickering wildly inside of her.

Before she could second-guess herself, Bethany took hold of the wet lapel of Wes's button-down flannel and walked him backward. He broke their ravenous kiss, anticipation lighting his eyes. He couldn't quite believe his luck and let her see his humble gratitude. His awe. His eagerness.

When they reached a stack of full cement bags, Bethany teased Wes's mouth while unbuckling his belt and lowering his zipper. His fast breaths could be heard over the storm now and they filled her ears with a sexy soundtrack. She reached into his briefs and circled a hand around his thick erection, loving the choked sound he made while she stroked it hard, nipping at his stubbled jawline. "You're too huge for these fitted cowboy jeans, Wes."

He watched her hand move, a muscle popping in his cheek. "You reckon I should switch to something else?"

"No." Bethany jacked him faster. "I didn't say I didn't like them."

"Baby, baby, baby." He caught her wrist, pushing through clenched teeth, "I've only got about ten seconds left of that."

A pulse boomed in her ears. She was completely and utterly absorbed by this moment, the outside world and her usual insecurities be damned. Her makeup had been washed away by the rain, her hair was a catastrophe—and she didn't even care. None of it mattered when she was being touched by this man. How was such a huge reversal possible? There might have been a trickle of nerves that she wasn't going to live up to his prolonged expectations, but it was a whisper compared to what was usually a roar.

She eased her wrist free of Wes's grip and worked his jeans down past his hips, leaving them gathered at his knees. Oh. Holy hell, the thighs. She'd never seen his thighs out in the open like this and they were rugged, muscular. They belonged on either side of a horse's back or in one of those dusty Wrangler ads. Forget crushing a walnut between them, he could snap a log in half. There was enough hair on them to make her blush, to make her weak-kneed for the chance to feel the tickle of it on her cheeks. And with that wicked vision in her head, Bethany went down on her knees.

"Ah, Jesus, you're really doing this," Wes gritted out, wrapping the hem of his T-shirt in his fist to give her access to his straining manhood—why was that so hot? "I shouldn't let this happen, but that mouth of yours, Bethany. That fucking mouth. I could draw it from memory. I'd die to watch it taste my cock."

His words heaped coal into the already wild fire inside of Bethany, his admission stealing any remaining trepidation. How could she be self-conscious when he wanted her so badly, he looked like he was in pain?

Those thighs called to her and she took her time kissing the rough insides of them, grazing him with her teeth and soothing the sting with long, thorough licks. As she switched to the other leg, she fisted his erection in her hand and pulled him off loosely, needing him to savor the experience, the way she was doing.

Finally, she reached the top of her nibbling hike up his sinewy thighs, treating him to a moment of blistering eye contact before wrapping her tongue around the base of his shaft as far as it would go, dragging her mouth to his engorged head.

Wes fell back on the stack of bagged concrete, the fingers of his right hand burrowing into her hair. "Bethany. Sweet Christ. What are you doing to me with that pretty mouth?" She performed the move again and his abdomen plummeted and flexed. "Ahhh, fuck. Trying to hold on, baby, but I'm hurting."

Talk about a power trip. Who knew it was possible to feel worshipped while on her own knees? But that's exactly how it felt. Instead of doing him a favor, Wes was paying homage to her mouth. She'd only gotten started, too.

Bethany closed her grip around his hard sex and pumped her fist, trailing her tongue through his sensitive slit. When his hips shot up off the concrete bags, his strangled shout echoing through the empty house, Bethany sunk her mouth down as far as possible, until she could feel her throat rejecting his ample size, then sucked her way up to the tip—hard.

Wes rasped her name once, twice, his chest shuddering, and he lost himself in her mouth. Lord, it was the sexiest moment of her life, the way the heels of his boots scraped on the floor trying to find purchase, the fervor with which he clutched the strands of her hair, his straining thighs. If ever there was a moment to believe she could orgasm without touching herself, this was it. Wes was the orgasm.

"Oh my God," he said in between heaved breaths. "Oh my God." Bethany yelped when Wes hauled her up onto his lap sideways. "All this time, I've been so smug knowing I'm going to rock your world and then you just go ahead and rock mine. Not even a polite warning."

A little butterfly danced around in her belly. "Are you waiting for an apology?"

"Hell no." He brushed a hand over Bethany's head and cupped her cheek, an unfamiliar light in those eyes that consumed her face. "I'm waiting to wake up."

Intimacy, the kind where she looked into someone's eyes and experienced unfiltered genuineness, was terrain she'd never walked before. It wasn't a skill she'd mastered, so she started to flounder. "Well." She straightened and laid a hard kiss on his cheek and then started to rise. "Don't think you're going to get special treatment at work tomorrow—"

Wes pulled her back down onto his lap. "Where do you think you're going?"

"I'm— Home," she sputtered.

"Is that so?" he drawled.

"Hmmm."

"No."

"No?"

His palm coasted up her inner thigh, slowing when he reached her center, placing two fingers over the soaked seam of her jeans and rubbing. Firmly. Confidently. Every iota of oxygen in Bethany's lungs whooshed out of her, lust turning the corner on two wheels and roaring down the avenue. She could only close her eyes and let Wes unzip her jeans, sliding his hands inside the denim, as well as her panties.

When his fingers made contact with her wetness, her hips hitched on a moan and heat flared in Wes's expression. "Still want to leave?"

"No."

He shook his head. "No, you don't. You don't want to leave my sight when you're this revved up." His middle and index finger parted her lips and teased her clit with a tight circle. "Not when I can make it so much better."

Her neck blew a fuse, head falling back. Wes's touch left her briefly to strip her jeans and panties off, and then she was naked from the waist down, draped across his lap, in the middle of their jobsite. Not that she could find the brain cells to care at that particular moment. The things he was doing to her with his fingers . . . it was as though Wes could actually read her reactions and interpret them in a way that afforded her more pleasure. Kind of like the object of sex, but this man actually did it, and his perceptiveness on top of her already monstrous attraction to him had Bethany so hot, her skin would surely singe if touched.

"Bethany . . . Jesus, look at you. How are you so fucking beautiful?"

Wes worked her swollen button of flesh between his knuckles, chuckling when her back arched. He cut off his own laughter by bending his head down and licking the tips of her breasts through her shirt—and then. Oh, then he bit down on a nipple and twisted his middle finger up inside of her. At the same time.

Deep.

"Wes, keep doing that," she said hoarsely. "Keep d-doing that."

"I'll do any damn thing you need," he groaned, adding a second finger and raking his teeth side to side over her sensitive nipple. "You want to fuck my fingers, darlin'? Move your hips. Move them around on my lap and feel how hard you've already made my dick again."

Her body followed his instructions before her mind got the chance, her backside writhing on his lap and enjoying the plump ridge of his arousal. Easy. Decadent. Until it became urgent that his fingers stroke her deeper. With her pulse points going off like little alarms, Bethany worked her hips in time with his big fingers. They slid in and out of her, faster and faster until she almost couldn't stand the oncoming pressure of imminent release. It built around her, the way an orchestra might during a piece of music's crescendo.

"Wes," she cried out, clutching at the front of his shirt. "I'm . . . yes. Yes."

The climax rippled through her middle and squeezed her muscles, blew embers at her nerves until she swore she was on fire. Wes pressed the pad of his finger to a secret spot inside of her and rubbed there with quick, sure movements, brewing a scream in the back of her throat.

"Go on, do it. You fucking scream if I make you scream."

She did and the freedom of it made her orgasm luminous and expansive, like she could dive through it and disappear. Maybe she did for a few moments, because when she opened her eyes again, there was only the smell of Wes's neck, the feel of his arms around her, though she had no memory of him pulling her close.

"Okay, so . . ." he began, his voice scratchy. "We'll take it slow starting now."

Bethany laughed, a full, spontaneous sound that was nothing like her usual one. It wasn't tempered or molded into what she thought a pretty laugh should sound like and as a result, it loosened something that had been unknowingly stuck inside of her. Wes's face softened at the sound and she felt . . . lighter.

Without warning, Wes surged to his feet with Bethany still in his arms. "It's your fault for being so irresistible," he said—and promptly blew a raspberry into her neck. Bethany was still slack-jawed when he settled her onto her feet and gave her bare ass a playful smack. "You've convinced me to forgive you for falling off the roof."

Bethany scrambled to get dressed and not ogle Wes's rock-solid buns before they winked out of sight, back inside their household of denim. "So we should maybe, um . . . figure out some ground rules."

"Nope."

She blinked. "Excuse me?"

"No ground rules. I'll try not to maul you on the jobsite,

but after hours . . ." He regarded her for a few seconds. "Just do what comes natural."

"I have no idea what comes natural," she whispered, her fingers tingling.

He came forward and kissed her softly on the mouth. "Figure it out with me."

CHAPTER NINETEEN

Balancing a tray of nachos, popcorn, and cotton candy, Wes and Laura made their way down the concrete tunnel toward the sounds of Travis's amplified voice. It boomed over the loudspeaker in Bombers Stadium and if Wes wasn't mistaken, there was an extra layer of smugness in the ex–professional baseball player's tone this brisk Wednesday evening. Understandable, since the man was fresh off his honeymoon in Italy.

Until the reminder came up on Wes's phone this morning, he'd forgotten about the complimentary tickets Travis had given him for tonight's game. Since neither Wes nor Laura had ever been to a baseball game and the flip was on schedule, he'd popped a hat on her head, bundled her up, and headed to the Bronx.

They sidestepped their way down the packed row and took seats overlooking the third baseline. Out on the expansive green field, the game was already in full swing, the Bombers in navy pinstripes, their opponent in teal. A baseball game was nothing like a rodeo, but the energy of the crowd, the swell of their periodic cheers, brought Wes back to the bull-riding arenas of the not-so-distant past.

Did he miss it?

He glanced over at Laura, who was devouring a cloud of pink cotton candy, and laughed under his breath. No, he didn't miss the past. There was a definite bittersweet spark inside of him knowing those days might never come to pass again. The lack of responsibility, the spontaneity. The cut-and-run mentality that kept him clear of any hurt or disappointment. He'd look back on that wild existence with fondness. But when he thought about bandaging up injuries wrought by being thrown from the back of a bull, he only appreciated where he sat now all the more.

Taking care of this kid could be the biggest adventure of all.

Did it scare him? Fuck yes.

Hell, if he wasn't nervous about potentially raising a daughter, he'd need to get his head checked.

His niece had become a part of his life that couldn't be carved out—and she wasn't the only one. Now there was Bethany.

Yes. There certainly was Bethany.

Wes slipped his fountain Pepsi out of the cup holder and took an icy-cold swallow, ordering himself not to think about Monday night. Not in public sitting beside his niece. He'd have to wait until tonight to remember the way Bethany had looked up at him from her knees.

He removed his hat and swiped a hand through his hair, muttering to himself about wayward thoughts and reckless blondes who fell off roofs. Christ, she'd damn near sent him into cardiac arrest when she'd lost her balance and slid over the edge. He'd still be in that house yelling himself hoarse if she hadn't shocked him into silence with that hug. If she hadn't looked up at him with her huge blue eyes full of tears and relief that he'd come back.

Oh mama, he was in deep.

Deep as the ocean floor.

So deep it scared him. But he could not, under any circumstances, let it show. Because they couldn't *both* be terrified. One of them had to be positive the relationship was going to work, despite their differences and tendencies to avoid lasting commitments. One of them had to be the weight on top of the stack of papers blowing in the wind. So it would be Wes.

He would not let her doubt.

As for himself, he was walking unfamiliar terrain and wasn't totally confident in his ability to catch a snag in the line before it turned into an issue. He'd never felt this way for someone. Nothing had ever come close to this tight sensation in his chest. Urgency to have her nearby. The drive to see her, talk to her, hold her. There was no outlet or relief—it only built.

Wasn't love supposed to be a euphoric rush of moonbeams and dandelions? His relationship with Bethany was kind of like walking through a minefield, but on the other side was the thing he wanted most. Her. Her trust. Her love.

Yeah, he loved her, all right.

Otherwise he wouldn't be opening himself up to what he'd avoided his whole life. Being a quick stop on the way to someone's real forever. He'd gone through it many times growing up and he was only starting to acknowledge the toll it had taken. Bethany was damn well worth facing his fears, though. The faith she'd slowly but surely put in him made Wes feel more equipped to fight for Laura, too. So she'd never have to experience the same hollowness he'd grown up with.

Wes sighed at his niece's sticky hands and sat forward to pull a Ziploc baggie of wet wipes out of his pocket, handing her one. "How's the cotton candy?"

Her wide smile revealed a row of pink teeth. "Good."

He laughed and took out his phone to snap a picture, noticing for the first time that he had a voicemail from an unknown number. Intuition blew a shiver up his spine, but he kept his features schooled. After all, he had a very perceptive kid watching him. Wes took a picture, saved it, and waited until Laura was preoccupied by the happenings on the field again before he put the phone to his ear and listened to the voicemail.

"Hey, it's me." His sister's voice was thin and quiet. "I thought about what you said and I think . . . I think you're right. I'm not sure when I can give Laura the kind of routine she needs. Not with me workin' nights. And I don't want to rip her out of school when she's only started kindergarten. If you still want to be her guardian, I think we should look into it. Not forever, you know? But for now. Just until I can figure some things out." There was a long pause during which Wes could only hear the rapid thumping of his heart, the sounds of the game faded away. "Problem is, I'm going to need the money from the house. I know you've been making the mortgage payments, but I need to sell it now. So . . . you'd have to find a new place with Laura. Look, just give me a call when you have time, okay?"

Wes dropped the cell to his thigh and stared into nothing.

Jesus. How had he overlooked the fact he didn't own the house where he and Laura were living? He'd moved in and taken over the monthly payments and forgotten all about the fact that his name wasn't even on the deed. Now his sister was going to put the house on the market and that left him—and her daughter—without a place to live. How the hell was he supposed to obtain guardianship when the sand beneath his feet was constantly shifting? If he was looking at his life on paper, he would never deem himself a suitable caretaker.

"Uncle Wes, can I have a sip of your soda?"

He swallowed hard. "Nope, you're on water, kid. You need to dilute the half pound of sugar you just consumed."

She threw back her head dramatically. "Water has no flavor."

"Sure it does." Her reluctant interest would have brought a smile to his face if his guts hadn't just been stomped on by an elephant. "Here," he said, uncapping the bottle and putting it in her hand. "Only the most refined taste buds can pick up on it. It's very hard to detect."

Laura nodded gravely and took a long sip. "Oh!" Her eyes flew wide. "I got it. I got the flavor."

"No way." He slapped a hand across his chest. "Almost no one tastes it. You're in a very exclusive club."

She sat up a little straighter. "I know."

They traded a serious nod and went back to watching the game, but Wes's mind was furiously trying to come up with a solution to the new problem that had been dropped into his lap.

Briefly, he thought of asking Bethany for help, but quickly discarded the idea. Their relationship was too new, too fragile to start heaping more onto their plate. If acknowledging that made the earth uneven between his feet, he'd just have to deal.

Wes settled the hard hat on Laura's head and hunkered down in front of her. He was going against his wiser judgment bringing his niece to the Project Doomsday site, but she'd been begging to come see where he and Bethany worked every day. She'd had a half day at school and the camera crew was filming at Stephen's flip today, so he'd left at lunchtime to bring her over for a quick visit before he dropped her off with the babysitter.

"Now remember, don't touch anything. Everything is dangerous."

Laura bounced around on the balls of her feet. "Is Bethany in there?"

"Yes."

A smile spread across her face. Yeah, he could relate.

He smiled every time he thought of Bethany, too. Unfortunately, it was now Friday, and most of the time they'd spent together since Monday night was inside this very house—working, not kissing. Even with the addition of a half dozen interns provided by the network, they were going to come in under the two-and-a-half-week deadline by the skin of their teeth. Bethany's nights had been spent pulling favors with décor companies to get furnishings shipped on time, and his nights had been spent researching guardianship.

Her smiles were all he was privy to lately—and he wasn't complaining about it.

Matter of fact, when he guided Laura through the front door, Bethany turned from her position at the top of a stepping stool and one of those very smiles bloomed across her face. God, he loved her like this, covered in drywall and paint speckles, hair in what he'd started referring to as her Sunday Bun. He was counting the days until this flip was over so he could steal more than the odd kiss between sanding and drilling.

"Hey, Laura!" Bethany called, climbing down off the stepping stool. "You look so official in your hard hat."

Laura beamed, showing off her missing bottom tooth. "Why aren't you wearing one?"

"My head is hard enough. Ask your uncle."

"I plead the Fifth."

Bethany stuck her tongue out at him and if his niece wasn't there, she would have been in trouble. The good kind. She seemed to know it, too. How long had they been staring at each other like there wasn't an unholy racket going on around them?

Bethany shook herself. "So how are Megan and Danielle? I bet you've been planning your next tea party."

"Yup." The little girl leapt in place, landing in a cloud of sawdust. "All the girls in my class are coming to the next one!"

"They are?" Wes and Bethany choked out at the same time.

Laura nodded vigorously. "Uh-huh. I told them they can ride in the back of Uncle Wes's truck and they're going to ask their moms." His niece shuffled in a circle and stooped down unexpectedly. "What's this?"

Wes sidestepped to determine what she was asking about—and it was already too late. She'd closed her grubby kid hand around a small chunk of plywood with a wayward staple sticking out of the end. Laura yanked her hand back and let out a howl that almost struck Wes dead on the spot. "Ow!"

"Why'd you touch that?" He took her wrist and turned it over, his windpipe closing at the sight of blood welling on her pointer finger. "Oh my God. Oh my God, she's bleeding."

"*What?*" Bethany screeched and bumped back into her stepping stool, sending it skittering back on the unfinished floor. "Oh my God. What do we do?"

"I don't know." Was that his hysterical voice? "She's never bled before." His vision winked brightly at the edges. "It's dripping now. *It's dripping!*"

Laura wailed, tears literally squirting from her eyes. Was that normal? Or was that a sign that she was going into shock. Was *he* going into shock?

"Okay. Okay." Bethany slid in front of Laura on her knees and ripped off the hem of her own T-shirt, wrapping it around the cut so many times it looked like Laura had a golf ball perched on her finger. "I . . . maybe . . . I think we just treat her like we'd treat an adult with a cut?"

"I don't know. They must have separate medicine aisles for children and adults in the drugstore for a reason, right?"

Bethany chewed on her lip. "I don't know how long that bandage will hold."

"Jesus." Wes picked up Laura in his arms and turned in every direction, no idea where to set her down. Were they the same blood type if she needed a transfusion? Could he give a transfusion if he was passed out cold? "What do we do?"

"This is my iPad finger," Laura sobbed.

"Your truck. There's a first-aid kit in your truck."

"Okay, yes. Okay." Wes carried Laura out the front door with Bethany right behind him. A moment later, he had Laura settled in the driver's seat of the truck, Bethany having sprinted around to the passenger side to retrieve the kit. She tossed it to him across the console, neither one of them registering the fact that Laura was now making *vroom-vroom* noises and trying to steer the stationary truck.

Holding his breath, Wes slowly unwound the scrap of fabric from Laura's finger and waited for the gore to show itself.

There was nothing.

He could barely make out the faint white line where the cut had been inflicted.

Slowly Wes lifted his gaze to Bethany, who was equally dumbstruck over the lack of bone protrusions and carnage. She let out a puff of laughter and slumped against the doorframe.

"You ripped your shirt," he said dazedly, relief making him dizzy.

"It's just a shirt." She looked at Laura for several beats before giving Wes her attention again, and something important seemed to be occurring in those blue eyes. "It's just a shirt."

Something happened between them in that moment. Sure,

her words weren't intended to have a deep meaning, but as soon as she uttered them, the final line tying him to the past frayed a little more. What came before would always be a part of Wes, but these people and their well-being was what mattered. Having them close so he could care for them when they were hurt. Why would he ever want to run away from that? From being needed by this woman and this child?

"Uncle Wes." Laura evaded Wes when he tried to apply Neosporin to her cut. "Can we take this thing out for a spin?"

He gave up on the Neosporin and pulled his niece into a hug instead. When he gestured for Bethany to join them, she seemed at a loss, but eventually climbed into the car and wrapped her arms around the two of them. And it was new and scary and he couldn't imagine himself being anywhere else in that moment.

Bethany dropped the freshly cut bouquet of roses into her favorite rose-gold Prouna vase and fluffed the stems. They fell into a less-than-perfect order and she was surprised to find herself okay with leaving them that way. Usually, she spent a good six to seven minutes organizing each flower just so in preparation for the Saturday night Just Us League meeting.

Had she really changed so much in the week and a half since starting the flip?

She propped a hip against the kitchen counter and reviewed the last eleven days. She'd gotten messy. Dirt-under-her-fingernails, hair-in-a-sagging-bun, clothes-covered-in-construction-fallout messy.

Somewhere in the middle, she'd given a blow job with her knees buried in sawdust.

Yes, that last one made flower arranging seem a little less pressing.

Thankful for her remaining few moments alone in the house, Bethany closed her eyes and remembered the taste of Wes's rain-slicked mouth, how sure his fingers had been moving in and out of her. God, had that been almost an entire week ago? How had she survived without more of his touch since then? Had he been employing reverse psychology by deciding to move slow? Because the suggestion of a prolonged timeline was making her Horny. With a capital *H*.

Long as you let me give this body what it needs, I can remember the boundaries tomorrow.

Sure, sure. Boundaries.

They needed to have those.

But like, how solid were those boundaries actually? What did they consist of?

The lack of ground rules was making her edgier than an unstyled bouquet of roses could ever hope to do. Maybe she would pay Wes a visit after the meeting. Just to clarify exactly what boundaries meant. No other reason.

Bethany realized she was fanning herself and pushed off the counter, flicking open another button on her blouse while making her final rounds of the house. Throw pillows were all aligned, snacks were placed strategically throughout the space, candles were lit, and the temperature was comfortable.

Standing in front of her couch, she drummed her fingers

against her mouth. Then she reached for one of the white throw pillows, turning it enough to let the small tag show. That itch on her neck woke up, demanding attention, but she ignored it and walked away in triumph. *Look at you. A rebel without a cause.*

Today? Pillow tags and messy flower arrangements.

Tomorrow? Who knew? Maybe she would forgo makeup at the next meeting.

What was responsible for these subtle changes in her? Was Project Doomsday acting as a radical immersion therapy for perfectionists? Or was it Wes?

Despite the attraction she'd nursed for him since he arrived in Port Jeff, she'd made Wes the enemy because he was the only one who saw her flaws. Now . . . now she wanted to be around him more for the very same reason. It made no sense.

None of what was happening with Wes made sense.

For once, though . . . she was considering leaving a relationship unarranged.

Messy.

If she could manage to let fate take its course, would she regret it?

A chorus of excited voices reached Bethany through the door before the doorbell started to ring. She smoothed her hair and made sure her bra straps weren't peeking out of her silver metallic wrap dress. Her outfit tonight was fancy even by her standards, but she'd chosen it mostly because she felt sexy and less because she wanted to impress everyone. It had been a really nice change, slipping the thin material up her freshly showered, bare skin and not being inundated with worries that it wouldn't be the perfect balance of understated and classy.

She'd gotten dressed for herself.

With a secret smile, which was also just for her, she opened the door and let in the milling group of women, greeting each of them with a kiss on the cheek and an inquiry about their job or family. And this time, she was really listening. Their words weren't dulled by the constant buzzing in her brain or pressure to come up with a witty response. She was actually enjoying herself. More than she had in a long time.

Rosie arrived on the heels of everyone, glowing as she always did now that her marriage had been repaired, carrying fogged-up Tupperware containers on her hip. With a fall bite in the air, the evening had a cozy ambiance. Talk of Halloween costumes and Thanksgiving plans circulated in the breeze while Bethany passed out wine and champagne.

For once, Bethany took a moment to savor what she'd built with her sister and Rosie. This club of women that had come together with the sole mission of being supportive of one another. Celebrating accomplishments and consoling each other when they didn't succeed. Bethany had been the one to come up with the initial idea for the Just Us League, but with a newfound clarity, she wondered if she'd done it for the right reasons. Had she hoped everyone else's problems would distract from what was wrong in her own life?

Starting now, she would be more present. She would lead this club with unselfish goals. Except maybe for one. She wanted to be kinder to herself. It would take time. And it might even take longer before she could voice that hope out loud to anyone, but there was a seed germinating and that was more than she had last week.

Wes's smile drifted through Bethany's mind and she found herself sighing dreamily into her glass of chilled champagne. How had he spent his day? She'd picked up her phone to text him several times, but whenever she'd tapped out a message, her old rules had prevented her from hitting send. If she didn't keep men at arm's length, they'd think she was needy. But if she showed too much interest, they might latch on too tight. And around and around she went.

"Rome wasn't built in a day," Bethany muttered, draining her glass and setting it on a leather coaster. She wove her way through the women standing in her living room and took her place at the whiteboard. "Everyone get comfortable," she chirped, uncapping her favorite marker. "Somebody tell me something good that happened this week!"

A local lawyer and longtime Just Us Leaguer named Trinisha put her hand up, sending her bracelets jangling down her umber skin. "I made partner this week. It was a total surprise and quite a few of my colleagues were not happy about being passed over. I started to feel guilty, like I always do, but"—she flicked a wrist—"I earned it."

The applause was enthusiastic, everyone toasting the accomplishment in a series of clinks and congratulations.

One of their newer members, a single mother with a short black bob, raised her hand. "I joined a dating site," she said, blushing. "I haven't been on a date in nine years, but . . . I'm meeting someone for coffee on Monday night."

On cue, everyone launched four hundred questions in her

direction, wanting to know his name, profession, eye color, and astrological sign. With amusement curving her lips, Bethany wrote "hot date" on the whiteboard and waited for the hubbub to die down. "That's amazing. Congratulations." She winked at the single mom. "Let me know if you want to borrow shoes."

"I'm not turning down that offer," the woman replied, still beautifully rosy from all the attention she was getting. "I'll be the envy of the club. We're all dying to get a peek at that collection."

What if it's not as amazing as they hoped?

What if they move something out of place?

"Really?" Bethany tucked some hair behind her ear and leaned into the rising tension in her midsection. "Well, go have a look, everyone. I-if you want."

The entire room went eerily still, before they all scrambled at once. They were up the stairs before Bethany could descend into a panic funnel. She waited with the marker clutched in her hand, telling herself it was stupid to worry what people thought about her shoe collection. But it wasn't really about the shoe collection, was it? It was any extension of herself. Project Doomsday, a tea party, her wall of shoes. How long had she been basing her value on how perfect she could make things *appear*?

The laces in Bethany's chest loosened when awed gasps traveled down the stairs. Her shoulders slumped in relief and only then did she realize Rosie was watching her with concern from the kitchen. Of course Rosie hadn't gone upstairs because she'd already seen Bethany's collection several

times. And wow, there was nothing quite as effective as seeing yourself reflected back in a friend's eyes.

She couldn't allow herself to be like this forever. Now that
she'd made a little progress, she was desperate for more.

Time to cut herself some slack.

Time to start taking more leaps without knowing where
she would land.

Starting tonight.

With Wes.

Bethany opened her mouth to call out to Rosie, but was cut
off when her front door shot wide open. Framed in the doorway was Georgie.

In a gondolier costume and a mustache.

"Buongiorno!"

With Bethany's and Rosie's laughter bouncing off the walls
of the living room, the Just Us League members came careening back down the stairs at a pace that had Bethany mentally
reviewing the details of her homeowner's insurance. Georgie
was wrapped in hugs from members, one by one, as if she'd
been gone for a year, instead of two weeks. Georgie wasn't
quite finished with her gondolier role-playing, however.

With a thick Italian accent, she waved a dismissive hand
at Bethany, demanding an Aperol Spritz and a selection of
cheese, dissolving the room into laughter.

"Get over here," Bethany said, pulling her sister into a hug.
"How dare you make me miss you so much."

"I missed you, too," Georgie responded, squeezing her
tight for a few seconds and then stepping back, a suspicious
glimmer in her eyes. "There's something different about you,

but I can't quite put my finger on it. Has someone else been putting their finger on it?"

"Georgette Castle." Bethany gave Rosie a stern look over her sister's shoulder. "You said you would intercept her."

"I did!"

"Come on. Me and Ro didn't get an ounce of privacy while we were dealing with our man woes. It's your turn, sister friend."

"What is she talking about?" Trinisha wanted to know. "Is it the cowboy?"

"Of course it's the cowboy," someone called. "He won't let it be anyone else."

A collective chant went up. "Details! Details! Details!"

Bethany's instinct was to shut down the interest. She'd only just allowed herself to board the relationship train, but . . . she wanted to share the silly flip-flop in her stomach. She wanted to be the one making a blushing confession because it would be an honest one. A rarity for her, but hopefully not for long.

Leaps. They were a-coming.

She shrugged and studied her fingernails. "The man hiatus is over."

The crowd went wild.

CHAPTER TWENTY

Wes tried to rub the blurred vision from his eyes and focus back on the laptop screen, on which he had approximately fifty browser tabs open. He'd gone from sitting at the kitchen table to lying against the headboard of his bed, hoping comfort might make sense of the legal terminology crowding his brain. In between bouts of reading through New York State's legal requirements for guardianship, he was apartment hunting.

He had a decent amount of money in the bank, but he needed a place fast and didn't want to rush into a house. Apartment it was. Although there were precious little of them in Port Jefferson. Most of the apartments were inside larger private residences or located over commercial stores. If they were nearer to the beginning of summer, he might have had better luck, but apartments were in short supply right now. He'd have to call Stephen in the morning on the off chance he knew of something that wasn't listed on the market yet.

Ordering himself to focus, Wes picked up the laptop and cradled it on his forearm, getting up to pace back and forth at the foot of his bed. If he understood the legalese correctly, he and Becky would need to file a Petition for Guardianship that could be approved or denied. If approved, someone would be appointed to inspect their living situation before they ever went before a judge for final approval, so he needed to get a place for them fast. And how the hell was he going to explain the sudden move to Laura? Or the fact that her mother wouldn't be coming back . . . indefinitely? Distraction wasn't going to work this time around.

A soft knock on the window brought Wes's rapid-fire thoughts to a screeching halt. Bethany stared back at him from the other side.

His feet moved of their own accord, carrying him toward the gorgeous image she made in a billowing silver dress, her light hair blowing in the wind.

Hi, she mouthed, her gaze raking his shirtless torso with interest.

Move, idiot.

Wes turned only long enough to drop his open laptop on the bed and lunged to open the window. Good Lord, without the pane of glass between them, she stole his damn breath faster than getting tossed off a bucking mustang. His cock turned full and hard behind the zipper of his jeans so quickly he almost got lightheaded. "Hey there, darlin'," Wes said, sticking his head out the window. "You forget how to find the front door?"

"No, I just saw the light on and I was worried knocking would wake up Laura." She looked down at her feet. Her bare feet. "Is this a bad time?"

"It's never a bad time for you. I'm just trying to wrap my head around Bethany Castle showing up at my window for a booty call."

She snorted. "This is not a booty call."

It was definitely a booty call, but he'd play her game. "Fine, then. You want to come in here and talk a while?"

"Sure," she said primly, reaching up to take his hand. A zing of electricity raced from wrist to elbow when their skin met and held, giving both of them a moment of breathless pause. Lord have mercy.

It was one of the greatest unexpected pleasures of his life to wrap an arm around Bethany and haul her through his window, carrying her into the room with the cold night air still clinging to her skin and clothes. The tips of her bare toes brushed the tops of his feet and they sunk into the feel of each other with drawn-out sighs humming in their throats.

"You have a few sips at your meeting tonight, baby?"

Her nose and mouth nuzzled the skin behind his ear and he pulled her higher, tighter, so she'd give him more. "Not enough to impair my judgment."

Wes caught their reflection in the top half of the mirror, watched himself breathing in this woman, and knew his life was here. In this room. In this town. All roads had led here—and to her. "How did you get here? Don't tell me you walked in the dark."

"Rosie dropped me off." She seemed to brace herself, tension stiffening her back. "I, um . . . told the club about us."

His heart grew ten sizes that day.

Couldn't she feel it testing the confines of his rib cage?

"If that bothers you, I'll tell them I had too much champagne," she said quickly. "People say silly things all the time at meetings—"

"What exactly did you say?"

Her swallow was audible. "That my man hiatus was over."

"I don't like the sound of that."

"You don't?" she wheezed, looking up at him.

"It makes me sound like the opening ceremonies to the man Olympics." He snuck his hand up the back of her dress and palmed her tight ass. "But I'll be the only one competing in the events from here on out."

She tucked her fingers into the waistband of his jeans, tugging just enough to make his life flash in front of his eyes. "Well. Your . . . javelin is definitely ready." She trailed a single finger down his distended fly and then danced away. "But like I said, this isn't a booty call."

He followed in her tracks like a hungry dog, tugging her hips back up against his lap and growling into her neck. "If that's true, it was evil to show up here looking so beautiful."

"Don't blame me," she murmured, rubbing her butt side to side against his groin. "You haven't even put sex back on the table yet."

Wait. What? Huh? Surely they'd moved past that initial agreement they'd made outside Project Doomsday. Felt like he'd laid down that regrettable gauntlet a decade ago. "What were my conditions for putting it back on the table?"

"When I stopped doubting your honorable intentions."

"Right." He traveled his open mouth up the side of her

exposed neck. "You thought I Zellweger'd so we could sleep together."

"Yes," she rasped. "I did."

"And now?"

"I . . . don't."

Victory tunneling through his bloodstream—*she trusts me*—Wes bunched the hem of her dress in his hands and groaned over the arousing picture she made, her thong-bedecked ass pressed to his bulge. "It's back on the table, Bethany."

She wiggled away. "Good to know." His low growl of frustration was followed by her tinkling laugh. And hell, the lightness in her tonight was kind of worth the pain, wasn't it? Who would have ever thought he'd have this incredible woman showing up at his window without shoes in the middle of the night, primed to tease him into begging? Not him. He sure as shit wasn't going to let a little—okay, a lot—of sexual frustration take away from how far they'd come. How far . . . she'd come.

Wes adjusted his erection and took a seat on the corner of the bed. "What else happened at your meeting tonight?"

She sauntered past, slowly plowing her fingers into his hair and taking them out. Fuck, Bethany was a queen every day of her life, but tonight she'd been transformed into a goddess, almost defying description with her sexual confidence. The last time they'd been intimate, she'd tried to run off before he could satisfy her. He couldn't see this woman trying to do the same. Naw, she looked ready to relish whatever came her way. "I let the tag on my throw pillow show.

And . . . I just let the flowers fall however they wanted. I let everyone go into my closet without me there to make sure they got the optimal effect. This probably all sounds totally ridiculous to you."

His heart turned over. "It doesn't," he said firmly. "But I want to know where this started, baby. What made you think everything you touched had to turn to gold?"

Bethany let a breath out. "It's hard to remember a time when I didn't operate this way. Stephen was the carrier of the legacy, but he made mistakes. Normal kid mistakes. I guess I thought that in these small ways, like dressing impeccably, getting straight As, or having my room organized, I could excel where he couldn't. He was top dog of everything else. Dad's affection. Mom's first-born." She paused, hands wringing at her waist. "It was always a competition, but I couldn't win at sports—I don't do sports. Or construction, because he was always learning at Dad's knee and I was never included. I just overcompensated more and more over time and it got out of control. It spread to everything."

He could see her as a young girl, studying late into the night, hoping a good grade would buy her more attention. Stressing until she got the test back. How easily that might have become a pattern if it wasn't corrected. "I did the opposite. Everything I did was an attempt to prove I didn't care if I got attention from my foster parents. Or anyone. I could go out and get it on the back of a bull. It only ever left me empty, though. Or landed me in the ER."

She dropped her hands. "I have great parents. I was so fortunate. I'm sure I sound so whiny to you—"

"Bethany, stop worrying how you sound or how you're coming across to me. If you're being honest, it's always good."

"That sounds so nice. Someone just knowing you mean well at all times."

"You can always assume that with me." He let that sink in. "And I'm proud of you for fucking with your pillows."

She huffed a bemused laugh. "I notice you didn't deny my whininess."

"You're not whiny, baby."

Pink stained her cheeks, her attention sliding toward the open laptop. "If you were watching porn, it's seriously going to detract from the poignancy of this conversation."

Wes reached for the computer and closed the lid, knowing full well he wouldn't be able to concentrate on anything but her for the rest of the night. He slid it under the bed, assured his browser tabs would be ready and waiting for him tomorrow. "Becky called me during the week. She's agreed to let me become Laura's guardian."

Her hands flew to her face. "Wes. Oh my God. That's wonderful."

He nodded, a little flustered by the wringing sensation in his sternum. "It's going to be a process. I don't even know if I can make it happen. She's selling the house right when I need to prove I can provide a stable environment. It's—" He cut himself off with a blown-out breath. "She's worth the trouble."

"Of course she is." A line formed between her brows. "Why didn't you tell me Becky had agreed to the guardianship?"

Truth was, he didn't want to overload her now, when everything between them was so new. But he kept that to himself, worried his reasons might hurt her feelings. "I just wanted to sound like I knew what the hell I was talking about first."

Bethany seemed happy but not quite convinced by his explanation. "I'll help. I'll help any way I can."

His lips ticked up at the corner. "You're going to be my Zellweger now?"

"It's my turn." She swayed closer until she was standing between his outstretched thighs, her fingernails scratching slow paths into his hair. "You're a good man, Wes. Every time I think I'm finally giving you enough credit, you go beyond it."

This was heaven. Right here. This woman playing with his hair, his mouth on level with her lush tits. Listening to her say words he'd been totally unaware of craving. Even with so much hanging in the balance, he'd never been more whole in his life. He leaned in and kissed the slopes of her cleavage, whispering, "How do I make you stay the night with me, Bethany?"

A shudder traveled through her body. "Oh, I don't think I'll need that much convincing."

Wes massaged his way up the backs of her thighs until they disappeared beneath her dress and clutched her butt, urging her closer until she climbed onto the bed. Straddling him. Their mouths clung during the whole maneuver, not kissing, just accepting and gifting breaths to each other until her pussy pressed down in agonizing degrees onto his erection and they moaned brokenly.

"Wes?"

He drew her into a breathless kiss, rocking her on his lap with shaking hands. "Anything, baby."

"I want you to make hard, messy love to me. I don't want to think."

She'd hardly finished issuing the request when Wes turned and threw her down onto the bed with enough force to make her gasp. Was he forceful because she'd asked him to be? Or because hearing the *L* word on her lips had been like shock paddles to his entire being? He didn't know. But her excited eyes stopped him from asking if she was all right. She was more than all right and wanted more.

"Our first time was always going to be hard and messy, darlin'." He reached up under her dress and ripped the thong down her legs, leaving the skirt bunched up around her waist—and God help him, he almost came seeing her pussy for the first time. It was blond and groomed like the rest of her, like he'd known it would be. But her obvious wetness was what made him hot. "Kind of assumed when we finally got here, it would be hate-fucking at its finest, but that's not what this is at all, is it, baby?" He gripped her sex and squeezed, making her back arch. "What I feel for you is the furthest thing from hate. But you might have a hard time believing that when I'm holding you down pumping like I blame you for this hurting dick."

Wes whipped the belt out of his jeans and tossed it on the floor, the resulting clang creating an army of goosebumps along her inner thighs, her neck. There was a part of him that wanted to make slow, sweet love to this perfect creature, but she needed to be overwhelmed into blanking her mind. He needed to give her that. Needed her to know it was possible. Then he'd prove to her he could do it every time, no matter how fast, slow, or rough they got.

He flipped open the snap of his jeans, lowered the zipper to give himself some breathing room and got down on his belly, appeasing his greed by pressing her thighs open wide. "All those eye rolls and insults. All those fights. I would have gotten down on my knees to lick this pussy in the middle of them all. One word out of your smart mouth and I'd have been panting and lapping between your thighs."

"Wes." She pulled down the bodice of her dress and palmed her tits, pinching her nipples, her hips writhing in front of him on the mattress. "The way you talk. I should smack you, but I love it. I love it."

His thumb traced the slit of her pussy and he watched it blossom open. "I know, baby."

Her laugh was a combination of incredulity and arousal. "Please. Please, j-just—"

A hard, thorough lick of his tongue stemmed the flow of her words, her whimper fueling his drive to please her. Sweet Lord. The flavor of this woman. He'd have chased her for fifty more decades just for the knowledge that she tasted like warm vanilla and turned-on woman. He'd only just buried his tongue in those folds and he was already worried about when he'd get the chance again. Fuck, her smooth texture was going to haunt him until the next time she let him get inside those designer panties.

In his periphery, he could see her hands settle on the comforter for purchase. His goal was to make her grip twist. That's when he'd know he'd found the right spot, the right speed, the right pressure. Jesus, though. It was a challenge to keep his eyes open and watch for those signals, because the taste of her drugged him.

Wes used the V of his fingers to keep her open for his ministrations, occasionally teasing her entrance with his thumb. Oh yeah, she liked that. Those hissed breaths confirmed it. So he trailed his tongue lower and tucked it inside her entrance, twisting his mouth to hit every one of her nerve endings. There. Her hands turned to claws in the bedclothes, more wetness slicking her pussy.

"Yes. There there there. Please."

He hummed to let her know they were on the same page, bringing his thumb to her clit and delivering light, massaging circles while his tongue continued to twist inside of her. *That's it, baby.* She couldn't stay still. Her thighs alternated between hugging the sides of his face and dropping open, little spasms against his tongue telling him she was already close. Where her words had been intelligible before, now they were nothing but syllables in between wails of his name.

His gaze devoured the sight of her heaving body, the fact that she was still wearing her dress while he ate her pussy making him so horny, he could only follow the urges of his body, humping the bed, slamming his hips against the edge repeatedly, rubbing when he found a decent angle. *Don't come. Don't come.*

Easier said than done when she was the hottest thing he'd ever seen. The fact that he knew this woman, that she knew him, and they'd both continued to gravitate toward each other despite fights, flaws, and firings, only made giving her pleasure more of a privilege. Throw in the obscenely delicious taste of her cunt and he was pushing the limits of his control. She had him on the edge with his jeans still on.

"I'm coming," she whispered choppily, then louder. "Oh my God, I'm coming."

Wes pushed his tongue deeper inside of her and worked her clit with his thumb, groaning when he encountered a new flavor. The best one. Her satisfaction. It made his tongue and lips slippery while she thrashed on the bed, her fingers ripping at his comforter.

She was limp and shaking when he managed to tear himself away from the place between her legs. Standing at the edge of the bed momentarily, he retrieved a condom from the nightstand before kicking off his pants and moving over her. He planted his knees on the bed between her legs and slid them wide. Opening her again, but this time for his cock.

There was a light sheen of sweat on Bethany's body, giving her the appearance of a glowing goddess. It rocked him. Humbled him. So much so that he almost fell on her like a starving man without putting on protection. Her fingers danced up the fronts of his thighs, her breath still coming in gusts, watching him with dazed eyes. "Wes," she murmured, shifting like a temptation. "Take me hard. Take me messy."

Thank God he'd gotten the condom in place when she issued that reminder, because he was reasonably sure he'd have thrust in bare. As it was, he dropped down on top of Bethany at the speed of sound, latching onto her neck with his teeth and entering her for the first time with a brutal drive.

He caught her scream at the last second with his left palm, but that was his last sensible action. Animal instinct took over and he was all feeling, all urgency. The viselike grip of her pussy made him thankful for the condom, because he would have busted immediately without it. She was slick, hot, and pulsing around him, making his balls fill with unbearable pressure. Best of his life. Best of the next life and the one after it and he hadn't even properly fucked her yet.

Time to fix that.

Bethany's nails raked up his ass, yanking him into movement and he went. Furiously. "It's a good thing this house has thick walls," he grated against her mouth, slap-slap-slapping his cock into her. "You a little screamer, baby?"

"No," she gasped.

He positioned her legs over his shoulders and bore down hard. "You are now." Jesus. The way she fit him was criminal. He continued to grind down into her hard, searching for spare space to get his whole cock inside of her, but there was none to be had. Didn't stop him from folding her in half, trying to find it—and there. There. She was taking all of him now, so wet and welcoming and snug. "Feels like I've waited my whole life to wreck this pussy, baby," he rasped thickly into her neck. "You have no idea. Knew it would feel like mine."

"It is." Their mouths collided in a series of hard, moaning kisses. "It's yours."

"I feel like yours, too?"

"Yes. Oh my God, yes."

Possessiveness had his teeth snapping at the pulse in her neck, had him throwing her legs back down and open on the mattress, his lower body pistoning, his mouth everywhere he could reach. Raking her neck, sucking at her nipples, on her mouth.

"What was that shit you used to worry about?" He licked a path between her bouncing tits. "Is the guy present during sex? Fuck yes I am. So are you. Your lighting makes me want to eat you alive. And I don't have a dog."

At the way he repeated back the words she'd spoken to him at the wedding, her eyes flared and he saw love in them. He saw it, goddammit, and he reeled it into his chest, braiding it with the love he felt for her. The amazing weight of it made him weak for a split second and Bethany used it to her advantage, rolling him onto his back without breaking their connection.

"You really do listen when I speak," she said breathily. "Now you're in trouble."

He lifted his hips and watched in awe as Bethany stripped off her dress, giving him the view of the fucking century. Bethany Castle, beautifully naked, sitting on his dick. Not to mention looking at him as if he'd been a very good boy. Someone up in heaven loved him. "I don't mind this kind of trouble." He rolled his lower back, lurching her up and back. "Ride it, darlin'. Make us come."

Using his shoulders for balance, she slid her sex up and down his shaft, testing the pressure, once, twice, oh . . . fuck. And then she fell onto his chest and started bucking her hips, stirring up that final kind of pressure at the base of his spine. "Ah, Christ. I'm not long for this world." He slapped his hands down on her ass cheeks and aided her movements roughly. "Don't stop. Don't stop."

Bethany, ever the overachiever, did that thing he'd only ever seen in porn. She curved the tops of her feet around his knees and worked him like a fucking pogo stick—and he couldn't last longer than ten seconds. Not with her mouth open with pleasure, her breasts shaking, and her pussy quickening around him, like she was going to come agai—

There she went, her fingernails scoring his chest, her body dropping down to rub and grind its way through her climax. It was too much, seeing her get outside of her head and take. Take from him.

He went hurtling through the sky, though he couldn't see any of his surroundings with blind eyes. Only knew he was wrapped in never-ending vastness and his body was a slave to relief. Fuck. Fuck. God. The draining of his need seemed to go on forever, ripping at his muscles and throat. Was that him growling like an animal?

Yes. And that was Bethany moaning brokenly into his neck, her sweaty body depleted on top of him. He was back down on earth again, but he was somehow still in heaven, too. Because she was there.

They lay there like that for long minutes, their breathing and heartbeats synced, bodies reshaping to fit each other.

Finally, responsibility knocked and Wes eased Bethany onto her side, kissing her shoulder before disposing of the condom.

Moments later, he returned to the bedroom to join Bethany, wondering how fast she'd climbed back into her head and already eager to help her crawl back out.

She was on her side, watching him with wide, unblinking eyes. "Hey."

Wes got into bed, pulled the woman into his chest, and kissed her hard on the forehead. "Hey. You were incredible. I'm a ruined man. I've never come that hard in my goddamn life. And you can go back to overthinking everything in the morning."

Her tension remained for another six seconds, then she wrapped herself up in Wes, like he was her favorite blanket, and passed out cold.

Afraid to shatter the perfection of the moment, the night, he whispered, "I love you," into the darkness.

CHAPTER TWENTY-ONE

For the first time in her adult life, Bethany woke to the sound of a child's voice. It was distant at first, kind of muffled—and then it was very loud and right in her ear.

"Elsa!" shrieked the child. "Uncle Wes, did you have a sleepover?"

Oh my God.

Oh my God.

Bethany's eyes flew open, determining from the shafts of sunlight painting the wall that it was well past her usual wake-up time of six A.M. Morning yoga: missed. She'd fallen asleep last night in Wes's bed. No, wait. What was that? An arm draped over her hip. Her naked hip? Those fingertips were dangerously close to the Promised Land and there was a child in the room. His niece. How were they going to explain this to her? How was she going to explain this to herself?

Wes set loose a smoky laugh in her ear, and abruptly, the building funnel cloud inside of her disintegrated. She let herself feel the flannel sheets—such a male choice—against her skin. She let herself enjoy the protective way his chest pressed to her back and the waft of pleasure that traveled up her spine when his fingertips brushed her tummy. One by one, her muscles relaxed and her pulse slowed.

"Before you turn over," he whispered into her ear, "I don't care about your smeared mascara and morning breath."

A smile had only begun to curve her mouth when Laura demanded her presence be acknowledged—by jumping on the edge of the bed.

"Uncle Wes, can we get a cat? Megan and Danielle have two cats and we don't have any. What are we doing today? What did you do at the sleepover?"

Wes's body vibrated against Bethany's, his low, scratchy morning laughter instantly becoming one of her favorite things about him. A thing she never would have known about unless she'd taken a leap. "Kid, can you do me a favor? There's a lollipop in the kitchen junk drawer. If you can find it, you can have it."

She was already sprinting down the hallway.

Bethany rolled over onto her back and got her first glimpse of sleep-mussed Wes. Wowza. Definitely worth missing yoga. Talk about a feast for her feminine senses. His strong, rangy body was outlined by sunlight, leaving his face shadowed but highlighting the pop of his shoulder muscles and triceps, the out-of-place hair. In a word, he was glorious. Perhaps the best part of all was Wes cataloguing the sight of her, the same way she was doing with him. "Lollipops for breakfast?" she managed.

He kissed her shoulder with a delicious scrape of morning beard. "I don't want to rush you, darlin', but we have about forty-five seconds to get dressed before she comes back."

They both sprung out of bed in a flurry of single-footed hopping and limbs thrown through openings in their clothes. They laughed when their eyes met across the bed and they were still laughing when Laura walked back into the room with a Dum Dums stick poking out of her mouth. "What?"

Wes sighed. "Bethany tooted."

She sputtered. "I did not!"

"What's the rule, Laura?"

"If you denied it, you supplied it," she said, giggling around her sucker. "Elsa tooted." The little girl sobered, whispering, "Did ice come out?"

Wes collapsed backward onto the bed in stitches and his niece took that as her cue to climb onto his shaking form. He immediately turned the tables, tossing the child sideways and tickling her ribs until she screamed.

Was Bethany seriously smiling over being accused of an ice fart? Growing up, being accused of a fart was grounds for assault among her siblings. Being accused as an adult was unheard of. But she was giggling uncontrollably now and she couldn't stop. Her vanity was on the couch requesting smelling salts, but she couldn't really find it in herself to care.

"Should we let her have pancakes, anyway?" Wes asked Laura.

"Pancakes," Laura hollered, flying back down the hallway toward the kitchen. As soon as they were alone again,

Wes rose from the bed and padded toward her in nothing but jeans and sunlight—and all sorts of visions from the night before rolled in like sexy hot rods. Best sex of her life? Um, putting it mildly, maybe. If her notions about sex were baseballs, Wes would have smacked them out of the park last night, into the lot where they'd shattered several windshields.

She'd definitely never had an orgasm from cunnilingus. Until last night, she didn't even like it. *Not for me*, she used to say with a mental shrug. So what?

The way he'd gone about it with such confidence and relish, like he'd been dying for the opportunity to pay her the sexual favor . . . that alone aroused her to a fever pitch. But then. God. What he'd done with his tongue. Inside of her.

"Bethany."

And then his penis.

"Bethany," Wes prompted again, stooping down until they were eye level. "Don't know if you've noticed, but we've got a five-year-old on the loose. Put that blush away before I start crying."

"Got it," she rasped, accepting a sweet kiss on the mouth, the forehead, the side of her chin. "Do you have chocolate chips for those pancakes?"

"Damn right I do." He snagged her hand and pulled her from the bedroom, like they'd done it a million times. "But be prepared for the fallout."

There was indeed fallout, not only from the sugar-high-inducing breakfast, but also from their night spent together. And that fallout was . . . happiness. It was kind of like trying on a brand-new pair of shoes at the store. She was walking around in them and they looked fabulous, but there was a little buzz of worry in the back of her mind that as soon as she wore them to work, they'd give her a blister in a place she wasn't expecting. Then where would she be? Hobbling around in a pair of deceptive shoes with blood oozing from a nasty cut.

Still, being with Wes in his kitchen felt so good. They laughed out of sheer silliness and came up with new ideas for the next tea party. When Laura eventually passed out on the couch from her sugar-induced hysteria, Bethany sat on Wes's lap in the backyard, wrapped in a blanket, and talked about the final-stage ideas for Project Doomsday.

Now that the layout and structure of the house had taken shape, she wanted a built-in banquet just off the kitchen and a skylight in the dark hallway. She was confident and talking to Wes about her ideas was so easy. He didn't discount anything she said, but he didn't yes her to death, either. He was genuine and insightful and they were dating.

That's what this was.

Her former enemy was now kind of on the way to being her boyfriend.

Actually, it seemed like more than that, somehow. "Boyfriend" sounded trivial compared to the way Bethany felt snuggled to his chest in the backyard or accepting a forkful of pancakes from him while leaning against the kitchen counter. The way he'd kissed her when they said good-bye on Sunday afternoon had been a stamp of definite ownership from which she was still reeling.

Now, on Monday morning, Bethany stood in the back-yard, watching Slade film promos through the giant space that would eventually contain a sliding glass door leading directly outside. Around her, the landscapers were hard at work, sectioning off flowerbeds and laying down sod. They'd arrived over the weekend to cart off a forest's worth of dead foliage and the results were amazing. Who knew they'd find an actual yard under all that excess nature?

To keep the job cost effective, Bethany had chosen stamped concrete for the back patio and it had just been poured. Two men were on the far side of the freshly dumped concrete smoothing it out with metal tools. Ollie was walking around the yard, shadowing one of the landscapers, with his wife on speakerphone giving what sounded like a whole lot of unsolicited advice about planting azaleas. Carl, as usual, was picking through the craft service table.

The job was coming along at a breakneck pace. Saturday they would announce the winner of *Flip Off*. She had no idea if it would be her and Wes. None whatsoever. But little by little, she was no longer feeling like a fraud.

"Hey, darlin'," Wes murmured, approaching from the side of the house where he'd been sawing lumber for her banquet. He gave her a long, hard once-over that made her nipples pucker inside her tank top. "God Almighty, I almost forgot for a second how beautiful you are. What's your policy on kissing in front of the cameras?"

"I already told you," she breathed, backing up.

He kept coming until the tips of his work boots bumped hers. "I forgot."

"My parents are going to watch this. Everyone is. They're not going to take me seriously if you're mauling me when we should be working. I can hear them all now if we lost. 'Well, maybe if they weren't so distracted, they'd have won.'"

"We'd win regardless," he said quietly, seemingly memorizing her features. "What are you doing standing out here, anyway?"

She pointed a toe at the house. "They kicked me out so Slade could film his update. Hopefully he'll be done soon; I really need to get back to sanding the master bedroom walls."

Wes grumbled a little with mock irritation until she poked him in the ribs to make him stop.

Turning his back to the house, he leaned down to speak directly above her ear. "I need to be alone with you, Bethany," he said gruffly. "Need you back underneath me so bad. I can't believe I've only been inside you once."

The string attached to all of her erogenous zones pulled taut in a way she'd never experienced. She'd been turned on plenty of times in her life. God knew she'd found the very bottom of internet porn during her self-imposed man hiatus. This was different. Her body was so awake and greedy, she didn't think it would be possible to deny this man ever again.

Her skin longed to soak in his heat, to be a victim to his teeth and weight and angst. With him standing so close to her, whispering her nerve endings into a flurry, she wanted this man she trusted to love her body without constraints or rules spoken aloud or time limits.

No time limits. That would have terrified her before.

Even now, a finger of apprehension traced up her spine, telling Bethany her worst flaws would show through over the passage of time, but she ignored it.

Wes studied her face and looked as if he wanted to say something else, but Slade's voice carried closer and he snapped his mouth shut. A playful twinkle entered his eye, though it didn't fully eradicate the lust. "Want to mess with him?"

Lightness blew through her chest. "How?"

He winked and crouched down, picking up a small stick from the lawn. He checked to make sure the patio guy's back was turned.

And then he drew a giant penis in the wet concrete, complete with smiley face.

"Wes," Bethany hissed. "I can't believe you did that."

Wes rose and tossed away the stick, then quickly wrapped an arm around her waist to pull her up against his body. He walked around to the side of the house and positioned them behind a pine tree. "Oh, come on. Yes, you can."

Trying not to laugh, she hid her face in his shoulder. Slade and the camera crew were slowly making their way to the backyard. They had a matter of seconds before Wes's handiwork was discovered. Tops. "Oh God. Oh God. They're going to see it. Smooth it back out. Do something—"

"If you'll recall, when we first arrived at Project Doomsday, the backyard was more like a jungle," came Slade's voice, his boots scraping to a stop at the very edge of the bedroom entrance. Bethany clutched the front of Wes's T-shirt and waited, a burst of laughter stuck in her throat. "Thanks to some extreme landscaping and Bethany's executive decision to save some cash with stamped concrete, the backyard living space is really starting to come together now. I can see the new homeowners enjoying many a margarita—" Slade cut himself off. "Oh. Uhhh. That's . . . not part of the design."

Bethany snort-giggled and Wes shushed her through his own shoulder-shaking laughter.

"All right," shouted the director. "Who drew the dick?"

She lost it, stumbling into Wes and knocking him backward into the side of the house. He caught her, both of them unable to hold back their amusement. At some point, they stopped laughing and just stared at each other, smiles fading. Need washed over her like foamy ocean water warmed by the sun—and it wasn't the kind of desire that could be delayed or tempered. No. It was big and overwhelming and glorious.

"I need you," she breathed. "Right now."

His lids hid his eyes momentarily. "Thank God." He chewed his lip, seeming to consider their options. "You trust me?"

"Yes," she said without hesitation.

A corner of his lips went up, his warm hand caressing the side of her face. "Good." His touch dropped to Bethany's wrist and he tugged her into the backyard, right into the throng of interns and cameramen—and Slade—who were gaping at the cement dick. "Wow," Wes said, stepping over the wet cement onto the set of stairs that led into the bedroom, helping Bethany up behind him. "You people will do anything for ratings."

The director glared. "Everyone take lunch," he muttered. "Can we get this dick cleaned up, please?"

They jogged side by side down the hallway of the house, both of them bursting at the seams with pent-up laughter. When they reached the bathroom, Wes hustled her inside and locked the door behind them. The new fixtures hadn't been installed yet, so the only light in the small room came from a sliver beneath the door. And that was a shame, because Bethany wanted to see him. She didn't want to close her eyes and just get through it, she wanted to revel in them being together like this. Breathless and horny and lacking any shame.

Wes wasted zero time pinning her to the far wall, their hands knocking together in their haste to get his pants unzipped. Judging that he had that vital part under control, Bethany scrubbed her palms all over his abs, going lower and fondling his beefy erection through his jeans. "Oh my God."

"What?" he rasped, stooping down long enough to yank off her yoga pants and panties, casting them aside into the darkness. A foil packet ripped, followed by the sound of latex unrolling. This was happening. They were really doing this. Having sex in a house full of people.

The illicitness of it only drove her urgency higher.

Who was she anymore?

"You just . . ." She responded to his pressing mouth, voice thready with unabashed honesty. "You get so hard so fast."

On a muffled groan, Wes boosted Bethany up against the wall. No sooner had she slung her legs around his hips did he clap a hand over her mouth and drive his thick shaft inside of her. Without an ounce of gentleness. Her eyes filled with tears from the sheer pleasure of the rough invasion. Oh, it felt so good. Incredible. She'd been more than ready for him and she loved that he hadn't made her wait. No games between them. Just giving and taking.

"Say that again," Wes demanded at her ear, slowly removing his hand from its position over her mouth.

"You get so hard so fast," she said in a rush, biting down on her bottom lip to trap a moan, because he was moving, moving, his hips rolling like a well-oiled machine.

"That's right." He wedged his hands between Bethany and the wall, taking tight hold of her bare butt, grinding into her and holding himself deep. "You're not complaining about my age anymore, are you, darlin'?"

"No," she gasped.

"No," he echoed on a groan, pumping his sex into hers slowly, snagging her top lip with his teeth. "The better to serve you with, Bethany."

A spasm caught her off guard, her intimate muscles squeezing around him. With enough force to make her suck in a shaking breath. "Don't stop." She wrapped her legs tighter around his moving hips. "Please. Please. I've never been this wet in my life."

Wes growled into the crook of her neck and his drives turned frenzied. "Fuck. You did not just say that to me. I'm going to blow so fast, baby. You have to come. You have to come."

Knowing Wes was teetering on the edge just like her was

intoxicating. She almost couldn't withstand the pressure building between her legs, his size increasing every time he entered her. Preparing for release. They were two straining, naked bodies in the dark, desperate as beggars.

She clawed at his neck, pulled his hair, dug her heels into his thrusting ass. There was no staying still when the huge stalk of his sex was rubbing her clit relentlessly and his finger was brushing the untouched ring of her back entrance, teasing it, jiggling it. God. God.

Voices passed in the hallway, the floor creaking. Even the bathroom door handle squeaked like someone was trying to turn it and Wes didn't stop. He fit their mouths together and kissed her like they'd never get another chance. His tongue moved in time with his lower body and it was too much. Sensory overload.

Wes's tempo turned bruising and Bethany's thighs trembled uncontrollably from their perch on his hips. "I'm going to," she whispered, clinging to his shoulders like a starfish to a rock. "I'm . . . ohhhhhh. Now now now."

"Ah Jesus, thank fuck," he confided hoarsely, slamming into her, relentlessly. "The pussy is too good, baby. I can't hold it back."

"Hard," she breathed, tunneling her fingers through his hair and yanking his mouth down to hers, gratified by the animalistic way he attacked her lips. Her climax signaled its imminent arrival with hot pulses that grew more and more intense. "Put it in me hard."

"Christ. Shut your perfect little mouth, Bethany. I'm trying not to rip the fucking condom," he gritted, but he pummeled her faster and harder regardless, his lips moving over hers, tasting, their tongues lapping and tangling. His hold on her butt turned brutal, using his grip to yank her down into his drives—and his ferocity flipped a switch inside of her, pleasure pouring into her midsection and flooding lower, pressure building to the point of pain before imploding. "Goddamn," Wes ground out, pressing her tight to the wall with his hips, his strong frame shaking violently. "God, baby," he pushed through gritted teeth, breath catching. "Beautiful woman. So beautiful, you know that? You make me come so hard."

They kind of just melted off the wall, Wes's arms coming up around her, his recovery breaths blowing around the hair at her temple. His sex slipped free of her and she immediately missed the connection, but was appeased when his thumb found the base of her neck and massaged circles there, his lips beginning to press kisses to her hairline. Reverently. Anticipating her need for reassurance before it even arose. And that consideration, that caring made the love inside her spout like a geyser.

It shook her with its strength.

Say it. Say you love him.

It had to be too soon to say those words. Eons too soon. They'd barely warmed to the idea of dating each other exclusively. What if she felt more deeply for Wes than Wes felt for her?

No, it was best to move slower.

Keep her finger on the pulse of reality and make sure Wes felt the same way about her before she revealed her feelings. Still . . .

Her heart ached to do something. To express the wild feeling inside of her.

She couldn't seem to suppress it.

"Bethany?"

"What if you and Laura move in with me?" Thank God for the darkness. As soon as those words came out of her mouth, she felt the magnitude of them and panic crammed like a fist into her throat. His face was probably a mask of utter horror. She couldn't even hear him breathing. Was he dead? Yes, probably from shock and fear of his bunny being boiled. "I meant like . . . l-like purely as a kind of business arrangement. You need a place to live and, well, you said the court will need to confirm the stability of her living environment and I just thought, you know, my house fits that bill. And I have two extra bedrooms no one is using. It just seems like, I don't know . . . I don't know."

"A business arrangement," Wes said slowly.

Grateful he'd spoken at all, Bethany continued in a rush. "Well, of course. I mean, we're not like, moving in together. That would be lunacy. This soon . . ."

Wes was silent for long moments. "I need to see your face while we're having this conversation, Bethany."

Was that a no?

The possibility of rejection clamped around her windpipe.

Oh God, she was getting dizzy.

She slid down the wall and felt around for her underwear and yoga pants, listening to the clang and zip of Wes fastening his jeans, disposing of the condom. The silence was stifling until the roar in her ears filled it. As soon as the door opened, she was going to make an excuse and go spend the afternoon hiding in her closet with a bottle of tequila. What in God's name had she been thinking?

Wes beat her to opening the door and his expression turned shocked at whatever he saw on her face. "Oh Jesus," he chuckled, catching her around the waist before she could flee. "Nope. You're staying put."

"I have to go—"

"You could, but I'd just chase you down."

Her mouth snapped into a straight line and she stared at his shoulder, willing her heart to stop doing cartwheels. "What?"

"What?" He tipped her chin up so she could witness his incredulity. "You asked me to move in with you and then you called it a business arrangement. About thirty seconds after we burned the fucking world down. Sue me if I can't figure out where the hell we stand."

"I just know I want to help," she whispered.

Wes scrutinized her face. "Is that the only reason you want me there?"

Of course it wasn't. Not only did she love the man, she adored the child. But exposed and vulnerable, Bethany could only give the slightest shake of her head.

It must have been enough, because affection kindled in Wes's eyes. He leaned down and kissed her forehead, saying, "I can work with that."

CHAPTER TWENTY-TWO

The Suffolk County Clerk's Office was quiet on a Tuesday afternoon. Wes stood outside turning his hat over in his hands, searching the parking lot for his sister. He'd offered to pick her up at the train station, but she'd opted to make her own way there, which made him nervous as hell. She'd agreed to meet him to file the Petition of Guardianship, but she wasn't reliable on her best day.

Come on, Becky. Come through just this once.

When he'd left, Bethany was hard at work on Project Doomsday laying tile in the bathroom, and he'd told the producer he was going out to grab some lunch. It didn't sit right with him, leaving without telling Bethany where he was going. Hell, he *wanted* her there. Badly. But she was already a deer in the headlights after her shocking offer to move them into her house yesterday, so he was forcing himself to give her some breathing room. Enough to relax her, but not enough to let her think he was going anywhere.

Yeah. Bethany Castle definitely had him walking on a tightrope.

Good thing he didn't want it any other way.

The woman was in his blood. He understood her a little more every time she let her guard drop, and those occurrences were becoming more and more frequent. He got the feeling she was terrified of him and magnetized by him, all at once. The same was true for him.

Love was open-heart surgery without anesthesia.

But he couldn't stay alive unless Bethany sewed him up with a shiny new ticker. One that would be bigger and hardier because it contained her love. Until then, he was just fighting for his life on the operating table.

He started to pace on the sidewalk, twirling his hat around and around on his index finger. He thought of Bethany as he'd left her, covered in grout, a line of concentration between her brows, that sweet tush in the air.

Okay, love wasn't all a touch-and-go operation.

There was the I-see-Jesus sex.

There was the way she'd become his best friend. The person he confided in.

The giggle she'd developed for him—just for him—was worth the niggling worry that she would change her mind. That she could move him and Laura into her house and get sick of him. He was trying so hard not to think of Bethany's house as the fifteenth home he'd lived in, but that's what it was. The doubt in his gut didn't much care that the woman he loved resided there. It only wanted to whisper in his ear that living with her would be temporary, like everything else.

But his heart said trust her. *Trust what you feel*.

Lord knew if there was an apartment in Port Jefferson available, he would consider taking it and giving Bethany more time to get used to him. To the fact that he was in this for the long haul. Not only being Laura's guardian or a Port Jefferson resident, but her man. *I am her man.* They were on an accelerated timeline and the possessive son of a bitch inside of him liked that, because the sooner it was understood by God and everyone that they were a couple, the sooner he could stop having nightmares about her dropping him for some appropriately aged chump with a seven-figure bank account.

A growl scraped around in his throat.

He slapped the hat down on his head and snatched the cell out of his jeans pocket, hitting Bethany's number on his favorites list. She answered on the second ring, the sound of power drills singing in the background.

"Hi."

Damn, she sounded so sweet. Did she miss him? He had been gone almost a full forty minutes, including the drive and the wait.

Christ. Listen to yourself. You're a goner.

"Hey," he said, willing firmness into his tone. "Is that offer to move in still good?"

"Yes, of course."

His heart got a running start and tackled his lungs. "Good. But let's get one thing straight, darlin'. I'm not sleeping in my girlfriend's guest room. You're getting me in your house and your bed, or nothing at all."

Bethany was silent long enough to make him sweat. "I think I can agree to those terms." Was that a smile in her voice?

The weight flew from his shoulders. "All right, then."

"Wes?"

"Yeah, baby?"

"What would you have done if I'd called your bluff?"

Admiration spread like butter in his chest, his mouth forming a slow smile. "Moved in anyway and seduced you."

There was that beautiful giggle. "Oh yeah? How?"

"Fought with you until you realized you're crazy about me," he drawled. "That method seems to work on you like a charm."

"You might be right," she murmured after several beats. "I was thinking you could bring some things tomorrow night after work. I should have the rooms ready by then."

"Room, Bethany. Singular."

"Oh yeahhh, that's right. Almost forgot."

He relaxed when he heard the cheeky smile in her tone. "Close the bathroom door until I get back. Your butt looks insane in those pants."

"Chauvinist."

"What's mine is mine."

She groaned, but he heard the door shut.

"What's yours is yours, too, Bethany. You going to hang on to me?"

Wes hung up before she could answer. He was afraid to hear a single note of uncertainty, worried what it would do to him. Hanging up without saying good-bye bothered him, however, so he started to dial her number again—but that was when a shadow darkened his shoes and he looked up to find his sister.

Slowly, he put away the cell phone. "Are you ready?"

"Yeah." She nodded jerkily, but he could see in her eyes that she'd realized letting him be Laura's guardian until she got back on her feet was the right thing to do. "Yeah, I'm ready."

A while later, when he signed the documents, he put down Bethany's address as Laura's permanent residence and ignored the feeling of diving without a parachute.

Wednesday wasn't so much a moving day as it was Wes and Laura throwing duffels into the back of his truck. Most of the things inside the house belonged to his sister, and at some point, he would probably need to help her move them, but as for his own possessions? There weren't many. He'd arrived in Port Jefferson with his wallet, some clothes, and a cowboy hat. Not much had been accumulated since then.

He'd come home last night after filing the papers with the county clerk and told Laura they were moving into Elsa's ice castle, but it had been disguised as a house to keep her powers a secret. At the time, she'd laughed and seemed excited. Now that they were en route, though, she was clutching her teddy bear a little too tightly, so instead of going straight to Bethany's house, he drove to Main Street and parked in front of the ice cream shop.

Wes unhooked her from her booster seat and held her hand on the way inside, letting her order an extra scoop with rainbow sprinkles and gummy bears. They sat in the window quietly for a few minutes while Wes tried to figure out how the hell to approach the topic of her obvious stress.

Two females and their complicated minds were going to kill him.

He could already tell.

"Hey." He nudged his vanilla-chocolate swirl across the table. "You want to try mine?"

"No."

He retreated. Took a few more bites. "What are you thinking about?"

"Nothing."

Inwardly he sighed. Looked like he would have to give a little of himself to get the truth out of her. Confiding in people was something he'd once avoided at all costs. Who wanted others knowing they had sore spots and weaknesses? But getting to know Bethany, Stephen, Travis, and Dominic had made him realize . . . everyone had weaknesses. They just came in different sizes and shapes. Maybe he could impart some of that wisdom on his niece. "You know, this is going to be the fifteenth house I've lived in."

She almost dropped her spoon. "Really?"

"Uh-huh."

"How many have I lived in?"

"I think this will be three or four, kid. But you know the good news? You're never going to catch up with me. Least not until you're an old lady with a cane. Maybe not even then, because I'm not going to let that happen." He paused, searching for the right words. "I know when I got here, it seemed like I was going to leave. That's what I was used to doing. But you had to go and be wonderful. My plans changed and they include you now."

A spark of joy went off in her eyes, but it faded little by little and she continued to tap her spoon against the tip of her ice cream mountain. "I want to move. I'm happy we get to live with Elsa."

Wes frowned. Didn't see that one coming. "Explain the pout, then."

"I'm not pouting," she exclaimed, rearing back.

He held up his hands. "My mistake."

They went back to eating silently for a while, but Wes could see she was working on whatever she wanted to say. "This means my mom isn't coming back."

His spoon slowed on its way to his mouth. "She wants to come back, Laura. This just means she needs more time to do it."

Slowly, she laid down her utensil and stared at the table. "It makes me feel bad to be happy."

It took him a beat to untangle that, but understanding dawned. "Ah. I see." He swallowed. "You feel guilty for not wanting your mom to come home."

She shrugged her tiny shoulders. "It's just better now. With you."

Wes chose his words carefully. If he'd learned anything from Bethany, it was that women didn't always need a solution, they just needed to get shit off their chests. His niece definitely didn't need to hear she was wrong for thinking a certain way, but he wanted to help absolve her of the natural guilt all the same. "Hey."

Laura glanced up. "What?"

"Did you know that only good people can feel guilty?"

She quirked a skeptical eyebrow, but he had her attention.

"It's true. Think about it. You feel guilty because you think your feelings might hurt your mom if she found out." He waited for her reluctant nod. "If you were a bad person, you wouldn't care if you hurt someone else."

"Oh," she murmured. "But it would still hurt her."

"Maybe. Yeah. But it's not your job to make other people happy, kid. Especially not the people who are supposed to be making you happy." He leaned back in his chair and gave her a narrow-eyed look. "Unless you want to let somebody sleep past six A.M. once in a while. That would be totally acceptable."

Finally, he caught the ghost of a smile, but her eyes were still troubled.

"Tell you what," he said. "I think it's okay to be happy we're moving in with Bethany. Why don't you let yourself be happy for now, as long as you give Mom a chance when she's able to come back? Does that seem fair?"

"I still won't want to. Because . . . if she comes back, you'll leave."

"No." He shook his head, mostly at himself, for neglecting to find the root of the problem sooner. He hadn't realized Laura was afraid of him leaving, because no one had ever really been afraid of that before. "I'm sticking around either way, Laura. This is my home now. With you."

Tears flooded her eyes. "And Elsa?"

"Yeah." His own voice was a little scratchy. "And Elsa."

Hopefully.

Laura hopped out of her seat and ran toward him around the table, wrapping her arms around his neck. "I love you."

A knot formed in his throat. "I love you, too."

"Can we go to the ice castle now?"

He laughed, trying to be inconspicuous about swiping at his eyes. "We'd better. It's rude to keep princesses waiting."

Wes was not supposed to be the nervous one. Bethany had enough nerves for the both of them. Not to mention, he needed to be confident for his niece's sake. He didn't want to present some mirage of stability for the courts—he needed it to be true.

But he probably should have paid a visit to Bethany's house prior to moving in because he was not prepared. It was like stepping into a *House Beautiful* centerfold. There was a plate of freshly baked chocolate chip cookies on the entry table, arranged in perfect stacks with purple flower petals serving as decoration. Candles flickered in huge glass globes from their places on shelves and her immaculate kitchen countertops.

Her carpet and furniture and goddamn near everything was pristine white.

He was moving a five-year-old into this place?

Bethany had stepped aside to let them in and was now crouched down offering Laura a cookie like some gorgeous domestic goddess, but his niece was too agog at her surroundings to reach for the perfectly rounded baked goods.

"It is an ice palace," Laura whispered.

Bethany's smile faltered a little and she stood, nearly fumbling the plate of cookies until Wes gripped her elbow and steadied her. "Hey." He leaned in and kissed her mouth softly. "Everything looks amazing."

She visibly calmed, and in turn, Wes did, too. Being able to pinpoint her insecurities and talk her out of them reassured him that they could do this.

They could not, however, keep this place sparkling clean forever.

Wes caught Laura by the back of her hoodie before she could step her dirty sneaker on the carpet. "Shoes off, kid." He toed off his boots. "Here, look. I'll do mine, too."

"Is everyone hungry?" Bethany asked brightly, sailing off toward the kitchen. "I made spaghetti sauce—I just have to heat it up. I was thinking we could go check out Laura's room first and then eat?"

Lord, the poor woman. Her heart had to be beating a thousand miles an hour. "That sounds perfect, darlin'."

"Great." She turned on a toe and gestured for them to follow her down the hallway. "Okay, so, it's not decorated for a young lady just yet, Laura, but I thought we could chat and come up with your own design? Or maybe you want a certain theme . . ."

She opened the door to reveal a room one might refer to as a chamber.

More flickering candles. A fluffy cream-colored bedspread.

A mountain of beaded throw pillows.

Thick maroon drapes.

A chandelier.

"This is my room?"

Wes held his breath, only letting it out when his niece squealed in delight and cannonballed into the center of the bed. Bethany slumped against the doorjamb, her eyes closing momentarily, and without needing to think, he reached over and braided their fingers together, bringing her hand to his mouth and resting his lips on her wired pulse. Willing it to settle.

But it spiked a second later when his niece rolled over and sat up, hair in eighteen directions. "Where are you sleeping, Uncle Wes?"

Bethany shifted. "Oh, um . . ."

Laura wiggled to the edge of the bed and leapt off, dashing between Wes and Bethany to an open door directly across the hall. She pushed the door open wider, disappearing into the darkness. Wes followed, flipping on the light to find a bedroom much like Laura's, only with a forest-green color scheme. "You'll be right across from me!"

Bethany turned to him with a bemused look. "Yes, isn't that awesome?"

"Guess we better ease into this," he muttered.

"I'll miss you tonight," she whispered on her way out the door.

"That's cute that you think you'll get the chance," Wes called after her.

As soon as Bethany was out of sight, he let out a breath and leaned back against the bedroom wall. If both females were happy, he would deem the move-in a success. He might be nursing the worry that he didn't belong in this perfect postcard of a house—hell, he'd once spent a week in between apartments sleeping in a buddy's van, and that had only been a goddamn year ago—but he needed to put his insecurities aside and focus on making their relationship stronger.

Having Bethany in his life was worth the self-doubt. She was worth everything. And when it came to stability, he couldn't ask for a better living situation for his niece. So if he was feeling completely out of place and his old fears of being someone's pit stop were starting to make their way to the forefront, he needed to suck it up and ignore them.

CHAPTER TWENTY-THREE

Bethany sat at the end of her bed slowly pulling a brush through her hair.

She'd lit the fire in her hearth for the first time this fall and she smiled into it now, the heat it exuded matching the warmth inside of her. The feel of Laura's bedtime hug still clung to her, as did the promissory kiss Wes delivered before she'd gone upstairs to bed—and if she kept thinking about it, she wasn't going to need the fire to stay warm.

Falling back on her bed, she let the hairbrush drop over the edge to the carpet and stay there. She'd pick it up when she darn well felt like it. These small acts of rebellion against her perfectionist nature were starting to come easier now. Though they would be a necessity now, with a child in the house. There were going to be stains and spilled food and tracked-in mud—and so what?

If she got this happiness in return? Worth it.

Worth it times a million.

Tonight after they'd eaten spaghetti and listened to stories about Laura's day at school, Wes had helped her clean up the kitchen while his niece literally crash-landed on the couch.

There had been a little lurch in her chest when the throw pillows went flying, and Laura definitely hadn't washed the marinara sauce off her face and hands, but it was nothing a little spot cleaner couldn't fix. And maybe it was time to think about new couches anyway! Something in a color that didn't show off every speck of dust that landed on it.

Maybe Wes could help her pick them out.

Wow, the mere act of thinking his name made the short silk robe feel extra decadent on her skin. She'd left the lights off, casting the room in nothing but firelight. The dancing flames flickered on the walls and her exposed flesh, reminding her of hands. His hands.

As much as she loved his ritual of reading to Laura in her room every night, she couldn't wait for him to come upstairs. Not only because she craved the confident, possessive, starving-man way he touched her, but because she wanted to talk to him. She wasn't the only one dealing with these huge changes. In the space of a week, he'd applied to become a child's guardian and moved in with his . . . girlfriend.

She was Wes's girlfriend.

The smile that transformed her mouth was kind of delirious—and it was still in place when there was a knock on her door. Bethany jackknifed so suddenly she got lightheaded, but managed to fall sideways onto her elbow in a seductive pose without tumbling off the bed. "Come in," she called.

The door swung open in a slow arc and there was Wes, proving their status as total opposites by arriving shirtless in sweatpants, while she was lotioned to death in a silk negligee.

"I feel overdressed," she said.

"Have to agree," he drawled, sauntering in, all loose-hipped and cocky, kicking the door shut behind him. "Don't worry, I have a plan to fix it."

"Oh, do you—"

Bethany broke off with a yelp when Wes snagged her ankle in a no-nonsense grip. She was flipped onto her back and pulled to the edge of the mattress, the silk of her lingerie dragging higher and higher, until it bunched beneath her breasts. With a dangerous wink, Wes leaned down and kissed her belly button with his hot breath. "That got your panties showing, anyway." He nipped the waistband with his teeth and her flesh sang like a choir of angels. "Pretty little thing, isn't it?" The tip of his tongue grazed the silk. "Let's see what it's hiding."

"Wait." She laughed through a wave of arousal. "Wait . . ."

Was she borrowing trouble or was Wes coming on even stronger than usual? God knew she didn't mind—she ached for his weight on top of her—but there was an almost inaudible whisper in her ear saying something was off. They'd just taken this huge step of moving in together and they should talk. How was he handling everything? How did he bring up the subject of moving to his niece and what did she say? Did he like her house or did he think it resembled an ice castle?

Wes dropped his forehead to her belly. "Stop thinking, Bethany."

Was there an edge to his voice? "I just thought we'd talk for a while," she said, scooting out from beneath him and rising from the bed, the heat from the fire licking her bare calves and thighs. "We have all night, right? We have every night."

When they found her, his eyes had softened somewhat. Did that mean they'd been hard before? "Of course we do." Wes closed the distance between them and used the tie of her robe to pull her into his arms, resting his cheek on the top of her head. "What's on your mind, baby?"

"You."

His hard body stiffened a degree. "Me?"

She leaned away to look up at him. "Uh. Yes, you, Wes. You're taking on all this new responsibility when you weren't even planning on staying in town—"

"Now I am staying," he broke in, reaching down to unknot the tie of her robe and push it off her shoulders. "It's as simple as that."

What was going on with him? "It's just a huge step."

"Why don't you just tell me what you're worried about?" he said calmly.

Too calmly?

"I'm not worried about anything," she said quietly. "I want to know if there is anything worrying you."

"Not a damn thing," he said in a firm voice, tipping up her chin so she could look him in the eye. "I'm rock solid, Bethany. Okay? Put your faith in me. I'm here with you because you've been my woman since the beginning, even before you realized or accepted it. I'm standing right here and

I'm staying right here. There is nothing you or anyone could do to make me want to be somewhere I couldn't hold you."

She was at a loss for words, her heart knocking wildly against her ears. What could she say to something so beautiful? That she loved him, yes. But God, they'd moved in together two hours ago; there was plenty of time for that. "Wes," she whispered, sliding her hands up his chest, into his hair. "I need you."

They weren't the words on her heart. But she still meant it in a way that went beyond physical need. She needed his presence, his love, his heart, his character, his humor, his selflessness, his loyalty, and his Texas temper. She needed all of it. And she wanted to clarify that to Wes, but he said, "Goddamn, I need you, too, baby," as his mouth traveled down the column of her throat, back up the side of her neck and into her hair, messing it up along with any semblance of rational thought or self-control.

Greedy hands shoved at the straps of her negligee, yanking it down to her waist so he could get his mouth on her breasts. As soon as the silk fell to the floor, leaving her in nothing but panties, his hands took hold of her backside and lifted Bethany onto her toes so he could suck her nipples, drawing them into the warmth of his mouth with long, guttural groans and teasing her with flickering licks.

Both times she and Wes had made love, there was a wicked urgency behind it, but Bethany sensed a change in him tonight. Something different. Almost like he was desperate to overwhelm her senses and fortunately—or unfortunately—it was working. So well. He didn't let her come up for air once, his mouth working magic on her breasts, his index fingers hooking in the sides of her panties and sending them floating to her ankles. It was everything she could do just to keep her balance.

"I'm rock solid," he said, finding her mouth once more and demolishing it with a hot, marauding tongue. "You're not just getting words tonight, either. You're going to feel it." He slapped her bottom, enough to smart, enough to rake her body with goosebumps and steal her breath. "You'll feel it best from your hands and knees. Will you do that for me?"

"Yes," she rasped, trembling. Like she could say no? Her sex was damp in his honor, clenching, looking for that hard part of him to fill it. None of her boyfriends had ever dared to spank her before, either, and a man she trusted doing such a thing allowed her to enjoy the exhilaration left in its wake—and God did she ever. She wanted to get on her hands and knees for him and be the object of his revelry.

Bethany turned and pressed her back to Wes's front, skimming the curve of her butt side to side on his lap, eliciting a frustrated male groan, before sinking to her knees. And then forward onto her hands. The fireplace cast a glow, allowing her to see the silhouette of her naked body on the opposite wall, and it ripped a moan from her throat. A moan that turned into a cry of "Now, now, now" when Wes positioned himself behind her, seeing to their protection before hefting her hips higher with a forearm. "Feel this, baby." He worked his shaft into her and pressed himself deep—God it was so good, so good—setting off an erotic tremble in

Bethany's thighs. "Does that feel like a man who doesn't know exactly what he wants?"

"No," she gasped when he started to move. "Wes . . ."

"How about now?" He fell on top of her, stopping just short of crushing her to the ground, always keeping her hips elevated with that powerful arm—and he slapped his lower body tight to her bottom over and over and over again, his erection filling her with deliberate, slippery drives. "That feel like I could live without you for a fucking second, Bethany?"

An intense shudder passed through her, making a stop at her heart, electrifying it. God, she loved this man. He could anchor her and send her soaring in the same moment. "No," she managed on an uneven exhale. "You couldn't."

"No. I couldn't," he gritted into the crook of her neck, the force of his thrusts turning punishing. "Fuck. You're even tighter like this. I can feel you getting ready to come, but you're going to stay with me a little longer. You work my cock so good when you're climbing. Dirty and desperate, huh?"

She nodded so she wouldn't have to issue a verbal guarantee that she'd hold off her climax. His thickness was entering her from an angle that gave her a new appreciation for math, because it doled out continuous friction to her clit and her G-spot until she was panting down at the rug and praying he didn't change the pace or those snapping upthrusts. *Don't change. Never change.* Good God, she sounded like a bad yearbook inscription.

"No you don't," Wes muttered hoarsely into her hair. "You're perfect."

Wait. Was she talking out loud? Who knew. Who cared? "More. Please."

"I'm here to give you everything you want," he growled, pressing his upper body down just those few inches more until her cheek was flush to the carpet, ass in the air, Wes's hips smacking into hers relentlessly. "I'm not going anywhere. Don't . . . let me go. Anywhere."

"I won't. I won't." Their voices sounded distant and she knew there was something she needed to remember. What did he mean, don't let him go? But the arm holding up her hips shifted and his fingers joined the sensual attack on her clit—and it was game over. Bethany spread her thighs to allow him even deeper and the pleasure rained down on her head like liquid candy. Her orgasm was so good, it was excruciating. And endless. But when Wes groaned her name above her head and slammed deep that final time, his big body shaking, she hit peak fulfillment.

Because they were there together.

Moments later, he cradled her boneless body in his arms and carried her to the bed. He settled Bethany carefully down on her back and climbed in beside her, curving his front to her back. Holding her tightly in the firelight.

Just before sleep claimed her, a worry crept in that nothing could remain this good for long, but it danced away with her consciousness before she could dwell on it.

CHAPTER TWENTY-FOUR

It was Friday morning, their final day to work on Project Doomsday, and everything was in a state of utter chaos. Ollie and Carl were in the hallway and the second bedroom applying last-minute coats of paint. Bethany was installing light fixtures and sconces from her perch on a stepladder while simultaneously directing the furniture deliverymen who were carting in the items she'd selected. Wes was putting finishing touches on the built-in bookcase, cowboy hat long since discarded on the floor. Even the production interns had hopped in to direct the plumbers and building inspectors who were making their final rounds and approving all the changes.

They had until tomorrow morning to make last-minute fixes, then the judges would arrive to film the final segment and declare a winner.

Bethany would likely spend the whole night staging so the house would be camera ready. It would be different this time, however. She'd had a hand in every little detail of this home, from the direction of the grain in the floorboards to the backsplash tile. She had grout under her fingernails from tiling the bathroom and a sore neck from painting the ceiling. Even though she'd almost gone ass-over-teakettle off the roof, she'd hauled her butt back up there and finished the job— Wes keeping a very close and irritable eye on her. But still.

When she'd thrown down the gauntlet with Stephen at the wedding, she'd thought the whole experience would be summed up by victory or defeat. That was no longer true. She'd already won.

Or, rather, she was winning.

She couldn't become a different person overnight, but changes were happening inside of her. Positive ones. She no longer had to hide the red mark on her neck because it was gone. When she stood in front of her closet in the morning, she no longer went through a mental checklist of everyone who would see her that day and dress accordingly. She didn't have to go through breathing exercises before setting foot on the jobsite. Every minute of her day didn't have to be spent trying to make the next minute count. And this morning when she'd driven Laura to school, she'd said, "I love you, too," when the crossing guard called, "Good morning," and she'd only dwelled on it for like, ten minutes.

Feeling a little zing in her spine, Bethany paused in the act of screwing in an energy-efficient light bulb and cast a look across the room to find Wes watching her. Watching and appreciating her as if there weren't two cameramen capturing their every move. He dragged his tongue along his lower lip and sent her a wink. There was a time when she would have rolled her eyes at him or flipped him the bird, but now? Oh, now all the elements of spring seemed to bloom in her belly at once. Flowers unfolded, birds chirped, sunshine blazed.

Bethany Castle had a live-in boyfriend.

Who would have believed it?

Not her, as little as two weeks ago.

Still, tiny fingers of skepticism skimmed the waters of her subconscious every once in a while, and she couldn't seem to help it. What if Wes hadn't needed a stable living environment for Laura? Would he ever have moved in? Would he have eventually gotten his fill of her and found someone less neurotic?

From across the room, Wes shook his head at Bethany and she quickly disguised her thoughts with a smile. Good God. Why was she borrowing trouble? She had a boyfriend who held her through the night like they were fending off a windstorm together—and she loved him. With a child in the house, her life was suddenly a Pandora's box of crayon crumbles and chocolate smears, but those things were slowly teaching her how overrated perfection was. Who cared what got messy as long as everyone was laughing?

And laugh they did. This morning, Laura had been lying in wait outside the bathroom to jump out and scare the shit out of her. She'd flailed like one of those used-car-lot inflatables and knocked a picture off the wall, landing smack on her butt, all while still in her towel. Wes had come rushing up the stairs to help her, his perplexed horror bringing the hilariousness of the whole situation into sharp focus. If they didn't have a house to finish flipping by tomorrow, Bethany might still be on the floor laughing facedown into the carpet with Laura perched on her back, hollering for Bethany to act like a bucking bronco.

How would she have spent the morning before?

Agonizing over flower arrangements and which flavor of tea to drink?

Oh, she still had things to agonize about. Her mother had caught wind of her new living arrangements and left approximately seventeen passive-aggressive messages on her voicemail. Bethany couldn't really blame her, either. A family dinner with everyone was long past due. Wes and Laura were a part of her life now and she needed to stop waiting for some nonexistent shoe to drop.

"Hey," she called to Wes.

Were his eyes sparkling as he sauntered closer? Was he magical? How had she ever spent a second denying her attraction to this man? "Yeah, darlin'?"

"I was thinking, you know . . . after tomorrow when everything dies down, we could invite—"

Wes's phone trilled, cutting her off. "Keep going," he said, waving it off.

"No, it could be something about Laura. You should get it."

He studied her for another beat, then answered. "Hello?" After a few seconds of listening, his demeanor changed. "Yes, this is Wes Daniels." He covered the receiver. "Family court."

Bethany wasn't given a chance to react. Without disconnecting the call, Wes wrapped an arm around Bethany's thighs and hauled her off the stepping stool and out of the house. They left a bunch of confusion and amusement in their wake, but she was way more interested in the phone call and the fact that Wes wanted her there by his side while he took it.

"Yes," he said, setting Bethany down and closing the door behind them, motioning for everyone on the lawn to be quiet. "You want to do the house visit tonight?" Wes turned in a circle while raking a hand through his hair and Bethany knew what he saw. Hours of manual labor that had yet to be completed. "Tonight is going to be hard. Is there any way we could shoot for—"

Bethany waved her hands at him. "Say yes," she whispered. "Yes. We'll make it work."

Wordlessly he asked if she was sure and Bethany nodded vigorously. "I . . . Yes, tonight is fine." He cleared his throat. "Six o'clock. We'll see you then."

Wes hung up the phone and reached for Bethany, but she was already on her way to him. He locked her in an embrace and they stayed that way for long moments, swaying side to side. "She says they'll likely approve the temporary guardianship if the visit goes well tonight," he said.

"It will," Bethany responded. "Of course it will."

If there was one thing Bethany knew how to do, it was charm. She might as well have majored in schmoozing in college, with a minor in sweet-talking people with clipboards. They had this in the bag. Wes and Laura were depending on her and she wouldn't let them down.

Something was eating at Wes's gut, but he couldn't quite give it a name.

He sat on the couch with Laura beside him, trying to concentrate on reading her Judy Moody, but Bethany kept drawing his attention to where she bustled back and forth in the kitchen.

She was in her element arranging chocolates on a plate and lighting candles. Her hair was pulled up, diamonds winking in her ears. She wore some kind of tight black one-shoulder dress that showed off her legs. Gone was the woman who'd been streaked with paint in lost-cause workout pants that afternoon. She was so beautiful; he could barely hear his own voice over the rap of his heartbeat. There was a jangle in her nerves, too, though, and it was impossible to ignore.

He'd done enough research to know that if the court-appointed visitor didn't approve the home as a suitable place for Laura, they could potentially appeal the decision and try again. He was going to see the guardianship through, one way or another. That's not what worried him. It was Bethany. Their relationship was so new, and while she'd grown more relaxed and comfortable in her own skin, he could still sense her occasional panic when their new living situation turned her into a fish out of water.

She might be worrying less and less about being perfect, but this single-minded intensity she was putting into tonight reminded him of Bethany Before. He was afraid if they failed, her old insecurities might come tumbling back out.

There was an anxious feeling in his gut telling him tonight's decision could put a crack down the center of what they'd built. Had he put too much pressure on her? He was the one who'd said they would take things slowly. Maybe he should have tried harder to find an apartment for him and Laura while he and Bethany grew stronger?

As swiftly as his worries rose to the surface, he stuffed them back down. There was only enough room for one nervous person in this house and he'd already decided it couldn't be him. He needed to be the picture of confidence at all times until Bethany knew for certain he wasn't budging. Until then and as long as she needed, he was a boulder without a single crack. Solid.

The doorbell rang and Laura's head popped up. "Is that them?"

His explanation to Laura had gone like this: The town had grown suspicious that Bethany's house really *was* an ice palace being disguised by magic. Someone needed to come over and confirm no shenanigans were taking place. "Yes, that's them." He rose from the couch and pulled his niece to her feet. "Why don't you go grab one of those chocolates Bethany put out? Wash your hands afterward."

"'Kay!"

Laura ran off and Wes let out a long breath, moving to the entryway and meeting Bethany in front of the door. She squeezed his hand and stepped back so he could open it, revealing a thin woman in her sixties, arms crossed, with not so much as a hint of a smile on her face. Once again, Wes experienced that ominous click in his gut. "Daniels and Castle residence?"

"Yes," Bethany said brightly. "Please come in."

The woman entered the house unceremoniously, her eyes seeming to land everywhere at once. "My name is Paula." She produced a business card from her jacket pocket and handed it over to Wes. "Just go about your night normally, please. I don't require a guided tour. I'll have a look around myself."

"Oh, okay," Bethany said haltingly. "Can I get you anything to drink? Coffee?"

"No, thank you," Paula replied, already breezing past them.

Wes stepped close to Bethany and took her hand, but it was clammy now where before it was warm. "Hey. Come read with us. It'll be fine."

Her smile wobbled. "It will be fine. I know."

Wes didn't hear a word of the story he read to Laura for the next fifteen minutes. He was only aware of the methodical footsteps moving through the house, entering and exiting rooms. Laura found a comfortable spot under Bethany's arm and started to nod off, and it seemed like nothing could go wrong. How could there be a negative outcome to anything when his niece was more relaxed than he'd ever seen her? Bethany had been transforming right in front of his eyes, slowly but surely, into someone who could laugh when pancake batter plopped on the ground and who didn't mind loud cartoons. She was fucking extraordinary and the kind of woman Laura could benefit from having in her life, before and after her mother returned—and he had faith that his sister could and would come back.

There was no better place for his niece, and God knew

there was nowhere else he wanted to be than right there with this woman he'd lost his heart to.

So why was his pulse ticking faster and faster in his ears?

He found out when Paula returned from her tour of the upstairs. One look at her pinched features and he knew.

"Can I speak with you outside, please?"

Bethany shot to her feet so fast, she almost lost her balance, but Wes caught her hand in time and brought her around the couch to the front door. He was grateful for the gentle snores coming from Laura because he didn't want her to hear the bad news obviously headed their way. It was already hitting him like a crowbar to the stomach, the blow sending out reverberations of numbness. How did this happen?

"I'm sorry to do this," Paula began, hesitantly. "I don't want you to think this is a poor reflection of yourselves or your home, but after examining Laura's environment, I can't recommend this as a qualified living space for a child her age. Either she's only moved in recently or no accommodations have been made to make this house kid friendly. It looks like an interior design showroom. Really, I find the home . . . cold." At that, Bethany flinched and Wes closed his eyes. "You'll have an opportunity to appeal the decision and I could be sent back for another visit, but for now . . . I'm recommending the temporary guardianship be put on hold . . ."

Wes didn't hear the rest because he was too busy watching Bethany's face and experiencing the slow erosion inside of his chest. And he couldn't help but want to grab Bethany by the shoulders and shake her. *Don't fucking shut down on me now when I need you.* It was too late, though. He could see that much clearly. Her brittle smile and distant expression had already moved into place, a mask to hide how she really felt about this failure.

No, not a failure. A setback.

Was there even the slightest chance he could make her see it like that? Did he even have the energy when his own disappointment was thick enough to choke him?

Thank you," Bethany said woodenly, as she closed the door behind Paula. They both stood there, but she was unable to make even the barest eye contact with Wes.

Humiliation ravaged her skin like fire ants.

Really, I find the home . . . cold.

The same had been said about her before by the men she put on ice, when they tried to get too close. All because she'd dreaded letting them in, all the way in, and having them come to that conclusion after meeting the real Bethany. That she was nothing more than an attractive package.

This home was an extension of her, wasn't it? She'd put her heart and soul into every single touch, floor to ceiling. And it had been deemed cold.

All she could think to do now was minimize the pain of such a stark failure. She'd fooled Wes and Laura into believing she was the warm, settling-down type. But this had to prove what she'd been afraid of all along. She wasn't the total package. She was an empty box dressed up in gift wrap.

"Don't do this, Bethany." She barely heard Wes's rasped plea over the roaring in her ears. "Please."

"Don't do what?" she asked, dazedly.

"First of all, fucking look at me." Oh God, she was. She was looking at this man she loved and he looked so defeated. She'd never seen him that way before, not even when she'd fired him. This was her fault. They'd cobbled together this wild idea that they could be a makeshift family and she'd been the wrong fit. What good was being a perfectionist if she couldn't be perfect when it really counted? "Look . . . we'll appeal it—"

"No, I . . . I mean, not here again. Obviously moving her . . . a-and you here was a bad choice." She flung a shaky hand out to indicate the house. "It's not for kids. Anyone can see that. This whole thing was crazy. It was crazy."

"It wasn't crazy. Stop saying that." He caught the bridge of his nose between two fingers. "You're not the only one who got punched in the gut here. I can be strong for both of us, but sometimes I need help. So I need you to keep it together for me right now."

"I am keeping it together," she said, making a break for the kitchen on wobbly legs. She just had to get away from the knowledge in his eyes. Bethany took a bottle of water out of the fridge, uncapped it, and took a hasty sip, desperately trying to control the chaos of her thoughts. The cool water sliding down her throat did nothing to help the sting of defeat, though.

"Bethany—"

"It's fine. We tried to fool them into thinking I was a mommy or some . . . happy homemaker, but I'm not. I'm not warm and welcoming. I never will be. I'm not even sure I *want* to be." Her words tripped over themselves. "And now you just have to adjust."

"*I* have to adjust. Just like that it's no longer *we*."

"Yup." She scoffed. "You would have been better off with almost anyone else."

His laughter was low and humorless. "Can't say I'm surprised."

With foreboding buzzing in her fingertips, she slowly set down the bottle of water. "What's that supposed to mean?"

"It means you were hunting for a flaw in what we've got here. A flaw in yourself. A flaw in us. So here you go, Bethany. Now you've got your excuse to cut and run."

"I wasn't *looking* for an excuse—"

"Bullshit." He dropped a fist onto the kitchen island. "You're pushing me away to minimize your own damage. And I can't talk you back from the edge every time. Sometimes I'm standing on it, too."

"I'm sorry," she whispered, stricken. "I just think our expectations for this relationship got too high, too fast, and this is proof." Oh God, she hated herself for every word coming out of her mouth, but she could only push, push until he finally left her alone where she could be mortified at her failure in peace. *That woman saw right through me to the fraud beneath.* "You'll have a better chance without me."

Wes appeared to be searching for patience, but he visibly couldn't find any. He raked a hand through his hair, opened his mouth to say something and closed it again. She almost got down on her knees and apologized for every single word she'd just said. Almost begged him to pretend the last five minutes never happened. After all, they could fix the house and make it warmer for Laura. She knew enough from reading over Wes's shoulder during the last week that unless the child was in danger in the home, the state wouldn't take her away and they could repair the problem. Appeal the decision.

But in that moment, she genuinely wondered if Wes could do better alone. All her efforts to make this place homey had been totally lacking—and there was no escaping that fact. It had just been confirmed.

"We'll be out of your hair as soon as possible," Wes said, turning and leaving the kitchen.

A hundred-pound weight dropped in Bethany's stomach. "Wait," she wheezed, knocking the bottle of water off the counter. Now? All of this was happening *now*? She'd reacted first without thinking through the consequences. Wes was supposed to *stop* her from spinning out, wasn't he? How had it gotten this far? "No. You don't have to leave."

Wes scooped his sleeping niece off the couch, stopping just before the hallway. "Yeah, I think we do." He looked down at Laura. "I'll let her sleep for now, but we'll be out in the morning."

CHAPTER TWENTY-FIVE

Bethany creaked down the hallway of Project Doomsday, dragging her fingertips along the wall. She'd traded places with the house. This morning, it had been a hollow vessel while she'd been so full of new life and hope. Now she was the empty one and the house was full of furniture waiting to be arranged.

After Wes had closed himself in his room, she'd returned to the jobsite alone, for once devoid of her usual excitement over that final stage of bringing a space to life. Everything was wrapped in plastic, placed in the appropriate room, but all four of her limbs were deadweights, so how those objects would find their way to the correct corners and angles, she had no idea.

An exhale stole the remaining energy in Bethany's body, sending her sliding sideways down the wall of the hallway and leaving her there in a heap.

What did you do?

She'd asked herself the same question ninety times since walking on unsteady legs out of her house and driving like a zombie across town. The answer was still hovering somewhere outside the reach of her consciousness, mostly because grasping anything beyond the pain of losing Wes was too hard.

A fresh wave of misery rose over her and she shivered.

Oh God. She'd lost Wes.

How, though?

How?

Their relationship had been new, but strong. Every time a worry bubble rose to her surface, he found a way to pop it. Found a way to make her forget it ever existed in the first place. He helped her laugh away her fears and focus on the good. No, he'd made her *feel* the good, not just look for it.

Wes had fought her dragons valiantly.

And she'd . . .

Kept letting them out, expecting him to crash back onto the scene in his suit of armor every time, sword at the ready. Had she stopped fighting her own mental battles and left the chore up to him too often?

Yes.

Yes, clearly she had. And everything he'd said to her in the kitchen tonight had been terribly accurate. She'd been looking for weaknesses in the foundation they were building together. She'd been up to her old tricks of searching for a way out so she wouldn't have to face her imperfections.

God, it would have slayed her if Wes had shown her kind of reticence. Instead he'd been the steadfast one, never letting her feel anything less than secure. Yes, she'd been working on herself, but not quickly enough. She couldn't sustain the blow of having her home deemed unsuitable and everything had fallen apart in the blink of an eye.

It was her fault. Entirely.

She'd folded like a cheap lawn chair and hurt the man she loved. And there was no mistaking that. He'd all but begged her with his eyes not to push him away. Now she'd lost the only person who'd ever looked over a list of her demons and signed up anyway.

Bethany pressed both hands to her face, letting salty tears trickle down along her palms to her lips, dripping onto her shirt. Oh man, she'd fucked up. She might have made herself more vulnerable to Wes than she ever had with another human being, but when it came down to brass tacks, she'd demanded a lot of Wes and given not enough in return. She was unreliable and wishy-washy and unworthy of someone with a heart that big.

Hastily, she wiped her eyes and looked up and down the hallway. It was the middle of the night, so there was nothing but lingering dust and a freshly cut lumber smell to keep her company. That's what she deserved—to be alone.

The Bethany she'd been before Wes would have preferred to be alone.

Did she prefer it now?

No. God, no. Nothing got accomplished that way.

Bethany sat up straighter.

At the outset of this project, she'd set out to prove she could flip a house alone and do a better job than her brother. A better job than anyone. That wasn't what she'd learned, though. She'd learned to accept help and be grateful for it.

She'd learned it took letting down her guard and admitting when she made a mistake—like firing Wes or ordering the wrong size tile for the bathroom and a million other things she'd done along the way—to be successful. Perfection wasn't success. It was impossible and frankly kind of boring.

It was the effort paid to the project that made her proud. Not the outcome.

If only she'd made the same effort with Wes.

Bethany pushed herself up off the floor and walked to the living room, using her fingernail to scratch a piece of tape off the plastic wrapped around the couch. Was she going to learn from her lesson? Or was she going to pretend the last two and a half weeks never happened and crawl off to lick her wounds?

Honestly, the latter held the most appeal. Her knees were rubber and her eyes were gritty from crying. She wanted a certain set of strong arms around her and the knowledge that she didn't deserve them was the most painful of all.

Still, she slipped her phone out of her pocket and dialed her sister, determined not to slip into the patterns that had landed her in this lonely, cold wasteland without the man who'd stood by her side when she didn't deserve it.

"What's wrong?" Georgie answered, sounding alarmed.

"Nothing is wrong," Bethany said quickly. "Sorry to call you in the middle of the night like this. I just . . . need some help." She swallowed. "I need your help staging the house for tomorrow. I can't do it alone."

A long pause. "Wait. Is this Bethany? My sister Bethany?"

A dull smile drifted across her lips. "Yes, it's me."

"Okay . . ." Georgie said slowly. "I'll leave Travis sleeping and be right over."

Travis piped up in the background. "Like hell."

"She needs help staging the house," came Georgie's muffled voice.

"Bethany needs help?"

"Yes!"

"Are you sure it's her?"

Their voices faded out for a few moments amid the sounds of covers rustling, then Georgie was back. "Travis is coming with me. He doesn't think I can handle the mean streets of Port Jefferson alone."

"The more the merrier. See you soon."

Georgie didn't come alone. She showed up with half of the Just Us League members, including a sleepy-eyed Rosie, Dominic in tow looking stoic and protective of his wife as usual. Bethany opened the front door of the house, so taken aback by the sea of smiling faces staring at her, she stumbled sideways. They didn't wait for her to greet them and they didn't ask for an explanation; they simply filed past her one by one, a couple of the older ladies patting her on the shoulder as they passed. The house went from eerily silent to extremely noisy, as plastic was ripped with Stanley knives, boxes were broken down, and furniture was dragged across floors. Bethany stared at the chaos with grateful tears in her eyes until her type A genes couldn't take it anymore and she joined the effort.

It took until dawn and a lot of hoarse instructions before the house was arranged as she'd envisioned. She didn't experience her usual dose of satisfaction, though, because the person she wanted to share the joy with the most wasn't there. He was getting ready to leave her—and rightly so.

With yawns aplenty, her impromptu decorating committee started to leave and she stood at the door, thanking each and every one of them until they'd all driven off to start their days, undoubtedly exhausted. Travis, Georgie, Rosie, and Dominic all lingered behind, cleaning up the last of the unpacking mess.

Georgie came up beside Bethany, laying her head on her shoulder. "It looks amazing. You should be really proud."

"I barely recognize it," Travis added, turning in a circle to take in what was once his childhood home. "And that's a damn good thing. Nice going, Bethany."

"Thanks." Her heart beat heavily in her chest. "I didn't do it alone."

Rosie handed her one of the coffees Dominic had gone out to pick up at the gas station, and asked gently, "Wes is home with Laura, I'm assuming?"

Bethany didn't miss the curiosity in her friend's tone. She'd obviously noticed that something was wrong. "They're at my house. They moved into my house."

Four sets of eyebrows shot up.

"I don't know how long they'll be there," Bethany continued stiltedly. "I've ruined everything."

"What is . . . everything? If you don't mind me asking." Travis shot his wife a look. "You're supposed to keep me abreast of the gossip."

"I wasn't abreast of it myself," Georgie murmured, studying Bethany's face. "Whatever it is you think you ruined, it's fixable. We'll help."

"I appreciate the offer." She thought of Wes the last time she saw him and shook her head. He'd been devastated over Paula's decision and she'd left him to flounder. She'd cut and run emotionally, just like he said. Abandoned him with cold words when he needed her the most. How could he trust her ever again?

He wouldn't.

But her journey to common ground with Wes had taught her so much, and she wouldn't abandon what she'd learned like she'd abandoned him in his moment of need.

"I have to tell you guys something." She paced away from the group to look out the window. "I second-guess myself constantly. I overthink every word and every decision and I push people away so they won't find out I'm actually a mess. I don't have it all together. I'm just pretending to be the . . . beautiful, dynamic creature you all see before you. All the time."

Everyone was silent for a few beats.

"Thank God," Georgie breathed, bringing Bethany around. "Bethany, congratulations, you're human. Nobody in this room is perfect."

"Not even me," Travis said, winking.

Georgie hip-checked him.

"If we made you feel like you needed to be faultless, we're sorry," Rosie said, coming forward. "You just make everything look so easy, it's hard to imagine you struggling like the rest of us."

"You asked for help tonight, though." Dominic coughed, visibly uneasy being the center of attention for even a second. "That probably wasn't easy. Wouldn't have been easy for me, either." He looked at his wife. "Before."

"And you're talking to us now," Georgie added. "Saying the problem out loud is half the battle. Like when I told you I was in love with Travis at Zumba class."

"Let's not refer to that as a problem," Travis growled.

"It was at the time," Georgie qualified, reaching out to take hold of her husband's hand. "But it grew into something beautiful. Problems don't have to go away—they can change shape or you can make them work for you."

"She's right," Rosie said with a soft smile. "You don't have to change everything about yourself. Sometimes you just have to add a little honesty and it makes all the difference."

Was Rosie right? It seemed like she might be. Bethany stood in front of her closest friends and family feeling exposed, yes, but also lighter. More herself than ever. Why did this lesson have to come a day late? Last night could have played out so differently. Instead of trying to push Wes away, she could have told him the truth. That she was embarrassed over the failure and horrified that she'd disappointed him. They could have talked about it and moved forward together. More than that, she could have found out how he felt about having their house deemed unprepared for guardianship of Laura.

She'd lost that privilege now, hadn't she?

He'd never take another risk on such a self-centered head case.

"Thanks, guys," Bethany said, clearing the rust from her throat. "And thanks for coming out in the middle of the night to help me. I never could have done this alone." She turned in a circle to observe the Cape Cod–style dwelling in all its spit-shined glory. "Now will it be enough to beat Stephen?"

The pit in Bethany's stomach yawned wider when she realized winning *Flip Off* was no longer important. Not when she'd already lost what mattered most.

The next morning, Wes discovered the true meaning of being a parent. Yeah, there was dress shopping and waking up at five A.M. But mostly it was smiling and being engaged through the terrible moments. When he got out of bed Saturday morning, after sleeping approximately twenty minutes the whole night, the house was empty. Bethany had to be off staging the house, and not being there with her didn't sit right. Not at all. They'd started the project together and they should be finishing it together.

As he leaned against the doorjamb watching Laura brush her teeth, he wished he could go back and handle his argument with Bethany differently. Lord, did he wish.

What good had it been for him to be the stabilizing presence for stupid little things like the mark on her neck? Or reassuring her that he didn't care about morning breath? If he couldn't be strong when she had a major spiral, none of that other shit meant a thing.

He could have wrapped his arms around her last night, kissed her, and said, "We got some bad news, baby. Let's sleep on it tonight and attack it fresh in the morning." What if that's all it would have taken to talk her back down?

Instead he'd blown out of there, pissed and hurt.

Hell, he still hurt. She'd thrown salt into his wound and he'd been too down to deal with it. But right now, he could only think of Bethany. Was she feeling this god-awful, too?

He might never know. She'd likely never want anything to do with him again. A man who couldn't be solid during her hardest moments didn't deserve her at all.

Eventually he would have to figure out a plan for him and Laura. If Bethany didn't want them living there, he'd respect that, even if he wasn't convinced that was the case. Bethany loved Laura. There was no mistaking the way she looked at his niece. The way she softened every time Laura said her name or sat on her lap. Still, he couldn't wait for Bethany to come down from the ledge to file the appeal for guardianship. It had to be sooner rather than later and he couldn't imagine putting that pressure on Bethany again right away.

"We're doing show-and-tell at school on Monday," Laura said, around her toothbrush.

"Oh yeah?" Wes tried to bury the heel of his hand in his eye socket. "What are you going to bring?"

"Bethany's magnolia candle. I already put it in my backpack."

"Why the candle?"

She spat into the sink. "It smells like her."

His heart lurched. "Yeah. It does."

"I like the way she smells. I like everything about her."

"I like everything about her, too." Even the crazy parts.

Last night in the kitchen, he'd loved her through that entire argument, hadn't he? He loved her so much now, his hands ached with the need to touch her face, stroke her hair. She must be working so hard staging the house and he wasn't there to tell her she was extraordinary. That she could do anything.

"Uncle Wes?"

"Yeah?"

She arched an eyebrow at him. "You haven't really been sleeping very much in the bedroom across the hall from me, have you?"

It hurt to smile, but he couldn't help it. "No, kid. Not really."

"Danielle told me what you and Bethany do at sleepovers."

He froze. "Oh yeah? What'd Danielle say?"

Laura hopped down off the stool Bethany had put in front of the sink, so she could reach the mirror. Had the home visitor even considered that? All the little touches Bethany had added, like a canister of Cheerios in the kitchen and the Disney princess shampoo in the shower? He hadn't even asked her to do those things. "She said when her mom and dad have sleepovers," Laura continued, popping his thought bubble, "they new their marriage vows."

Christ. He was not mentally prepared for this conversation when his head felt like it was buried in cement. "New? Do you mean . . . *re*new?"

"Yeah." She smiled brightly. "They new them."

Wes stayed really still, hoping his lack of movement might work the same way as avoiding a bear attack. "Okay. That's nice, I guess."

"Yeah, but you and Bethany aren't married."

This was it. He was going to be mauled by a bear. He'd never wished harder for Bethany to be standing next to him. She wouldn't know what the hell to say, either, but that was the beauty of the relationship. Whether it was an impromptu tea party or a bleeding finger, they muddled through it together. Fuck, he'd blown it with her. His first and only time in love and he'd barely made it out of the starting gate before letting Bethany down.

He'd let Laura down, too.

Look how happy she is. How is she going to react to moving again?

"No," he rasped, finally. "Bethany and I aren't married."

"Then what vows are you newing in there? Can people make vows even if they aren't married?"

She nudged him out of the way and he followed her into the hallway, toward her room. And it was a good thing her back was turned, because he was probably white as a sheet. "Yeah, sure . . ." he started, and thought of words he'd spoken to Bethany in the dark.

I'm rock solid, Bethany. Okay? Put your faith in me. I'm here with you because you've been my woman since the beginning, even before you realized or accepted it. I'm standing right here and I'm staying right here. There is nothing you or anyone could do to make me want to be somewhere I couldn't hold you.

Something jagged lanced his throat. He'd said that to Bethany.

He'd meant it, too. What the hell had he been thinking,

telling her they were going to leave? Would she ever believe another word out of his mouth?

"Yeah, people who aren't married can make vows," he finished, dropping onto the edge of Laura's bed and burying his pounding head in his hands.

"Oh." Laura sounded disappointed. "But you can still also make the married kind, right?"

"Why?"

He lifted his head to find Laura sprawled out on the bed beside him. It struck Wes how comfortable she was in this room, no matter what the hell it looked like. It wasn't about the décor . . . it was the feeling she got being inside the room. Inside this house.

Where the hell did anyone get off saying Bethany's home wasn't suitable?

Laura spoke again, diverting his anger. "I don't know. I have a mom already. But I could have two. Couldn't I?"

A rake clawed at his insides. "You want Bethany to be your mom?"

He swore there were stars in her eyes when she sighed. "Yeah. Do you?"

"No, I don't want her to be my mom."

Laura giggled and his lips curved into a smile, despite the desolation making his chest burn. This whole situation suddenly struck him as unfair. Sure, he knew the court had a responsibility to make sure kids went to a safe home, but Lord, what he would have given back in the day for someone who cared about him the way Bethany cared about Laura.

She'd set aside her insecurities and become a fixture in his niece's life, picking her up from school, protecting her from potential pain when Becky showed up, given her a home. A *warm* one, to hell with what that woman said about it. They were just new at this.

But he didn't want to be new at anything without Bethany. He needed her.

Laura needed her, too. And he'd completely failed to let her know that when she needed to be reassured most. She'd given him an out, because she'd been scared, and he wanted to punch himself in the face for taking it.

She needed to know he would never, ever take an out.

That he would never even think about it.

"You mind spending a few hours with Let's Color, kid? I've got some work to do."

CHAPTER TWENTY-SIX

In an effort to juice every ounce of drama from the competition, the producer sent Bethany across town with the camera crew—and Slade—to have her tour Stephen's flip prior to the winner being announced. When they parked at the curb, Wes's truck was no longer in her driveway across the street. Had him and Laura left for good?

Her stomach took a dive at the thought.

Just get through this morning.

Easier said than done. Her knees almost buckled upon stepping over the threshold of Stephen's flip. The first-glance effect was spectacular. He'd opened up the entryway and carved a little mudroom into the east wall. A pendant light caught the sunshine and projected fragments of rainbows on the lemon sorbet–colored walls. Oak floors beckoned her deeper into the open floor plan and she could only gape at the changes. Bethany was well aware that the cameras were documenting her every reaction, but she didn't have room to care.

Right in this spot, just under three weeks ago, Wes had Zellweger'd for her.

"If we can get through a meeting without biting each other's heads off, then we'll consider working together."

"We're just going to pretend you have other options, huh?"

"Are we having a meeting or not?"

"Yeah."

Even then, he'd been winding through her insecurities like a maze. How could it have taken her so long to realize Wes was a hero in disguise?

"How are you feeling about your chances?" Slade asked, coming up beside her in a classic construction-man pose, arms crossed, legs braced. "Are you surprised by what your brother managed to pull off without you?"

"Yes, actually. I am." She let out a long exhale and advanced into the living area, shocked once again by the tasteful elegance. "Looks like I'm not the only decorator in the family. I couldn't have done it better myself."

Slade displayed a half grin. "You sound worried."

His cajoling tone, along with the bright camera lights, amplified her headache. "We could definitely lose. But losing won't make me any less proud of our house."

"Speaking of *we*, where is your foreman?"

A pang caught her in the sternum. "I don't know."

Around her, the camera operators shifted, as if they were excited by the subject of Wes and wanted to get a better angle. "Do you have any regrets about trusting him with so much responsibility?"

"No. No, I have a lot of regrets, but trusting Wes will never be one of them. I'm not sure if he could say the same about me." Burning pressure greeted the backs of her eyes, and she cut through Slade and the director, heading for the door. She piled into the middle seat of the network van and took deep breaths to steady herself. And then the van was moving, Slade and the director chatting loudly in the front seat about potentially changing his wardrobe for the big announcement. It made her wish for Wes so badly. Made her wish for one of his eye rolls or drawled comments in her ear.

Chaos reigned back at Project Doomsday, interns running between trailers and the house, landscapers helping to set up shots of the exterior—Ollie and Carl being interviewed out front in tuxedos, which would have made her laugh out loud if her heart wasn't dragging behind her like tin cans.

The van door slid open to Bethany's right, drawing her attention. "Both houses have been toured by three impartial real estate agents and given an unofficial appraisal. Your brother is inside touring Project Doomsday so we can bank his reaction shots. When that's over, we're going to bring you both out on the lawn and announce the winner. Your friends and family are already being arranged in the shot."

"Oh." Sure enough, in the distance she could see everyone on her favorites list, including her parents. Her mother was wearing the same dress she'd worn to Georgie's wedding and applying lipstick in an endless coral oval. "Great."

As Bethany was escorted from the van to the staged filming area, butterflies swept through her stomach, surprising her. All morning, she'd been hollow and calm—heartbroken, to get technical—but now . . . she wanted to win. She needed the win. Not for herself, but for her and Wes. She desperately needed something positive to come from their relationship.

Sure it had been painfully short, but it had impacted her like nothing else. Their time together might as well have lasted a decade and she needed something to show for it. For the changes he'd inspired in her, for the unconditional support he'd given.

Bethany reached the crowd of family and friends, everyone speaking to her at once and none of the words penetrating. Stephen exited the house, capturing her attention. He was wearing a shirt that read ONE HUNDRED PERCENT THAT FATHER without an iota of shame and Bethany could only shake her head.

"You're really going to wear that on television."

"Kristin got one for you, too."

"Do either of you need a bottle of water?" a harried intern asked.

"We're fine," Stephen answered for them, sending the young man scurrying off into the swelling crowd of crewmembers. "It's okay, Bethany, you don't have to congratulate me on the pregnancy. Saying congratulations twice in one day would be too much."

"Oooh, you should have saved that zinger until the cameras were rolling."

Her brother shrugged. "I've got plenty of them."

"All right, everyone," shouted the director, holding up a hand. "I like the energy here. Let's keep it going, so I can get a panning shot of the audience. On my signal, everyone cheer like your lives depend on it. Like you're outside of a Best Buy on Black Friday, or whatever excites suburbanites."

"What a tool," Bethany muttered.

"We can agree on that," Stephen said out of the corner of his mouth. "So who is going to crack first and ask for an opinion on their flip?"

"Not it."

Stephen cursed.

"All right! Here we go! Black Friday energy!" The director settled his hands on his knees. "Action."

Behind Stephen and Bethany, whistles and woos filled the mid-morning atmosphere, calling more attention to her loneliness. This wasn't right. She wasn't supposed to be standing there by herself.

Slade disrupted her thoughts by stepping between her and Stephen, rubbing his hands together. "Two small-town flips, condensed into an incredibly short time frame. Brother versus sister. Ultimate bragging rights on the line." Dramatic pause. "I have to say, both of you delivered beyond our expectations. But who will come away victorious?" He fired a finger gun at the camera. "Stay with us. We'll be announcing the winner after the break."

"Cut! Perfect, Slade," called the director. "Let's go right into the announcement next. Build the drama. Stretch it out. Folks, on my signal, cheer your faces off. Cameras ready?" He waited for a nod from the cameraman. "And . . . we're rolling."

Once again, the sounds of clapping and cheering filled Bethany's ears, the bright lights blinding her until all she could see were vague outlines of human beings and blurs of color.

Slade's voice cut through the noise like a buzz saw. *"Flip Off* is back, coming to you from Port Jefferson, Long Island! If you're just joining us, we're primed to announce the winner of a brother-sister showdown of epic proportions. How are you feeling, Stephen? Confident?"

Bethany's brother puffed up his chest. "Always."

"Bethany? What about you?"

"Nervous," she breathed, the honesty beginning to come easier.

She only caught a hint of Stephen's frown before Slade blocked her view. "Our judges have done a thorough inspection of both houses, and while both of you did an outstanding job, there can only be one winner. Without further ado . . . we're going to announce who impressed them the most. The winner of *Flip Off* is . . ." He stopped talking for so long, Bethany almost pinched the host to see if he was alive. "Stephen! Congratulations, buddy."

Bethany felt every camera train on her face and knew she should grin and bear the news, but she couldn't seem to make it happen. It was insult to injury. She'd lost Wes, and now this home they'd worked on tirelessly for weeks had been declared a loser, just like their relationship. It hurt, like a nail in the coffin.

Still, she stepped around Slade, prepared to shake Stephen's hand. "Hey, congratulations. It's a well-deserved vict—"

"Now, hold on one second," Stephen blustered, avoiding her hand. "What exactly were the judges' criteria? Because my sister started with a ramshackle nightmare and I started with a slightly outdated house. And she had little to no experience, on top of everything." His face was starting to turn red. "I just went in there and . . . Bethany, you killed it. All those little details are going to sell the place. The broken-up backsplash in the kitchen, those built-in bookshelves, and the ornamental trim you ran along the middle of the bedroom walls. I mean, what the hell were the judges even looking at?" He jabbed a finger at Slade. "My sister won. Announce it again."

Somewhere in the distance, Bethany heard her mother burst into tears. "My children love each other."

"Stephen," Bethany said thickly. "You don't have to do that."

"I'm not blowing smoke, Bethany. You won."

"Your house was beautiful, though. Your staging was spot-on."

"You know why? I pulled up one of your past furniture orders and put everything exactly where you did." He threw up his hands. "I just copied one of your old stages."

A gasp went up from the crowd.

"Oh. Come to think of it, the arrangement did look pretty familiar," she murmured to herself.

"The twists and turns keep coming on *Flip Off*," crowed Slade.

Bethany swiped at the gathering moisture in her eyes. "You know what? I wanted to win. I wanted to have something positive to hold on to in the middle of the mess I made, but . . ."

"But what?" prompted the host.

She stared into the abyss of people behind the cameras. "It doesn't feel right accepting the win without Wes here. My foreman. My . . . ex-boyfriend, I guess?"

Her mother was in full vapors now. "She already broke up with him? I didn't even get a Sunday dinner out of it."

"Wes saw every side of me while flipping this house. Stubborn Bethany. Scared, stressed, and silly Bethany. And he stuck it out. He was patient. More patient than I deserved. I would have spun out so many times if he wasn't standing beside me, making me fall in love with him." She could practically feel the cameras zooming in on her face, but she'd stopped hearing anything but the rapid pound of her heart. "So, maybe . . . hopefully six to eight months from now he'll watch this show on his couch and he'll hear he made a difference. Wes, you were always more than a pit stop for me. You were the destination. I just got lost on my way there one too many times—"

Wes stepped out of the blur of bodies and slowly removed his cowboy hat.

They stared at each other, five feet apart, the cacophony of noise falling into a hush around them.

"You're here," she whispered, rooted to the spot. Held there by the sheer overwhelming pleasure of being near Wes, seeing him, absorbing his presence. How did she ever go a day without him? How would she ever do it in the future?

"I'm here," he echoed, taking a step closer. "Right where I'm going to stay. What about rock solid didn't you understand?"

Bethany started to tremble. Was he forgiving her? Was she dreaming?

"I'm late because I was filing the appeal. Next time I saw you, I wanted to have a next time on the horizon. We don't quit, Bethany. We muddle through it together. We're in *everything* together."

Her lungs released their contents in a rush. "I love you so much."

His eyes became suspiciously damp. "I heard."

Neither of them moved to close the gap between them.

"I promise to be rock solid for you, too." A sound welled up in her chest and burst free. "I'm so sorry—"

Wes surged forward, dropping his hat at her feet in favor of cradling her face in both hands. He took a moment to search her gaze before his mouth landed on hers with eager precision. Determined fingers tangled in her hair, his tongue stroking hers in a way that was at once tender and hungry. "You're my first home, Bethany, and my last," he rasped against her lips. "I'm yours, too. And sometimes a floorboard is going to get creaky or a porch light will need fixing. We'll repair it and be good as new. That's love. I wouldn't have known what love felt like without tea parties. Or a beautiful woman showing up at my window at midnight. Or that same woman opening up her home even though it scared her." He kissed the tears off her cheeks. "I am your destination. And you didn't get lost on the way to me, you just circled the block one extra time. Now park the goddamn car, darlin', come inside and tell me you love me again."

Her laugh was joyful and watery. This man was a marvel. Her marvel. Not to mention her future. "I love you."

Wes pulled her into a tight embrace and kissed her forehead. "I love you, too, Bethany."

"Hate to interrupt," Slade broke in, making Wes growl, "but I don't think you'll mind what I have to tell you. There is an actual prize for this competition. Something slightly more substantial than bragging rights."

"Make it good, Slade," Wes said, never taking his eyes off Bethany. "I need to kiss this woman until she can't taste the word 'ex-boyfriend' anymore."

Slade laughed. "Stephen has officially conceded victory, making Bethany and Wes the winners of *Flip Off*." He dangled a set of keys in front of their faces. "You've raised the house value and you'll be receiving a check for the difference, plus a year in paid property taxes. How does that sound?"

Bethany and Wes turned to each other with identical expressions of shock. Wes recovered first, scooping Bethany up into his arms, parting the sea of crew members as he carried her toward the house—and over the threshold.

"What do you think?" Bethany smiled into Wes's neck. "Should we keep flipping houses? We make a pretty good team."

"We make the best team." He set Bethany down and pressed her to the closest wall, letting his mouth travel over hers slowly, adoringly. "Just stay off rooftops during storms."

"It's a deal."

Their shared laughter lifted and faded. "There's one more reason I was late this morning, Bethany." He reached into his pocket and took out a ring box, lifting it between them to the soundtrack of Bethany's gasp. "We can wait a week or ten years, but I want you to know I plan on loving you straight through eternity. "

How much happiness could one heart withstand? "I'll love you, too, Wes. Fiercely. Even when we fight. Especially when we fight," she vowed, her voice shaking. "And I would be honored to be your wife."

His lips jumped at one corner. "Don't you want to see the ring?"

"No. All I need to see is you."

EPILOGUE

Eight Months Later

They were the scourge of the kindergarten graduation ceremony.

The Castle-Daniels contingent required an entire row to cheer on Laura as she accepted her diploma. Bethany winced over the dirty looks they were receiving from the other parents, but what could she say? She'd gotten there an hour early to secure seating. When you snooze, you lose.

Crammed into the front row of the elementary school auditorium were her parents, Georgie, Travis, Dominic, and Rosie. Kristin and Stephen were there, too, behaving as if Kristin had the future king of England strapped to her chest, glaring at anyone who sneezed or spoke too loudly in his vicinity.

Bethany had to agree about one thing. Her new nephew was pretty great. Bethany, Laura, and Wes had a secret pact to expose the kid to as much normalcy as possible, in the hopes he turned out slightly less bananas than his parents.

Although, to be fair, Bethany and Stephen had grown a lot closer post-flip. She'd even let him sit in on a Just Us League meeting around Kristin's due date, because he'd been too paranoid leaving her there alone.

He'd ended up buzzed on tequila and engaged in a group hug, crying and promising to be a better friend to women. Bethany was still traumatized.

But she loved her big brother. Or whatever.

The day he'd conceded *Flip Off* to her, she knew he'd meant it. And along with her own growth during those wild three weeks, she'd truly started trusting herself. Believing in herself. And now she never questioned her ability to love or be loved.

Love wasn't perfect.

Well, some days it was. Other times, it was just muddling through and ripping off your T-shirt to make a bandage. Or her, Wes, and Laura all getting a cold at the same time and piling like zombies in her once-pristine bed for days on end.

They did what worked—and the result was wild, chaotic, beautiful happiness.

Bethany craned her neck to see if Wes had arrived yet. She was saving the seats next to her, right on the aisle, so Laura would be able to see him. And their special guest, if she was able to make it.

The school principal tapped on the microphone, unleashing a peal of feedback. He welcomed everyone to the graduation ceremony, but Bethany was only half listening. For one, she was worried Wes wouldn't make it on time. But mainly, she couldn't help but reflect on how much things had changed over the last eight months.

For one, she'd married Wes.

Had she planned a big, perfect wedding?

No, they'd invited everyone to their new house, formerly known as Project Doomsday, and ambushed them with a surprise wedding, right there in the living room. A living room full of finger paintings and framed pictures and dust on the mantel. That's right, Bethany Castle had gotten married barefoot in a messy house without a single stroke of professional makeup. There was no place she'd rather be.

They didn't leave her home behind due to a lack of warmth or hominess. They'd simply wanted to create their own space top to bottom, as a family. She'd stood in that haphazard living room with a smile on her face a mile wide. Why wouldn't she be smiling when she was marrying the most incredible, loyal, steadfast man on all of planet earth and gaining a quasi-daughter in the process?

Now, months later, every single person in the front row had fallen in love with Laura. She didn't have merely one home, she had several—and in about a decade, she was going to be the busiest babysitter in town, because Rosie and Dominic were expecting twins, Travis and Georgie had a little girl on the way, and, not to be outdone, Stephen and Kristin were already trying for another.

As for Bethany and Wes?

They had their girl and she was more than they could ever want.

Speaking of whom, with the last name Daniels, she was going to be one of the first handful of kids to cross the stage. Where was Wes?

Her thought barely had time to finish before her husband appeared in the entrance of the auditorium, dressed in his signature cowboy hat and too-tight jeans. A look of relief crossed his face when he saw the ceremony hadn't started yet and Bethany waved him down to the front row. His lips curved at her and he shook his head a little, as if to say, *Of course you snagged the front row.* Also, *I love you.*

His expression said that as well. It always did.

She was confused when Wes stepped back out of the auditorium momentarily. Until he walked back in with his half sister at his side.

Bethany breathed a sigh of relief. She'd made it.

After the appeal was filed with the court to grant Wes temporary guardianship of Laura, they didn't hear from Becky for several months. They'd been so busy moving into their new house, those months had flown by so fast that Bethany had been stunned to open her front door one evening and find Becky standing there.

As luck would have it, there'd been a Just Us League meeting on that night. Becky stayed for it. And then she showed up for the next one, and the one after that. She still hadn't opened up about everything in her past, but it was impossible not to see the positivity of the club take effect, little by little. With Bethany and Wes's help, Becky had completed rehabilitation and was now sober, living in Freeport.

With Brick & Morty expanding to take on two flip teams

instead of one—Bethany and Wes making up the additional crew—Bethany had been in need of a new stager. She was training Becky for the position.

Her husband and his sister slid into their seats, just in time for the principal to start calling the names of the kindergartners.

"Hey!" Bethany whispered, reaching out to squeeze Becky's hand and accepting a kiss on the forehead from Wes. "I'm glad you made it."

Me too, mouthed Becky, seeming a little uncomfortable in her surroundings. Compared to how she'd been at Laura's Christmas show, however, she was definitely growing more relaxed in family situations. For Laura's sake, Bethany couldn't be more pleased about that. Laura had been standoffish with her mother during their first few visits, but the more commitment Becky showed, the more Laura warmed—and Bethany had faith it would only get better from there on out.

Laura's name was called and the front row broke out the noisemakers, causing Laura's clear, happy giggle to ring out on stage. She waved at the front row and held up her diploma like Thor's hammer. Oh yeah, she was done with princesses.

It was all about superheroes now.

Wes's fingers threaded through Bethany's, squeezing and drawing her attention. She was surprised to find emotion shining in her husband's eyes.

He looked down the row of friends and family, then back at her.

"Look at what we've got, baby," he said quietly, brushing a kiss across her wedding ring. "We've got everything."

"Everything," she breathed.

He leaned in and kissed her mouth, lingering a moment before repeating the vow he'd made on their wedding day and every day since. "You and me. In it together."

"Forever and ever."

The End

Already wishing for more Just Us League? Good news! Your favorite side characters star in their own stories . . .

See Georgie and Travis fall head-over-clown-shoes in

FIX HER UP

Watch Rosie and Dominic renovate their rocky relationship in

LOVE HER OR LOSE HER

Available wherever books are sold!

ABOUT THE AUTHOR

TESSA BAILEY is originally from Carlsbad, California. The day after high school graduation, she packed her yearbook, ripped jeans, and laptop and drove cross-country to New York City in under four days. Her most valuable life experiences were learned thereafter while waitressing at K-Dees, a Manhattan pub owned by her uncle. Inside those four walls, she met her husband and her best friend and discovered the magic of classic rock, and she managed to put herself through Kingsborough Community College and the English program at Pace University at the same time. Several stunted attempts to enter the workforce as a journalist followed, but romance writing continued to demand her attention.

She now lives in Long Island, New York, with her husband and daughter. Although she is severely sleep-deprived, she is incredibly happy to be living her dream of writing about people falling in love.

BOOKS BY TESSA BAILEY

FIX HER UP

A steamy, hilarious romantic comedy perfect for fans of Christina Lauren and Sally Thorne!

> "*Fix Her Up* ticks all my romance boxes. Not only is it hilarious, it's sweet, endearing, heartwarming and downright sexy. It's a recipe for the perfect love story."
>
> —Helena Hunting, *New York Times* bestselling author of *Meet Cute*

LOVE HER OR LOSE HER

A unique, sexy romantic comedy about a young married couple whose rocky relationship needs a serious renovation . . .

> "Bailey writes banter and rom-com scenarios with aplomb, but for those who like their romance on the spicier side, she's also the Michelangelo of dirty talk. She wields filth like Da Vinci does a paintbrush, and there's a lot to be said for an author who can fill such exchanges with all the requisite heat, enthusiastic consent, and yes, even humor, of such a scenario without veering into corny territory."
>
> —*Entertainment Weekly*

TOOLS OF ENGAGEMENT

Two enemies team up to flip a house . . . and the sparks between them might burn the place down or ignite a passion that neither can ignore!

> "Her voice feels as fresh and contemporary as a Netflix rom-com."
>
> —*Entertainment Weekly*

🔥 HarperCollins*Publishers*

BAILE FLT
BAILEY TESSA.
TOOLS OF ENGAGEMENT.

10/20